PRAISE FOR KATHRYN HARVEY'S
BUTTERFLY

"A steamy story of violence, sin and corruption."

—San Francisco Chronicle

"Sizzling!"

—New York Daily News

"Glamour, wickedness and passion . . . A vivid, imaginative tale . . . Builds to a dramatic and unexpected conclusion."

—Publishers Weekly

"Pacing that hurtles you through the pages."

—Washington Post Book World

"Erotic . . . An immensely readable yarn."

—Chicago Tribune

"Gripping . . . Builds in intensity until the dramatic denouement that is not easy to forget."

—Rave Reviews

Other Books By
KATHRYN HARVEY
Butterfly
Stars

Books By
BARBARA WOOD
Virgins of Paradise
The Dreaming
Green City in the Sun
Soul Flame
Vital Signs
Domina
The Watch Gods
Childsong
Night Trains
Yesterday's Child
Curse This House
Hounds and Jackals
This Golden Land
The Divining

PRIVATE ENTRANCE

PRIVATE ENTRANCE

BARBARA WOOD

TURNER

Turner Publishing Company

200 4th Avenue North • Suite 950
Nashville, Tennessee 37219

445 Park Avenue • 9th Floor
New York, NY 10022

www.turnerpublishing.com

Private Entrance is a work of fiction. Although some events and people
in this book are based on historical fact, others are the products of
the author's imagination.

Cover design by Gina Binkley
Interior design by Mike Penticost

Library of Congress Cataloging-in-Publication Data

Harvey, Kathryn.
Private entrance / Kathryn Harvey.
p. cm.
ISBN 978-1-59652-874-1
1. Businesswomen--Fiction. 2. Health resorts--Fiction. I. Title.
PS3573.O5877P75 2012
813'.54--dc23
                    2012006385

Printed in the United States of America
12 13 14 15 16 17 18—0 9 8 7 6 5 4 3 2 1

For Sharon Stewart—dear friend and beautiful lady. May you win a week's stay at The Grove!

PROLOGUE

*I*N THE EARLY HOURS BEFORE DAWN, AT A LONELY CROSSROADS in the middle of nowhere, a man stood shivering in a phone booth, mentally urging the person at the other end to pick up. The desert air was killer-cold and the frigid stars didn't help.

Parked beside the booth was a dusty old Chevy with a woman inside, holding a baby in her arms, a newborn she was coaxing to drink from a bottle. In the back seat, three other babies slumbered, wrapped in blankets and protected with cushions.

All four babies had been stolen.

The man in the phone booth heard the other end pick up. "It's Boudreaux," he said quietly into the phone, as if anyone could possibly overhear, he and the woman miles from civilization. "I've got the merchandise."

He listened, nodding, shoulders hunched against the whistling wind that found its way through cracks in the booth. "Okay," he said after he received his instructions. "We'll be there in an hour. Yeah, that's right. Four. All girls. All white."

He hung up and ran back to the car, rubbing his hands as he got behind the wheel and slammed the door shut. "Guess what I done, Muriel!" he said gloatingly. "I got him to agree to a extra thousand dollars for each baby!"

"We should get more," she groused. "These're pedigreed. Come from rich families."

"That don't mean nothing to the buyers. All's they care is race and sex."

Muriel frowned, set the bottle down and bent closer to the baby in her arms. "Hey Spencer," she said. "This one's dead."

"What! You sure?"

She covered the little face with the blanket and Boudreaux pounded the steering wheel. "Shit!" There went a thousand bucks.

PRIVATE ENTRANCE

CHAPTER ONE

HIS EYES MEET HERS ACROSS THE AISLE OF THE FIRST CLASS cabin. There is a message in his glance that says: the in-flight movie is over, dinner is history, and the other passengers are reading or snoozing. At thirty thousand feet, what else is there to do?

He unbuckles his seat belt and stands up to stretch. Custom tailored shirt of pale blue silk pulls tight over defined musculature. No golfer, this man. Extreme sports are his thing.

He turns. Coco feels the breath catch in her throat when she sees a hint of heaven in the pleated slacks.

A flicker of dark, inviting eyes before he makes his way down the aisle. As he passes Coco's seat, she picks up his manly scent, feels the air around her crackle with electricity, as if a god had just walked past. She doesn't have to turn and look to know he has made his way to the restroom.

Coco's pulse races. She's never done it in the john of a 747 before.

Dare she?

Casually, she gets out of her seat and moves down the aisle. Are people aware of what these two strangers are up to, what they are about to do?

She doesn't know his name, his profession, if he's married. It doesn't matter. They are drawn together in primal need.

As she nears, she sees him slip inside. He does not turn the knob to "Occupied."

He is waiting.

She licks her lips. She has never felt so excited, so keenly sexual. She reaches for the door and slips inside. The compartment is so small they are pressed together as soon as she closes and locks the door. No words, just instant mouth on mouth, arms encircling, fabulous erection pressing against her groin. His hands travel up her thigh and under her skirt. Coco fumbles at the zipper, setting him free. They don't stop kissing, tongues and lips hot and voracious as her panties come away with one tug. He is so strong he lifts her off the floor and perches her on the edge of the sink. He spreads her legs and—

"Ms. McCarthy? Can I get you another drink?"

Coco looked up, startled. The flight attendant was smiling down at her. "Um," Coco said. "Yes. Please. Another drink would be great. How soon do we land?"

The attendant consulted her watch. "We should be arriving in Los Angeles in forty-five minutes."

"Make it a double."

Coco sighed and looked at the handsome stranger seated across the aisle, his head bent over a magazine. A man she would never meet, let alone have sex with at thirty thousand feet. The story of her life. Sexual fantasies with strangers, one night stands with men who had promise until they found out what she did for a living. One relationship had actually lasted six months—she and Larry had even moved in together and the air had prickled with the hint of marriage. And then the police had called, the homicide detectives had arrived at her door and Larry ("I can't take it any more.") was history.

But all that was about to change.

Coco was on her way to a place called The Grove and although she had never been there she had heard about it.

The tabloids called it a sex club. But The Grove was more than that—an emerald oasis in the Southern California Desert that offered romance, fantasy, escape; gourmet food, vintage wine, imported spirits; aromatherapy, facials, mineral baths; exclusive shops, top flight entertainment, escort services; anonymity, privacy, no questions asked. But mostly everyone remembered the sex. As one Hollywood columnist quipped: "The Grove is a place where the sex is elegant and the elegance is sexy."

The Grove didn't advertise, its number wasn't listed, you didn't find it written up in the glossy magazines of the very rich. As far as Coco knew, you had to hear about the place from a friend who told you how to contact the reservations desk, how to find the private terminal at LAX. Which was where Coco was now headed, on this flight from New York—to catch the private jet to The Grove to begin her week's free stay there.

She had won a contest.

The 747 finally landed and Coco made a hasty exit with a forlorn glance at the handsome stranger who would never know what fabulous sex he had shared with her in the john of a jumbo jet. She collected her luggage and found the chauffeur assigned to drive her to the small terminal on the other side of the airport. "The Grove," with palm trees on the sign. A small jet stood on the tarmac, people in the boarding lounge were helping themselves to complimentary cocktails and hors d'oeuvres.

Accepting a screwdriver from the foxy bartender, Coco looked out at the twenty-passenger DHC-6 Twin Otter painted in lush azure and green hues as if the craft had been built out of palm trees and blue skies. She saw the pilot walking across the tarmac with his black bag. Tall and square-shouldered in a dashing uniform that sent delicious signals. *Come fly with me.*

Coco tried not to stare at her fellow passengers. Movie stars and celebrities enjoying piña coladas and crab cakes.

Then she spotted a man who gave her pause.

Wearing reflective aviator glasses, jeans and a leather jacket while everyone else was in Aloha casual, he seemed to be keeping apart from the others, but watching. Instinct told her he was a cop. Not that there were any outward signs—no badge or gun or Sam Browne. But Coco knew. And she wondered why a cop was going to The Grove. He didn't have the vacation look about him, he wasn't relaxed, wasn't eating or drinking. He looked exactly like a cop on duty. What possible assignment could a cop have at The Grove? She sized him up with her inner eye and thought: Detective. Homicide.

"Isn't this exciting?"

Coco turned and looked into a pair of pale green eyes.

"I mean, the movie stars! I'm Sissy Whitboro. We don't run into many movie stars in Rockford, Illinois. I don't suppose we can ask for autographs."

Coco judged Sissy to be in her early thirties, like herself. Pale skin, carrot-colored hair done in a tidy librarian's bun. Cotton shirtwaist dress and sensible shoes. She had housewife written all over her. "I think they'd rather be left alone," Coco said.

"I could never afford a vacation like this," Sissy said. "I won a contest."

Coco gave her a surprised look. "So did I. But I don't remember entering one. I don't like contests."

"Me neither. How do you suppose it happened? I mean, from what I've heard of the place, it isn't the sort to run contests and give away vacations to just anybody. It's exclusive and pricey."

"I'm sure they'll tell us."

"I wasn't even going to come," Sissy said, stirring her frosty, fruity cocktail, "but my husband insisted. He said I've earned a vacation. Strange that the prize wasn't for two. Just me. I didn't want to leave Ed and the kids, but he said it would be a shame to pass up a chance to stay at a resort where celebrities go."

While Mrs. Whitboro went on about movie stars, Coco's eyes slid back to the guy in the reflective aviator glasses and, thinking of the secret reason why she had accepted the contest prize, had a sudden, startling thought. Was *he* the one?

She smiled to herself. Wouldn't that be a kick, that the man she was searching for turned out to be a cop?

They were finally called to board the plane. As Sissy set her glass down, her purse slipped from beneath her arm and dropped to the floor. "I've got it," Coco said as she retrieved it. But the minute her fingers grasped the leather strap, a flash went through her.

She gave Sissy a searching look and decided not to say anything. It wasn't her business. But Mrs. Ed Whitboro of Rockford, Illinois was in for a big surprise during her stay at The Grove.

As they took their seats and buckled in, Coco's vagrant thoughts meandered down the aisle and found themselves in the cockpit where the handsome pilot was running his final check.

She settled back and closed her eyes. *Once airborne, the captain puts the jet on autopilot, fixes his hat onto his head and comes out to smile at the passengers. When he nears Coco his eyes linger on her, his smile wicked and secretive. Up close, she sees the lines of maturity on his face, the years of wisdom in his eyes. He has flown missions in the Gulf War, 747s to France, bush planes in Australia, trimotors over the Amazon. A seasoned pilot who could fly by the seat of his pants.*

Pants that Coco would very much like to remove.

"Ladies and gentlemen," came the captain's voice over the intercom. "We will be landing in a few minutes. Please make sure your seat belts are fastened..."

The jet taxied to a stop, the door opened and stairs unfolded to the ground. Coco joined the others in retrieving carry-ons and saying thank you to the captain who stood there to wish everyone a nice stay. Close up, he had the sexiest gray eyes.

As soon as she stepped out into the desert evening, Coco was reminded of the Maria Muldaur song back in the seventies: *"Midnight at the oasis, Send your camel to bed..."* There were a million dazzling stars in the black sky, and palm trees swayed in the breeze. The air was crisp and clear and intoxicating. It was a whole new world, a fantasy world. It was definitely not New York.

When she stepped down to the tarmac, Coco noticed two women at the end of the landing strip, protected by huge waxy banana plant leaves and dense palms, as if they didn't want to be seen. She surmised one of them to be the owner of The Grove, a woman of mystery from what Coco had heard.

"Have fun," Sissy Whitboro said as they headed for their separate carts.

"You, too," said Coco. "Maybe we'll run into each other." And then, re-membering the flash she had experienced when she touched Sissy's hand-bag, added, "I'll give you a reading, if you like." Back in the boarding lounge, she had confided in Sissy what she did for a living. Women tended to be more accepting of it than men. And Coco had a feeling Sissy Whitboro was going to be in need of help while she was here.

The new arrivals were met individually by attractive male escorts in white Bermuda shorts and colorful Hawaiian shirts, and female hostesses in curve-hugging sarongs, who took the guests in little covered golf carts to their individual accommodations—lavish suites in the main building, or private cottages and bungalows spread out among the lush foliage and greenery. There was no check-in, no front desk. All this had been handled in Los Angeles before take-off.

The carts hummed past landscaped gardens filled with flowering mi-mosas and hibiscus, groves of orange trees and cedars, waterfalls and ponds and streams fed by The Grove's own artesian springs, deep beneath the desert floor. And when they arrived at their various accommodations, the guests marveled at the silence around them. All credit to the genius of the woman who had created this paradise: you would not know there were other people nearby. Clever landscaping and the ingenious positioning of guest quarters provided for the quietest possible atmosphere. And the utmost in privacy.

Perfect for letting loose.

Coco could barely contain her excitement as the little cart carried her along the paved paths. There were men everywhere! In Hawaiian shirts and shorts, in pale slacks and tennis shirts. Old men, young men, tall and short, chunky and thin.

And one of them was hers.

Coco's accommodations were a garden cottage with its own pool in a walled garden. A place made for partying. The mini-bar was bigger than her fridge at home; the TV was a massive home entertainment center, and there were sofas enough for a gang of Monday Night football fans. Yet it was just her.

It was always just her.

But that was going to change.

The young woman in the Tahitian sarong offered to unpack for her but

Coco declined. Bad enough when people said, "What do you do for a living?" But to have someone see the contents of her luggage?

As she took the suitcase from her, wrapping her hand for a moment around the young woman's hand, Coco saw something all in an instant. "Marry him," she said on an impulse.

"I beg your pardon?"

"Don't let his family stand in the way. It's *your* life, not theirs."

The young woman's eyes widened. Then, with a baffled smile, she said thank you and left. It was a habit Coco was trying to kick. Not everybody wanted their fortunes told. Not everybody sought psychic advice. But she couldn't help it. She would get a flash— especially if it involved a difficult decision—and she saw the answer clearer than the person wrestling with the dilemma. Sometimes, though, instead of helping, she only made matters worse.

She carefully unpacked her things, working up to the "special" case—the strangely shaped, custom-made case that carried the most precious cargo she owned—putting her bras and panties away, hanging up her clothes, shoes in the closet, toiletries and cosmetics in the bathroom, everything perfect and in place so that the atmosphere was just right to address the contents of the special case.

Finally she was ready to unlock the bag and lift out the cube-shaped, sturdy velvet case within. Setting it on the dresser, she lifted the lid to expose the instrument that was the cornerstone of her life's work.

"What do you do for a living?" people would ask—men at parties, women at card clubs, the grocery store checker.

Coco had stopped telling the truth long ago.

And she certainly never told anyone about the crystal ball.

Before getting started, she went into the bathroom to splash cold water on her face, chase away the cobwebs of flying and alcohol. She ran her long acrylic fingernails through her burgundy-dyed hair, frizzing it out even bigger, checked her make-up (you never knew who was going to come to the door) and decided to change out of her traveling clothes into a comfortable ankle-length shirt and gypsy blouse.

Pouring a chilled glass of Evian, she was ready.

Gently cradling the crystal in her hands, she brought it to the sofa and set it on the coffee table where it sparkled in emerald and turquoise highlights. Opening the sliding glass door to the private patio to admit desert breezes and the lonely call of a night bird, Coco addressed the shimmering globe. With a deep breath, she closed her eyes, hummed a soothing mantra, felt her body relax, then she opened her eyes and stretched her hands out over the globe. As perfume drifted in from the garden where flowers were bursting on their stems, as the draperies stirred and the call of a loon filled the air, Coco drove her gaze into the heart of the crystal.

She felt guilty. She should not be doing this. "Your gift is to help others, not yourself," her mother frequently admonished, adding that, to use her psychic gift for selfish reasons, Coco was inviting disaster. But she couldn't help it. She was desperate. Years of failed relationships, one night stands that went no where, men giving her strange looks because of her gift. Coco had come to The Grove to find a man.

Not just any man. Her soul mate. Her Romeo, her Antony, with whom she was destined to spend eternity in deep love and passion.

But first she had to find out who he was.

CHAPTER TWO

*F*ROM THE PROTECTION OF LUSH BANANA PLANTS AND FERNS, THE owner of The Grove anxiously watched the passengers disembark and gather on the tarmac to be greeted by personal hosts and hostesses. She rarely met new arrivals—but tonight was special.

Abby Tyler watched tensely as the aircraft's propellers feathered to a stop and the door opened, stairs unfolding to the ground. She held her breath as the first disembarking guest stepped into the desert evening: a man who owned a company that made risqué toys for adults—pornographic jigsaw puzzles, Strip Checkers, Dirty-Words Crosswords. Business was booming and he was there to reward himself. The woman with him was not his wife (*she* was vacationing in Jamaica with her personal trainer). Behind them came a famous movie star wearing large sunglasses and a wide brimmed hat to hide recent plastic surgery scars; he had had a facelift, an eye job, a chin implant. Behind him were two brothers who had come to The Grove to cheat on their wives (who thought their husbands were golfing in Indian Wells). These were followed by a burned-out writer who hadn't published anything in four years and had come to the desert oasis in hopes of finding inspiration; two sisters eager to get laid (they had already flirted with the two cheating husbands during the short flight); the famous singer-actress who had had her eyebrows lifted so many times her face wore a permanent surprised expression; a widow who had come to The Grove to enact a cherished fantasy from her past; and a couple who had come for the sex games. Lastly, two women looking hesitant and uncertain because they did not know why they were there, only that they had won a contest they didn't remember entering.

"Coco McCarthy and Sissy Whitboro," Vanessa Nichols said. Vanessa was the resort's General Manager and Abby Tyler's best friend. "Ophelia Kaplan didn't come."

That puzzled Abby. Why would anyone turn down a chance to stay at an exclusive resort for free?

"Dr. Kaplan is a very busy woman," Vanessa said, reading her friend's thoughts.

When all twenty new arrivals were gathered on the tarmac, Abby expected the turboprop to taxi away. It did not. An additional guest suddenly appeared at the top of the stairway. The manifest had listed twenty passengers. Abby hadn't known about a twenty-first. "Who's that?" she asked.

Vanessa consulted her clipboard. "Jack Burns. From Los Angeles." Occasionally, when the flight was full a last minute passenger was given the co-pilot's seat.

"Why wasn't I told?"

"I'm sorry, Abby, I thought you were."

She studied the latecomer. In his jeans and leather jacket, he didn't seem to fit in with the rest of the crowd. Something about him sent alarms off at the back of her head. Perhaps it was the way he paused at the top of the stairs to look her way, his shiny reflective aviator glasses homing in on her, flashing sharply in the moonlight. He watched Abby for a long moment, then started down the stairs.

"What's wrong?" Vanessa asked. She knew why her friend was edgy this evening. It had nothing to do with the unexpected stranger in the aviator glasses.

"I don't know. I just got the oddest feeling about that man."

"Do you know him?"

Abby shook her head, short dark curls dancing in the breeze.

Vanessa gave Jack Burns a long look and suddenly felt a stab of fear. "My God, Abby, you don't think—"

"Keep an eye on him." As Abby started to turn away, Vanessa put a hand on her arm and said quietly, "You don't have to go through with this. We can stop it right now." Meaning something other than the twenty-first passenger.

Abby looked into Vanessa's solemn eyes and knew her friend was speaking only from concern. But there was no stopping this. That moment had come and gone. Something that had begun long ago had inexorably caught up with her, as she had known it someday must, like an old fashioned showdown. "And what about you? Are *you* all right with this?"

Vanessa smiled. "You know me. Fearless."

"Then let's get ready," Abby said, and turned toward the heart of the resort.

But Vanessa paused. "When are you going to tell them the *real* reason they're here?" She was referring to the two "contest winners."

"Tomorrow," Abby said. "I will have lunch with Sissy and Coco. And please check into Ophelia Kaplan. Find out why she didn't accept the contest prize."

As she delivered herself back into the protection of ferns and fronds and blossoms, Abby Tyler thought of Dr. Ophelia Kaplan, wondering why she had not accepted the free vacation. Abby would have to think of a way to convince her to come so that all three would be at The Grove at the same time: Sissy, Coco and Ophelia—three women from three different cities and three different walks of life; one single, one married, one engaged; one Jewish, one Catholic, one a self-professed Pagan. A university professor, a police psychic, and a homemaker. Three women who, if they met in a room together, would think they hadn't a single thing in common—until they learned that all three had been born on the same day, thirty-three years ago.

Abby thought of the manila folders back in her office, files containing information that went back over three decades, accompanied by photographs secretly shot with a telephoto lens. Sissy Whitboro, Coco McCarthy and Ophelia Kaplan, going about their business, not knowing they were being photographed.

And as Abby thought of those three faces in the photographs, as she searched for clues, for recognizable traits, hints of herself in their features, she silently asked: *Which one of you is my daughter?*

CHAPTER THREE

*T*HE SEXY ROOM SERVICE WAITER WHEELED THE CART ONTO Sissy Whitboro's private patio and set up breakfast while she watched. He was olive-skinned and wore tight pants. And when he winked she felt her heart skip.

He couldn't have been a day over twenty, and she was in her thirties!

Still, Sissy was flattered and tried to tip him as he left. But tips weren't allowed at The Grove, he said. She went back to the cart, relishing the desert morning sunshine, the fresh air, and plants and flowers in her walled garden. She was glad she had accepted the prize, even though she didn't know what the contest was. As she lightly buttered her toast, she felt a pang of guilt. Ed at home with the kids while she was here in this luxurious silence. She shouldn't be enjoying herself, but she was. And she was reminded once again that lately she had felt something missing from her life. She didn't know what it was, and she never admitted it because it felt like a betrayal of Ed, whom she loved very much.

As she sipped her orange juice she heard a sound on the breeze. Someone moaning!

She looked around. It sounded like they were sick or hurt. Creeping around her garden, Sissy listened until she homed in on the source. The groaning was coming from the other side of the wall. She tried to peer over but it was too high. Then she saw the wooden gate. It was locked on her side. Drawing back the latch, she pushed through.

It took a minute for her eyes to register what they saw. Two people on a chaise lounge, completely naked, the woman with her legs and arms flung back, the man's pale buttocks going up and down.

"Oh!" Sissy said. The man looked up. He grinned without stopping his rhythm. His partner didn't even open her eyes.

"I'm sorry!" Sissy mumbled, backing away and closing the gate. It took her a minute to regain her breath. She stayed by the gate as she heard the chaise continue to creak and she found herself fascinated by the sound, unable to pull herself away.

The woman moaned again, and the rhythm increased. Now she began to cry out, and urge him on faster, faster, while Sissy held her breath and listened, picturing them, shocked at herself yet unable to retreat. As the creaking increased in speed, so did Sissy's pulse. She placed her hand on her chest and felt her heart thump as the two thumped together in the next garden.

Finally the woman gave a yell and the man released a strangled grunt. And then they were laughing and Sissy heard one of them say, "Woman next door," and she ran away, cheeks burning.

Flustered, she hurried back inside, pulling the room service cart with her, and closed the sliding glass door as if to cover her faux pas. Blundering into someone's private garden was something the very proper and polite Sissy Whitboro of Rockford, Illinois would never do. And she had never seen two people "do it" before. Not in real life.

As she collected herself and sat down to eggs and toast (guiltily thinking that the man next door had taken a lot longer than Ed ever did) she saw an envelope standing between the silver salt and pepper shakers. It appeared to be an invitation.

Made of pale pink and cream paper, the outside of the card said *Fantasy*

Encounters. Sissy opened it and scanned it in puzzlement. *"Enjoy your special fantasy in one of our richly appointed rooms: the Castle Tower, the Spanish Parlor, the Robert E. Lee Drawing Room...May we recommend Antony and Cleopatra or Robin Hood and Maid Marian...We offer a wide variety of costumes and special accessories...Male and female companions...Complete discretion and privacy."*

Sissy was shocked. First her neighbors and now this. What kind of a place had she come to?

The night before, while she was unpacking in this lovely little dwelling done in bright orange, purple and yellow, aptly called the Bird of Paradise Cottage, the manager of The Grove, Ms. Vanessa Nichols, had paid Sissy a visit, welcoming her to the resort and to let her know she would be having a private luncheon with The Grove's owner, Ms. Abby Tyler, at noon today. Ms. Nichols had gone on to explain that the week's stay was all expenses paid and that Mrs. Whitboro was invited to avail herself of all services. But Sissy had no intention of making use of the resort's dubious services—fantasy companions!—she had come for just one reason. She hadn't said as much to Ms. Nichols of course, but she did ask one question: How was it possible she had won a contest she didn't remember entering?

Ms. Nichols had replied vaguely, "It's something we do now and then."

Whatever the reason, Sissy had decided she was going to take advantage of her good fortune. It was a perfect opportunity, with no demands from her kids, husband and the many committees and clubs she belonged to, to put together the family album—a project she had been putting off for too long.

So now she proceeded, on this beautiful Monday morning, with desert sunshine streaming through diaphanous draperies, spotlighting the remnants of her eggs and toast breakfast, to unpack all the treasures she had brought with her.

When she had packed for the trip, she had reserved an extra suitcase just for the project and had gone into Ed's den, to the closet where they threw everything that "someday" would receive attention, and she had grabbed boxes, envelopes, and bags stuffed with photos, souvenirs and memorabilia, and crammed them into the suitcase to be sorted at the other end.

The photographs and mementoes went back fifteen years and represented a good life. A full life.

Ed had done very well for himself as the general manager of a factory that made machine tools. With over a thousand employees under him, Ed was an important man in town. A devoted, faithful husband, not one to begrudge his wife luxuries and pleasures. Ed was very generous, including to himself, having recently joined the very expensive Rockford Men's Racquet Club. It had been at the suggestion of Hank Curly, his new sales manager, who was a fitness freak. Ed and Hank went two and three nights a week to play racquet ball, and the results showed: Ed's incipient paunch had vanished and his arms grew hard biceps. The change had made him, curiously, even more generous. A new car for Sissy, all the charge accounts and new clothes she could want. Dinner every Saturday at the country club. Add to that the beautiful home and three wonderful kids, and it was a perfect life.

So why had Sissy started thinking something was missing?

She couldn't get those people next door out of her mind, on the chaise lounge. Other than R-rated movies, Sissy had never witnessed a sex act. It had left her feeling strangely unsettled. And restless, so that now, as she surveyed all the photos and mementoes, scrapbook supplies, it suddenly struck her as being a very unimaginative and prosaic endeavor. Who came to a resort like this to do a family scrapbook?

A good mother did, she told herself, that was who. Everyone was always telling Sissy Whitboro what a good mother she was. The day Adrian was born, Sissy had vowed to raise her as a real mother should, not in the cold, aloof way her own mother had—"Don't muss Mother's hair. Don't touch Mother's make-up." A woman who never hugged her child, or said I love you, or did silly things to make her kid laugh. Or created a family album.

"You are the best mother in the world," her best friend, Linda, had said when she drove Sissy to the airport. "Now leave your family at home and enjoy yourself!" Linda was divorced with two kids and had a slightly wild and racy nature. She had given Sissy a "care" package before she left, with instructions not to open it until she was alone in her room. Sissy had unwrapped it the night before and found flavored condoms, chocolate body paint and a dildo covered in smileys. The card said, "I am with you in spirit!"

Linda was far more liberal about sex than Sissy was. When Linda had heard of a bordello for women in Beverly Hills, she had flown there to see for herself. She had found it, Butterfly on Rodeo Drive, but you had to be a member, and to be a member you had to get someone to sponsor you. Linda had come home disappointed, but when they all read the about the bordello being raided by the police several months later, Linda said, "Pity," but was secretly glad she hadn't joined. The town of Rockford would never have gotten over the scandal. "I wonder if The Grove is owned by the same woman," Linda had speculated while watching Sissy pack for her free week at the resort. "Beverly Highland disappeared, and they say the woman who owns The Grove is very mysterious and secretive."

Sissy suddenly heard laughter outside. Her cheeks burned when she recalled the way the man next door had grinned at her as he pumped away—a wicked grin, as if inviting Sissy to join them.

She shook her head and addressed the project, laying out tweezers, scissors, silhouette punches; trimmers, stickers, rubber stamps; colored pens, pencils and markers. Sissy had gone wild at the craft store back home—

How *did* a threesome work anyway? Could one man satisfy two women?

Her thoughts shocked her. Raised a strict Catholic, the most Sissy had done with boys in high school was make-out. She lost her virginity on her wedding night and had been with no other man since. Ed was a considerate lover, every Saturday night after dinner at the Country Club, and he even stayed awake a little afterward. It wasn't skyrockets for Sissy, but she didn't believe women were supposed to feel that way.

She began sorting the photos and theater stubs and little bits and pieces of happy moments, wondering, should she place the photos and mementoes chronologically or grouped into themes?

She frowned. Where was the glue? She searched through the adhesives and mounting tabs and photo corners but found no glue. Maybe she had hastily thrown it in with something else. She went through the boxes and manila envelopes. No glue. The last item she inspected was something unfamiliar to her. She had grabbed it in her sweep of everything off the closet shelf. A brown accordion file secured with a black elastic band. She couldn't recall ever seeing it before. It must have been tucked away at the back of the closet for a long time for her not to even recognize it. The pictures in it must be very old.

She opened it and looked inside. Her frown deepened as she brought out the contents. Bank and credit card statements. But whose? Ed was very careful about their financial files and kept them in neatly organized folders in a metal filing cabinet. Perhaps they had been left behind by the people they had bought the house from, six years ago. But the dates on the credit card statements were recent. And they all had Ed's name on them.

What on earth *was* all this?

She scrutinized the charges more closely and saw that none were familiar to her—jewelry stores, florists, expensive restaurants, even hotel charges. It had to be an error. That was it. Identity theft. Someone using Ed's name. He was most likely fighting it out right now with the credit card company and hadn't told Sissy because he didn't want to worry her.

She gazed into the sunbeams slicing through the diaphanous drapes, saw golden dust motes dancing in the light. And got a very strange feeling.

She rarely called Ed at work, but this was something that needed explaining. "Sorry, Mrs. Whitboro," his secretary said now. "He's out with a supplier at the moment."

"Would you ask him to call me please?" And she gave the woman the number at the resort.

One of the file pockets contained phone bills stapled together. Sissy didn't recognize the number on the account. It was a cellular service. Did Ed have a second cell phone she didn't know about? She noticed that one number appeared numerous times. Out of curiosity, she dialed.

A woman's voice, deep and sultry, answered. "Hi, this is Tiffany. What can I do for you?"

Tiffany? "Is Ed there?"

"If you say so, sugar. What would you like Ed and me to be doing?"

Sissy frowned. "I'd rather you weren't doing anything."

"Okay, sugar. I get it. You want Ed to watch while you and I get it on? Tell me what you're wearing. Describe your breasts to me—"

"I'm looking for my husband! I found this number. He's been calling you."

A brief silence and then, "Jesus. You're a *wife!*" Sultriness gone.

"Where is Ed?"

"Look, honey, I don't know where Ed is and you still gotta pay for this call."

The connection broke, leaving Sissy to sit in bafflement.

Selecting another number on the phone bill, she dialed and heard a recording: "Hi, I'm Bambi," breathy and soft, "and I'm not in right now. I'm out buying lingerie, the crotchless panties you like so much. But, ooh, I want to talk to you, I'm here for you and I'm hot and ready. Just leave your number and—"

Sissy quickly hung up. She scanned the lists of numbers, the minutes, and the total at the end. One month's phone bill came to over five hundred dollars.

Sissy knew she was not worldly when it came to certain matters, but it did not take a genius to recognize what these calls meant. Her head swam. Ed was into phone sex?

No, it was a mistake. It had to be. It wasn't like him. She and Ed went to church every Sunday. Ed coached their kids' soccer team, was a member of the Kiwanis and the Knights of Columbus. He led retreats for Christian youth on the weekends. Ed never even looked at another woman, not even at the company Christmas parties where everybody got drunk and flirted. He and Sissy had been devoted to each other for fifteen years.

She was sure there was a reasonable explanation for what she had found inside the accordion file.

And then she saw that there was more in there, and she was suddenly afraid to look.

CHAPTER FOUR

*A*BBY! ARE YOU AWAKE? WE HAVE AN EMERGENCY!"

Abby Tyler opened the door wearing a silk dressing gown, her hair damp from the shower. "What is it?"

"Trouble," Vanessa said, hurrying inside, closing the door behind herself. "It's the kitchen again. The lobsters did not arrive on this morning's flight, and the caviar that came is not Beluga. On top of that, someone left the *foie gras* out overnight so that it has spoiled. Maurice is throwing a fit."

The kitchen was the heart of the resort, known for its fabulous menus, and Maurice, the head chef, trained at Cordon Bleu and world-famous for his quail in port sauce, possessed a temperament that was as changeable and extreme as the desert surrounding the resort. If he walked out it would bring the Grove to a standstill.

"I'll go talk to him." Abby hurried back into her bedroom where she had been in the middle of selecting her wardrobe. She was to have lunch with Sissy Whitboro and Coco McCarthy. Now it would have to be rescheduled. And dealing with Maurice could take all day, calling for psychology, diplomacy, emergency phone calls, and sending the plane to Los Angeles on an emergency run.

Vanessa followed her friend into the bedroom. "Abby, you look awful. Did you get any sleep at all?"

"No, I was up all night." Coco and Sissy. Two of the three women the private detective had tracked down. *Three babies kidnapped three decades ago, stolen from their mothers and sold to desperate families.*

As she snapped a brush through her short dark hair, she looked at the woman in the mirror, in her late forties but looking younger because of careful avoidance of sun and smog. A face she had kept hidden. "Were you able to get through to Ophelia Kaplan?"

"I placed a call to her home last night but haven't yet received a response. Abby, what if she doesn't accept the prize?"

"We'll cross that bridge when we come to it." Maybe, for the first time in fourteen years, Abby was going to have to leave The Grove. She had invented the contest as a way to get the three to come to her because she couldn't go to *them.* But if she had to, to see Ophelia Kaplan face to face and learn the truth, she would do it.

She reached for a sweater. "What about the man I asked you to keep an eye on?" The surprise twenty-first passenger. Mr. Aviator Glasses.

"Jack Burns. He hasn't requested anything so far. No special services. Hasn't signed up for the spas or tennis. Dined alone in his room last night—steak and fries. Ordered a bottle of Black Opal Shiraz."

That surprised Abby. Few of her guests were hip to southeastern Australian wines.

"Female companionship?"

"Nothing."

Abby headed for the front door. "When did he make his reservation?"

"He's been on stand-by for three weeks. We got a cancellation. Burns was notified and he came right out."

"From where?"

"Los Angeles."

Stand-bys were not unusual, but the fact that he wasn't taking advantage of the resort's many offerings was. No one ever came here to do *nothing.*

"Paparazzi?" Vanessa suggested. "Or a celebrity stalker?" The Grove saw more than its share of famous people. Those who wanted to get into the "business" came here hoping to make connections. Security was constantly on the watch for guests pestering the celebrities. Maybe this one had a screenplay to shop, or an idea to pitch, a portfolio to show. "Do you want security to have a look in his room?"

Abby shook her head. Privacy was her number one rule. She had never snooped in a guest's room and wasn't about to start now. Pushing Jack Burns from her mind, she focused on damage control in the kitchen and averting a disaster with Maurice the head chef.

"We need fingerprints, Jack," his friend at the forensics lab had said. That was why Jack was here. To get fingerprints from a woman known never to socialize with her guests. "Buy her a drink. Take the glass."

Easier said than done.

But he had made a promise over a coffin, and so now he was here, in the morning sunshine exploring The Grove, figuring out a way to get Abby Tyler's fingerprints.

The night before, when the plane landed, he had seen her at the edge of the tarmac, observing the arriving passengers. She had looked younger than he expected. Attractive, too. To his surprise, she had also looked vulnerable, standing there anxiously surveying the new arrivals. He had seen her stiffen when she saw him, her guard suddenly up. Did she know? Had she guessed why he was there?

In the desert sunshine, tall and slender palm trees bent seductively in the breeze, long green fronds swaying like hula skirts. The sky was so blue and sharp it hurt the eyes. A waterfall splashed nearby. Jack was approached by a young woman in a curvy sarong carrying a tray of colorful drinks, paper umbrellas sticking out of them. She gave him the once over and smiled in a flattering way. An act? Part of the resort's policy to entertain guests? Perhaps not. Jack had encountered such smiles before. He had been told by various ladies that he "wasn't bad looking." A bit weathered, they said, but what man would-n't be in his line of work? You don't squint at a city's underbelly for years without carving a few creases and lines in your face. At forty-seven, Jack kept himself in shape, not overly so, just enough to outrun a purse snatcher if he had to.

He politely returned the smile and strolled on. Recreational sex wasn't his scene. Jack preferred emotional attachment with his bed partners. Which was why his bed had been empty of late.

Finally he saw her, hurrying past a giant aviary filled with exotic birds.

He followed, watching the long stride and confident step, hands tucked into the pockets of her tailored slacks, silk blouse fluttering in the breeze, molding to her form so that he couldn't help notice nicely rounded breasts. He knew how old she was. He grudgingly admitted she kept herself in good shape. Her colors surprised him—Jack thought a woman in hiding would try to be as invisible as possible. But Abby Tyler's slacks were crimson, her blouse flame-colored

Last night she had looked vulnerable. But looks can be deceiving.

And then he saw on the path ahead one of the housekeeping maids struggling with a large load of linen. A small Hispanic woman in a green and blue uniform, she was wrestling with a duffle nearly her own size, and blocking the path.

Jack knew what would happen next. He had witnessed it before in other retreats that catered to the very rich and spoiled. The maid would be ordered to remove the cart from the path and to see to it that she never again made her self so visible. Some hotels, guests never even saw housekeeping personnel, they were that adept at keeping themselves invisible.

Jack hung back as he watched Abby Tyler and her companion, a tall woman in a long white caftan, stop and say something to the maid. The breeze carried their voices so that Jack could hear. To his surprise, no reprimand from Tyler. Instead she took the large bundle from the maid and lifted it up and over into the clumsy cart. Jack caught bits of what Tyler said: "Never lift heavy things…must think of your baby…call one of the men to help."

Jack noticed the young woman's rounded abdomen and realized she was pregnant. Tyler addressed her as Maria and patted her on the shoulder. Maria blushed and smiled. Then Tyler and her companion hurried on.

That gave Jack pause, forcing him to make an adjustment to his preconceived character assessment of Abby Tyler.

Picking up his pace, he hurried after her. "Miss Tyler!"

She turned. For an unguarded instant, she looked preoccupied, troubled almost, and then a mask went up. "Jack Burns," he said, holding out his hand.

Her handshake was unexpected—two-handed, taking his between hers in a welcoming grip. And then she smiled and that further surprised him—a sunny, confident smile. Closer up now, he saw the crinkles around her eyes, not from being out in the sun but from smiling a lot. He sensed a warmth deep within her as she tilted her head and her dark curls caught the sunlight in copper streaks. "Have we met before, Mr. Burns? Your name seems familiar to me."

"It's possible," he said, offering nothing more.

Her perfume was delicate and feminine, wafting over him when the desert breeze shifted. She seemed to be studying him. It caught him off guard. He knew she had a reputation for rarely mingling with guests. He was unprepared for such a direct confrontation. He removed his aviator glasses to give her look for look.

As the breeze swirled around them, Abby studied him, wondering why his name was so familiar. He himself was a stranger: the shiny aviator glasses, the leather jacket, the stance, the shortly trimmed hair that had never seen a comb. Then, remembering the crisis in the kitchen, she withdrew her hands. "I hope you are enjoying your stay. If you will please excuse me…"

He looked this way and that, like a man not wanting to be overheard, or plotting his next words, a cautious man, Abby thought, and the gesture gave her a good look at both sides of his jaw, his sinewy neck, the trim hair buzzed halfway up his skull. "Maybe I could buy you a drink later?" he said.

She had not expected the invitation. "Thank you, but I am really very busy. It was a pleasure meeting you, Mr. Burns." And she moved on.

She had gone a few yards when she turned to look back to find him still standing there watching her behind those silvery glasses again.

As she felt the sharp desert air on her face, Abby felt fresh new fear. She had the feeling he was sizing her up, that he was here on a fact-finding mission. Where did she know him from? Were you ever in Little Pecos, Texas? she wanted to ask. She searched her memory…

The summer of 1971, an innocent sixteen-year-old girl named Emmy

Lou Pagan was living alone with her grandfather in a roadside nursery and feed store on a stretch of Texas highway when she met and fell in love with a nameless drifter. She had known nothing about the stranger, and he had volunteered no information about himself, so that when she fell in love with him it was with a phantom of her own imagination. She had not known, as she lay in his arms beneath the Texas stars, that he had a black soul and that he would commit murder for fifty cents.

The drifter stealing her grandfather's truck to kill an elderly woman for her money, and the local sheriff arresting Emmy Lou, believing she had done the killing.

Did Jack Burns know about the trial in which flimsy circumstantial evidence led to a guilty verdict by a jury of twelve good Christian men and women, not because they thought she had committed the crime but because, in the course of the trial, it was discovered she was pregnant—sixteen and unmarried in Texas Bible country—and therefore they could not let her go unpunished?

Did he know that Emmy Lou's sentence of life in prison had caused her grandfather to drop dead of a heart attack, leaving his sixteen-year-old granddaughter alone in the world except for the baby growing within her?

Did Jack Burns know that Emmy Lou Pagan was now Abilene Tyler, owner of The Grove, and that she had been in hiding for over thirty years?

Abby was brought back to the present by Vanessa's voice. "Do you think he knows something?" her best friend was asking.

If he did, the two of them might have to move on. It wouldn't be the first time they had had to flee. But this time Abby didn't *want* to run. Not now that she was so close to finding her daughter at long last…

CHAPTER FIVE

*C*OCO McCARTHY HAD HAD TOO MUCH TO DRINK WHICH WAS WHY *she was letting Rodrigo slide his magnificent hands under her blouse to feel her breasts. He was a fantastic kisser and his body was hard all over, not just down* there.

Coco was on fire. She had had the secret hots for Sergeant Rodrigo Diaz for months and hadn't thought he was aware she was alive. Yet here he was, getting her under the mistletoe, pressing up to her and seducing her with his melting black eyes.

Now his hands were on her thighs, lifting her skirt. Coco squirmed against him, unable to get away even if she wanted to because he had her pinned to the wall. My God, everyone could see! Was he actually going to give it to her right there, in the middle of 17th Precinct squad room, in the middle of this wild Christmas party?

What had the captain put in the punch anyway? Because Coco's right leg was moving on its own, creeping up until it hooked around Rodrigo's perfect rear, giving him wide access. The flimsy panties came away and the sergeant's fingers were inside, exploring.

Coco thought she would faint with desire. She felt the eyes of everyone on her, all the cops, their dates, the prisoners in lock-up, all watching what Ro-drigo Diaz was about to do to her. It excited her beyond belief.

"Yes," she whispered against his olive-skinned ear. "Yes, yessss..."

Coco's eyes snapped open.

She blinked.

Where the hell was she?

She rolled her head on the pillow and squinted at blinding sunlight pouring through the window. What happened? Had she left the Christmas party with Rodrigo? Was she at his place?

And then she remembered: It wasn't Christmas. It was April. And she had won a contest. She was at a place called The Grove.

She sighed. Rodrigo had been but a dream. They had never kissed under the mistletoe. She had never felt those wonderful fingers deliciously inside her. Not in real life, just in her fantasies.

But that was about to change because she had come to The Grove to find her soul mate!

Jumping out of bed, Coco made a hasty room service call for a breakfast of lox and bagels and cream cheese, then she dashed into the shower which she set at an energizingly low temperature.

"He is well traveled. He knows the world."

That was what her crystal ball had said the night before, although not in exactly those words, and not in an actual voice. The crystal communicated in ideas and images. And it wasn't the crystal itself speaking, but Coco's spirit guide, Daisy.

What Coco needed were details. The first time the message had come through was several weeks ago, when Coco was working on a missing child case. She had been con

sulting the crystal when her phone rang. Gerard, the cute African American detective who looked like the cop on *Law & Order*, calling to break their date.

Big surprise there. Men thought she was great—Coco had a bubbly per-sonality, voluptuous figure, and a fabulous smile—until they learned she was a psychic and worked for the police. Gerard had said he could handle it, after all his own grandmother was psychic (she predicted rain storms). But when Coco voiced what she saw in her famous "flashes"—usually mundane things, such as "your car keys fell behind the dresser," but sometimes she saw secrets—Gerard had started acting uneasy. That night was to have been their first date—dinner and a movie. But he had called with a lame excuse and that was it. Bye bye Gerard.

Depressed over the sorry state of her love life—at thirty-three Coco was starting to yearn for the white picket fence—she had looked at the crystal that was trying to tell her where a lost child had wandered to, and a forbidden thought had come to her: *Ask the crystal if there is a man somewhere in the world just for you.*

Coco had been psychic from an early age and her mother, recognizing that her daughter's gift was unique and precious, had admonished Coco that she use her talents only to benefit others. "If you work it for your own personal gain," she had said many times, "you invite disaster."

Coco had heeded that advice until Gerard's phone call. It was the final straw. For years she had helped the police find murderers, kidnap victims, lost children—wasn't it time to get something in return? It wasn't selfish, was it? After all, as a sideline Coco offered psychic advice to friends and relatives. Her own sister had found her soul mate through Coco and the crystal ball. Why *was* it wrong for Coco to consult the orb for herself? Who besides her mother said it would bring bad luck?

So Coco had relaxed herself, spread her hands over the orb and opened her mind to Daisy, and the message had come through loud and clear. *Yes, there is a soul mate waiting for you.*

Excited, Coco had asked: Where?

Behind her eyes, she had received a vision: the setting sun.

But the crystal would reveal no more. And then the FedEx envelope had arrived containing the announcement that she had won a contest, a week's stay at a desert resort in California. *Setting sun.* West! It could not be a coincidence. Coco had accepted at once, cancelled all readings and séances, informed the local police she was going out of town, and jumped on a plane for the West Coast.

And now here she was, getting dolled up for her first foray into the land where her soul mate dwelled.

Her long session with the crystal the night before, after she had checked into her private cottage, had not revealed the man's name, nor what he looked like, nor anything useful. The message that Daisy, through the crystal, kept sending was: He is well traveled.

Great. That could describe every guest in the place. People who could afford The Grove could also afford to globe trot.

She must not waste any time. All the crystal could do was advise—it did not arrange introductions. The rest was up to Coco. And if she wasn't on her toes, she could miss her soul mate and never again have the chance to find him.

As she stepped out of the shower and vigorously toweled off, she knew exactly where to start looking. Morris What's His Name, the man she had flirted with the night before in the bar at The Grille. They had had something going until Coco felt inexplicably sleepy. Remembering that her inner clock was set three hours ahead, she had made excuses and left. She would look for him now. Last night he had said he wrote travel books and had been all over the world. Exactly the man Daisy had told her to look for.

As she was about to leave, her phone rang. It was the manager, Vanessa Nichols, rescheduling Coco's lunch date with Abby Tyler. "Something has come up." It was fine with Coco. More time to find the man of her dreams.

The Grove was alive with morning birdsong, not only from the aviary that dominated the center of the resort, but all the wildlife that inhabited the imported trees that grew there. The shaded path led her to one of the swimming pools, where happy guests were splashing and sunning and flirting in the bright desert sun. Coco selected a stool at the bar and ordered a Bloody Mary with extra salt and the first sip immediately put her in an upbeat mood.

As she scanned the scene for Morris the travel writer, she spotted famous faces cavorting in and around the waterfall and fountains. A sexy young man with a cute butt came by with an armload of towels. When he offered her one, Coco said, "No thanks, I'm allergic to swimming."

She had loved pools when she was younger, but when she and her waistline both reached thirty—years and inches, respectively—she had put away her bathing suit. With a sigh she watched the cute butt walk away. Had he given her the come-on? She had heard stories about this place, the rampant sex, that everyone was into it.

"Excuse me."

Coco turned to find a familiar face smiling at her: the man from the boarding lounge the night before, whom she had pegged as a cop. She liked the look of him—salt and pepper hair, lined face, hard eyes. And was that a gun bulge under the leather jacket?

"Yes?" she said.

He put his hands on his hips and looked this way and that. "I'm trying to find a magazine kiosk. Somewhere I can buy a newspaper. But this place is so big and I keep getting lost."

"Sorry, I'm new here myself," she said.

"It's quite a resort. Never seen anything like it. Do you come a lot?"

It sounded like a pick-up line, yet she had the feeling he wasn't hitting on her. "This is my first time. Believe it or not, I won a contest I don't even remember entering! A week's stay at the Grove."

He surveyed the exotic scene. "The owner must be rich."

Coco shrugged. "I wouldn't know. I don't know anything about the owner."

He settled his eyes on her, from behind silver aviator glasses. "Abby Tyler, I think that's her name."

Coco sipped her umbrella drink. He wasn't the one, and he clearly wasn't "looking." And Coco certainly did not want to get into a relationship with another cop.

"This place was recommended to me by a friend, Nina Burns," he said and waited for a reaction. There was none. Either Coco didn't recall her telephone conversation with Nina, or Nina had used a fake name.

He reached for the peanut bowl and when the sleeve of his leather jacket brushed her arm, Coco received a flash. He was here on a case. Homicide. "Hope you catch your killer," she quipped, and when he gave her a startled look, she added, "I'm a psychic. I work with the police in New York."

He nodded. "Some guys on the force think it's a waste of public funds.

But I've seen police psychics in action, cases solved where the police were ready to give up."

They chatted for a few more minutes, about the resort, its mysterious owner, and why people came here, until he finally said he would continue his prowl for a newsstand. Coco watched him go, her eyes on his tight sexy butt, and then she turned back to her drink and that was when she saw him: Morris from the night before.

He was attractively dressed in a Geoffrey Beene polo shirt and expensive looking tailored slacks, all in pale pastels to fetchingly set off his tan.

"Hi there," he called, looking decidedly pleased to see her.

As he ordered a wine spritzer and took the stool next to her, Coco waited for the chemistry to happen. Morris wasn't bad looking, if a bit wasted close up—watery bloodshot eyes and a pouchy chin—and last night he had been witty and entertaining. But that was in a dark bar. It was amazing how sunlight could change things.

But Daisy and the crystal had said her soul mate was well traveled, and Morris had been to Egypt and Antarctica. So Coco would give him a chance.

As they chatted and drank, and exchanged meaningful looks, Coco made herself vibrant and open, waiting for the fireworks. Maybe she should just reach out and touch him, see if she received a flash. But it didn't always work that way. And Coco only occasionally received psychic flashes from men. She was more successful connecting with women.

"What say we take a walk?" Morris said as he slid off his stool.

As they skirted the pool area, he impulsively pulled her into a cabana and closed the door. Coco was instantly excited—all those people out there! It was dark and warm inside the little dressing hut, and very cramped, no place to lie down.

They started kissing, but the chemistry wasn't happening. Morris was too eager, and his lips didn't fit hers. He rushed into her panties and did some inexplicable fiddling. "Wait—" she began, wrenching her mouth away from his, but he pressed himself against her, whispering, "Oh baby," as he rubbed his body up and down hers with such vigor she thought the cabana was going to fall over.

"Slow down," she hissed. Too late. He suddenly gave a great shudder and a moment later she felt wetness seep through the front of her dress.

"Oh God," he said, mortified. "I've never done *that* before."

Coco pushed past him and out into the daylight, holding her purse in front of herself as she dashed through the pool area and off down another path.

The desert safari sounded interesting, so after a change of clothes, Coco headed off for the pavilion where the safari vehicles were parked.

The manager of the resort, Vanessa Nichols, was there with her clipboard, checking off names as guests boarded the SUV. It was obvious Ms. Nichols' lipstick had been freshly applied, and she self-consciously brushed a speck of dust from her immaculate caftan. Coco got a flash from her. Ms. Nichols was secretly in love with the driver, an attractive older man named Zeb.

Why keep it a secret? Coco wondered as she climbed into the SUV. Zeb was attractive in an exotic way. His smile looked genuine. Maybe it was the racial issue. Did Ms. Nichols think Zeb preferred his own kind? Coco had never understood color bias. A man was a man.

Zeb (his name tag didn't give a last name) was wearing khaki shorts, olive knee socks, boots and a safari hat that sported a leopard hatband. But his loose shirt was made of a colorful fabric that Coco recognized as traditional *kanga* fabric, handwoven by the native women of Tanzania. Zeb also wore an elephant hair bracelet, known for good luck.

It said in the brochure that Zeb, the caretaker of The Grove's many species of wildlife and birdlife, was born and raised in Kenya. Coco thought he was attractive in a dissolute, Hemingway-esque kind of way. But a man burdened with secrets, she sensed. A heavy drinker. And Coco sensed conflicted feelings from him when he looked at Vanessa. If the difference in their race wasn't the problem, then what could it be? Coco thought Vanessa was a knock out: generous of bosom, wide-hipped and plump-thighed, wearing a flowing Moroccan caftan and sandals with her long sleek black hair hanging in corn-rowed braids. Coco thought it ironic that Vanessa would be called

African while the man who was actually from Africa, would only be called "white."

Coco took a window seat and body-languaged herself in a way to let the guy next to her know she was open to conversation. But his arms brushed hers and she received a flash. He had a boyfriend back home.

Zeb climbed behind the wheel, said "Welcome everyone," in his classy East African accent, and they were on their way.

Coco was so busy sending feelers out to the men in the van that she was only vaguely aware of rocks, cacti, wildflowers blooming in carpets of color, and red tailed hawks wheeling overhead. "Those giant rocks you see up ahead," Zeb pointed out, "form the entrance to a series of caves once considered haunted by the local Indians." Camera shutters clicked like crickets on a spring night.

"A word of caution, my friends. If we come across coyotes, please remember that they are wild. Do not attempt to feed them or pet them. Coyotes are not your average Fido—they can be dangerous."

Coco leaned her forehead against the window and realized she had made a mistake. Only ten minutes into the desert and she knew that none of the men in the SUV was her soulmate.

"Mr. Memory!" the sign outside the cocktail lounge shouted. "Challenge him and win a fabulous prize!"

It was afternoon and Coco needed a drink.

After the desert safari, she had walked all over the resort, which turned out to be surprisingly big, and finally found herself at the main building that looked like any posh hotel except it didn't have cars out front or valet parkers or bellmen carrying luggage in and out. The lobby was cool and desert-spacious, with fountains and palms and parrots on perches.

She had come upon the Java Club, and a sign advertising an act. "Mr. Memory."

Coco was drawn to such attractions—magicians, mind readers, hypnotists. She had been one herself once, during a desperate period in her life.

The hostess led her to a small table with a candle glowing in a ruby globe. Coco ordered a cappuccino and turned her attention to the stage. The place was packed. The act must be good.

Her drink came and the lights dimmed. First an introduction by the emcee, and then the star came out. Tallish, blondish, medium build, wearing an opera cape and top hat. He gave the audience a brief talk about how he was able to remember anything and then he asked the audience to make lists of twenty words. That was when Coco noticed the pad of paper and pencil on her table. She watched others madly scribble and was curious to hear what they would come up with. This was an act she had never seen before.

A plump woman in floral print dress stood and read from her list: "Jezebel, Magdalene, Elizabeth, Eve…" Coco realized they were women from the Bible. When the woman was finished, Mr. Memory repeated the list back to her, word for word without a single mistake or hesitation.

The audience applauded.

Next, a small man with a shiny bald head who had to be asked twice to speak up: "Falcon, penguin, buzzard, peacock…" Coco thought surely Mr. Memory would stumble. He did not as he rattled off the twenty words in one breath. The applause was louder.

Coco's interest was piqued. More people stood and recited lists, each more tongue-twisting and esoteric than the last, and Mr. Memory didn't miss a word, a syllable, a beat. How did he do it?

Coco picked up a pen and wrote ferociously.

When a woman failed to challenge Mr. Memory with a list of fruits and vegetables, Coco didn't even raise her hand to be chosen, she just stood up and said, "I'm next!"

The spotlight swiveled to her and all heads turned. She cleared her throat and recited: "Cat fat rat bat ball wall fall tall tell well sell bell bill till will kill kid rid bid lid." When she was finished she heard a chuckle go through the audience and she knew people thought she hadn't challenged him, but when she raised her eyes, she saw something on Mr. Memory's face she hadn't seen with the others: a flicker of admiration.

He glibly recited her list but she detected the briefest hesitation between "bill" and "bell" and when he was done, the applause wasn't as enthusiastic.

But while everyone clapped politely, Mr. Memory looked right at Coco, across the crowded, dimly lit room, finding her eyes in the reflection of the little ruby globe candle, and she felt him from all the way across the room touch her, saw his lips lift in a knowing smile, felt her heart do a somersault. And then she saw that he really was quite good looking, cute more than handsome, and oh so sexy in black tie and tails, red-satin lined opera cape and tall hat, so that Coco wondered if he was the one.

She wasted no time going back stage after the act and insinuating herself in his path as he came toward the dressing room. With the top hat removed, she saw surfer-blond hair beneath the lights, and when he smiled at her she thought: Boy next door.

"You were good," they both said at the same time.

They laughed. "You first," Mr. Memory said.

"I've never seen an act like that before."

He removed the cape, set it on a tall stool with the top hat, and said, "And I haven't had a challenge like that before. Let me buy you a cup of coffee."

Most of the audience had left, so that the little club was quiet and cozy. "My name's Kenny," he said as their cappuccinos arrived.

Coco couldn't get over how *ordinary* everything about him was—his name, his beach boy looks, his pleasant personality. Yet his act on the stage had been extraordinary. "How do you do it, the memory thing?"

"It's something I was born with."

"A gift?"

"Or a curse, depending on how you look at it. I don't have the ability to forget. Everything I read, or see, or hear, everything I experience, I remember. All the way back to my childhood. Nothing is ever lost." Their eyes met over the ruby globe and Coco felt the chemistry begin.

She thought he would explain more about his memory gift, but instead he said, "So, Coco, you were named for Chanel?"

"It's a nickname," realizing he didn't want to talk about it, just as she never liked to talk about her own gift/curse. "My real name is Colleen but my older sister, who was two when I was born, couldn't say Colleen. She said Coco and it stuck."

"Coco," Kenny said. Not addressing her, just saying her name. "Makes me think of a hot, sweet drink."

"What's the prize?"

"Prize?"

"The sign says outside to challenge Mr. Memory and win a fabulous prize."

"Oh that." He laughed. "First prize is a week in Fresno. And the second prize—"

"Is *two* weeks in Fresno." They laughed together and Coco felt the connection. "So you liked my challenge?" It was a blatant bid for a compliment, but what the heck. She watched him as she sipped her drink.

"Did you notice that I didn't get as much applause for your list? The audience didn't get it that your list was more difficult. It was clever in fact." His eyes twinkled in admiration. "The harder lists, or the ones that look harder, are in fact easier to remember. Words are distinct separate entities, they form pictures in the mind. And most people choose categories without realizing it—Biblical names, birds, gemstones. But *your* list, bland almost meaningless monosyllables, all running together, 'fat rat bat,' making it difficult to hear the breaks. As if you threw me one long twenty-syllable word. Very smart. How did you know?"

"A hunch."

"Do you get a lot of hunches?"

She paused. This was the moment of truth, when most men turned off. She would see the little switch in their eyes, the interest dimming, and she could see them mentally search for reasons to leave. But she needed to know. "I'm a psychic reader."

"Really?" he said. "Interesting." Accepting it just like that.

And Coco's heart did a flip-flop.

"How do you do it? Ouija board?"

Full marks to him. "I read people. Usually by touch. It's called psychometry. I hold an object and read its history. I'll be happy to give you a reading sometime." Any excuse to touch him. "And incidentally, ouija boards are not genuine psychic tools. They were invented as a parlor game in the nineteenth century. The name is 'yes' in French and German—*oui* and *ja*."

"That's almost interesting," Kenny said with a dimpled smile and Coco felt another sweet jolt in her heart.

"What brings you to The Grove?" he asked. "It certainly can't be for any beauty treatments. What's to improve?"

This was getting better by the minute. "I won a contest. In fact, I'm going to have dinner with your boss tonight. Who is this Abby Tyler anyway?"

"A very nice lady who rescued me. Literally saved my life."

Coco waited but he looked away and addressed his coffee. "A story for another time."

A man with a secret. Coco was a sucker for men with secrets. If she reached out right now and touched him, would his secret be revealed to her? She cleared her throat and casually stirred her drink and tried to sound offhanded as she said, "So you, um, must travel a lot with your act."

"No. Never been away from the West Coast."

"Oh?"

"Born in Seattle, grew up in Seattle, got my degree in computer engineering there, then moved down to Silicon Valley. I was doing my nightclub act in San Francisco when I was approached with a job offer to work here at The Grove."

"But you would *like* to travel someday? See the world?" she asked hopefully.

"I'm happy where I am."

"Do you read a lot of travel and geography books?" Her hope was growing thin.

"Not particularly. My hobby is mathematics. I like to work difficult equations. Why this interest in travel? Is it what you do?"

Coco was disappointed. She had pinned such hopes on him, she was *warming* to him, but he wasn't the one. "I'm sorry," she said, pushing her chair back and standing up. She had to nip this in the bud before her heart became entangled. "I just remembered something I have to do."

"But—"

"Thanks for the coffee," she said and was gone, out of the main hotel, down the myriad paths where guests strolled and laughed, through the trees and shrubs until she was back at her own cottage, slamming the door behind herself, throwing her purse onto the sofa and reaching for the crystal ball.

CHAPTER SIX

*I*T WAS THE GETAWAY SUITCASE.

After thirty-three years, Abby still hadn't thrown it out. The case was old and battered, the handle broken and repaired, locks replaced, the inside lining still torn. For years she had kept it as a reminder. Should she ever get over-confident and relax her guard, the suitcase brought her back to reality.

But that was not why she took it down now from the top shelf of her closet, her hands trembling, her heart filling with pain and memories, drawing the old suitcase into the noon sunlight that streamed through her bedroom window. She brought it out because of what was inside.

The issues of the day weighed upon her—Maurice threatening to quit; the nagging feeling that Jack Burns should be watched; and Sissy and Coco—*one of you might be my daughter.* Abby had a million things that needed seeing to, but emotion overcame her, so that she sat on the bed to run her hand over the worn leather of the suitcase.

And remember…

The inmate's name was Mercy, a young black woman whose head was shaved smooth as a billiard ball. Skinny with haunted eyes, Mercy didn't speak as they crossed the dusty yard.

"What about my suitcase?" Emmy Lou said as she followed Mercy through the cool dusk. It was 1971, the trial was over, the jury found her guilty of a crime she did not commit, and now she was at the prison to serve her life sentence. She had been processed through and she wanted her suitcase. Granddaddy Jericho had packed it for her.

Mercy didn't answer and Emmy Lou noticed there was something wrong with her mouth.

Barrack Twelve was a long building made of wooden siding and a tar paper roof. Inside, two rows of beds stood beneath barred windows, with a narrow aisle down the center. Some of the beds were occupied, women lying down or sitting, some reading, others playing solitaire or checkers, and some just staring into space.

"There's your bed," Mercy said and Emmy Lou saw that she had no teeth, even though she didn't look older than twenty.

When Mercy started to turn away, Emmy Lou said, "Wait, please. My suitcase. How can I get it?"

"We ain't allowed personal possessions." And Mercy was gone.

White Hills Prison was a garment factory, and the inmates earned eleven cents an hour for their labor. As soon as she could, Emmy Lou purchased a writing tablet, envelopes and pencils and spent her free time writing letters to her public defender, the judge at her trial, the sheriff who had arrested her, the county prosecutor, even the editor of the Pecos newspaper—anyone she could think of who might have the clout to get her case re-examined. She protested her innocence, but never mentioned the drifter with whom she had had a brief summer romance. Although her suspicion that he was the one who killed Avis grew with each day that she didn't hear from him, she had no proof, and perhaps a small part of her held out hope that he wasn't guilty after all. Her letters were filled with her fondness and high regard for Avis and about the fact that she used that shovel all the time, which was why her fingerprints were on it. Emmy Lou poured her heart into those letters, and sent them off every week like doves of peace, to wait hopefully for responses.

In the meantime, there was her baby, growing within her, and which she loved with all her heart.

Emmy Lou hated the words "bastard" and "out of wedlock." Artificial, manmade words that had nothing to do with nature's law. How could a baby be illegitimate? Might as well call a seedling illegitimate, or force male and female flowers to marry before they could cross-pollinate. And it wasn't even one of the Ten Commandments: *Thou shalt not bear bastard children.* The inmates told her that because she wasn't eligible for parole for fifteen years, she couldn't keep her baby, that it would be taken from her. So Emmy Lou wrote letters to her grandfather and the other folks in Little Pecos, begging them to take care of her baby until her appeal came through.

She was in the recreation room writing letters when they came for Mercy—the matrons, with their clippers and shavers and anti-lice shampoo, chasing her around the room until they tackled her and scraped the "pickaninny fuzz," as they called it, off her scalp. Once a month they did it, and Emmy Lou didn't know why, because none of the other prisoners had their heads shaved, just Mercy.

It was a cold January day and she thought Mercy would be better off with hair on her head, but the matrons had their way until Mercy's head was smooth. No one came to her rescue, and when Emmy Lou went to Mercy's side, some of the others muttered, "Nigger lover," but Emmy Lou ignored them.

They had nicked Mercy's scalp so Emmy Lou got a wet towel from the bathroom.

"It's coz I'm Negro," Mercy said, running her hand under her nose. "They don't like the new de-segregation laws so they punishing me."

It was strange to see a young woman with not a tooth in her mouth. And was it her imagination or did Mercy look even thinner than when Emmy Lou had first arrived, four months ago? "You need teeth," she finally said because it had to be said.

Mercy nodded. "I fell in with a bad man. Thought he loved me. He tried to force me to prostitution, but I ain't no whore. First john he connected me with, I nearly bit his cock off. My so-called boyfriend knocked all my teeth out, said I wouldn't be doing *that* again. Why I killt him."

"Can't you get dentures?" knowing that some of the women took advantage of the prison having a dentist.

"Got 'em," Mercy said unhappily. "But I can't wear 'em. They hurt." She pulled back her lips to expose sore gums. "Why I don't eat, why I don't talk to no one. I look like a freak, girl like me looking like a old lady."

Emmy Lou wrote to her grandfather and asked for magazines and gum, and for a special item, which she told him to label "vitamins" as she suspected the prison authorities wouldn't let her have it.

The package came a week later. She gave the magazines and gum away and found Mercy out in the yard, at the edge where the chainlink fence met freedom.

"Got something for you, Mercy."

The black girl shivered in the biting winter wind. "Go away. They all laugh at me, say I'm fallin' for a do-gooding white girl."

"Here," Emmy Lou said, holding out the small bottle.

Mercy narrowed her eyes. "What is it?"

"It's called Tincture of Cloves. My Granddaddy makes it from his own clove tree. Rub a little on your gums, it makes the pain go away. Put some on and wear your dentures for five minutes. Do it a little longer each time, pretty soon your dentures will feel as comfortable as an old pair of shoes."

It was the beginning of April when Emmy Lou was in the mess hall eating a potato and corn dinner when the hall fell silent. They all turned to see, walking proudly with her head high, Mercy grinning with a mouthful of white teeth.

She had done as Emmy Lou said, using the tincture to get her mouth accustomed to the dentures, eating porridge and mashed potatoes, graduating to vegetables and bread until she could wear her teeth all the time and eat anything.

The transformation was stunning. Cheeks and lips no longer falling in, Mercy walking with a straight back and meeting people in the eye. A new, strong Mercy that no one would mess with, not even the matrons with their clippers.

There was no stopping her from talking after that. "Momma was a scrub-woman," she told Emmy Lou as they walked in the exercise yard, Emmy Lou supporting her back now that she was eight months pregnant. "It might have been dirty work, but she was proud and she had her dignity. She coulda sold her body to feed us kids, men comin' around all the time on account of she was so beautiful. But Momma was a good Christian woman and said if she got down on her knees it would be either to pray or to scrub floors, not to satisfy some man's need."

They stopped at the chainlink fence to ponder the plains that vanished into eternity. "You have a dream, Emmy Lou? Something you want to do before you die?" A twenty-year-old asking this. "My dream is to see the fog rolling into the San Francisco Bay. I come from the dustiest spot in Texas, where the dust gets under your skin and behind your eyes, and I saw this travelogue at the picture show, San Francisco with hills and cable cars, and this big white cloud sailing across the water from the ocean, swallowing up that big red bridge, lonesome foghorn calling out in the mist, and it like to have cleaned that Texas dust right out of me. Came right here," she said, tapping her breast, "and settled there, calling me to go someday."

Emmy Lou's dream was to get out of prison before her baby was born. She would have her baby in freedom, they would go back to Little Pecos and live with Jericho, and the two of them would teach the child how to grow God's green things.

Emmy Lou was fastening hooks to men's zippered prison pants when she was ordered to the infirmary for a vitamin shot. Her pains started soon after, as she was taking her tray to the cafeteria window. She cried out and slumped, and Mercy was there to grab her, so it was Mercy who got her to the infirmary and Mercy who was recruited to help because the usual infirmary trusty was laid up with adult tonsillitis.

"It's too soon," Emmy Lou cried, shocked at the severity of the pain. She still had three weeks to go. Was something wrong? "Call my grandfather! Promise me! He must come and take my baby."

The doctor promised her.

"Let my grandfather know," Emmy Lou said to Mercy who was holding her hand. "Tell him he has to come for the baby. Don't let it go to an orphanage."

"Don't you worry none," Mercy said, patting Emmy Lou's shoulder.

Mercy was looking at the scalpel and clamps and large obstetric forceps being laid out on a table.

Emmy Lou clutched her abdomen: *Not yet little one. Wait. Stay with me a while longer. There's no rush to be in this world.*

When the doctor said, "Put her to sleep," Emmy Lou held on tight to Mercy's strong hand.

As the drug began to work, Emmy Lou felt a sharp pain, and then no pain, and then the sensation of a velvet curtain being drawn around her. After that she saw, heard, felt nothing.

When she woke she was in an infirmary bed with sunlight streaming across her blanket. A nurse was taking her pulse. "My...baby...?"

"It died, sugar. Just a little bit of a thing, not fully formed."

There was no cemetery at White Hills. When an inmate died, a mortician came from Amarillo to pick up the body. If there was no family to take care of the arrangements, the deceased went into the Potter's Field. That was where Emmy Lou's baby had gone, into an unmarked grave.

She lay on her cot trying to imagine the little grave that contained a tiny wooden box, her baby lying cold and alone in the dark. Why had it died? Was it something she did, or didn't do? If she had eaten right would her baby have lived? If she had prayed harder, slept longer, fought for her innocence, written just one more letter, could she have saved it?

Her thoughts were dark and jumbled, like the clouds grumbling over the Texas Panhandle, grief encompassing her like the gray blanket on her bed. Why was she still here, in this terrible place? Why was she being punished for a crime she did not commit? Why had the world forgotten her?

The final straw was the letter from a neighbor back home: "Sorry to have to tell you this but yore Granddaddy died of a heart attack. I'd of come and told you myself in person excepting my arther-itis is acting up and the trip is just too long, you being up Amarillo way and all. Jericho was never the same after you was put away. Folks stopped coming to the nursery. Business went bad. The bank took the nursery and all the property, cause of back taxes. Jericho died broke. He didn't leave you nothing."

Emmy Lou drifted off into a fitful sleep and dreamed she was burning in hell. It was hot and thick with smoke. She had always thought hell would stink of sulfur, but it didn't, more like burning tar paper. And then a devil's imp had its clawed hand on her shoulder, shaking her.

Her eyes snapped open. She looked up into Mercy's wide eyes as she bent over her in the dark. "Get up!" she hissed. "Come on!"

Before Emmy Lou could ask why, Mercy had her wrist in a strong grip—since her teeth fit Mercy had put on pounds and muscle—and pulled her from the bed. Wordlessly, Emmy Lou stumbled after her, down the center of the rows of sleeping women and out into the night that was suddenly full of smoke.

"This way!" Mercy said, and she took Emmy Lou a way she had never been before, in the direction of the guards' dormitories. She looked back to see flames leaping from the main building, and people running out now in night dresses, screaming as alarms rang shrilly in the night. More than one fire raged, Emmy Lou saw—the mess hall, the garment factory, the warden's office.

They ducked behind a building as the guards came pouring from the dorms, pulling up pants, opening the locked gates, racing toward the barracks and huts that were bursting into flame they were so dry and old and wooden.

Mercy ran through the open gate, and Emmy Lou saw now that she was carrying a suitcase.

When they got to the guards' cars, they ran from one to another until they found one unlocked. Throwing the suitcase in the back, Mercy jumped behind the wheel, found keys in the sun visor, and shouted, "Get in!"

Emmy Lou climbed in and Mercy took off before her door was closed. They shot through the parking lot, over the dirt and onto the highway, Mercy saying, "Keep a lookout if we followed."

Emmy Lou kept looking back, as the blazing prison receded until she couldn't see it anymore, but saw no cars chasing them, no lights or siren on the deserted highway. Then she faced forward scared out of her skin as they plunged into the darkness ahead.

After miles of not speaking or slowing the car, Mercy finally stopped at a crossroads that couldn't even have a name it was so small, smaller even than Little Pecos. But there was a bus stop sign that said Greyhound, and they were out of Texas because they had crossed the state line into New Mexico.

It was still dark but would soon be dawn, and Mercy spoke her first words since the escape. "I set those fires back there coz I had to get out and it was the only way. I brought you with me coz you made it possible for me to smile and eat. I will never forget what you did for me, Emmy Lou Pagan. You gave me back my pride and with it came my old fighting spirit, and I remembered that I am a human being not an animal, and I knew I had to burn that place down. But here we part ways. You have your own road, I have mine. I'm going to ditch this car and head east. You take the bus. One's bound to come along. I will never forget you, first white person ever to treat me with respect."

She reached into the back and pulled the suitcase to the front, and Emmy Lou realized it was hers. "Before I set the fires, I got this for you. I remembered how important it was to you."

Emmy Lou opened it and saw magazines, coins for the phone, stationery and stamps, gum and candy gone stale, lipsticks, photographs of the mother who died when she was little. An envelope containing a thousand dollars in cash. All tenderly packed by her grandfather before she was put away.

She started to hand the cash to Mercy, but Mercy pushed it back. "I got money. Took it out of Warden's desk. Figure she owes me, all those haircuts they forced on me. Now I got some advice for you. Change your name, they be looking for Emmy Lou Pagan."

"No," Emmy Lou said. "I'm going back."

"What!"

"I'm innocent. My granddaddy died of shame because of me. I am going to clear our name. I can't do it if I'm on the run."

"You go back they lock you up for good."

"I have to fight them, Mercy. I'll get a lawyer. I'll fight."

Emmy Lou didn't know what else to do then except reach for the door handle. There were some big boulders at the side of the highway, she would hide behind them to change out of her prison nightdress and into the clothes in the suitcase, then wait for the Greyhound—the one that would take her back to White Hills.

"One last thing you oughta know," Mercy said. "Your labor was induced. I heard them say. That wasn't no vitamin shot they give you, but some drug that makes the contractions come on. They was in a hurry to take your baby outa you."

Emmy Lou stared at her. "Why?"

"Coz your baby ain't dead. She was born alive and healthy with a good set of lungs. Ten fingers and ten toes, we counted. Warden give her to a man come to the prison and drive off with her. Warden told me to keep my mouth shut or she'd make it permanent I never have teeth again."

Emmy Lou sat like a stone. Her eyes said it all, the big question.

Mercy's voice softened. "I don't know where your baby went, hon. But I heard Warden say to the doc, 'Bakersfield is in a hurry.'"

Emmy Lou had to squeeze breath from her lungs, her chest was so tight. "Bakersfield? Is that a person?"

"Could be, or it could be short talkin', you know, like *the man in* Bakersfield."

"Where is that?"

Mercy shrugged. "Car had California license plates. I carried the baby out, wrapped in a blanket. The warden give her to this man driving a white Impala from California. There was a woman in the front seat, and there were two babies bundled in the back. Driver give your baby to the woman and she had a baby bottle for it. That's all I know."

Emmy Lou stared through the pitted windshield, at the ribbon of highway that rolled off to the horizon. Everything was different now. Her baby was alive. She couldn't go back to White Hills. Not until she had found her child.

Mercy rested a strong black hand on Emmy Lou's arm, her eyes full of wisdom at twenty. "Remember something as you go through this life. It's men makes the rules. You and I was put in prison coz we are women and coz we would not abide by men's rules. They make us have babies, then they punish us for having babies, and then they take our babies away. I killt a no good pimp and you didn't kill nobody. We wasn't convicted for that. We was convicted because we are women and we wanted to rule our own bodies."

They were both crying now and using their sleeves. Wondering if there were tissues in the glove box, Emmy Lou opened it and something black and heavy tumbled out.

"Good Lord," Mercy said.

Emmy Lou stared at the gun. It belonged to the prison guard whose car this was. Gingerly picking it up, she put it back in the glove box, slamming it shut.

Then she said, "I'm going to find her," meaning her baby.

"Be careful when you do, coz you will be crossing more men and breaking more men's rules and they won't like that. Men who steal and sell babies can't be saints. They be dangerous. And we runaways now, wouldn't stay put in a man's prison. Just you be careful. And change your name," she said again.

Emmy Lou looked at the photograph of her mother, that Jericho had put in the suitcase, a smiling young woman with red-gold hair like her own. Tyler Abilene Pagan—named for the town she was conceived in and the town she was born in—tragically dying in a car accident with her young husband. Emmy Lou would adopt her mother's name.

"I will never forget this, Mercy. Someday I will repay you."

The hugged each other and kissed damp cheeks, then Emmy Lou got out of the car and watched Mercy drive off and disappear into the rising sun. Then she turned her face to the west. Toward California and the town of Bakersfield.

Standing out there alone on the desert highway with nothing but cactus and wind for miles, Emily Louise Pagan, now Abilene Tyler, still sixteen soon to be seventeen and promising herself she would never fall in love for the rest of her life, made two vows: to find her child, and never to be a victim again...

She had kept both vows, and now, thirty-three years later, looking at the battered suitcase, she was prepared to use it again. In it she had packed a change of clothes, toiletries, toothbrush, and a one-way airline ticket. Before the week was out, Abby would be gone from this place she had so lovingly created and never come back.

CHAPTER SEVEN

OH YES!" THE GIRL SCREAMED. "DO IT! HARDER!"

And Fallon did it, just as she asked, hard and fast and deep. The seamstress—Fallon didn't know her name—loved getting it from behind, which suited him fine because she had an ass like a bass fiddle.

He had come looking for Francesca and had found the seamstress in the penthouse suite at the top of the Las Vegas Atlantis Casino Hotel. The girl was on her knees making adjustments to the hem of the wedding gown. She told him everyone had gone to lunch and then batted her eyes at him the way she had during the several fittings he had attended, so he had known she wanted it. Fallon made it a policy never to screw women of his own social standing, they got too demanding afterward. But the seamstress would be history after the wedding on Saturday. And to Fallon's pleasant surprise, having sex among virginal lace and bridal satin and maidenly petticoats gave it a uniquely erotic edge.

Michael Fallon, owner of the Atlantis, the biggest and flashiest casino hotel on the Vegas Strip, was fifty-eight years old, rich and Italian-good-looking. He had been born out of wedlock to a Las Vegas waitress whose Irish-immigrant parents had come to Nevada in search of work. Her father helped build Hoover Dam and had died in a dramatic plunge into what would one day be Lake Mead. Mrs. Fallon died of a broken heart, leaving eighteen-year-old Lucy to fend for herself. Her beauty and sweet personality had landed her a job at the new Flamingo Hotel, which opened in December 1946 to much publicity and fanfare. She had even had her picture taken with notorious mobster, Bugsy Siegel. When her baby was born the following summer, Lucy was twenty years old, unmarried and waitressing at the Wagon Wheel casino hotel on Highway 91.

She baptized her baby in the Catholic church, took him to Mass every Sunday, and when he was eight Michael received his First Holy Communion. She never told anyone, not even her son, who the boy's father was, and so, from the start, the kid had problems with his ancestry.

"Ma, who was my father?" And she would say, "You're too young to understand." Apparently he never got old enough to understand because to this day Mike Fallon still didn't know who his father was.

"Then how do you know you're half-Italian?" Uri Edelstein, his best friend, had once asked.

"'Cause I can *feel* it," Fallon had replied. And it was true. Besides, in those days, in 1946 when Eastern mobs were moving in and taking over Vegas, the big juices were all wops. And since his mother wouldn't talk about it, it only stood to reason she was ashamed because she'd gotten into bed with a gangster.

Michael didn't like doing *all* the work, so he pulled out of the big-hipped seamstress and switched places with her, lying on his back so she could climb on top and ride him, giving him a good view of her jiggling tits.

Not knowing who his father was hadn't really bothered Fallon because he'd drifted into a life of crime himself, doing jobs for the local mob. But then Francesca was born. That was when Fallon's life did a complete turn around and he decided to go straight. He had worked hard all the years since, to create his sterling image. Michael Fallon was now a respectable businessman, serving on the boards of several charities, a deacon in his church, but his crowning achievement was going to take place the coming

Saturday, at the wedding that was going to grant him admission at last into the oldest, richest echelons of Nevada.

He had to make sure there were no loose ends.

It was not only his father's identity he was worried about, but his own underworld activities when he was young and fancied himself a Vegas high-roller, working any scheme he could that made money, even driving kidnapped babies across state lines.

"Oh Mr. Fallon!" the jiggly seamstress cried.

Time to end this. Clamping his hands on her hips, he lifted her off his cock and pulled her head down, saying, "Suck it." His mind was on other things now. The important phone call he was expecting. Michael tangled his fingers in her hair as he came in her mouth, then he slipped out from under her and said, "Better get back to work, doll." There were still yards of white lace to hem.

He dressed quickly but paused to retrieve his money clip and peel off a hundred-dollar bill. "Here you go, sweetheart," he said, giving it to the seamstress, adding a wink and a smile.

On the way out, he stopped at the wedding veil hanging by the door. Made of hand-beaded imported Italian lace, it was so heavy it was going to require three little flower girls to carry it.

Michael trembled to touch it, remembering the night Francesca was born, the night his life turned around. His beautiful Gayane, lying dead on bloody sheets, the helpless infant in his arms. Something had flipped in Fallon that fateful night as he had held the tender little bundle in his arms, driving him to take his first step in cleaning up his life.

He had found Karl Bakersfelt at home, making arrangements to pick up three illegally obtained babies.

Michael had walked in holding out a cigar, that night years ago. "Congratulate me, I'm a daddy."

"Hey," Bakersfelt said, accepting the fine Havana. He had heard Fallon's wife, Gayane Simonian, was knocked up. He waited. This meeting had to do with more than a cigar. Michael had an odd look about him, his manner was strange.

Then it came: "Gayane is dead. She gave her life delivering my daughter."

"Oh, I'm sorry about that," said Karl Bakersfelt who had purchased more babies than he could count, and never knew the mothers, whether they were alive or dead, and he didn't care.

Michael had got a faraway look in his eye which, under other circumstances, would have alarmed Bakersfelt. But he understood where it came from. Man's wife dying like that. "She screamed, Karl. And there was so much blood. The doctor said he could save only one—my wife or the baby. I had to choose. What could I do?"

"You chose the baby," Bakersfelt said unnecessarily, wondering why Michael had come, wishing he would get to the point because Karl had people waiting for infants.

"I'm leaving the life, Karl," Michael said at last. "I'm making a clean break. I held that little creature in my arms and my heart melted like chocolate on a Vegas sidewalk in August. I vowed there and then to go straight."

Karl grinned and reached for his lighter. "Fatherhood'll do that to ya. Okay, I won't call you no more. I'll find another hand-over guy."

"The thing is," Fallon said cautiously, still unclear on all the nuts and bolts of his major life-changing decision. "I have to ask myself: can I trust old friends never to talk about the past?"

The gold lighter froze in Bakersfelt's hand. "You can trust me, Michael."

"Well, you see. I did some work for Joey Franchimoni, coupla hits, and I don't think Joey would keep quiet, especially as the Feds are pressuring him to sell his casino and leave town. Joey's the sort who might talk to get himself a break."

"Yeah," Karl said, nodding. Joey the Nose, so named on account of he didn't have one, was known for his loose tongue.

"So I visited him an hour ago and slipped him the salt," Fallon said, meaning he stuffed bichloride-of-mercury tablets down Joey's throat—a metallic poison favored by the Mob.

"I ain't no stoolie," Bakersfelt said. "You can count on me."

"Good, I just wanted to have your word on that. I'm a father now, gotta be respectable. No more ties with the old gang. No more hits or dirty stuff. My kid grows up, I can't be always worrying my past is going to come out. Know what I mean?"

Bakersfelt nodded, he knew what Fallon meant, and he thumbed the gold lighter and produced flame, touching it to his fine Havana cigar. The explosion took away half his face, spattering his desk with blood and bone and black powder.

"*Now* I have your guarantee," Fallon said to the dead man. Then he went around the house with a can of lighter fluid, squirting extra hard into the file cabinets that held records of blackmarket flesh peddling.

It only took one match. The house went up like the rotted piece of tinder it was and cinders flew to the sky carrying the names of young mothers, adoptive parents, cities of birth, dates, routes driven, cash amounts—leaving no record of Bakersfelt's years of black-market baby trafficking, especially Michael Fallon's involvement in it.

That was years ago and Fallon had believed he was safe. But recently he learned there were still a few loose ends that could connect him to Bakersfelt and the baby business.

Leaving the seamstress to her work, Fallon made his way upstairs to the penthouse where he stripped off his clothes and stepped into the spacious marble shower. As he lathered his athletic body, Fallon thought about those days back in the late sixties, early seventies, when he ran blackmarket babies across the Western states. It was big money in those days, and easy. Just a driver and a nursemaid, picking up kids from other drivers— you never knew where they came from, mostly they were stolen, though—and dropping them off at their new families. All so damned illegal that there was no way to trace any of it, so Mike Fallon had rested easy with the thought that his own involvement in the operation would never be uncovered.

And yet it had. By a certain nosy bitch named Abby Tyler who owned a resort outside of Palm Springs.

Turning off the shower and wrapping himself in a robe, Fallon went to the window that overlooked Las Vegas. In the distance, buildings and grass met the edge of a vast ochre sea: the desert.

Michael Fallon hated the desert because it reminded him of infinity. It just went on and on with no beginning, no ending, no purpose, no point. The desert gave him the creeps because there was no way of knowing or understanding it, no way of getting along with it, and no way of beating it because the desert, like the house, always won. Therefore he embraced the concrete and glass and neon and cheap carpeting of the casino hotels, sucked in the bracing air-conditioning the way mountain climbers inhaled alpine air, and reveled in the hot bright lights the way most people worshiped the sun.

He poured himself a scotch and wondered if the fucking phone would ever ring.

Karl Bakersfelt had been only the first. Michael had then drawn up a list of people who knew too much and had gone about systematically silencing them. All these years later, with the wedding just days away, he was down to five on the list.

The first involved a certain Nevada newspaper editor. The day after Fallon, at the time twenty-five years old, had married Gayane Simonian, the man had written: "Gregory Simonian, considered to be the founder of the famous Strip, has long been held in esteem for his refusal to do business with gangsters. The Wagon Wheel is considered the one casino not tied to 'outside' interests. But yesterday's wedding indicates a changing wind for Mr. Simonian, who now counts Michael Fallon as his son-in-law."

Fallon and his gunmen broke into the editor's home in the middle of the night and ordered him and his wife out of bed. Fallon had the editor tied to a chair, hands and feet, and when the man said, "What are you going to do?" Fallon had quipped, "I'm going to shoot you, of course. It's what *gangsters* do, isn't it?"

Fallon had then made the wife take off her nightgown and kneel naked before him. While one of his goons held a gun to the editor's head, Fallon had unzipped his pants, pulled out his erect member and said to the kneeling wife, "Kiss it."

When she refused, he said, "You only get one more chance. Then my friend there pulls the trigger."

The terrified woman did as told, and as soon as her lips met turgid flesh, a blinding flash filled the room. Quickly restoring himself and zipping up his pants, Fallon gestured to the camera in Uri Edelstein's hands. Then he shook a threatening finger in the editor's face and said, "You say one more word about me in that filthy rag of yours and this picture is plastered all over the fuckin' United States." On his way out, he had added with a cocky smile, "I told you I was going to shoot you."

It wasn't the editor Fallon worried about now—that man had long since gone to his reward—but the henchman who had held the gun to the editor's head, one of Fallon's old goons. He was still alive somewhere in the United States and Fallon was worried that if he read about the upcoming wedding, he might get it into his mind to try a little blackmail.

The second loose end went back to a day back in '72. A job in the desert, Rocco Guzman, buried up to his neck in sand.

A pair of vultures, perched on a nearby mesquite bush, had watched in anticipation while another variety of vulture—in trousers and overcoats and hats—stood in a circle around the hapless Guzman. There wasn't another soul for miles. Across the desert, barely visible in the distance, were the towers of Las Vegas, adult playground of the Western world, affectionately known as Sin City.

But those men had not been there for fun. Despite the golf clubs in their hands.

"Where's the money, Rocco?" Michael Fallon had asked. It was before Francesca was born, back when he still worked for the Syndicate and hadn't yet started cleaning up his act.

The man in the ground, his face growing purple, could barely talk, the sand constricted his rib cage and choked his throat. They had done a good job of burying him. Having his hands and feet bound in electrical tape had helped. He gasped something out.

Fallon bent over. "What was that, Rocco?"

Rocco, a flat-nosed hoodlum, couldn't talk. While the vultures watched.

Michael Fallon, in long black cashmere coat and old fashioned wide-brimmed fedora on his head—an admitted affectation—wasn't really expecting a response from his erstwhile henchman. The money Rocco had stolen had been recovered. Fallon had brought him here to teach a lesson to the others. You work for Michael Fallon—whether it was drugs, prostitution, extortion, racketeering—you'd better be honest.

Giving his men the signal, he had turned and headed back to one of the black sedans parked across the dunes. The golf clubs made cracking and thudding sounds and Rocco managed enough breath to scream a few times before he was silent. Fallon wasn't worried about the body being found. The vultures on the mesquite bush would take care of that.

But now, on this Monday afternoon as he got ready to make his walk-through in the casino downstairs, he was worried about those men. Two had died of natural causes, one had gotten killed in a gang hit, leaving two who could still talk. Fallon had ordered them taken care of.

The main chink in his armor, however, was still his mother, living in a Miami nursing home. No matter how much Michael had begged, pleaded, cajoled or threatened, his mother would not talk about his father. Wouldn't reveal his name. But if she were to do so now...

The phone rang at last. Private line. "Fallon here." The news was good. All three men had been taken care of. That left just two people who could still ruin everything between now and the wedding.

His mother. And Abby Tyler.

CHAPTER EIGHT

*Y*OU NEED FINGERPRINTS, JACK," HIS FRIEND IN FORENSICS HAD said. "Buy Tyler a drink. Have dinner with her. When she isn't looking, take the glass. Without prints there's not much we can do." Jack returned to his room to check the fax machine, see if there was any new information on Abby Tyler. But there was still nothing from his contact at Hollywood Station.

Thumbing through the CDs he had brought with him, he selected a disc, slipped it into the player and a moment later Chopin filled the air.

Going into the bathroom to wash his hands, he looked in the mirror and glowered at the stranger glowering back at him. The man had deep lines on either side of his mouth, his hair was too gray for his age, and his brown eyes looked as if they had seen too much.

Jack had had the dream again last night and had wakened that morning in sweat-soaked sheets. Fainting at the crime scene when the medical examiner rolled the corpse onto her back. When Jack had first gotten the call he had thought it was a routine investigation, just another od'd junkie, they said on the police radio. And it *was* a junkie, the needle was still in her arm, heroin tracks on her white skin.

Jack had stared at the pale face, thinking he knew it from somewhere. That nagging familiarity. And when it had come to him, and he had whispered, "Nina," his knees had given way and the floor had rushed up to slam him in the face so that he lay crumpled next to the naked corpse.

What haunted him now was not the shock of seeing his sister's body, but the message she had left on his telephone answering machine just a few hours prior to her death: "Jack, I've managed to contact some of the names on my list. There's one in New York, one in Illinois and one in Santa Barbara. I told them I'm doing an article and would like to talk with them in person. The strangest thing, Jack, two of them said they were going away on a holiday. They had won a week's stay at a resort called The Grove. These women don't know each other, and they said it was a prize for a contest they don't remember entering. Jack, I think it has something to do with the owner of The Grove. Listen, something big is coming together. I don't want to say anything more until I've met with a contact tonight. He says he will only talk to me on condition of anonymity. I'll tell you all about it at breakfast. Wish me luck!"

They were the last words he had heard his sister speak.

Savagely drying his hands, he slipped into his leather jacket, set protective silver glasses in place and left his room in search of Abby Tyler.

Abby studied her face in the mirror. She was worried about being recognized.

Vanessa had urged her friend time and again to get plastic surgery, to alter her face, but Abby wouldn't hear of it. "Someday I am going to find my daughter," she would say, "and I want to be able to stand in front of a mirror with her and say, 'We look alike.'" Vanessa herself was lucky. She bore no resemblance to the waif-like creature who had made a daring escape from prison. Changing her hair, getting dental implants and putting on weight had altered her appearance so much that no one would connect Vanessa Nichols to the girl who was once victimized by sadistic prison matrons.

Vanessa thought back to the day Abby found her, in 1985, thirteen years after they had parted company at a lonely crossroads in the New Mexico desert. Abby's search was inspired, having nothing more to go on than a dream Mercy had once voiced. Abby had found Mercy—by then Vanessa Nichols—sitting at the view point on the City end of the Golden Gate Bridge, watching the fog roll in. By that time, Mercy had changed her name, gotten fake ID and birth certificate, scrubbed floors during the day and gone to school at night, landing a job at a large hospital on the housekeeping staff, cleaning patients' rooms and working her way up until, that foggy day in 1985 when Abby found her, Vanessa was the assistant supervisor for the entire housekeeping department.

Abby had asked Vanessa to move back to Los Angeles with her, saying that she missed her, that Vanessa was the only person in the world she could trust, her only friend, who had been there when her baby was born—and Vanessa felt the same way, being powerfully lonely in such a crowded city, with no one to tell her story to, no one to say, "Hey, remember that time," to. But Vanessa had hesitated. "We're still fugitives, and if we are fugitives together, we have twice as much chance getting caught."

"*Half* the chance," Abby had corrected. "Because we will watch each other's back."

They had watched each other's back since.

Especially now. When Vanessa saw her friend's eyes stray to the window, her gaze filled with pain and longing, Vanessa knew what was on her mind. To run over to Sissy's and Coco's cottages and find out which was her daughter. "Abby," Vanessa cautioned now, "go slowly. You're walking a tightrope. One slip-up and you will lose everything—this resort, your daughter, your freedom, even your life! You can't blunder into this. There might be ears listening. And Jack Burns, whoever the heck he is, I don't trust him. Abby, you've waited thirty-three years, another day won't hurt."

When Abby brought her eyes from the window and looked at Vanessa, there was such naked want in them that Vanessa was briefly taken aback. "Shouldn't a mother know her own child," Abby asked with passion, "even if they have never met?"

"I don't see a strong resemblance to you in any of them." But she knew that didn't necessarily mean anything. Vanessa's sister Ruby didn't look at all like her parents or her siblings yet was the image of a great-aunt on her mother's side.

"That wasn't what I meant," Abby said. "I'm talking about instinct, knowing something in your soul."

"Have you decided how you are going to approach them?"

What do you say to a daughter who didn't know she was adopted? Or, if she knew, that she had been adopted through illegal means, that she was stolen from her birth mother, and that her birth mother was serving a life sentence for murder at the time?

Jack Burns found himself at the departure pavilion by the airstrip where a few guests were waiting to leave. Everyone was cheery and up-beat, talking, laughing, a few kissing and holding hands, not at all the way vacationers looked at the end of a trip: tired, beaten, worn out. These people looked as if they had imbibed a potent tonic. And seeing the romantic smiles and dreamy eyes (and the ladies definitely glowed) Jack guessed what the tonic was.

Winding his way through the heart of the resort, past a magnificent aviary filled with colorful exotic birdlife, he came upon one of the smaller of The Grove's pools—created out of rocks and surrounded by dense ferns so that it looked like a natural lagoon. He grudgingly admitted that he would love to strip off his jeans and leather jacket and dive in.

On a small grassy area next to the lagoon, lounge chairs and tables had been set out, and a group of people were paying obeisance to a man in a tank top and shorts, who was talking in a too-loud voice about what a "pussy magnet" his recently won Oscar statuette was. "I tell you, the babes come panting for it. Got it over my fireplace, they take one look at the statuette and cream their pants. They spread for it, I tell you!"

Jack knew him. Ivar Manguson, the famous director of titanic mega-hits involving state-of-the art special effects. He was known for carrying on a passionate affair with each current leading lady and then dumping her when the film was finished. He had even married one—the star of a disaster epic that broke box office records—and when he divorced her at the end of production had said it was because "she was no longer the character she played but an ordinary woman again."

Jack was about to move on when he saw a cocktail waitress arrive with a loaded tray. One of the men in the group shot out a grabby hand and tried to catch her ass. She sidestepped, but it unbalanced her and the tray went sliding.

Cold drinks, ice and paper umbrellas fell everywhere.

A frosty Mai-Tai landed in Manguson's lap. He jumped up, hands on his crotch, shouting, "Ow! Ow!" Dancing around in his two-hundred-dollar sandals. "Shit!" he shouted at the waitress. "You made it look like I've pissed my pants!"

The flustered waitress snatched up a napkin from the table and tried to wipe him off.

"Get away from me, you stupid bitch!" Shoving her so hard she fell to the ground.

Jack ran over and helped her up. "Are you okay?"

She nodded, in tears.

Jack turned to the cursing and swearing man, who was trying madly to mop the cocktail out of his shorts, and said, "Apologize."

Manguson gave him a dumb look. "What?"

"Apologize to the lady."

"Like fuck I will."

Jack shrugged, looked at the waitress as if to say, What can you do? and grabbed Manguson's wrist, swung him around and, holding him in a painful arm-lock, said, "Apologize."

"Go fuck yourself."

Jack twisted the arm higher. Manguson grimaced and his face turned red. "You're breaking it, man!"

"Say you're sorry to the lady and I'll let go."

Two security men appeared through the trees just then, and behind them, Abby Tyler. "Is there a problem here?"

"That bitch—" The man in the wet shorts began. But Jack cut him off. "This gentleman laid a hand on one of your staff. I am asking him to apologize to her."

Abby sized up the scene, the frazzled waitress, the staring faces of the other guests, the beet-red cheeks of the man Jack Burns held in a clinch, and then at Burns himself who appeared calm yet had a strong hold on his captive who was now yelling, *"Don't you know who I am?"*

"Please release him, Mr. Burns," Abby said calmly.

Jack said, "Just one word of apology is all I ask."

"Please, Mr. Burns."

He saw her steady gaze, the look of expectancy, felt Manguson struggle against his hold and, in disgust, released him.

"That's more like it," the hot shot said as he rubbed his arm. "Get this idiot out of here," he said to Abby's security guards, gesturing at Jack.

But the security men didn't move.

"Hey," said Manguson. "Are you deaf?"

Abby addressed him. "We will be happy to refund your money, Mr. Manguson, and make room for you on the next flight back to Los Angeles."

He ogled at her. "What?"

"You are clearly unhappy with our services. You will be reimbursed completely. My staff here will escort you back to your room and assist you in packing."

"You're out of your mind!" he shouted, neck veins bulging. And then he saw the calm demeanor, the unflappable stance, frowned, tried to understand what had just happened. Then he said, "Fuck it. I'm outa here. And you can be sure I'm going to spread the word about this dump."

He stalked off.

Abby turned to Jack. "Thank you. It was nice, what you did."

He looked at her in surprise. He had expected her to kiss up to the offended guest, offer to have the waitress fired. He had seen it in other places.

"M-Ms. Tyler?"

Abby looked at the young waitress who, although she had just addressed her employer, still had her eyes fixed on Jack. And Abby saw in those wide, grateful pupils what the girl saw: a man on a white charger, shield in one hand, lance in the other, a magnificent plume rising from the top of his shining helmet.

Some women fell in love easily.

"It's okay, Robin. Take the rest of the day off."

After the waitress vanished through the trees, Jack said, "Your security men got here fast."

"All of our staff wear small pagers that send signals in case of emergency. A push of a button and security is alerted."

"Do you always come with your security men in an emergency?"

"I happened to be in the security office when the alarm sounded." Abby removed her sunglasses to look right at Jack with that steady gaze again. "You handled Mr. Manguson well."

He shrugged. "I'm used to dealing with people like him."

"Oh?"

"I'm a cop," he said, watching her.

She didn't blink. "I hope you are enjoying your stay with us, Mr. Burns. Or should I call you Officer?"

"It's detective, actually. LAPD."

A twitch at the corner of her mouth. "I see."

A bee flew between them, buzzing first around Jack, then around Abby, lingering near her perfume before buzzing away.

"It's a nice hideaway you have here," he said, choosing the word on purpose.

Her eyes remained steady. "Yes, it is a hideaway for my guests and I am very protective of them. To a degree."

Jack felt grudging admiration. He had been to enough posh hotels, mostly on police business, to see managers pandering to assholes like Mr. Oscar Winner. But not Abby Tyler. She had integrity, he gave her that.

"I'd like to buy you a drink, cup of coffee maybe," he said.

Her guard went up as her instincts told her it was not a casual invitation. And it was the second one—why was he so eager to have a drink with her?

"Mr. Burns, I would love to have coffee with you. Why don't you come to my bungalow this evening. Say, around ten o'clock?"

He promised he would be there.

CHAPTER NINE

SISSY WHITBORO STOOD IN THE CENTER OF THE SMALL
bookstore in shock. She had been casually browsing through
Travel and Cookbooks when she came upon: *Sex for Dummies, The
Joy of Sex, The Book of Sexual World Records, Sex and the Married Woman.*

After making the dismaying discovery about her husband's phone sex,
she had put the accordion file aside, afraid of what else it contained, afraid
of the conclusions she might jump to (certainly those statements and credit
charges had nothing to do with Ed). One phone call would clear it up and
she could get back to concentrating on her scrapbook.

However, she had been unable to bear sitting in her room waiting for
Ed to call, unable to address the scrapbook project, and definitely unable
to sit there and listen to the sounds of her neighbors doing it *yet again* on
the chaise lounge. On top of that, her luncheon with Abby Tyler had been
re-scheduled. So, tying her pale orange hair into a pony tail and donning
twill capris and a crewneck sweater, she had gone out for air and to walk
off the tension. Beyond her door Sissy had discovered a wonderland she

had not seen the evening before, when the plane landed and a hostess had whisked her away in a little cart. Now Sissy saw the fabulous greenery, the little paths meandering through jungle growth, people cavorting in swimming pools, laughing at outdoor bars, even openly making out.

Sissy started to turn away from the sex books. And then curiosity got the better of her. Glancing over her shoulder to make sure no one saw, she pulled one of the volumes off the shelf and flipped through it. The illustrations made her face burn. She just *knew* Father Ignatius was hiding behind the cookbooks watching her. She stopped at one picture and ogled. Sissy hadn't even known people could *do* that.

Ed wasn't one for sexual experimentation. In fact, he was predictable. But he was loving so you couldn't fault him for not being a Casanova.

Her thoughts shocked her and her conscience screamed at her to put the book back. But her hands would not obey. More illustrations flipped past, naked people doing things together. Her curiosity mounted, as well as a strange little hot feeling deep in her abdomen.

And then an even more shameful thought occurred to her. To buy the book.

Well, why not? Sissy was a grown woman, a wife and a mother. She bought all four.

When she returned to her cottage, she found the phone message light blinking. Ed had called!

But it turned out to be a message from Vanessa Nichols, apologizing for having to reschedule Sissy's dinner with Abby Tyler, adding that she hoped it wasn't a terrible inconvenience. The truth was, Sissy had been so preoccupied with the discovery of Ed's secret phone sex activities that she had forgotten all about her date with Ms. Tyler.

And now Ed hadn't returned her call.

It was nine o'clock in Rockford, he would have gotten the message from his secretary by now. Feeling an unpleasant foreboding steal into her bones, Sissy ordered room service—bacon, lettuce and tomato on rye toast, salad and a side of fries—and stepped onto the patio to decide what to do next. A spring moon was rising. Music and perfume filled the dusk. Sissy felt as if she were living inside someone's dream. Her real life—kids and husband and friends—was miles away in another world.

She found herself listening for sounds in the next garden, almost hoping to hear the noise of lovemaking.

Her dinner was delivered and she let it sit there while she stared at the phone. Ed's secretary was a very efficient woman. He would have gotten the message that Sissy had called. So why hadn't he called back?

Finally, unable to eat until the mystery was solved, Sissy took the initiative and dialed home. She was pleased to hear her fourteen-year-old's voice at the other end. "Mom! Are you having a good time? Have you see any movie stars?"

Sissy offered her daughter a few names and heard Adrian swoon with envy. Then she asked for Ed.

"Daddy isn't here. Grandma's here."

"Put her on please. Mom!" Ed's mother, not hers. Sissy's mother didn't have time for her grandchildren. No surprise, since she never had time for her own daughter. "What are you doing there?"

"Ed asked me to sit with the kids tonight."

"When?"

"A couple of hours ago. He called from the factory and asked me to pick the kids up from school. Said he was going straight to his sports club with that friend of his, Hank Curly."

"Thanks. I'll call over there."

Hank Curly wasn't exactly Ed's friend. He was the factory's Sales Manager and had been working under Ed for three years. It was Hank who had persuaded Ed to join the Rockford Men's Racquet Club, a very expensive place, and they had been going two and three times a week since.

As she called Directory Assistance for the club's number, it occurred to her that in all the time Ed had been a member she had never called him there. But this was something of an emergency. It troubled her that he hadn't returned her call from that morning.

"Hello," she said when she was put through to the reception center. "I need to get in touch with my husband. He's playing racquet ball there."

"Certainly. The member's name?"

"Ed Whitboro." She spelled it.

While she waited, Sissy heard footsteps pass her window. Stiletto heels on concrete and a giggle she was becoming familiar with. The couple next door must have gone out and were now coming back. Would they do it outside in the moonlight, she wondered?

"I'm sorry, we don't have any Ed Whitboro registered as a member."

Sissy blinked. "He joined three years ago."

"I'm sorry."

She tried to think. She had obviously gotten the name of the club wrong. "Is there another men's racquet club in Rockford?"

"No, maam."

Maybe he had been attending as Hank's guest? Ed said Hank was one of the founding members, nine years ago. "Then would you please page Hank Curly? It's rather urgent."

She heard the door to the next cottage open and slam shut, and then silence.

"Sorry," came the person at the other end. "We don't have a Hank Curly registered either."

Sissy frowned. "Please look again. He is one of the founding members."

"Sorry."

Sissy hung up and stared at the phone in perplexity. She then spent the next fifteen minutes calling every fitness club in the Rockford area. Ed and Hank weren't members of any of them.

Where was her husband?

She called home again and asked her mother-in-law for Ed's secretary's number. "Is something wrong?" Mrs. Whitboro asked, sounding worried.

"Oh no," Sissy said. "I just got some dates on my calendar mixed up." It occurred to her to say, "Are you sure Ed said he was playing racquet ball tonight?" but that would only alarm his mother, and plant unnecessary suspicions. Sissy was sure everything was all right. Ed was probably at Hanks' house right now, asking to use the phone to call Sissy.

Ed's secretary was home. "Hi Susan, Sissy Whitboro. I'm sorry to bother you but I was wondering if you could give me Hank Curly's home number?"

"Who?"

Sissy gripped the phone. "Hank Curly. The company Sales Manager."

"I'm sorry, Mrs. Whitboro, I don't know any Hank Curly. Our Sales Manager is Jim Phelan. He has been for six years."

Sissy stared at her living room wall. Through the brick and paint and plants outside, and stretch of grass between the cottages, and more brick and paint, she was sure her neighbors were engaged in love making.

"Mrs. Whitboro? Are you all right?"

She apologized, hung up, and dialed Directory Assistance. There was no Hank Curly listed in Rockford, or Illinois, or the surrounding states.

As she sat holding the phone, her heart thumping, the sense of foreboding growing, Sissy began to remember things. At the company Christmas party, Ed saying, "Honey, you just missed Hank. He had to leave. One of his kids slipped on some ice..." At a barbecue at their home: Ed waiting for Hank, going into the house because he said he heard the phone ringing, coming back out to say, "That was Hank, he had to cancel." All those times she had "just missed" Hank, and Ed feeding her enough information for her to form a picture in her mind—"I envy Hank his thick hair," "Hank's got perfect vision, doesn't need to wear glasses like I do"—making her think she had actually *met* him, when in fact she never had.

The shattering truth hit her like a cold storm: Hank Curly, the man with whom Ed had supposedly played handball two or three nights a week for the past three years, did not exist.

She seized the accordion file and upended it so that the rest of the contents tumbled onto her bed like autumn leaves. Now she saw more damning evidence: restaurant receipts, stubs from airport boarding passes, car rental charge cards, and cancelled checks with Ed's unmistakable signature. But she went through them all the same, still hoping to catch the lie, the stolen identity, the forgery, the terrible crime that was afoot here. But in the end she realized that the crime was Ed's. This was no identity theft. Her husband had opened a secret bank account, made secret deposits, and paid off secret credit cards with it.

The statements went back five years.

When I was pregnant with the twins.

She closed her eyes. The phone sex, the credit charges for flowers and hotels. Ed going on a diet, changing his clothing style, buying a sports car. Ed insisting she come to The Grove, practically packing her suitcases for her. "You deserve a vacation. I'll hold down the fort."

The classic signs.

Through tears she looked more closely at the credit card statements and remembered some of the dates when Ed was supposedly in Seattle or St. Louis. Yet here it said he was in Chicago. And now that she thought back, whenever Ed went out of town he would call when he checked in and then tell her he was going to be busy all day. He would call each evening and each morning—to head her off, to insure that she would never need to call *him*? Not once, whenever he went away, did he leave a number where he could be reached, and say, "Call me if you miss me." And now that she thought about it, did he ever tell her the name of the hotel where he was staying? It was always, "I don't know. My secretary booked me into one of those chains, the Marriott or Holiday Inn. They're all alike to me."

But according to the credit statements, he had been in Chicago at the Palmer House every time.

She felt dizzy.

And then outraged.

She had to dial the phone three times before she got the number right, her hands shook so badly. Linda answered and Sissy blurted the whole thing, the horrible discovery she had made. "I can't believe Ed is cheating on me!"

Linda's tone was sympathetic. "Girlfriend, all men cheat at one time or another. They can't help it. It's in their nature. I suggest you do the same. Goose and gander and all that."

"I couldn't!"

"From what I've heard, you're in the perfect place for it. Private, safe, anonymous. God I envy you."

That would serve him right. Find a man and do to Ed what he was doing to her! But Sissy knew she could never do something like that.

After she hung up, she realized that Linda had sounded odd. Her tone guarded. As if she were holding something back. But that wasn't Linda's style. Sissy chalked it up to her own shaky nerves and imagination.

She had not meant to open the wine. She never drank. But she went to the mini-bar in search of cold water and looked at the small bottle of burgundy and brought it out and unscrewed the cap and drank straight from the bottle.

A few swallows and she wanted to cry. A few more swallows and she was blazing mad.

How dare he! Bad enough to call strange women and talk dirty to them, bad enough to run around behind her back, but to invent a friend, a Sales Manager, to lie about his whereabouts three nights a week? And the hotel charges on the credit card statements! Weekends when he had said he was on Christian youth retreats. When he had gone to Washington on sales trips. When he was supposedly attending machine manufacturers conventions in other states! And the whole time he was at the Palmer House, ninety miles away!

She dressed with fury, yanking a sleeveless dress from the closet, snapping the hairbrush through her shoulder length hair that she insisted was orange but which friends kindly said was strawberry blond. Then a dusting of face powder over her freckles and she grabbed her purse and the wine bottle, and fled into the cool night where crickets chirped and an owl hooted and wind rustled dry palm fronds. She had no idea where she was going. Her eyes were blinded by angry tears. How could Ed do this to her? What had she done to drive him to such deception?—and suddenly she came upon a beautiful little scene that made her stop and stare and sniff back her tears.

The path ended at an arching wooden bridge, the type seen in Japanese gardens, curving over a pond so still it looked like glass. Moonlight reflected on the water like a perfect pale opal on black velvet. The bridge and pond were secluded amid dense shrub and tall trees. Sound was blocked out. Not even a breeze got in. A place suspended in time.

Sissy walked to the center of the bridge and leaned on the rail to look at the water, noticing an occasional gold glint as exotic fish swam about.

Her world had disintegrated. Ed cheating on her. Lying. Hotels, jewelers, florists. *Spending money on other women.* She felt betrayed and furious beyond belief.

The tears started up again. She couldn't help it. And because she was completely alone, she let herself break into sobs.

"Why are you sad?" a deep voice gently asked. And Sissy was startled to see a perfectly starched and folded handkerchief enter her vision.

She looked up into a pair of searching eyes. He was a older than she, his dark hair silvered at the temples and his mouth nicely framed by lines of maturity. Impeccably dressed in a blue blazer, white shirt with a maroon tie, and casual gray slacks. He looked rich, a gentleman. She took the mono-grammed handkerchief and dried her eyes.

"Why are you sad?" he asked again.

Because my husband has been cheating on me. God, what sort of fool did that make her? For five years it had been going on and Sissy had not had a clue.

"I'm sorry you're sad," the handsome stranger said softly.

He had a hypnotic voice. And eyes so blue you could swim in them. Sissy couldn't speak, couldn't breathe.

"A beautiful lady shouldn't be crying."

She handed him the damp handkerchief. Fingertips touched. The only men Sissy had ever touched were relatives or close friends. She wondered where the stranger had come from. Had he materialized from the stars and moon and the pond?

"I'm Alistair," he said, holding out his hand.

To her amazement, Sissy delivered her own into his, clasping his hand as if it were a life preserver. She tried to say her name but the jolt she felt from his touch did something to her throat.

He smelled good.

"Do you want to talk about it?"

"I've...lost someone," she said.

"Ah." He nodded, knowingly, as if she had spoken a thousand words. "I sympathize." And a new look came into his eyes, one of pain and sadness and Sissy thought: He has lost someone, too.

She saw his eyes in the moonlight and they reminded her of a boy she had known in high school, before Ed, when she was a virgin. He had been a good kisser, that boy. She looked at this man's lips, wondering if he was a good kisser. Impulsively, she lifted up on tip-toe and touched her mouth to his. He didn't flinch or frown or draw back or look sur-prised. He gave her a secretive smile, bent his head and kissed her right back.

"I'm sorry," she said. "I'm married and I should never drink wine."

He placed a fingertip to her lips. "This is no place for apologies," he said softly. "You're supposed to be happy here."

"Is that why you're here?" She couldn't believe she was asking such a personal question of this stranger. But she suddenly wanted to know.

"I'm here because," he began, leaving the sentence unfinished and full of mystery. He looked out over the pond into the night darkness as if searching for ghosts.

"I'm sorry," she said again.

He brought his eyes back to hers. "You keep apologizing."

"No, this time it was for you. I'm sorry for your loss."

"You're amazing," he said.

"I am?"

"You came here sad, and now you're worried about a stranger's unhappiness. That's a rare quality." He gave her a long look. "I came looking for happiness."

"Have you found it?"

"At this moment, I think so."

His voice caressed her ears, insinuated itself into her brain, and made its warm way down to her insides where she felt a little engine start to heat up. Sissy's heart pounded. She hadn't felt this way since her first dates with Ed.

Alistair in his elegant navy blazer made her think of yachts and oceans and freedom. Oh to sail away...

She lifted her face again and he brought his mouth down on hers. She snaked her arms around him, and he pulled her to him. The embrace grew tight, the kiss intimate. In that instant, Sissy Whitboro could have done anything with this stranger. The feel of him against her made the pain go away. The sudden desire within her drove out the anger and made her forget the terrible things she had found by accident. She had felt like such a fool on the phone, insisting that her husband was a member of the racquet club. But this man didn't make her feel like a fool, he had said she was amazing.

He ran his hands over her back, she drove her fingers through his hair. He was hard and she suddenly wanted to reach down for him. She wanted to lie beneath the stars and open herself to him. She had never been with another man. It felt delicious and sexy and wonderful, and her head was filled with wine.

He drew back for a moment, looking at her with sea-colored eyes, a question in them. "Yes," she whispered, feeling so warm she wondered if summer had suddenly come to the desert.

Taking her hand, he led her from the bridge and through the trees where they came upon a tiny clearing, completely private, with a carpet of cool grass. The heat built in Sissy. It occurred to her she was out of control, but a hunger deeper than common sense had taken over. When Alistair laid her on the grass, she pulled him down onto her. She kissed him as if she were starving. His hands found her bare skin and caressed, teased. *New* hands. Another man's hands. And the feeling of them drove her mad.

She opened his shirt, he unbuttoned her blouse. He lifted her skirt and she unzipped his pants. They did not get all the way undressed, which made the act all the more erotic for Sissy—as if their bodies met only at the crucial points, all else being superfluous. His penis felt strange in her hand, but good too. And when she felt him explore inside her, it too felt strange, but exciting beyond belief. In that moment she wanted nothing more in the world than to feel him inside her, filling her, and smothering her mouth with his electric kisses.

She guided him into her and held tight as he moved with a steady rhythm. Her eyes shut against the moon and stars, trees and wind, so that she went deep inside herself to that delicious spot where Alistair was stoking a fire so hot she thought she would burst into flame.

The orgasm caught her by surprise. Her eyes flew open, she looked at him, his eyes watching her, and she said, "Yes yes yes," holding tighter as the delicious wave began to grow. Oh my God, she thought as the pleasure crested and broke and a sound that could not have come from Mrs. Sissy Whitboro exploded from her throat.

When the paroxysms subsided, Sissy was aware of the grass, the breeze, her exposed breasts, her parted legs. And Alistair smiling at her in a gentle, mysterious way. And then reality hit. My God, she thought in shock. *What have I done?*

CHAPTER TEN

*A*RE YOU SAYING, DR. KAPLAN, THAT HUMANS ARE BY nature promiscuous?"

Ophelia tried to hide her irritation. She had been invited on the TV talk show to discuss her book, *not* her theories on human mating practices. "Well, John," she said, "archaeological evidence shows that our cave dwelling ancestors did not live in male-female pair bonds but in separate male-female groups. But this has nothing to do with my—"

"So there was a lot of sneaking back and forth between these groups?" he said, interrupting her yet again. "Those caves must have been pretty cozy!"

Laughter from the studio audience. Ophelia kept herself in check. She had already come out onto the stage in a mild stew, having watched the host's opening monologue from a monitor in the famous Blue Room. "Tonight's guest, Dr. Ophelia Kaplan," he had said, "who has single-handedly turned Americans into Neanderthals."

The audience, getting the inside joke, had loved it and Ophelia had wanted to march out and drive straight home. But Ophelia never backed down from a fight. Now she wished she had as she tried to clarify her theory to this cocky talk show host. "Prior to twenty thousand years ago, John, humans did not know that the male had anything to do with procreation. Birth was strictly the purview of females. Sexual intercourse was simply another bodily impulse and it was gratified randomly."

He turned to the audience. "Sounds like things haven't changed much in twenty thousand years."

More laughter, at the expense of Dr. Ophelia Kaplan who took her theories and scholarship very seriously. Why he was doing this to her she had no idea, since they were supposed to be discussing her book, not her controversial theories on human pair-bonding. But when the next guest came out, she realized what was going on, realized with burning cheeks that she had been duped, and worse, realized that she should have seen it coming.

But her mind was on other things.

The other guest was the thirty-something salsa singer who had just dumped husband number four and was already running around Hollywood with a new boyfriend (the fraternity brat famous for romantic comedy leads). The singer was known for her notorious entourage—she never traveled anywhere with less than eighty hangers-on. Ophelia had observed the phenomenon first hand in the Blue Room, where one make-up specialist had taken care of just the singer's eyebrows while another had applied the famous fox fur eyelashes.

After the applause for the singer-actress died down, the host leaned toward her and said, "Magdalena, I assume you've been following the show so far. What do *you* think of Dr. Kaplan's theory that it's in our genes to have sex with as many partners as we can."

"Well, John, I don't know about Dr. Kaplan, but I prefer to have sex *outside* my jeans."

After the laughter died down, the host said, "Speaking of jeans. Dr. Kaplan, I read somewhere that you don't believe in shoes. Is that right?"

"I was referring to high heels. They are unnatural. We evolved with a flat-footed gait. We force our bodies into contortions that were not meant to be."

"How about bras," he said, eyes going to the salsa singer's cleavage. "Are we meant to wear bras?"

"*You* might consider it," she said, making reference to the host's obesity.

"Where are you going?" David asked one hour later as Ophelia angrily threw clothes and toiletries into a suitcase. "Look, the show wasn't that bad. Everyone knows how John Simon twists everything around. I mean, this isn't like you, Ophelia."

She turned to him and he was shocked to see how white-faced she was. "That isn't it. It wasn't the show."

"Then what?"

It was the fact that I didn't see it coming. The attack on my theories. Twisting everything around. Ophelia was usually sharper than that. "Nothing. Never mind." She clicked the suitcase shut.

David put his hand on her arm. "Ophelia," he said gently. "I know you. Something's bothering you. It has been for a couple of weeks. I didn't want to pry. I've just been waiting for you to come to me about it."

She looked into David's dark eyes and recalled the day she had seduced him. "This is something I have to sort out myself."

"By going away? Ophelia, I've never known you to run from anything in your life. What about your classes, the lectures you have lined up, the awards banquet?"

"I've canceled them. I need to get away to think." And to make a life and death decision.

"That contest prize?" he said, meaning the FedEx envelope that had arrived three weeks prior. The whole thing sounded suspicious to David. What sort of exclusive resort lets people in for free?

Three weeks ago Ophelia had tossed the FedEx envelope aside, saying she didn't have time. Now, all of a sudden, she wanted to go. David took her by the shoulders and drew her away from the bed. "No," she said, understanding his intention and trying to wrench free. But he imprisoned her mouth with an insistent kiss. She pushed him back. "I'm angry, David. This is no way to make love."

"It's the *only* way." He pulled her hard against him, smothering her mouth with his, and she responded with sudden, equal ardor. Roughly he tugged at her clothes, sending a button flying. Ophelia tore at his shirt, fingernails raking his bare chest, anger fueling her desire. David sucked the breath out of her as she ripped the shirt from his back.

Her blouse slipped from her shoulders, David drew down a bra strap, yanked the lacy cup to free a breast, then resumed sucking down there.

Ophelia drove her hand into his trousers and took a firm hold of him. He moaned. David had the loveliest cock she had ever met. He had once joked that that was what she loved about him. It was partly true. She loved the taste, feel, shape and size of it, and by great good fortune, David came attached to it.

Ophelia dropped to her knees and feasted on him. But when she sensed he was about to climax, she drew back and brought him down to the carpet, pulling him on top of her as she spread her legs. David thrust hard. Ophelia cried out, clamping her legs around his thighs.

Considerately, he let her come first, enjoying the look of ecstasy on her face, eyelids fluttering, head pushed back, an animal sound coming from her throat. And then he allowed himself release, exploding as she clasped him tightly inside her.

Ophelia dozed off, she always did after sex. When she woke, she found the two of them in bed, naked, David asleep at her side. Quietly, so as not to disturb him, she slipped out, showered, dressed, finished packing her suitcase and, grabbing her laptop, left.

"What do you mean I missed the flight?"

"I'm sorry, Dr. Kaplan," the pretty desk clerk at The Grove's private air terminal said. The place was quiet and deserted. "There are no more flights tonight. The aircraft will stay at the resort and return in the morning. I can make room for you on that—"

"Then I'll drive. Just give me the directions."

"Cars are not allowed—"

"Look, I know you're not supposed to give out that information. But it is really vital that I get to The Grove tonight."

"I'm sorry, ma'am. We will be happy to put you up at a hotel here at the airport for the night and you can fly out first thing in the morning."

The brochure that came with the ticket and letter of congratulations described the resort as being thirty miles northeast of Palm Springs. How hard could it be to find?

By the time she was on the freeway heading east into the night, Ophelia's anger had not subsided. In fact, it grew with each mile. She had hated running out on David like that, hated to cut him out of her private fear. But she needed to be alone, to decide what to do. Her life was falling apart and she was helpless to pick up the pieces.

She knew she had hit the desert when she started passing billboards that said *Play the Slots On the Morongo Indian Reservation*, and *Can't Get A Date? Try Us*. It was for a date farm.

Her first two attempts led her nowhere so that she had to backtrack each time and start again from Palm Springs. Local inquiries produced no information, but at the gas station where she filled her tank, the proprietor said The Grove was off Indian Canyon road and about twenty miles beyond that. "In the middle of nowhere," he added as a warning. "Dirt track, very hard to follow. Especially at night."

She drove like a maniac under the stars, swerving around potholes, jolting over rocks. If she had a tire blowout she would be in a jam. But she didn't care.

And then she saw a chainlink fence ahead, and a padlocked gate with a sign that read PRIVATE ENTRANCE. As she inspected the lock, wondering if a hairpin would do the trick, she saw headlights in the distance, coming toward her.

Two men in smart blazers and flannel slacks got out and met her at the gate. They knew who she was. The desk clerk at the airport had called ahead and warned them. "Follow us, please, Dr. Kaplan."

At the resort, Ophelia was greeted by Vanessa Nichols, the manager, who said they were glad she had changed her mind. Nichols took her in a small golf cart to accommodations in the resort's main building. "Where the private suites are," Vanessa said.

Ophelia marched wordlessly at her hostess's side, oblivious of the desert wind in her short black hair, oblivious, too, of the looks she got from passersby when they saw her T-shirt. A tight black top over faded denim jeans, the T was printed with white letters that read: *Homo erectus isn't funny.* Her assistant had given it to her one birthday, because it was the opening statement of Ophelia's lecture in her course, Introduction to Physical Anthropology. Whenever she made her first mention of Homo erectus, a few students always giggled, and so she now opened the class with, "Homo erectus isn't funny." To show them she brooked no nonsense in her class.

Ophelia's room was the Marie Antoinette Suite, a lavish boudoir of white and gold appointments and Louise IV furniture that conjured powdered wigs and masqued balls. When Ms Nichols drew the heavy drapes aside, Ophelia received a shock. The view was not of the resort nor the desert that surrounded it, but a lifelike vista of Paris, with the Eiffel Tower in the near distance.

"Please feel free to enjoy our many services and amenities," the manager said as she said good-night and left.

Briefly pondering the error of placing the Eiffel Tower in the wrong historical period—"Must you always be the academician, can't you ever relax?" her sister once asked—Ophelia turned away from the view and went to her overnight bag, removing a paper sack from an all-night drugstore in Palm Springs where she had made an impulsive purchase. She took the sack into the gold and marble bathroom, removed the box from the bag and set it, unopened, by the sink.

She stared at it in icy fear. The box contained a pregnancy test kit. And herein lay her fears, the nightmares that had been hounding her, the secret she kept from David, the worry that had so preoccupied her that a fat talk show host had blindsided her.

As she stared at the test kit, she thought: *I can't be pregnant.*

In fact, it was impossible.

CHAPTER ELEVEN

OCO HAD SPENT THE AFTERNOON WITH THE CRYSTAL AND ALL SHE had gotten from it was a headache. Daisy, her spirit guide, had not spoken.

So it was time to take action. Since her dinner with Abby Tyler had been re-scheduled, it meant she was free for the evening. Dressing in stone-washed jeans and an oversized shirt, she decided to prowl the resort again in search of the man of her dreams. During her afternoon consultation with the crystal, she had tried not to think of "Mr. Memory" Kenny and his sweetness—"You're not here for beauty treatments. What's to improve?"— and tonight she would definitely *not* stop by the Java Club and catch his evening performance.

But as she stepped outside her cottage and locked her door, Coco turned and saw the blond hair in the lamplight that illuminated the walkway.

"Hi," Kenny said.

Her traitorous heart skipped a beat. "How did you find me?"

"Insider knowledge." Kenny grinned. He wasn't wearing his stage costume but beige slacks and an Oxford shirt that made him look younger. Like a frat boy, Coco thought. She wondered how old he was. "My show doesn't start for an hour. I thought you might join me for a drink."

When she hesitated, he added, "You left so quickly this afternoon, I thought maybe..."

Was he trying to lay a guilt trip on her? But his eyes were open and direct. No games being played here. "I'm sorry about that," she said. "I just suddenly had to be somewhere."

"I understand." He lifted a blond eyebrow. That drink?

They found an outdoor bar built into the side of the resort's magnificent aviary. Couples sat at tables, minding their own business. The air was misty from a waterfall, it felt like the ocean, which was a hundred miles away.

"So how did you become Mr. Memory?" she asked, wanting to be sitting there with him, *enjoying* it, but eager to be moving on as well.

"The nightclub act isn't my real profession."

It wasn't exactly a straight answer. "Then what is?"

"I write code."

"Secret codes! How fascinating. Navajo Wind Talkers. ULTRA in World War II. Hidden messages leading to the Holy Grail."

He cleared his throat. "Actually, I write code for computer software."

"I knew that." She sipped her Tequila Sunrise. "So how did you become Mr. Memory?"

He shrugged. "It was something to do. My excellent memory and all. So how is it you can read people?"

His evasive answers piqued her interest. So did the sprinkling of blond hairs on his forearms. He had nicely shaped hands. She wondered what Kenny was like in bed. "I have a spirit guide named Daisy," she said, watching him. This was when most guys said they needed to buy a pack of cigarettes and didn't come back. "She was sixteen and died in a house fire in London in 1868. She first spoke to me when I was eight."

"That must have been weird. I'll bet your parents thought it was an invisible friend."

"As a matter of fact, they did." She twirled the little paper umbrella between her fingers. She would rather have been touching something else, but

Kenny wasn't the one and she didn't want to get anything started. "If you write computer code, how did you wind up here? We're a long way from Silicon Valley."

"I was recruited. Vanessa Nichols caught my night club act and invited me."

"What do your folks think of your act?"

"No problems there," he said vaguely, and Coco sensed deeper secrets, something that even she couldn't reach.

"So you were born with a good memory," she said, feeling her heart tug in his direction. She sensed something vulnerable about him, even though he was about six feet tall and looked like he could handle himself in a fight.

"A good memory?" he said. "I guess you could say that." He looked into his drink, an Irish coffee that he had yet to taste, and a dark look flew briefly across his face. "I remember everything, Coco. The bad things as well as the good. Most people can repress bad memories, not think about the terrible things in their past. I can't. Every moment of my life is recorded permanently up here." He tapped his temple. "I've tried everything—drugs, hypnosis, therapy. I spent six months at the Carl Jung Institute for Memory in Switzerland where they watched me, measured me, tested me. I was a lab rat and finally I had to escape."

Coco didn't know what to say. She had never met anyone like him. "I would think having a memory like that would be a plus in relationships. You'd never forget birthdays or anniversaries."

"That's the trouble. One woman I was seeing, I knew when her birthday was, and when the day came I knew it was her birthday, and I knew what she would like, remembering from birthdays past. The problem was, I was swamped at work, had to work overtime, barely got home in time for bed. I arrived with no gift. She knew I had remembered her birthday yet I had done nothing about it. Which is a bigger sin than forgetting altogether. Another lady I was seeing—we got into an argument over something and she called me a freak. We kissed and made up but the next morning she said, 'You're never going to forget that, are you?' She couldn't live with that, because with me there is no 'forgive and forget.' I can forgive, but I can never forget."

It was the saddest thing Coco had ever heard. The sounds of the aviary and the other couples receded so that all she heard was Kenny's soft voice. "And then there was the performing. I worked at many jobs because I was always having to move on. Invariably my memory would be discovered, and the guys at the water cooler would challenge me, they'd place bets and see who could stump me. At parties people egged me on. 'Watch Kenny recite the Periodic Table backward!' They'd pile money on the table and cheer."

Coco closed her eyes. Her sisters: "Come on, Coco, tell us when we'll get married. Who's taking us to the prom? Will I get into UCLA? Hey everybody, watch what Coco does with this crystal, it's uncanny." She knew exactly how Kenny felt.

"So what about you?" he said, stirring his Irish coffee. "What is it like being a psychic?"

"Someone convinced me years ago that I must share my gift with the world, that I was being selfish by not sharing it. So I hung out a shingle and gave psychic readings. Since my success rate was high, word of my so-called powers spread and I had more clients than I could handle. But what I really couldn't handle was everyone's neediness. Will I get the job? Will he ask me to marry him? Do I have cancer? People waiting to hear from bosses and boyfriends and doctors came to me because they couldn't stand the wait, the not-knowing. Instead of waiting for the phone call with the dreaded or desired news, they came to me, jumping the gun. I read many accurate prophecies, but no one was satisfied. If I said, 'No, you don't have cancer,' they would badger me: 'Are you sure?' Or if I said, 'You have cancer,' they would shout, 'How do you know, you're not a doctor.' If I gave them bad news they hated me, if it was good news they were greedy for more. I ended up satisfying nobody so I took my shingle down and looked for a way to devote my gift to just one worthwhile endeavor."

"Which is?"

"I find missing people."

"Sounds rewarding."

"I also work homicide cases, to help the cops find the perpetrator."

He fell silent, then he said, "I see."

"I work in Manhattan. Sometimes I get requests from Jersey or as far north as Boston. I don't like to go farther than that because they'd have me hopping night and day."

"You must be good."

"I am." She didn't say it in a prideful way. "And I wish I weren't."

"Have you ever tried to get rid of it, your gift?"

"Countless times. Shrinks, therapy, even drugs." She shook her head.

"We have something in common," Kenny said. "You see things you don't want to see, and I remember things I don't want to remember."

She stared at him. It had been a long time since she had had anything in common with a guy. Now that she thought about it, this was the *first* time.

"Does anyone else in your family have this talent?" he asked.

"No. When I was little, before I realized I had this skill, my mother was always telling me how special I was. I never knew why. Maybe she knew this was in me."

"Do you take after her?"

"I don't take after either of my parents. My sister looks like my mother and my brother looks like my father, but my genes got so scrambled I don't look like anyone."

Kenny looked at his watch and said, "I have a show to do. Will you come and watch?"

"Actually," she said as she slipped from the barstool, "there is somewhere I have to be."

"You said that this afternoon. A woman of mystery." He put his hand on her arm. The touch was electric. It startled her.

And then came the flood of emotions. Loneliness, pain, desire, *reaching out…*

Coco broke away and left him standing there, telling herself it was best to end it this way, before it really began.

She found herself at the edge of the resort, on the tarmac for the landing strip. There were no passengers in the deserted pavilion, and the private jet stood pale and ghostly in the moonlight, like an airliner out of a *Twilight Zone* episode, Coco thought.

She struggled with her emotions. Kenny standing back there at the aviary, the disappointment on his face. But Coco had spent her life connecting with men who eventually left her. She was just protecting herself. Both of them.

She heard voices. Following them, she came to a wooden shack with a windsock on top. Two men were chatting—a man in mechanics coveralls, wiping his hands on a rag, the other Coco recognized as the pilot, the one she had fantasized about Sunday night. And now he was standing there in the flesh, a man who traveled a lot.

He was tall and angular, very straight-backed as if he carried his morals on his shoulders. A square-jawed Dudley Do-Right who filled out his uniform very nicely. Remembering that one way to fight a fire was to light another fire, Coco waited until the mechanic said, "Good night," and headed in one direction, while the pilot, overnight bag in his hand, headed for another.

She stepped out. "Hi. I think I'm lost." A quick glance at his left hand. Enough moonlight to show no wedding ring. These types *always* wore a wedding band if they were married.

"I'll be happy to help," he said in his professional, intercom voice. Polite but impervious to the flirtations and come-ons from lady passengers. Those were the best kind.

Up close, he was very attractive, eyes looking at her from the beneath the bill of his pilot's hat. No jacket, but a white tailored shirt with captain's bars on the shoulders. He was an adventurer, Coco decided, a survivor, a man who pulled off daring rescues. This milk-run between LA and The Grove was just a breather between hazardous missions.

"Where are you trying to get to?" he asked.

She pointed at the jet. "I would love to see your cockpit."

A mild look of surprise, and then eyes crinkling at the corners.

The stairs were still unfolded down from the door. He invited her to go up first. The cockpit was small and cramped. Coco looked at all the dials and switches and instruments and thought of his hands commanding such power. "Do you always stay the night here at the resort?" she asked, feeling his warm breath on her face.

"There are two of us," he said, running his hand up her back, resting it on her shoulder. He caught on quick, she thought. "We take turns staying with the aircraft, and alternate weekends."

She turned to give him access to her mouth, and their lips met in a kiss. As Coco waited for the flash that sometimes happened, sometimes didn't, it occurred to her that he had done this before.

There was no room to maneuver. He quickly had her against an instrument panel, his erection pressing rock-hard against her.

Coco put her hand on his chest and felt something in the shirt pocket. Something small and round.

She drew back. "What's this?"

He turned bright red.

Coco fished in and brought out a gold band.

Now the flash came to her: wife and kids back in Los Angeles, he removed his ring whenever he got to The Grove.

"Sorry," he said.

No sorrier than Coco.

CHAPTER TWELVE

As Jack made his way down the path illuminated by soft lamps, toward the private entrance to Abby Tyler's bungalow, he saw lights on in the windows. She was waiting for him.

He knocked and Vanessa answered the door, inviting him in. The place was decorated tastefully with antiques and objet's d'art. Nothing ostentatious. Understated and classy. Like the woman who lived here.

He was momentarily arrested by a stunning painting over the fireplace: clouds at sunset, blazing scarlet and orange. The décor of the living room was done in warm tones— peach, tangerine and flame—as if the sunset in the painting were casting the furnishings in the glow of a dying day.

Abby came out in a rose-pink silk dressing gown, smiling when she saw him. Once again Jack sensed a deep warmth within her, but that she held it in check. He wondered what it would be like to set that fire free.

He was suddenly annoyed with himself. Jack had always prided himself on his firm resolve. Officers back at the station called him a bloodhound, because once he was on the scent, he didn't give up. But Abby Tyler was consistently throwing him curve balls.

"Forgive me, detective…" she said, holding out her hand. "It's been a day. I had to help out in the main kitchen." All afternoon and evening, while Maurice the head chef had sulked. Abby was exhausted and would like to have rested, but she was curious about the mysterious Jack Burns. He was a policeman and he didn't look like he was here on vacation. Should she be concerned?

She invited him to sit while Vanessa brought in tea service on a silver platter, and then discreetly left.

"It's Hawaiian hazelnut," Abby said as she poured and handed him the china cup. "I hope you like it."

Jack stirred in cream and sugar and thought of her name—ABBY TYLER—printed in large letters and circled in red on a note among his sister's papers. The name was followed by three exclamation points. But Nina had written nothing further. Was Tyler the anonymous person she was meeting with the night she was murdered?

"How are you enjoying your stay here, detective?"

"Call me Jack," he said and then watched her carefully as he said, "Actually, Ms Tyler, I'm not here on vacation. I'm working on a case."

She brought her cup to her lips. "What sort of case?"

"Homicide."

Her coffee did not get touched. She lowered the cup and said, "Is one of my guests a suspect?"

"More like a *lead* to a suspect. I can't say anything more right now, and I'd rather no one knew. You might say I'm undercover."

"Certainly, detective," she said as she sipped her coffee. But he saw worry in her eyes. "When did this murder take place?"

That startled him. Most people asked how and where about a murder, but rarely when. Did she have a specific murder in mind? "A few weeks ago."

He saw the barest relaxation in her manner. So, there *was* another murder. Something she had been involved in? "The murder victim was Nina burns," he said, watching her for a reaction.

"Should I know that name?"

"She was a rather successful businesswoman and well known in the professional community. She was my sister."

Abby set her cup down. "I'm sorry. How awful for you. No, I have never heard of her. But you think you might find a lead to her murderer here, in my resort?"

He didn't want to say anything more, and he saw that she was tired. So he drank in silence, commented on the weather, the artwork on her walls, how efficiently she ran her resort, then he stood and said he had to be going.

He paused to look at the cup cradled in her hands and realized he was not going to manage a way to get it for the fingerprints. He had hoped she would meet him in one of the restaurants where he could take an opportunity to lift her cup or glass. Now he would have to try again.

He was surprised to find himself looking forward to another meeting with Abby Tyler.

"If there is anything I can to do help in your investigation," she said at the door.

"As a matter of fact there is," Jack said, trying not to notice how the silk flowed over her body, the hint of cleavage where the dressing gown opened beneath her throat. "I would like your permission to look around the resort, maybe talk to a few employees." When he saw her alarm, he quickly added, "I would be very discreet. I won't mention murder or that I'm a cop. Just casual conversation."

She thought for a moment, then said, "Let me give you a security pass. I'll be right back."

She disappeared into the next room and closed the door. While he waited, he strolled around the spacious living room, impressed by its taste and classiness. When he came to an old fashioned roll top desk he surveyed the feminine pens and notepads and—

His eyes stopped on a stack of file folders. The top three were labeled *Ophelia Kaplan, Coco McCarthy, Sissy Whitboro*. The three women Nina had wanted to talk to—the three women who had been born the same week as Nina.

Glancing quickly over his shoulder, he tapped the stack of folders with a fingertip so that he could read the tabs underneath, and he received a jolt when he read: *Nina Burns*.

He stared in shock. Abby Tyler had lied to him.

Hearing the latch on the door, he quickly stepped away from the desk. Abby came forward holding out a card laminated in plastic. "This will give you access to any area in the resort, detective. I only ask that you be discreet."

He took the card.

"Is something wrong?" she asked.

"No. Nothing. Thank you for the coffee, Ms. Tyler. Good night."

After Abby closed the door, she turned to Vanessa and said, "Jack Burns makes me nervous."

"Don't worry. If he was here to arrest you, he'd have done it already."

Abby forced Jack Burns out of her mind. She had other things to think about. Ophelia Kaplan had arrived earlier and was settled in the Marie Antoinette Suite. Now Abby could go forward with her plan.

But she must take the next step with extreme caution. One reckless move and all would be lost. Going to her wall safe, she unlocked it and brought out a rolled-up yellowed poster with thumb tack holes in the corners. She remembered the day she had torn it down from a Post Office bulletin board, thirty-three years ago...

She was in Bakersfield, California, because Mercy had said she heard the warden say to the doctor "Bakersfield is in a hurry." It was 1972 and a young and scared Emmy Lou Pagan, going under a new name, praying the police didn't find her and send her back to prison, went through the phone book and wrote down all the addresses of adoption lawyers and agencies, desperately hoping to find the man and woman who had driven off with her baby. She made discreet inquiries, pretending she was pregnant, saying she needed money, hoping that it would give her a lead on the blackmarket baby ring.

But by Christmas she still had not found the man in the white Impala and her daughter was now six months old! Abby couldn't ask the authorities for help because they might still be looking for her after the prison fire. They might even think she caused it.

With each passing day, that lonely year in Bakersfield, Abby's panic had grown. Where was her baby? Who had adopted her? What sort of people adopted babies through a blackmarket service? Abby had tried to find out when she visited lawyers, telling them she was pregnant. "I want my child to go to good people."

"We screen our applicants thoroughly," they all said. "We make sure the adoptive couples are stable, financially comfortable, mentally sound."

Mentally sound! It had not occurred to Abby that unbalanced people who wanted babies would be turned down by a legitimate agency. They would resort to illegal means, getting babies from people who cared only about the money, not the welfare of the children.

Abby had gone frantic with worry. Was her baby in the hands of crazy people?

She had been on her way to an agency she found in the Yellow Pages when it had suddenly begun to rain and she had ducked into the post office for shelter, and as she waited for the storm to pass, she saw something that turned her world upside down.

On the wall above the counter that held various postal and tax forms was a bulletin board pinned with FBI Wanted Posters. Among the pictures of men wanted for armed robbery, murder, and sex offenses was the sharp likeness of a very familiar face. Beneath it, in bold letters:

Emily Louise Pagan. Wanted for Murder, Arson with Intent to Murder, Grand Theft Auto, Armed Robbery, and Escape.

Aliases: Emmy Lou Pagan.
Date of Birth: June 3, 1955
Place of birth: Little Pecos, Texas
Hair: reddish gold.
Eyes: green Height: 5'7"
Weight: 135 pounds
Sex: Female
Race: White
Occupation: Unknown
Scars and Marks: Heavy facial freckles

Remarks: Pagan is fond of gardening and has great horticultural knowledge, is known to visit gardens and might frequent nurseries or wherever plants are cultivated and sold. Might also be seen in the company of a Negro woman named Mercy. CAUTION: EMILY LOUISE PAGAN ESCAPED FROM PRISON BY SETTING FIRE TO THE FACILITY. WITH AN ACCOMPLICE SHE STOLE AN OFFICIAL CAR AND USED A POLICE WEAPON IN THE COMMISSION OF A HOLD-UP IN WHICH TWO PEOPLE WERE KILLED. SHE IS CONSIDERED ARMED AND EXTREMELY DANGEROUS. IF YOU HAVE ANY INFORMATION CONCERNING THIS PERSON, PLEASE CONTACT YOUR LOCAL FBI OFFICE OR THE NEAREST POLICE. The FBI is offering a $50,000 reward for information leading directly to the arrest of Emily Louise Pagan.

CHAPTER THIRTEEN

*A*BBY WAS WALKING TOWARD HIM THROUGH THE MIST, HER *garments long and white and pure. Her hair was longer than he remembered, tumbling over her shoulders, and as she drew near, Jack saw that one strap of her gown had slipped down to expose the swelling of a pale breast.*

They were in a forest, Jack could smell the loam and dampness, heard the call of a bird overhead. Stillness lay all around them as if time had stopped. He realized he was naked from the waist up, and when he looked down, saw that his trousers were leather, and his feet were clad in fur boots.

He felt raw. Primal. He wanted only one thing.

By the time she reached him, Abby's hair had grown down to her waist. Now the top of her gown was down around her hips, but her bare breasts were hidden behind long dark tresses.

She smiled, but there was mystery in it, and her eyes were shadowed. She lifted milky arms and Jack took a step toward her. When his fingertips touched her cool flesh, she closed her eyes and bent her head back to expose her white throat. The air was chill. Snow lay on the ground. He wanted to warm her.

She slipped smoothly into his embrace, face upturned for the kiss, her body molding to his. Her lips were cool, her kiss impersonal. It inflamed him all the more because he knew there was heat within her, and he wanted to draw it out.

A fur cape materialized on his shoulders. He spread it on the ground and lay Abby upon it. Her smile was serene as she kept her eyes on him, but she remained aloof, all Mystery.

He lay by her side and explored her ivory body, touching, caressing, watching her face as he searched for the heat. She smiled enigmatically, as if challenging him, and it heightened his ardor. He slid the white gown up her thigh and explored until he found her sweet spot. At his first touch, she moaned, and suddenly the forest vanished and they were on top of a desert butte with vast wilderness stretching to the far horizons and a blazing sunset scorching the western sky.

Abby circled her arms around his neck and he felt heat on her skin. Her lips had turned scarlet, parted and moist, her tongue pink and inviting. A hot wind blew as he kissed her deeply, and when he reached for the gown, which had turned the color of pomegranate, Abby parted her legs and a wave of heat engulfed him.

His hands possessed her breasts, warm in his fingers. Moans escaped her throat, which had turned blush-colored, as if she burned. Her mouth was hungry on his, as if she wanted to devour him, and she curved her leg around his thighs, urging him to delve into her heat.

He nearly exploded with the first thrust, and when she cried out, the cry echoed in the red canyons of the desert.

Jack awoke with a start and found himself drenched in sweat. He lay there stunned. It had been a long time since he had had an erotic dream. And with Abby Tyler of all people.

After he had discovered a file on Nina in Abby's bungalow, the night before, he had returned to his room with a sick feeling in his stomach. She had blatantly lied to him about knowing his sister. Not only did she know Nina, she possessed a file that, from what he could see, held several papers plus photographs. He felt betrayed. He realized he had been softening toward Tyler and his police instincts were being overridden by his male appreciation of her. From now on he was going to keep his guard up and trust no one.

Especially not Abby Tyler.

Remember why you are here. Do not be seduced by this place.

That was it, of course. It wasn't just Tyler, it was this resort. Insidiously seductive, getting under your skin and into your soul without your knowing it, until it was too late.

He didn't bother to try for more sleep, even though he had had only four hours. Jack Burns had not slept more than four hours straight in weeks. Not since he had been called to a crime scene and fainted at the sight of the corpse.

It hadn't been his first corpse either.

After a cold shower, which shocked his body back into obedience although Abby Tyler was still on his mind, he went to the stereo and slipped in a Beethoven CD. As the emotionally turbulent *Appassionata* filled the air, Jack turned his eye to the photograph on his nightstand, Nina.

He was still reeling from the shock of four years ago when, sitting at the bedside of their dying mother, he and Nina had heard a startling confession. Monica Burns' voice came out feathery and light on her last breath: "You were fourteen, Jack, away at boarding school. I wanted another child but I couldn't conceive. So we went to an adoption agency. They said we were too old, that babies were being placed with younger couples. We found a lawyer who handled what he called specialty cases. He said he could guarantee a baby, but it would cost a lot of money. We came up with the cash, and you were brought to us, Nina. The minute you were placed in my arms, you were no longer adopted. You were my child. That's why I never told you. Jack, you came home from school and you believed I had been pregnant. I left it at that.

"But now that I am leaving you and will no longer be around, you should know the truth, Nina..."

Nina had begun her investigation the next day, going through her mother's papers, finding the lawyer who had handled the adoption, retired and living in Phoenix. He couldn't give her much to go on, but what he was able to provide had sent Nina all over the country. With old adoption records opening up, she had been able to follow leads, interview people from thirty-three years ago, and start to put a picture together.

What she discovered had come as a shock: Nina had been bought through an illegal adoption ring.

It haunted her. Had she been kidnapped? Had her teenage mother been coerced into giving up her child? Was her real mother searching for her at that very moment? Four years of obsessive searching had brought Nina to the last phone call she had made to Jack a few weeks ago, saying she wondered what Coco McCarthy, Sissy Whitboro and Ophelia Kaplan had in common, and why were they going to a resort they knew nothing about? The phone call in which Nina said she was meeting someone that night and it could lead to something big.

And then next day she was found murdered.

Jack looked at the file folders spread across his desk. The sum of his sister's exhaustive research into a blackmarket adoption ring over thirty years ago. Unfortunately, her notes did not clarify everything. She had written the name Abby Tyler in large letters and circled it in red.

Why?

And who was Nina meeting with the night she was murdered?

Jack had run a check on Abby Tyler and discovered she owned the resort the three women had won prizes for. He had then run background checks on Tyler but had not been able to find much. In fact, Tyler's history seemed to go back only to 1974. And that was why he needed her fingerprints.

Paperclipped to Nina's photo was a glossy brochure for a beautiful place called Crystal Creek Winery. He had clipped it to the photo because it, too, was a reminder of his mission. The winery was for sale and Jack had been negotiating with the owner when he got the call about Nina. The winery was his lifelong dream; he wanted to retire there and collect his police pension while growing grapes and making wines. The brochure had been in his pocket the night he fainted. He never got back to the owner. His life had stopped at that moment, next to Nina's corpse, like a clock with hands frozen in time. The winery, archery contests, plans for travel—Jack's entire life was put on hold the night Nina died, and it was still on hold, to move forward again only when he had the answers.

Jack was restless. Nervous energy flowed through his muscles and bones. He had to get out of there, this place with the magic, away from the woman who was doing things to his mind. Peering through the glass door that led to his private patio, he noted the beginning of sunrise behind the distant mountains. Jack decided it was a good time to do some shooting.

Holstering his police revolver beneath his jacket, he perused the Guest Services book. *"The desert area beyond the periphery of The Grove is laid with delightful and romantic nature trails that guests are free to use. We do request, however, that you inform Management before you leave the resort grounds. We also recommend you check weather ahead of time as there can be the danger of flashfloods and sandstorms. If you wish a ride, please call Reservations."*

"Excellent hunting in Africa," Zeb said twenty minutes later as he guided the SUV along the desert track.

The sun had cleared the horizon and was washing the landscape in breathtaking hues of pink and gold. Spring wildflowers were in bloom, spread out in carpets of blue and yellow and scenting the morning air with exotic perfumes.

Jack didn't respond to Zeb's comment. He had never cared for hunting, didn't see the appeal. Noticing the elephant hair bracelet on Zeb's arm, he wondered if Zeb missed the "real" game of Africa—the giraffes and lions and rhino—because the wildlife of the Mojave must seem tame by comparison.

"Here we are, sir, Indian Rocks." A massive geologic formation of rounded boulders that looked as if they had melted. Recent signs had been posted: DANGER! Caves Unsafe! Do Not Enter!

Jack looked around at the surrounding wilderness and saw emptiness and desolation, not a building or road or habitation for miles.

Perfect.

"Do you have a cell phone on you, sir?" Zeb asked after Jack had gotten out of the vehicle.

"Yes, why?"

"In case of emergencies." Zeb handed him a small card with the resort's security number on it. "This line is monitored twenty-four hours."

Jack squinted around at the rocks and sand. "Looks safe enough."

"We've had high coyote activity lately. We suspect there is a den on the north side of these rocks. Would you like a driver to return for you?"

Jack looked back at the dense growth of trees, white domes peeping through. What was it? Three miles away? "I can walk back."

"If you change your mind," Zeb said. Then he gave Jack a friendly salute and drove off.

Despite the sharp sunlight flooding the sandy plain, the air was biting cold. It whipped through the massive boulders that comprised Indian Rocks, whistled through cracks and crevices, raced around Jack, tugging at his clothes, nipping at his face and hands. The place felt ancient and sacred. Jack could almost believe he was the last man on earth.

Unfolding the portable target that was designed to stop broadhead or field point tipped arrows, Jack wedged it between two boulders and then paced a hundred feet from it, back to where he had left the rest of his equipment. He removed his jacket and folded it onto a rock so that he stood in jeans and a T-shirt that was tight fitting both for safety and better accuracy. Loose clothing was a hazard in archery, and could also throw one's aim off. He also removed the gun and shoulder holster.

Noting the direction of the wind and the angle of the sun, Jack slipped the shooting glove onto his right hand, hooked the quiver to his belt, and picked up his bow that was already strung.

Jack had discovered archery when he was a boy at one of the expensive summer camps his wealthy parents were always sending him to, places where movie stars' kids went. He had taken immediately to the bow and arrow, the feeling of control, the moment of tension, the pulling back and letting go, the satisfaction of the bull's eye. Jack occasionally entered competitions, to test himself and evaluate his skills—his favorite being unmarked-distance archery—but he had never joined a team. Jack Burns was a solitary archer.

His bow was a Hatfield Take-Down Recurve with sixty pounds of draw weight, custom crafted right-hand grip, fiberglass surfaced laminated limbs finished in satin gloss, and reinforced tips for fast flight string.

This was Jack's world now, he was in his element, where it was just he and the target and the wide, wide world stretching away to the far horizons.

All of existence, life, the universe were reduced to the bow, the string and the arrow, and Jack's keen eye, strong muscles, and determination to hit the bull's eye.

"It's a nasty one, Detective," the uniformed cop said. "Young and pretty."

He took his stance, planting his feet firmly with his left toe pointed toward the target, right toe pointed away. *She was nude, lying face down in her own vomit.*

He selected an arrow and nocked it on the bowstring. *"Looks like semen on her thighs and buttocks," the man from the coroner's office said as he scraped samples into a plastic bag. "She had sex before she checked out."*

With his back straight and head upright, he raised the bow and addressed the target.

"Cause of death?"

Extending his bow arm, he kept his shoulder locked down and his elbow relaxed. *"Hard to tell. Drugs most likely, judging by the paraphernalia."*

Drew the bowstring back, anchoring it at his jaw. *"Accidental overdose?" Jack asked as he watched the coroner reach for the girl's cold shoulder to turn her over.*

Taking aim. Feeling the tension in his back. Eye on the target. His mind and body focused. *The corpse was turned over onto her back and blond hair fell away from her face—his sister's face.*

He released the bowstring. *Jack Burns fainted on the spot.*

The arrow flew through the air and went straight into the bull's eye but because he was at The Grove for one reason, to catch a killer, in Jack's mind it wasn't a bull's eye but a human heart.

The heart of Nina's killer.

Vanessa arrived with her usual flourish of swirling caftan, clattering beads and musky scent. "It's all arranged. Dinner tonight with Coco Mc-Carthy."

Abby had planned to dine with all three at the same time, but Ophelia had declined, saying that she preferred to be alone. And Sissy said she was expecting some important phone calls, but would be happy to re-schedule. Abby's anxiousness was growing. She should just go to their rooms and knock on the door, look into the eyes of Coco and Sissy and Ophelia and see if she *knew*. But Ophelia Kaplan seemed troubled. And Sissy was embroiled in a personal matter. Abby didn't want to intrude.

As Vanessa helped herself to a cup of fresh Kona blend coffee, she said, "Abby, I still think you should just do DNA testing." It would simplify everything. A strand of hair taken from each of the three hair brushes, and a lab analysis to compare with Abby's own DNA.

But Abby was adamant. She would never invade another person's privacy. Not even for something as important as this. She had vowed long ago that she would not to do others what had been done to her…

Sixteen-year-old Emmy Lou, arrested in front of her friends and taken to jail, the police going through her personal things, reading her diary, the prosecutor displaying her private possessions during the trial, to prove to the world what a bad girl she was, innocent objects—travel brochures to gardens around the world, true confession magazines, romance novels. He had read aloud the lurid titles of the confession stories and romance novels and told the jury that Emmy Lou wanted Avis Yocum's money to run away because the United States wasn't good enough for her, this girl who had been seen in the frequent company of a draft-dodging hippy.

And then after sentencing, being taken to White Hills Prison, ordered to strip for a physical exam and humiliating rectal search, sprayed with green soap and hosed down, ending with a physical exam by a doctor who didn't even look Emmy Lou in the eye as he asked, "How far along are you?" in such a distracted tone that Emmy Lou didn't know he was talking to her. Emmy Lou on her back, her feet in stirrups, the doctor's fingers probing, and his declaration: "Looks like two months." The snap of rubber gloves as they came off his hands. "She's healthy. She can work."

The final insult: chopping off her long copper-gold braids, "For safety," and being issued used underwear and a loose cotton dress, and from then on forced to bathe in open shower stalls with male guards watching, and using toilets that had no doors.

No, Abby would not invade Coco's and Sissy's and Ophelia's privacy by testing their DNA without their permission.

Abby knew little about the three women other than the basic facts the private investigator had collected. They *were* adopted. That fact was beyond doubt. But what if they had never been told? Things were different in 1972, when adoption records were sealed and it was nearly impossible for mothers and children to trace one another. Only in the last decade had old records started opening up. And the things people had found, shocked them. Many of the adoptive parents had believed they were dealing with legitimate attorneys and agencies, that the babies had been willingly given up for adoption. Many had no idea they had been given kidnapped babies, or infants sold by desperate mothers.

The word "sold" had haunted Abby for years. Sold for *what*? As if her child were a piece of furniture. Or a dog. Nightmares had haunted her. And guilt. She should have known her baby was born alive. She should have fought to keep it. She should have demanded legal aid, demanded to know what her rights were. Through Abby's ignorance and naiveté, her child could be living the worst life. But now, at least, knowing what she knew of Ophelia's and Sissy's and Coco's lives and their families, Abby received some consolation that her worst nightmare never came true.

But another terrible thought continued to haunt her: that her daughter *did* know she was adopted, and had been told that her mother was a convicted murderer. Abby wanted to set the record straight.

Vanessa watched the struggle on her friend's face, knew the agonizing indecision that gripped Abby, and made an observation: that her friend had created this oasis of healing, yet could not herself be healed.

"By the way," Vanessa said. "I checked with the LAPD, to see if Jack Burns really is one of their detectives."

Abby snapped her head up. "And?"

"He is."

"Investigating his sister's murder?"

"They wouldn't say. Do you believe him, Abby? What if it's just a cover for the *real* reason he's here?"

Abby shivered with premonition. Was it here at last? The showdown that she had feared someday would come?

Not now! she wanted to shout. Not yet. Just a little more time. Let me be reunited with my daughter as a free woman...

CHAPTER FOURTEEN

*U*RI EDELSTEIN WAS INVISIBLE.

Sitting in his boss's bullet-proof office on the second floor of the Las Vegas Atlantis Casino Hotel, the senior accountant and best friend of Michael Fallon watched the action below on a special closed-circuit TV.

He saw Michael down there, handsome and charming in a black hand-tailored suit, gray shirt and pearl-white silk tie, thousand-dollar lizard skin shoes, dark hair slicked back, two pinkie rings flashing gold and diamond. Fallon greeted the hotel guests and casino customers as if they were personal friends, shaking their hands, effusively welcoming them to the Atlantis.

Everyone loved Fallon. When he took over the Wagon Wheel back in 1976, after the death of Gregory Simonian who had built the first casino on the Strip, Michael had established an open-door policy with his employees, inviting anyone with a complaint to come straight into his office and speak directly to him. He would sometimes circulate through the casinos and hand out cash to gamblers who had gone bust. If a police officer was killed in the line of duty in the Vegas area, Fallon would send a generous check to the family. He donated millions to charity and was seen in church every Sunday. He hobnobbed with the cream of Vegas society, hot shot politicians, movers and shakers. They clapped him on the back and said, "What can we do for you, Michael?"

It was a different Las Vegas from the one Uri and Michael had grown up in. The sixties had seen the pinnacle of Vegas mob crime when Robert Kennedy had spearheaded the fight to rid Nevada of organized crime, and the old boys got out. But no amount of federal investigating could tie Mike Fallon to the syndicate he had once worked for. He had turned legitimate the night Francesca was born. He had done it for her. And the wedding this coming Saturday, costing in the hundred thousands, was all for her.

But now it was threatened.

Uri figured gangsters killing gangsters was one thing, and he looked the other way. But the baby trafficking had come as a shock. He hadn't known Mike was involved in that. He learned about it when Fallon came to him with an outlandish story about a man named Bakersfelt who had run a lucrative network of black market adoptions years back, and now a woman named Abby Tyler was poking around into all that old business. "She'll uncover my name, Uri. I can't allow it. If the Vandenbergs find out…"

Vandenberg, Nevada royalty, the richest of the rich, and Fallon's ticket at last into the blue-blood echelons he had craved to belong to—the family Francesca was marrying into on Saturday.

So Uri had made a few phone calls and was awaiting the response.

Down below, among the busy roulette tables, he saw Michael stop and exchange pleasantries with a pit boss named Julio. Fallon was grinning and Julio laughing, sharing a private joke. Then Fallon pointed to the ceiling, gave Julio a friendly pat on the back and moved on.

Uri knew what the gesture meant. Julio had been ordered up to the office.

As Fallon stepped into the private elevator, he sent Julio a wink and a smile and pressed the button.

The doors whispered closed and Fallon let the smile drop. Some days his face ached from all the smiling.

But it was what got him where he was today, that smile.

Marrying Simonian's daughter had not launched Michael Fallon in the echelons he aspired to. Nor had inheriting the Wagon Wheel. No matter what he did, no matter that he was good looking, or how hard he tried to charm, he was still Mike Fallon, petty thug. When Francesca entered his life and his goals became for her instead of for himself, Fallon had made a frank appraisal of the man in the mirror and saw the flaws. It wasn't enough to be smart and ruthless and handsome. You had to have charisma. He saw it in all successful men.

So he went to Hollywood and hired a make-over artist, a personal trainer, a movie director and an acting coach. They assessed him and analyzed him, they made him walk and talk and eat and drink while they watched and conferred. Then they trained him and coached him, made him posture in front of mirrors, took movies of him and showed them on a big screen. And what he learned was that it took a lot of phoniness to look sincere.

It was hard work. They had to search for and find the one feature that would be Fallon's trademark, that would make men drop their guard and women want to hop into his bed. They found it in his laugh. But he didn't laugh much and that had to change. The team coached him on timing, how to blush on command, how to close his eyes as if he had committed a gaff. They brought in actors who showed him how it was done and pretty soon Mike Fallon got good at laughing in a self-conscious, self-mocking way. It was funny, sexy and so opposite from his dark side that even he believed the aw-shucks guy in the mirror. His rivals would never know what he was thinking, and no woman would turn him down.

Fallon returned to Vegas a changed man. The thug was gone, the charmer was in his place.

"Good house tonight," he declared to Uri as walked into his office. Fallon said it every night, the Atlantis always hopping.

Uri saw his friend glance in the gold-veined mirror over the bar. Fallon never failed to check out his reflection, ever since his vacation in Hollywood and he had come back with a new laugh and a bounce in his step. "I'm going places, my friend," Fallon had said when he returned from California three decades ago. There had been a new light in his eyes, as if he had done some house cleaning in his head. A new energy filled him, as if he were plugged into a dynamo. "I don't believe in luck," the new Mike Fallon had said, "not like those schmucks in my casino. Luck is for losers. I am going to *make* my way in this world, carve me a big chunk of it and hand it to Francesca on a platinum platter." And Uri, who knew Mike better than anyone, had fallen under the magic spell and decided that this was a star he wanted to hitch himself to.

"I invited Julio up," Fallon said as he poured himself a scotch. Uri wondered if it was to give the man a bonus. Mike did that when he was feeling generous, and it kept the employees on their toes.

Judging by the grin on Julio's face when he was escorted in, he was thinking the same thing.

"You're doing a good job, Julio," Fallon said, patting the middle-aged man on the shoulder. "I wanted you to know that."

Flanked by two bodyguards—no one ever had a meeting with Fallon alone—Julio muttered a modest, "Thanks." But excitement shone in his eyes. Only last week Manny Rosenbloom got a brand-new Cadillac for catching a crooked dealer. You never knew.

"Hey," Fallon said, tapping Julio's abdomen. "What's this? Putting on extra luggage there?"

"You know how it is."

Fallon blushed and laughed as he patted his own abdomen. "You and me, Julio, we're entering our spare tire years."

And Julio laughed in agreement.

Fallon sipped his scotch. "So, Julio, I saw you talking to my daughter this morning."

Julio shrugged. "I said hello. You know."

"You put your hand on her arm."

"I did?"

"She was wearing a tennis dress. Sleeveless. Her arm was bare. You touched it."

"I did?" he said again, his forehead suddenly sprouting sweat. "I don't remember. I mean, I didn't intend any disrespect. You know that, Michael. I wasn't thinking."

"Sure," Fallon said with ease. "I understand. We all do things without thinking. But I don't like anyone touching my daughter."

His nod to the two bodyguards was so subtle that Julio didn't see the first punch coming. It snapped his head sideways and sent a tooth flying out of his mouth. The second punch knocked the air out of his lungs, making him double over in agony, and the third dropped him to his knees. The men alternately punched and kicked him, their feet making sick thudding sounds, Julio sobbing and then silent, the sound of a bone snapping, until he was unconscious and blood streamed from his nose and mouth and the cuts on his face.

"Drop him in the desert," Fallon said dismissively. Then with a tug on his French cuffs, said to Uri, "Keep me informed on that business with Abby Tyler. I'll be upstairs saying good night to Francesca." It was Michael's nightly ritual. But as he started to leave, he stopped and said, "What?"

Uri raised his eyebrows.

"You look funny," Fallon said.

"I do?"

"You have a problem with how I handled Julio?"

Uri met his friend's eyes and for the first time in their four decades together, felt a prickle of fear. "No, not at all, Mike."

"Hey," Fallon put a hand on Uri's shoulder, "you and me go back a long way, don't we?" Fallon had asked Uri to be his daughter's godfather, and at the christening, a big affair in a Catholic church, Uri had worn a yarmulke and had sung a Hebrew prayer over the baptismal font. The priest had been a little nonplussed but everyone loved it and Michael Fallon cried with unabashed sentimentality.

But now the hand on Uri's shoulder felt heavier than it should. "No problems," he said, for the first time in his life uncomfortable beneath his friend's scrutiny.

The moment stretched, Uri's Adam's apple went up and down, and finally Fallon's face broke into a sunny grin. He slapped his old friend on the back and said, "Just fucking with you!" and, with a laugh, walked out.

Pulling out a handkerchief, Uri mopped his forehead. He had never passed judgment on Fallon's brutal form of justice. But he didn't think Julio deserved getting beaten up like that. Mike was tense these days, because of the wedding. Uri just hoped no one else got in his way.

In high school she had been voted the girl most likely to keep her head in a disaster, and her friends at Harvard Business School had teasingly called her Ms. Spock, after the Star Trek character—Francesca was that level-headed.

Wouldn't they all be surprised to see her tonight, looking at her fiancé's picture and wondering why she was marrying him?

She wouldn't be the first daughter in history to get married just to get away from an overbearing father. But at least *she* had chosen Stephen, she had that consolation. And the fact that her father had taken an instant liking to him. Her father had disapproved of all her previous relationships.

Francesca had an MBA from Harvard. It was her father's dream for her to go into business law. If Francesca had ever had a dream of her own, she had long forgotten it. She had met Stephen through a mutual client named Featherstone, who wanted to create a chain of fitness centers for women around the country. When she had told Mr. Featherstone the growth potential was tremendous, he had brought in a venture capitalist from Carson City, Stephen Vandenberg. During the months they had worked putting the plan together, romance had blossomed.

But now, with the wedding only four days away, Francesca felt doubts niggling at her. Was it really love she felt for Stephen? All her life, her emotions had been overshadowed by her father. They only ever had each other—no aunts or uncles or cousins. She didn't remember her grandfather, Gregory Simonian, who died in a freak accident when she was four. Nothing Francesca did or felt was ever separate from her father and her feelings for him. How could she expect to ever know anything about herself?

She knew what had triggered these fresh doubts: her father's wedding gift to her and Stephen—a brand new house in a gated community, right next to his own.

She had hoped she and Stephen would move to Reno, be independent of their parents as they started their new life together. But her father had looked so hurt when she hadn't gushed with excitement over his gift that she had given in. They were to stay in Vegas.

At least, she reminded herself once more time, *I* chose Stephen. It was one of the few decisions in Francesca's life that had come from her. And that, she decided, was reason enough to marry him.

Wasn't it?

When Fallon reached the top floor of the hotel, he thought of how close he had come to losing all this, back when Francesca was a little girl.

The story went that a crazy Armenian named Gregory Simonian was driving from Los Angeles to Las Vegas back in 1941 when he stopped on the side of the highway to take a piss. As he was watering the sand he noticed the traffic whizzing by: all those California suckers heading for Glitter Gulch on Fremont Street to gamble away their money. It occurred to Simonian that someone should build a place out *here*, four miles south of downtown, on this strip of desert highway, catch the suckers before they got to Fremont. Everyone called him crazy for building his casino hotel in the middle of nowhere. But it worked. Folks stopped at the Wagon Wheel, stayed and gambled, Simonian got rich, and other men came to build casinos in this so-called middle of nowhere that was once the Los Angeles Highway but was now called The Strip.

When Michael was young he had seen how everyone respected Gregory Simonian. That was the life Michael wanted. But being Simonian's son-in-law turned out not to be enough. Michael wanted to make his mark on Vegas. The Wagon Wheel was still the Wagon Wheel. What was needed was an eye-popping, show-stopping casino hotel outclassing all the others.

His father-in-law lived at that time in a big house in the better part of town, with a water-guzzling lawn and six car garage. He was watching a boxing match on TV when Michael arrived to discuss making changes to the Wagon wheel. His wife, Gayane, had been dead four years. The only connection between the two men was little Francesca.

Simonian wasn't interested in Michael's plans but Michael persisted. "You've been to Glitter Gulch," he had said that day, talking over the TV, "you've seen the kids waiting outside the casinos while their parents are inside gambling. We should create a place where parents can park the kids *inside* the casino. We offer games for the kids, make a mint."

Simonian had kept his eyes on the TV and made a loopy gesture around his ear.

"And there's a lot more working stiffs out there than high rollers. We should cater to factory workers and truck drivers, not the whales."

"You're crazy."

"I *know* how much money can be won from the smaller gamblers."

Simonian had continued to shake his head, as he always did, until Michael suggested installing "loose" slot machines. Now Simonian lost his temper, jumping to his fee and shouting, "You're talking about paying out *more* jackpots? Are you out of your mind?"

"Come on, Gregory. You and I both know that very little of those winnings ever leave the casino. It's a fever. And we feed it. Keep 'em winning and they keep pouring the coins back into the machines. We still win in the end."

Simonian gave him a disgusted look. "You know? For a smart wop you sure are a dummy."

Fallon's face darkened. "Gayane might not be around, but I am still the father of your grandchild and I demand respect."

"You get nothing from me!" Simonian yelled. "I gave you job of casino boss so I can keep an eye on you. So you don't go back to working for your mobster friends. So my little Francesca is kept safe."

"And what I'm talking about is *for* Francesca! You don't want her to inherit a third-rate casino, do you? I want to build it into something big. Into the biggest goddam attraction in Las Vegas."

"You," Simonian said, pointing in Fallon's face, "son of a bitch, you don't get my casino, you don't get nothing!"

Simonian paused to watch a punch thrown on TV, then returned to his son-in-law. "And another thing, Mr. Big Shot Gangster. Don't get any ideas about making me disappear the way you do everybody else. I got the goods on you, good and proper. I found out about the baby selling business, you running kidnapped kids across state lines. I got papers to prove it. And those papers are in safe keeping with two men," he had lifted his thumb, "my lawyer," he lifted his index finger, "and my priest. Sealed so they don't know what's in them, but insurance for me. They got instructions—I get shot or stabbed or poisoned, or I vanish, or anything, they take those papers to the Feds and you're put away for life. *You got that*?"

Michael had gotten it.

Seven months later, on May 16, 1977, the right landing gear of a New York Airways Sikorsky 5–61L helicopter failed while the aircraft was parked, with rotors turning, on the rooftop heliport of the Pan Am Building. The aircraft rolled over, killing passengers who had been waiting to board. The National Transportation Safety Board determined that the cause of the accident was fatigue failure of the right main landing gear assembly.

Among the fatalities was Mr. Gregory Simonian, Las Vegas hotel owner, who had literally lost his head in the accident.

The tampering had cost Michael plenty, enough to keep the helicopter mechanic in tropical luxury for the rest of his life, but worth every penny because it had looked like such a freak accident that Simonian's attorney and Father Diran Papazian of the Las Vegas Armenian Church did not connect it to Fallon and so the sealed papers in their care, proof of Fallon's days as a baby-runner, remained sealed.

Just to be sure, however, a month later, Fallon saw to it that the lawyer and the priest died in separate, unrelated accidents. No one reported certain documents missing from their respective offices because no one else had known about them. His secret had remained secret so that nothing had stopped Michael Fallon from going all the way to the top—the king of Las Vegas, with Francesca as his queen.

He knocked lightly on the double doors of her suite, because sometimes Francesca was already asleep and he did not want to wake her. But she was awake—reviewing legal contracts, she said. So typical of his level-headed, focused daughter. Instead of fussing over guests lists and flower arrangements and which bridesmaid was to stand where, work came first for Francesca Fallon.

The sight of her, as always, slammed him back to the night she was placed in his arms. His wife, Gayane, pale and bloody from hours of difficult labor, lying dead on the sheets. He had held the little newborn life in his arms and had cried like a baby himself, sobbing so hard he shed hot tears on the little pink thing, dropping into her open mouth so that the first thing Francesca tasted in life were her father's tears.

He had not been prepared for the love. It had crashed into him like a desert twister, picking him off the ground and spinning him around until he didn't know up from down.

Now he knew his own father hadn't abandoned him. Because Fallon understood a father's love, the utter depth of it. It was his mother's doing, keeping Fallon's father out of the picture. And because he knew this, he hated her all the more. The night Francesca was born, he went to the little house in the middle of dust fields, where his mother was ironing her waitress uniform, and told her she was moving to Florida. And so Francesca grew up not knowing she had an Irish grandmother named Lucy Fallon living in Miami.

And if there were other Fallons, Michael didn't care. He despised his Irish half and embraced his Italian side with even more zest and gusto, passing this passion along to his daughter, teaching her how to say her nightly prayers in Italian, how to order in an Italian restaurant. Even her name, Francesca, was Italian. A baccarat dealer had once innocently commented on her Armenian eyes and the man was fired on the spot.

Only one thing Michael didn't tell his daughter—that her Italian grandfather was most likely a mobster. There had been a lot of Italians in Vegas at the time of Fallon's conception: Michael Cornero, king of the western rum runners, and his crime partner, Pietro Silvagni. The boys from Chicago, Vito Basso and Carlo Bellagamba. The guys from Florida, Angelo Siciliano and Frank Taglia. And Nevada's own Joey "the Nose" Franchimoni. Michael would have been proud to be the son of any one of them—with the exception of Franchimoni who had been so determined to kick the Jewish mob out of Vegas that his anti-Semitic proclivities offended Michael's best friend, Uri Edelstein.

Of course, they were all dead or retired by now, Michael having survived and come out on top. And not a single person had the goods on him.

With two exceptions. And both were women.

"Can I fix you a drink, Daddy?" Francesca asked, rising from her desk, tall and slim, shining chestnut hair dancing on her shoulders. A brilliant lawyer with a brilliant future. Everything perfect. And after Saturday, nobody was ever again going to call Mike Fallon a "dumb wop bastard" like the kids in school long ago. Michael silently congratulated himself for a job well done. Francesca had no idea that her meeting Stephen had been arranged by her father. Selecting Stephen Vandenberg from a list of twenty eligible bachelors, Fallon had then laid his plan: creating a dummy client who went to Francesca with an idea for a chain of fitness centers. "Mr. Featherstone" had then brought in Stephen Vandenberg and, as Fallon had hoped, a few months of the two working closely together and nature had taken his course. Mike Fallon, matchmaker, he thought with a grin.

"A scotch, please, sweetheart," he said as he settled into a padded club chair.

The phone rang and Francesca picked it up. "It's for you," she said, handing him the phone. "Uncle Uri."

"Fallon here." As he listened to Edelstein's report, his smile stretched into a grin. "Good work. Keep me informed."

Good work indeed. Uri had found a way to get a man into The Grove. The same reliable hit man who had discreetly taken care of the other "loose ends." On a signal from Fallon, Abby Tyler would no longer be a threat.

CHAPTER FIFTEEN

*S*ISSY FELT AS IF SHE WERE WEARING A NEW SKIN. IT HAD MORE nerve endings, danced with electricity, and felt hungry all over. Alistair, the night before.

It was the first time she had had an orgasm during sex. Sissy always had to do it on her own, usually in the shower, the one place she knew she wouldn't be interrupted. Which was where she was now on this Tuesday morning that hummed with life and surprise. As she lathered the soap over her skin, she closed her eyes and relished the sensation, imagining that it was Alistair. She soaped her breasts and nipples, then moved over her abdomen and lower. She had been taught it was a sin but she couldn't help herself. Alistair so crisp in her mind, the imprint of his lips still on her mouth. She brought herself to a climax within seconds and had to grab onto the towel bar to keep from falling.

What was it about this place? Did they put something in the coffee? Did they spray pheromones into the air?

Had Alistair even really existed? She had left him there, in that little glade, and run back to her cottage. Ashamed, filled with guilt, but confused as well. And her sleep had been far from restful, visited with erotic dreams.

As she stepped out of the shower and toweled off, she thought about her previous night's encounter. How surprising, the feel of another man. Alistair's body had been so different from Ed's, his penis slightly longer, narrower. He kissed differently, lingered over her nipples the way Ed never did, and when she clasped his bare butt with her hands, they had felt fuller, firmer. Sissy had assumed all men were the same in the dark. But they weren't.

Was that what happened to Ed? Did he get bored with their routine, wonder what another woman's body felt like, and decided to experiment?

Wrapped in one of The Grove's luxurious bathrobes, she went into the living room and saw the phone message light blinking.

It was Ed: "Hi, hon. My secretary said you called yesterday. She only just now gave me the message. Sorry. A big storm moved in last night so Hank and I stayed at the club. I'll be with buyers all day today. Will call tonight. Hope you're enjoying yourself. Love you."

She frowned. He didn't *sound* like he was cheating. Had she made some sort of horrendous error? Just because his secretary didn't know Hank Curly, or that Hank wasn't listed in a phone book didn't mean he didn't exist. And maybe Sissy *had* gotten the name of the sports club wrong.

She got a terrible feeling in the pit of her stomach. She had cheated on Ed.

If only she hadn't missed his call, she could have cleared everything up. As it was, she would have to wait for his call tonight.

How was she going to get through the day?

Thinking of her best friend, she tried Linda's number but got the machine instead. Sissy wished she could talk to someone. But it would be too humiliating to tell any of her friends what she suspected was going on. And although Ed's mother was a nice, understanding woman, she would draw the line at hearing accusations of her son cheating. That left Sissy's mother. And in all her life, not once had Sissy been able to go to *her* with a problem.

Going out onto the patio where desert sunlight glowed like gold, Sissy heard moans and giggles on the other side of the wall.

She felt a pang of envy.

It surprised her. Sissy had never envied anyone. Ed had been captain of the high school football team, a young man destined to succeed. Girls had fallen all over him, and he had chosen Sissy. He never forgot a birthday or anniversary, and always, regular as clockwork, made love to her on Saturday nights (even if it *was* with the lights out and in a somewhat predictable pattern). Sissy had always thought herself the luckiest of women, with a beautiful home and wonderful kids, and anything she asked for Ed gave to her. But lately there *had* been that strange, nagging feeling creeping into her life… that something was missing.

And now she was experiencing envy.

"Where did you find such a big vibrator?" the woman in the next garden squealed, and Sissy hastily retreated into her living room. It was disgusting, she told herself, to be so obvious about it, so vulgar.

They're in their own garden, she scolded herself. *It's not as though they're doing it in the middle of Safeway.*

But her curiosity was piqued. Linda had once shown her the vibrator she never traveled without and Sissy was shocked. A sexually active woman and she still needed a vibrator? Linda had suggested she get one and try it but Sissy with her regular Saturday nights with Ed didn't need such things.

She turned to the sliding glass door and squinted at the golden patio beyond. What *would* it be like to do it outside in the daytime?

Where was Alistair at that moment?

Her thoughts shocking her, and then frightening her—would she dare go in search of him?—she turned her back on the inviting sunshine and spread her scrapbook supplies out on the large coffee table. Her eye caught on something that belonged in the brown accordion file: a claim ticket to a jewelry store.

She stared at it.

The date was a week ago, the ticket was for an expensive ladies' watch.

Sissy's birthday was coming up, obviously Ed was going to surprise her with a fancy gift. Or maybe he *had* had some sort of midlife fling and now it was over and he was going to make it up to her. A diamond watch was certainly a nice first step toward apologizing. Sissy would just put the claim ticket back in the file and pretend she never saw it, never saw any of this stuff. But her hand wouldn't obey.

Clutching the ticket, she paced the rich royal blue carpet, then went to stand at the scarlet and gold drapes, to looked out at her private garden. Even with the sliding glass door closed, she could hear the giggles and the woman squealing, "Get away from me with that thing! Are you trying to *kill* me?"

Sissy went to the phone and looked at it as if it were an animal that had crawled in from the desert. Would calling the jeweler be an admission that she did not trust her husband?

As she reached for it, there was a knock at her door. Sissy jumped. The neighbors, inviting her for a threesome!

But it was Vanessa Nichols, with a big friendly smile and apologies for disturbing her. "I just wanted to invite you to dine with Ms. Tyler tomorrow night."

Sissy thought of her neighbors and realized with a shock that she was disappointed it wasn't them at the door, inviting her to join them. "Yes, that would be fine. I look forward to meeting her."

But once she closed her door, everything was forgotten except for one thing. She picked up the phone and dialed the number on the claim ticket.

"Ah yes, madam," a nasal voice on the other end said. "The watch is ready. Inscribed as requested."

Inscribed! "Would you read the inscription to me, please?"

"Certainly," the nasal voice said. "The inscription reads: 'To Linda, You Have Made Me A New Man, Ed.'"

CHAPTER SIXTEEN

OPHELIA HADN'T PLANNED TO FALL IN LOVE.

She had been having trouble sleeping, difficulty concentrating, her temper was short. It was because of her busy class schedule, and her book had just been published and she was in demand for signings and appearances. As a social and political activist, there were demonstrations at abortion clinics that needed to be organized, tracts to be written and distributed. Her colleagues in anthropology were attacking her controversial theory that, prior to ten thousand years ago, sex was random, promiscuous, and outside of the laws of men. Ophelia's critics accused her of making a claim for promiscuity, that lifelong marriage was "unnatural," and demanded she explain how she reconciled this with the laws of God which she purported to follow. Finally, a male student had filed a complaint with the university that Dr. Kaplan had given him a failing grade because he was male.

And the unexpected controversy her book, *Bread Kills*, had triggered! What had shocked her most was her own family's reaction. Bread was the most elemental of foods, her mother had strongly reminded her, it was always served at meals, even the unleavened kind. Bread was holy, a gift from God. And then her brother the rabbi quoted Solzhenitsyn: "Bread is hope, bread is encouragement, bread is strength. Bread never speaks of the grave, is not sentimental about despair. Even a stale ration of this mystery can, crust by crust, wage a valiant campaign against starvation."

It was as if Ophelia had attacked God and Judaism and their ancestors.

She had thought she was going to lose her mind.

At the urging of her mother and sister (and her dean and her publisher and fellow professors) Ophelia had acquiesced and agreed to seek help. She didn't believe in counselors and therapists, thought they were crutches for weak people, Ophelia Kaplan having always worked through her own troubles. But her work was starting to suffer—she was making herself less available to her students, she tossed and turned at night, and she was pushing herself twice as hard at her fitness clubs, to the brink of exhaustion. A friend had recommended a "good man."

Ophelia had spent the next weeks pouring out her hurts and fears to him, baring her flaws and weaknesses, making herself totally vulnerable, which was not Ophelia Kaplan's style, and he had just been so understanding as she had laid her soul at his feet, that she arrived at a startling realization: he had changed in her eyes, from therapist to desired lover.

It wasn't a true seduction, she told herself now as she completed her fiftieth lap in the resort's largest swimming pool. She had executed it unconsciously. Hadn't she? What sort of woman sets out to seduce her analyst?

She had begun to dress for it: button-front blouses instead of pullover sweaters, skirts instead of slacks. Even her shoes, strap-heels replaced no-nonsense pumps. Sending him signals until one day he caught them. It was the end of a visit, she remembered it was raining, making his office even cozier, more insulated against the big, scary, demanding world. He rose from his chair to offer her a hand up from the sofa, but this time he drew her to him, and took her into his arms. He caressed and stroked while she sighed and moaned. His cool fingers explored the smooth crevice between her breasts, and then the hardened nipples, placing his lips on them and suckling gently. Her own hands reached down and caressed him until he hardened.

He broke away, that rainy day, flustered, mumbling he was sorry, that it was wrong, unethical, but Ophelia was determined. She had never really fallen in love before because she always kept up a tough, impenetrable front to men, fighting for a woman's place in a man's jealously guarded world, earning for herself a reputation around campus of being an emasculating bitch. But with *him* she could be frail and powerless, give her feminine self over to his strong masculinity, a feeling charged with such eroticism that it became an obsession.

It was another rainy day and this time he had a fire going in the fireplace. Cold outside yet she wore a diaphanous blouse so that pale blue lingerie was visible underneath. When he saw that she wore no stockings, that her legs were bare and exposed, he pulled her to him and kissed her. It happened quickly. Later he would describe it as like "a hot knife sliding into soft butter," she was that ready. They lay on the soft carpet and when he entered her again, to make love more slowly, Ophelia cried out with a joy she had never felt before. David was hers at last.

That was a year ago and now she wore his engagement ring and was terrified she was carrying his child.

Her laps finished, Ophelia pulled herself out of the pool and into the sparkling morning sunshine. It had been a good work-out and she must get back to her room, face the pregnancy test. She hadn't tested herself last night when she arrived at the resort because it was so late and she had been exhausted from the talk show and the long drive. And this morning she had left the kit unopened because she had wanted her morning workout first.

Ophelia chided herself for putting it off. Procrastination was a weakness she despised. Yet here she was doing it. Time to face up to taking the test.

As she towel-dried her short black hair, she noticed a couple of women on the lounges reading her book. She shook her head in amazement. No one, absolutely *no one*, believed her when she said she had not set out to write a popular diet book.

Well, David believed her. But then, David was in love with her.

Dr. Ophelia Kaplan, university professor of anthropology, had unwittingly caused a sensation three years prior when she published a book titled *Bread Kills*. A diatribe against the consumption of flour-based products, she had gotten the idea while comparing the teeth of prehistoric people with those of the ancient Egyptians. Mummies showed that the Nile Valley dwellers suffered from shocking, almost epidemic, gum disease, tooth decay, dental abscesses. Along with circulatory diseases and other evidence that pointed to widespread diabetes.

Ophelia had asked herself what could have caused such a drastic and radical change in health from pre-pharaonic times to pharaonic? There was only one answer: bread

"Human physiology," she had stated in her thesis, "evolved over four million years, adapting to the environment around it. Our hominid ancestors scavenged for eggs, lizards, birds, roots, seeds and berries. Occasionally they killed larger game. But our digestive systems, our pancreases, our metabolisms evolved to suit the food we were taking in. And then, a mere ten thousand years ago, suddenly we were making bread, eating honey, drinking alcohol. These three poisons—refined flour, sugar and ethanol—were never meant to be ingested by humans. Ten thousand years has not been long enough for our digestive systems to adapt and evolve to handle these substances. This is why we are so overweight today, why we suffer myriad health problems and why Type II diabetes is on the rise. We are born with the digestive tracts of hunter-scavengers. Perhaps in four million years we will evolve a pancreas and fat-storage system that can handle such an overload of sugar—for that is what flour is—but until then we are poisoning ourselves."

The book was originally small, academic, and not meant for popular consumption: *The Shift From Hunter-Gatherer Society to Agrarianism and Its Impact On the Pathology of Bronze Age Peoples.* The initial printing was intended only for college bookstores, but word of mouth had spread among students and then into the public sector because, to everyone's amazement, those who adopted the prehistoric diet found their excess pounds melting away.

The University Press re-vamped the book, giving it a hip new cover and a new title derived from one of the chapters because it had consumer appeal. Ophelia's book was currently condemned by The Physician's Committee for Responsible Medicine, the American Heart Association, the Surgeon General, and the U.S. Department of Health because they said she wasn't a qualified dietician or medical doctor. Ophelia's response was she hadn't written a diet book. It was a *history* book. If people chose to use it as a template for eating habits, it was their responsibility.

Finally she arrived at her room in the main building, the lavish rococo of the Marie Antoinette Suite, and her heart began to race.

The box in the bathroom. The pregnancy test kit. It frightened her. The box, placed among her toiletries, stood ironically next to her birth control pills.

What if I am pregnant?

Get a hold of yourself, Ophelia. You are strong, you are a fighter.

She called room service and ordered lunch, then she showered and dressed and finally reached for the box.

She looked at herself in the mirror. Her body was sinewy with not an ounce of fat. Sleek and strong. Put a club in her hand and she could be an Australopithecine foraging in Olduvai Gorge. She could fight saber-tooth tigers.

When she saw how her hands shook as she opened the package, she mentally scolded herself. This was no time for irrational fears. Where was her scientific objectivity? Ophelia reminded herself that she was first and foremost a scientist and should take the rational approach to this, as she would to any laboratory test.

The insert read: *This product can detect the pregnancy hormone as early as three days before you expect your period. The amount of pregnancy hormone increases as pregnancy progresses.*

Which meant there would be no false positive, not a whole month after her period was due.

Test any time of day.

Now was as good a time as any.

Two pink lines pregnant; one pink line not pregnant.

Was it too late to pray for one pink line?

Result in three minutes.

The longest three minutes of her life.

Ophelia unwrapped the test stick and read the instructions: *Hold test stick in your urine stream for five seconds. Lay the test stick down on a flat surface with the clear side facing up. You will see a pink color moving across the clear top to indicate that the test is working. Read your result after three minutes.*

Ophelia had never been so nervous in her life. Not when she had read from the Torah before the congregation at her Bat Mitzvah, not when she had applied for post-grad studies under one of the most stellar anthropologists in the world, not when she had sat for her oral exams for her PhD. No courage in the world could hold up to two pink lines.

She closed her eyes. The phone call from her sister five years ago: "*Ophelia, little Sophie has stopped crawling! And she won't reach out for anything. She was so active last week and now—*"

Her mouth ran dry and she scolded herself again for being afraid. It's a simple chemical test, that's all. Just pretend you're in a lab, running a fluorine analysis of fossilized bones. Place the ion selective electrode on the specimen, make three replicate measurements, calculate fluoride content, enter the data on a spread sheet for statistical evaluation.

Removing her panties, she straddled the toilet and started to pee. With a trembling hand, she lowered the test strip and—

Dropped it.

Right into the toilet.

"No!" she shouted, jumping away from the porcelain bowl before she was finished. She stared in horror at the plastic strip floating on the surface of the water. She started to reach down but stopped when she thought of germs. The water might be clean but how clean was the bowl?

Traipsing back into the living room, furious with herself—this would never would have happened in a laboratory! Had her hand really been shaking, she who was *always* in control, or was it an unconscious act of sabotage?—she picked up the Guest Services book and frantically flipped through it, wondering where she could find an emergency pregnancy test kit.

A resort that specialized in romance and sex, that offered on the Room Service menu flavored body paints and candy sex toys, would they have pregnancy test kits? She found it: a drugstore for the convenience of the guests was located in a place called the Village.

CHAPTER SEVENTEEN

*W*HEN COCO AWOKE, THE FIRST THING THAT CAME TO HER mind was Kenny and how sexy he was in a hometown boyishly innocent way.

And his electric touch.

As she lay in the crisp, clean sheets, listening to birdsong on her patio, and relishing the soft fuzzy realm between sleep and wakefulness, she closed her eyes...

I open my door and Kenny is standing there. He is wearing his sexy tuxedo, but I notice he has no shirt on under the jacket. "I need your help," he says, blushing shyly. He has three shirts on hangers. "I don't know which to wear for my performance tonight."

I let him in and pick up the scent of his cologne as he passes. He has just showered. I wonder if his skin is still damp. His blond hair is spiky in the back where the comb missed. I reach up and rake those naughty little spikes down with my fingernails.

Kenny turns, surprise on his face, his cheeks flushed. "Which shirt?" he asks.

I pretend to be interested when all I care about is seeing what's under the tuxedo. "Try them on, that way I can tell."

He slips out of the jacket. He is slender and pale, not surfer-tanned as I had imagined. But the paleness excites me, it makes me think of imprisoned men in need of being set free.

When I see that the zipper of his trousers isn't done all the way up, but open just below his navel, my breath catches in my throat. He has a nice abdomen. It looks hard. I wonder how hard the rest of him is.

He puts the pale pink shirt on, with ruffles at the front. He doesn't button it, but lets pale chest show through as he says, "What do you think of this one?"

I have to make sure the shirt fits. I slide my hands under the starched fabric and around to the back until my fingers meet so that Kenny and I are chest to breast. I remember with a shock that I haven't finished dressing! I am only in bra and panties. No wonder he blushed when I opened the door.

"Feels like a good fit," I murmur and feel his breath minty and cool on my cheek. "I'm not sure about the pants, though. I think you could use a smaller size."

My hands slip down to his lower back, making him groan, and then farther still until I clasp his tight round ass.

Kenny's hands are on me now, tentatively, as if in scary uncharted territory. I gasp. He knows how to explore a woman's back, teasingly up to the bra hooks and down, making me think he is going to set my breasts free, and then not, turning my heat up.

I am about to insist he get on with it, but he steps back and says, "Maybe I should try on another shirt."

I allow him to slip out of the pink one but stop him from reaching for the blue. "The trousers," I say, "are wrong." I tug at the waistband and he says in embarrassment, "I'm not wearing shorts."

I know this. It's why I want the pants off.

"Wait," he says, backing away. "I came for another reason. I've decided to add an assistant to my act. Would you like the job?"

"What would I have to do?"

"Just look pretty and wear this." Now I see that, along with the shirts on hangers, he has brought a small bag.

"What is it?"

"A magician's assistant costume. If you can fit into it, you have the job."

He withdraws two tiny swatches of sequined material. Is he kidding? That costume would-n't fit a mouse. But there is challenge in his tone and I'll be darned if I will back down.

"Very well," I say, "but you have to close your eyes. No peeking." I know I can go into the bathroom to change, or just turn my back, but I'm putting him to a test. If he peeks, he's no gentleman. But I run into a snag. The hooks at the back of my bra won't cooperate. The drawback of having large breasts, it requires four hooks to defy gravity. With my long acrylic fingernails, I am helpless to undo the fasteners.

Kenny's eyes are still shut. I press against him and whisper, "Unhook my bra. But don't look. If you peek, I will have to punish you."

He fumbles around in back and gets the job done. I toss the lacy cups to the floor, my eyes on his eyes. He hasn't peeked so far, but the way his eyelids are fluttering, I can tell it's a struggle.

The costume is impossibly small. I remove my panties and step into the sequined thong, but can get it only halfway up my thighs. This costume was made for Twiggy!

I give up, and when I straighten, I catch Kenny with his eyes open. Now I shall have to punish him…

"Whoa!" Coco said out loud.

This was not a good sign. Time was passing and she had a man to find.

After a cold shower and a hot breakfast, keeping Kenny and his electric touch—and gentle voice and sad story and sexy hands—as far from her thoughts as she could, Coco consulted the crystal. "Daisy, don't let me down," she said, sitting in the sunshine, hoping the desert ethers would open up the spirit world and give her a break. "Tell me something more about the man I am supposed to find here."

She closed her eyes and held her hands over the sparkling orb. Slowed her breathing, relaxed her body. She started to feel something. A tingling. Daisy trying to come through. "Give me a name—a specific detail…"

Ring!

She nearly jumped off the sofa.

Coco glared at the phone as if it had interrupted her on purpose, debated answering it, considered throwing it outside, then couldn't resist.

It was Kenny. His voice making her heart skip as he asked her to meet him for cocktails later. Coco frowned. It was only morning. How could she possibly think that far into the future? But he was persistent in a pleasant, polite and, frankly, flattering way—and she was so damned attracted to him—so she agreed, thinking it wouldn't hurt to share a drink or two with him. And the time *would* be limited because she had a date to have dinner with Abby Tyler afterward.

Returning to the crystal, and forcing Kenny from her mind, but deep down glad he had called and looking forward to seeing him, wishing she weren't—her emotions at odds—she returned herself to a spiritually receptive state and once again invited Daisy into her mind.

A message came through!

No words, really, or images, nothing substantial or concrete. More of a *sense* of something. A slight adjustment to what Daisy had said the day before. Not "well traveled" but "worldly."

Coco opened her eyes and stared at the crystal. Worldly! Not exactly the same as having a heavily stamped passport. A person could circumnavigate the globe and not be aware of worldly things.

She briefly thought of Kenny but had to eliminate him. He did not strike her as being sophisticated or experienced in global matters. *He writes code and tries not to remember things.*

Full of optimism, she spruced herself up, using her long red acrylic nails to frizz out her hair (the curls and burgundy color were salon-created), a touch of blush, eyebrows penciled, and four layers of lipstick to give her that kissable look. Sandals, gypsy skirt, off-the-shoulder blouse and she was off.

The jungle paths and paved walkways of The Grove were alive with men. Fresh and jaded, vain and modest, dressed tastefully, plainly, hot, or as if they had dressed in the dark. They smiled at Coco, they nodded, they made eye contact. But nothing jumped out at her. She knew these guys were on the prowl for sex and Coco wasn't looking for sex. Sex was easy. All you had to do was hang around places where the manly men hung out—cops, firefighters, paramedics—and the bed partners were there for the picking.

The stone path led through a growth of thick banana plants and on the other side she found a man sitting on a verdigris wrought iron bench, his head bent over a newspaper. More publications lay at his side: *Wall Street Journal*, *New York Times* and the *International Herald*. Coco knew at once that he was experienced, knowing, sophisticated. Knowledgeable in the affairs of the world. *Worldly.*

He was fortyish with thinning hair but his profile was strong, and keen eyes peered from behind wire-rimmed glasses. Tan chinos and a madras shirt with button-down collar. A college-campus man. If the day were chilly he would be wearing a tweed jacket with elbow patches.

He looked up. Nice smile.

"Hi," Coco said.

He introduced himself as Dr. Charles—"But everyone calls me Charlie"—Barnhart, and said he was a geologist at Caltech, heading up the earthquake department.

Coco's radar blipped. Not only did he keep up on world events but he was smart to boot.

He invited her to sit and they made interesting small talk, with Coco liking his eyes and his voice and wondering if this brainy, worldly Caltech seismologist had plans for lunch when he said, "Want to see something interesting?"

He led her around the small glade, through dense trees, past a formal garden, taking deserted paths until she thought he was going to walk her back to Palm Springs when he stopped suddenly and said, "There!"

Coco stared. Beyond the edge of the verdant resort, where the tawny desert stretched away to the horizon, she saw a shimmering lake of sun-golden water.

"It's beautiful!" she said.

"It isn't real."

"What do you mean?"

"It's a mirage. I hiked out there yesterday and it's just sand. Do you know what causes a mirage? The refraction of light through air layers of different density."

Brains had always turned her on so when he kissed her suddenly she kissed him right back. His hands were good, knew exactly where to go and what to do. She found him a little soft around the middle but that could be sexy, too. As he unbuttoned her blouse and his lips traced a moist path to her nipple, she observed the desert from beneath her eyelids. The mirage sparkled and vibrated with such intensity that she felt its heat. She felt Dr. Barnhart's erection as well and it made Coco sparkle and vibrate with intensity. He slipped inside with ease and while he didn't last as long as she had hoped, he felt good and Coco was able to sneak a hand down and give herself an orgasm. In future sessions, Charlie would make an interesting pupil.

They restored their clothing, smoothed their hair and, belatedly, looked around to see if they had been observed. But they were still isolated at the edge of the resort, with the mirage continuing its miraculous shimmer a few miles distant.

"I want to know more about you, Charlie," Coco said as she looped her arm through his. "Like, what are your hobbies?"

"I collect antique scientific equipment. I even own one of the original Richter scales. Early model. Excellent condition. Worth a mint."

Coco stared at him, blinked, then felt something inside herself go cold with disappointment. She withdrew her arm. "If you don't mind, I'm not in the mood for lunch, after all."

"What's wrong?"

She gave him a sad shake of her head. "Are you really a scientist, Charlie?"

His cheeks pinked. "Why do you ask?"

"Because you need to work on your act. Charlie, the Richter Scale isn't a machine, it's an *equation*!"

CHAPTER EIGHTEEN

*A*BBY WATCHED HIM APPROACH. ZEB HAD TOLD HER THAT Jack Burns had gone into the desert to shoot a bow and arrow. It surprised her. And now, seeing him walking toward her— enormous bow slung over his shoulder, quiver of arrows hanging from his belt, the tight T-shirt showing off taught muscles—he looked primitive, powerful. And very sexy.

She introduced Jack to the man at her side. "This is Elias Salazar, the head of security here at The Grove. I have apprised him of your purpose here and he will be at your service, should you require help."

"Thanks," Jack said, surprised that she was being so forthcoming with help. He wished he could ask for his sister's file, ask what she knew about Nina and why she had lied about knowing her. But Jack didn't want to tip his hand.

As he thanked her and Mr. Salazar, he headed back to his room, thinking it puzzling that Tyler should be so helpful on the one hand, yet secretive on the other. He also wished she weren't such an attractive woman. It made being suspicious of her more difficult.

He went straight into the bathroom where he splashed cold water on his face. The crime scene image had followed him from Indian Rocks, where he had relived discovering Nina's body.

Whoever had killed Nina had raped her first and then rigged it to look like a drug overdose. Nina who wouldn't even take an aspirin! It killed Jack to imagine what her final minutes had been like.

He had not cried at her funeral. For Nina, he would hold himself together. He would stay focused and find her killer. But more than that: he had taken up her personal cause to find her real birth mother. If it took him the rest of his life, he would track down the woman who had given life to Nina.

Before leaving his room, he checked the files he had been studying the night before, which Nina had collected. He knew Ophelia Kaplan had finally arrived at the resort because he had overheard buzz about it when he had walked by the main swimming pool. Because of her diet book, Kaplan was a celebrity. He would seek her out and chat her up as he had done Coco McCarthy. While his partner and the other cops at the station were spending an all-out effort to investigate Nina's murder—"Don't worry, Jack, we will leave no stone unturned"—interrogating witnesses, analyzing crime scene evidence, retracing Nina's steps in the days leading to her death, Jack had come to The Grove to follow a different sort of trail: the trail Nina herself had been following.

The answers were here. He was sure of it. As he slipped into his jacket and picked up his sunglasses, with Sissy Whitboro and Ophelia Kaplan as his goals, he thought again of the file he had found on Abby Tyler's desk. What did Tyler have on his sister? Maybe he should find a way to borrow it without Abby Tyler knowing.

As he struck out into the noon sun, he thought of Coco McCarthy and their brief conversation the day before. He had found nothing in her manner out of the ordinary or suspicious. She appeared to be exactly what she was supposed to be: a guest at a resort having a good time. Yet he could not shake the hunch that the so-called contest she and the other two women had won was but a ruse to get them here. Why? What did these women, besides having been adopted, have to do with each other and with Abby Tyler? According to Nina's data, Coco and Sissy and Ophelia had been born in the same year, and in the same week as Nina herself. By tracking *their* birth parents she had hoped to find her own. But Nina's life had ended before she could find the answers.

He strolled through the village, looking in the shop windows, smiling at passersby, and as luck would have it, spotted Mrs. Whitboro in a small clothing boutique, browsing through the racks

Tucking his glasses into the pocket of his leather jacket, he slipped into the cozy store and carelessly worked his way to the men's corner where Aloha shirts were on sale.

He watched Sissy Whitboro in the security mirror. With her pale orange hair tied back, and dressed in white pleated Bermuda shorts and a striped polo shirt, she looked like a typical resort resident. Yet, upon watching her more closely, Jack saw that her manner was distracted and her eyes were puffy, as if she had been crying.

Grabbing two shirts from the rack, he approached Sissy and said, "Excuse me, I wonder if you could help me out. I came here on short notice. I was on standby and they called and said there was a free seat on the plane. Unfortunately I came dressed incorrectly. I notice you have a wedding ring so I assume you help your husband pick out clothes." He held up the two shirts. "What do you think? Which one?"

She barely looked at them. "The palm trees."

"My wife usually helps me pick out my clothes. Unfortunately she couldn't come with me."

Sissy smiled politely. "Home with the kids?"

"We don't have children. But we're thinking of adopting." He shook his head. "I don't know…They say you love them just the same…"

If Sissy Whitboro knew she herself had been adopted she gave no indication, but merely smiled absently and moved on.

Jack contrived to arrive at the cash register at the same time, and while the clerk ran his credit card, he said pleasantly to Sissy, "This is an amazing resort. I would think the owner would be someone famous. Do you know who she is?"

Sissy shook her head. "All I know is I won a contest prize so I'm making the best of it. Have fun with your new shirt."

And she was gone.

CHAPTER NINETEEN

OFFICIALLY IT WAS THE WEDDING REHEARSAL DINNER. FOR Michael Fallon, it was another excuse to hold a monster barbecue at his sprawling, multi-million-dollar estate in Henderson— a huge affair with more food than anyone could eat, lively music from a five-piece band, and free-flowing champagne. The late afternoon sun shone down on the happy, well-dressed crowd.

And Mike Fallon, mogul of the gambling scene, famous for bringing the masses to Las Vegas and turning it into a thrill-seeker's paradise, Fallon in his white slacks and open-necked shirt to show off his olive skinned chest, his black hair showing not a strand of gray despite his sixtieth birthday being just two years away, observed it all with intense pride. A secret vow he had made on the night of his daughter's birth had come true at last. He and Francesca, ruling the world.

"She's beautiful," said the blonde next to him. She wore a smart sailor outfit of white and navy with little gold stars over each breast. Fallon vaguely recalled having had her in bed—she had been wild and insatiable and particularly liked sucking on him. He had given her a rare opal ring and told her she was the best.

Fallon looked over at Francesca sharing a joke with the Bishop of Las Vegas, who stood out in the crowd in his long black cassock and purple sash, three-cornered *biretta* on his head. The Bishop was going to personally conduct the wedding ceremony and Fallon was going to show his appreciation by donating a new building to the Catholic school.

Francesca was tall, her chestnut hair radiant in the setting sun. Francesca, the center of Fallon's universe. On Saturday, she would enter the rarified world of Nevada royalty, when she married Stephen Vandenberg III.

After renovating the Wagon Wheel, changing the name to Atlantis, and making it the most profitable casino hotel on the Strip, Fallon had learned that money wasn't enough. People like the Vandenbergs even looked down their noses at millionaires, if the millionaire's bloodline was questionable. That was when he had realized the only entry into their world was through marriage. They would accept him then because they had to.

Fallon searched the crowd for his future son-in-law and found Stephen deep in conversation with a state supreme court judge. From their gestures, it looked like they were discussing golf. Stephen's parents weren't at the party. They lived in a massive historical mansion in Carson City and had been unable to cancel plans to fly down. Fallon didn't mind. He also didn't mind that they disapproved of the marriage. There wasn't a damn thing they could do about it.

Fallon had experienced a moment of panic six years back, when Francesca had fallen in love with a professional skydiver. She had breathlessly confessed to her father that she had found her soul mate. The man was penniless and performed at air shows. If it hadn't been for the tragic accident with the parachute, Michael Fallon might have had to call the young man "son" for the rest of his life. Luckily, a pair of scissors in the right hands could be bought for five grand.

Francesca's grief over the boy's death had startled Michael. He hadn't thought her love for the skydiver ran that deep. What had worried him even more was her vow that she would never fall in love again because it was in Michael Fallon's plans for Francesca to marry. She was his ticket into the world he had hungered to join.

Fortunately, by the time Fallon contrived for her path to cross that of venture capitalist Stephen Vandenberg III, Francesca had gotten over the skydiver and was receptive once again to love.

Fallon left the flirty blonde and went to mingle with his guests like a king greeting peasants. There were bodyguards in the crowd. Francesca didn't know it. He knew how she felt about his obsessive protection. Years ago he had pretended to ease up and give her more freedom. Fallon had simply turned the personal surveillance into a covert operation.

Fallon knew first hand how easy it was to steal a baby.

As he moved through the crowd, enjoying the warmth of the late sun on his shoulders, he spotted Uri Edelstein over by one of the outdoor bars, chatting with the Mayor of Las Vegas. Fallon noticed the mayor's wife giving Uri the once-over—at fifty-seven, Edelstein was himself in fit shape and attractive in a horn-rimmed glasses, cerebral way. But Uri was pointedly ignoring the woman. His sex life baffled Michael. Still with the same woman, after all these years. How could he stand it? Where was the mystery? Women were like fortune cookies—crack them open and you never knew what you were going to get. But who ever cracked open a fortune cookie *twice*?

Michael was on top of the world. Or nearly so. Saturday's wedding was going to clinch it. As long as word about his past didn't get out. He had spent years diligently plugging leaks here and there, silencing anyone who might talk. Two remained. Abby Tyler, whom Fallon was keeping a close eye on, and his mother who still carried a secret that, if found out, could destroy everything.

Francesca still didn't know about a grandmother tucked away in Florida, the Irish Lucy Fallon. And Francesca certainly hadn't a clue that her father might be the bastard of a Vegas mobster. Years ago Michael invented a story to explain their last name. "When my great-granddaddy immigrated to America, his name was Antonio Falconelli. But the immigration agent at Ellis Island wrote it down as Fallonelli. His grandson, my father, shortened it to Fallon to make it sound more American. But you're a Falconelli through and through, sweetheart," he had assured her.

Fallon blinked suddenly into the setting sun. All this thinking about his father must have created a hallucination because, if he didn't know better, he would swear that standing at the gate, arguing with the armed guards, was none other than Gino Gamboni, a crony from his past.

Jesus. It *was* Gamboni.

Michael strode over, instructing the bodyguards to let the man in. They embraced. Gino Gamboni smelled of moth balls. He had prison pallor and fleshy, liver-colored lips. His sorry story was that he had kept working for the Chicago mob long after Michael was smart enough to quit. Arrested and convicted for tax fraud back in '74 and had been in and out of prison since.

"Just got out again," the old man said as he gulped his first whiskey in five years. "You was smart, Michael. You saw it coming, the change in Vegas, back then. You knew it wouldn't be long before the Feds cleaned up the town. Spilotro and them, they didn't know their days were numbered. But you knew." He offered his glass for a refill.

The bartender was generous with the Glenlivet.

"Beautiful little girl you got there, Michael. A real princess." He looked at the tables groaning beneath ravioli, spaghetti, veal marsala. "I ain't tasted good Italian cooking in ages," Gino Gamboni said.

Michael nodded in sympathy. What was life without lasagna and Chianti? But he had thought Gamboni was dead. Michael had to do some quick thinking. "How you doing, Gino? I mean, you gotta place to stay? You got money?"

"Aw shit, Michael. It's rough. The world don't need guys like us any more."

Without another word, Fallon reached into his pocket and pulled out a platinum money clip. Gamboni saw a lot of bills there. All hundreds. Michael counted out ten and pressed them into his old comrade's hand.

"You need a job," Michael said, "you come by tomorrow. No friend of mine goes wanting in this town."

Gamboni started to cry. "We come a long way from running drugs up from Mexico, hey Michael?"

Fallon smiled. "Sure, Gino. It was a hundred years ago."

Gamboni slugged back his drink. "Remember those baby trips we did? Back in sixty-eight? You know what I did one time? I get to Fresno with one of the babies and I tell the happy couple it was twice the amount. I said it was outa my hands because I was told to collect twenty thousand. They want the baby bad. I say I have to take it back, they don't have all the cash. You know that? They come up with the extra ten grand and I keep it and that bastard Bakersfelt he didn't know a thing. Those runs were easy money," he added wistfully.

"Hey Gino," Michael said, clapping him on the back. "Go easy on the liquor, okay? It's a celebration honoring my daughter, after all. Listen, I'm no snob, you know that. But you're not dressed for this occasion. No offense, but it's for my daughter. You know."

"Yeah, sure Mike."

"Listen, I'll have one of my men take you to the Atlantis. Set you up in a suite. You order from room service, anything you want. Play the tables. Whaddya say?"

Gamboni cried openly. "You're the best, Mike. All heart."

Gamboni was sleeping off a binge when something woke him in the dark. It took him a minute to remember he wasn't in a prison cell but one of the Atlantis' luxury suites. "What?" he said muddily and then the lights went on.

Mike Fallon stood over him.

"Listen to me you disrespectful piece of shit," Fallon said, pulling the man from the bed. "I take you into my home and I give you money, and you talk trash. The past is gone, Gamboni. I got nothing to do with it anymore. You don't ever mention the past again. Not to me, and especially not in front of my daughter. You got that?"

Gamboni blinked owlishly as Michael dragged him to the room service cart covered in the remnants of Gamboni's steak dinner. Before he knew it, Michael had his hand pinned to the table and in the next instant speared it with a steak knife.

Gamboni howled.

"You spread the word, *capisce*? Nobody talks about the past. They do, they lose more than a hand. I take their dicks next time. Is that clear?"

Gamboni nodded, his lips pressed together, eyes screwed shut tight in pain. He had gone white and sweat ran down his face. Blood streamed from his hand, pinned to the table like a New York cut.

Michael beckoned to the two bodyguards at the door. "Take him to a hospital. Make sure he lives so he can pass the word to anyone else who's still alive from the old days."

CHAPTER TWENTY

*T*o Linda, You Have Made Me A New Man, Ed.

After she had broken the connection with the jeweler, Sissy had sat in shocked silence, staring at the primary colors of Bird of Paradise Cottage, desperately trying to convince herself that there must be some mistake.

But in the end she could only put two and two together and come up with the unbearable fact that Ed was having an affair with her best friend.

She had dialed Linda and when she got the machine again, dialed Linda's pager, something Sissy rarely did as Linda sold real estate and was often in the middle of a sale. She caught Linda in her car and at the sound of her friend's breezy voice, Sissy lost her cool. She had promised herself she would be adult and calm about the whole thing but it was just too much.

Linda pulled her car over to the side of the highway and, when Sissy's tirade ran out of steam, said, "Girlfriend, I might be the horniest female in the state of Illinois and parts of Wisconsin but I would never do it with my best friend's husband."

Sissy started to cry. Somehow, if Ed had to have a fling, there was some comfort in at least knowing who the woman was. Now it was with a stranger. "I'm sorry I thought it was you," she said, pressing a tissue to her eyes. "It's just such a blow. The rejection—"

Sissy didn't have to explain. Linda knew all about Sissy's deep rooted fear of rejection. It went back to the day she found out she was adopted. "My birth mother gave me up!" Sissy had screamed. "What mother rejects her baby?" But it had explained why her adoptive mother—the woman she had thought for years *was* her mother—had raised her with such cool indifference. To be rejected by two mothers was devastating enough, but now to think that her husband...

"Linda," she said, suddenly remembering something, "last night on the phone, you sounded guarded, like you were keeping something from me."

With traffic whizzing by in the background, Linda said, "I was. Last year, when you said Ed was in Seattle on a sales trip, I saw him in Chicago. At a restaurant with an attractive blonde. She did not look like a machine parts buyer."

"Why didn't you tell me?"

"Sometimes it's best not to know these things. A husband has a one-off fling and that's all. Why ruin a good marriage because of one miss-step?"

After she hung up Sissy had flown into a rage, screaming at Ed, cursing him, throwing anything she could get her hands on which resulted in a few shattered vases. Her tirade had alarmed the people in the next cottage, so that they had come running and banged on her door until she opened it.

The sight of her neighbors had sobered her instantly. The woman in a black and white French maid's uniform, bare breasts hanging out, the man in jodhpurs and boots and gripping a riding crop. They had come to see if she was all right, and when she calmed down and dried her eyes and told them she had just received some bad news, they had cheered right back up and invited her to a luncheon party.

Considering the state of their dress and Sissy's own emotional state, she had declined. Instead she had gone into the little village at the heart of the resort where she had tried to distract herself with shopping, but only ended up helping a stranger to choose a shirt, and now it was eight o'clock in the evening and Ed had still not called back as he had said in his morning phone message he would.

The credit card statements listed the Palmer House in Chicago for all those times Ed was supposedly out of state. Dialing Directory Assistance, she obtained the number of the Palmer House, dialed, and asked for Ed Whitboro's room. A small spark of hope in her was snuffed when the desk clerk said, "Certainly," and put her through. She had hoped they would say no one by that name was registered there.

But Ed *was* registered there. He wasn't in and this was not something to leave on voice mail, so she hung up.

This time Sissy didn't reach for wine. In a fury she stripped off her clothes and plunged into a steaming bath, scrubbing herself all over as if to scrub Ed off her skin, to erase all the imprints he had left on her over the past fifteen years. She scrubbed her face and lips and plunged her head under the water to get Ed out of her hair like the song in *South Pacific*.

She had brought a couple of good dresses with her, chose the pink silk. Applied a little make-up and left her hair loose instead of up in its usual modest bun, so that it felt strange flowing loosely about her neck.

Anger drove her into the night through the trees, past flickering tiki lights, around a lime-shimmering pool where people swam and splashed, until she came upon the enormous aviary where winged creatures flew about, trapped.

She didn't know where she was going, only that she had to move. And she wasn't aware that she was nearly running until she rounded a private path and slammed into a warm, hard wall that said, "Oof!"

Sissy bounced off and would have landed on the stone path were it not for two large hands grabbing her arms and holding her upright. "Steady there," a stern voice said. "Where's the fire?"

But he was smiling and when she apologized for running into him he just laughed. "I've had worse things happen in my life." His accent was slightly Southern. He wore a black baseball-style cap with gold stitching that said *United States Marine Corps.* And he was wearing green and black camouflage fatigues. It crossed her mind that he might be on his way to visit her kinky neighbors when she stepped back, out of his strong grasp, and nearly fell again.

She had twisted her ankle.

"Let me help you, miss," he said, holding out an arm.

But Sissy couldn't walk.

"I'd better take you to the nurse." And before she could utter a word, he swept her up into his arms so that she floated parallel to the ground. She quickly hooked an arm around his neck so she wouldn't fall, and then realized there was no risk of falling, his grip on her was so tight.

"This really isn't necessary," she said, feeling foolish, but feeling a thrill as well. He smelled of manly aftershave and she saw the slight stubble of beard on his jaw.

"I know a back way," he said, understanding that she wouldn't want people to see her like this. As they followed a dark path illuminated only by moonlight, he introduced himself as First Lieutenant John Parker.

"Just take me back to my room, please," she said, barely able to breathe. He had impressive eyebrows, dark and thick and lowered over shadowed eyes—a man used to giving commands. "I don't need the nurse."

He grinned with splendid white teeth. "Whatever the lady wants."

Once inside her cottage, Lieutenant Parker deposited Sissy gently on the sofa and went to the mini-bar for a chilled bottle of water, as if he lived there, taking control.

Unscrewing the cap and handing Sissy the bottle, he knelt before her and tenderly manipulated her ankle, asking, "How does this feel?"

He had removed his black cap and she saw the blond military buzz cut. His fatigues were clean and crisply pressed—loose trousers with cargo pockets, shirt with the sleeves rolled up and unbuttoned at the throat. Gold insignia glinted on the collar. He explained that he had just come back from a tour of combat and was taking some R&R at the resort. Sissy asked politely where he had been but he wouldn't talk about it. He wanted to put it behind him, he said. Sissy was spellbound. She had never met a soldier before. The closest she had ever come to a man in uniform was when a policeman gave her a ticket for jaywalking. The soldier took her breath away. Just the thought of what he had seen, been through, and had to endure—

Sissy was startled by her reaction. She found herself studying his jaw, so square and clearly defined, with just a hint of stubble, a man too preoccupied with deep issues to even think of shaving. But he was clean. He smelled clean. He looked scrubbed, in fact. His forearms were sunburnt, as was his face and neck. Desert Storm. The Middle East.

It made her pulse race.

Finally, he stood and recommended she stay off her feet for a while. Then he went to the door where he turned and looked at her with shadowed eyes. She felt his scrutiny, the power emanating from him. Her lungs struggled for air.

"Are you all right?" he said in a throaty voice, as if she were having an effect on him as well. "Would you like me to stay?"

No! Go, quickly! "Yes," she whispered.

He reached her in three strides, lifting her off the sofa, lifting her with power and force and bringing her face to his. The kiss was hard and possessive. Everything about him was hard—his back, arms, legs. He carried her to the bed and when she thought he would be rough, rip her clothes off and have his way with her, he surprised her by standing over her, undressing her first with his eyes, then reaching down with calloused fingers to gently unbutton her, draw silk away from silk, lingerie from her skin, exposing her with such maddening slowness that she wanted to scream for him to hurry up.

She lay mesmerized as he continued to stand over her when she was completely naked, and then began to undress himself—the shirt, the olive undershirt where dog tags jingled at the end of a chain. Next the shiny combat boots, then the trousers to reveal olive shorts that could not contain his erection.

When he was completely undressed, he stood over her like a statue, but smiling, and Sissy was mad with desire. She looked at his magnificent member and suddenly she wanted to do something she had never done before in her life. She reached for him without even thinking. She didn't plan it, the gesture came naturally as she slipped her hands over his sculpted buttocks and took him into her mouth.

It was another new sensation, and one that so intoxicated her she became ravenous. He stood for only a few seconds before drawing back and pressing Sissy down on the bed. He was big—bigger than Ed and Alistair, and heavier, and it was powerfully erotic to have him on top, pushing down, and then opening her legs to fill her with himself. Sissy closed her eyes and reveled in a new kind of lovemaking, because her soldier was neither gentle nor slow, but all male, dominant, and went about his business with force.

He was danger and combat, warrior and courage, guns and fighter jets. His kisses were forceful. His stamina astonished her. When she had thought he would finish, he kept going so that she experienced one orgasm after another until, sweating and exhausted, she begged him to stop.

She tried to stay awake, but she felt so delicious and satisfied, that she dozed off in his arms. And when she awoke later, he was gone. All that lingered was his scent on her skin.

Her ankle didn't hurt any more either.

CHAPTER TWENTY-ONE

OPHELIA SCANNED THE SHELVES IN THE SMALL DRUGSTORE IN THE Grove's little village and found everything from eye drops to foot powder. But no pregnancy test kits.

"I'm glad you're taking this holiday," her mother had said. "You're worn out, *bubeleh*."

David had been equally as supportive. "You push yourself too hard, Ophelia." Back when she was in therapy with him he had asked her if she knew why she pushed herself so, why she needed always to be the best, the smartest, the fastest. Who was she competing with? She had said she was just that way and dropped it and he never asked again. But his encouragement that she take this free week at a resort, to relax and think, implied the question was still there. He wanted to know what drove her—more, he wanted Ophelia herself to know what drove her.

An admitted workaholic, she had even brought her current project with her to The Grove, a book titled, *In Defense of Our Ancestors*. Her theories so misunderstood, attacked and ridiculed, that she felt a rebuttal was in order.

In her laptop was stored the transcripts of all the TV and radio shows she had been on, plus print media—articles, book reviews and interviews. David had suggested that the title was misleading—she wasn't really defending cave dwelling forebears but herself. Ophelia thought that sometimes it was a pain to be married to a Freudian psychoanalyst. It wasn't necessary to analyze *everything*.

But none of that had anything to do with why she had decided to accept the contest prize for a week's stay at a resort.

A young woman staffed the counter, dispensing aspirin and lip balm. "May I help you?"

Ophelia asked for a pregnancy test kit and the young woman directed her to the infirmary. "We have a nurse practitioner in residence. She works with a doctor in Palm Springs. She's very capable and discreet."

The two-room infirmary was located in the main hotel building, behind the business offices. The nurse was young and hip, quick to explain that she wasn't "just an R.N." but a licensed physician's assistant trained to diagnose and prescribe, under the aegis of a doctor who came to the resort twice monthly to go over the medical records.

When Ophelia told her what she needed, the nurse went into the back to look through her supplies, and as she waited anxiously, Ophelia thought of little Sophie, how her illness had changed her sister's and brother-in-law's lives. Everything had revolved around the illness. Their every thought and action, what movies they saw, what they had for dinner, was ruled by a damaged gene. Her sister became obsessed with it. Sophie almost became a secondary player in the drama.

"I'm sorry," the nurse said, returning to the outer room. "We are out of pregnancy test kits. I can call the order now and have the kit flown in with our evening supply delivery."

Evening. Ophelia checked her watch. It was noon. She could wait. She would work on her book. Swim more laps. Call David. Act normal.

CHAPTER TWENTY-TWO

HE HAD COME TO MY ROOM TO ASK ADVICE ON WHAT SHIRT TO wear, and while I was changing out of my bra and panties and attempting to get into the little sequined costume, Kenny peeked and he was not supposed to.

So now I pretend to be annoyed with him and tell him he must be punished. "You expect me to get into this silly costume, you put it on me." It is an order. "But you must keep your eyes closed."

He kneels in front of me with his eyes closed and tugs at the thong, pulling it up my thighs. He pauses. His hands abandon their task and swarm over my thighs and butt, as if he were reading Braille. I feel his breath on my groin. His fingers return to the thong, but instead of pulling it up, he draws it down. Now I close my eyes, as I stand before him, relishing his exploration of me. I know his eyes are open now, I feel the flutter of his eyelashes against my skin. I am very tender down there, the slightest touch ignites my inner fire.

I widen my stance to give him greater opportunity. He spreads me open and teases me with his tongue. I grow dizzy and drive my fingers through his hair. I feel like a goddess and Kenny is kneeling at my altar. But his offering is driving me mad. One more touch and I will explode. I want him inside me. I want to be on my back, my legs as wide as they will go, Kenny heavily on top of me, thrusting, taking me to exquisite heights.

I fall to my knees. I engage his mouth, where I taste myself. I am salty and sweet. His arms encircling me, we slide to the carpet, thick and luxurious against my bare back, and Kenny's magnificent cock takes its rightful place. I want it to go on forever. His deep, slow thrusts send shockwaves of pleasure through my body.

When Coco nearly knocked someone off the path, she was startled to realize she had no idea where she was. She had struck off from her bungalow for the aviary. Amazingly, she discovered she was in the right place.

Kenny was up ahead, waiting.

"Sorry I'm late," she said, adding that she couldn't stay long as she had a dinner date with Abby Tyler. He was wearing his tuxedo for the evening performance. It was on her lips to say, "You chose the pink shirt," when she realized that was only in her fantasy.

They explored the aviary that rose in tiers and was landscaped like a jungle and smelled of loam and soil and primeval life. They didn't speak until they reached the end, where night hawks perched and Kenny suggested they go somewhere for a drink.

They found the bar next to the largest swimming pool, where lights glowed brightly against the darkness and people laughed and swam and filled the air with party sounds. Kenny ordered two Chardonnays.

As Coco sipped her wine, she watched Kenny. His mouth intrigued her. She was dying for him to kiss her. While he talked she watched his lips move and imagined them moving on her mouth and on the secret places of her body. She wondered if he would be anything like he was in her fantasy.

"Ken, listen—"

"Kenny, please. Ken is Barbie's boyfriend."

"I came to this resort for a reason."

She hadn't planned to tell him. Like her flashes, it just came out. But as she poured out the story of the crystal and Daisy and the promise that she would find her soulmate here in the "setting sun," part of her hoped he would shout, "Yes! I've had a dream just like that! It's me you're looking for!" And part of her hoped he would say, "Well, it clearly isn't me, so I will leave you alone."

He listened thoughtfully, then said, "How do you know it isn't me?"

"Daisy insists he's worldly and well traveled."

"Then let's fly to Paris."

Oh God I want to.

"Coco, why can't you just let it happen naturally, like with other people?"

"I've tried! Kenny, I long for the kind of relationship my parents have. The joys they have experienced together."

"You and I can share that," Kenny said softly.

"I've been in so many failed relationships—"

"How do you know ours will fail when you won't even let it begin? Listen, I long for those things, too. A family. Loving parents. But not for the same reasons as you. Coco, I'm an orphan."

She stared at him. She had never met an orphan before.

"My birth mother couldn't keep me, and the people who adopted me changed their minds, so I was placed in foster care. I lived with a lot of different families after that, but never long enough to bond with them."

Coco's throat closed up and she felt her emotions ride a Tilt-A-Whirl. For the first time in her life, she was speechless.

"Ms. McCarthy?" Coco nearly jumped. It was Vanessa Nichols, looking knock-out in a vibrant blue caftan with stunning gold trim. "Sorry to interrupt. I've come to escort you to Ms. Tyler's residence."

Coco had forgotten. Her dinner with their host. She said good-bye to Kenny and went off with Vanessa, to leave him sitting there, watching her disappear.

Abby was nervous. After three decades of searching for her daughter, were they about to be reunited at last?

Sissy had cancelled their dinner date. She sounded upset. Abby wanted to enquire but left it alone. And Ophelia had declined again, saying she had work to do. So it was just Coco.

As she tried on one outfit after another, worried about making an impression, she recalled the night her child was conceived. Abby might have lain with a stranger but the baby had been conceived in love. And now, after years of searching, of following false leads and running into dead ends, was she about to be reunited with her daughter at last?

"Here we are," Vanessa said as they approached the private residence. She looked at Coco with shining eyes and wondered: Are you the little baby I carried out of the prison thirty-three years ago? "Good luck," she said, and knocked on the door.

Coco was thinking those were odd words when Vanessa's caftan brushed against her and she received a flash. Something very strange about this woman. A feeling of transience, as if she weren't permanent, a soul on the move. Or ready to flee.

Remembering that Vanessa was secretly in love with Zeb, the white hunter from Africa, it was on Coco's lips to tell her that she should let Zeb know her feelings before they became separated, because Coco knew for certain that Vanessa would not be in this place much longer, that a long flight lay ahead of her, and that if she did not declare her feelings to Zeb soon, she would lose him forever.

But it was a habit Coco was trying to break, so she kept her silence. And her intrusion into Vanessa's personal life might not be welcome.

Abby Tyler opened the door and greeted Coco with a warm smile.

They shook hands and Coco couldn't help herself, the flash was so strong. "You're worried about something," she said.

"Yes," Abby said guardedly, knowing about Coco's psychic abilities, wondering how strong they were. "Management problems."

Coco gave her an odd look. That wasn't the flash she had gotten. Abby Tyler was worried about a child.

Cold seafood salads were already set out, chilled wine, fresh bread and sweet butter. Light from the chandelier glittered on china and crystal, and the sliding glass doors stood open to admit the perfumed evening.

"So tell me about this contest," Coco said, reaching for her wine. "I never enter contests. How did I manage to win this fabulous vacation?"

"The man whose land this once was wanted to create a sanctuary for people seeking peace. But he was a philanthropist and it troubled him that

The Grove would be available only to people with money. So he established a kind of random lottery."

Abby was trying not to stare at her guest. Were Coco's eyes her own, had she gotten her nose and chin from the drifter? Beneath the burgundy dye, what was the true color of her hair?

Shouldn't a mother instinctively know her own child?

And how on earth was she going to broach the subject of parenthood and adoption? Did Coco even know she was adopted?

Abby asked if she was enjoying her stay and Coco mentioned Kenny.

"Yes, he's very talented," Abby said, adding nothing more because that was up to Kenny. Abby had found him during one of her adoption searches. The private investigator had been following a lead on orphans that had taken him to San Francisco. Although Abby knew her child was a girl, her heart went out to Kenny all the same because he, too, had been a stolen baby. Abby had subsequently learned of the rejection by the adoptive parents and the string of foster homes and she wanted to do something for him. Especially when she saw how he was suffering from his secret addiction. He needed to heal and so, by way of Vanessa, she had invited him to work at The Grove.

Abby casually asked questions of Coco without appearing to pry. But she had to know. For thirty-three years she had celebrated every birthday, had thought of her child's first tooth, her first step, her first word. Imagining her daughter's first day in school, picturing herself doing things with her little girl, things that had become the privilege of another woman.

"I accepted the contest prize as a birthday present to myself," Coco said. "I have a birthday coming up."

"Oh?"

"May 17. I was born in Fresno."

In the private investigator's report: *Baby girl, born Amarillo, Texas, May 17, sold to McCarthy family in Fresno, California.*

"Is anyone else in your family psychic?"

"No. I was different from the start. From the minute I was born."

Abby was suddenly alert. "How so?"

"I was born with polydactyly." Coco held up her hands and wiggled her fingers, pointing out tiny scars on the sides. "Six fingers on each hand. They were removed when I was little. Imagine what a pianist I could have been!"

Abby heard Mercy's words: *"A perfect baby, ten fingers, ten toes. We counted."*

Coco McCarthy was not her daughter.

CHAPTER TWENTY-THREE

*T*HE DESERT NIGHT WAS FILLED WITH THE HOWLS OF coyotes.

As Jack stood at the open door to his patio, he thought the wild creatures sounded close to the resort. They also sounded hungry and agitated.

Turning away, he went back inside, to stay focused on his work.

Jack was good at what he did. Investigating and solving cases. He had won a commendation or two, a handshake from the Mayor. Fellow detectives came to him when they were stumped. Except that this time, Jack was the one who was stumped.

Nina's notes baffled him. She seemed to think a vital element to her search lay in this resort. Yet he was unable to find it. Perhaps the key was Ophelia Kaplan. He needed an excuse to knock on her door, and as luck would have it, the resort's small bookstore was open at this late hour, so he left the coyotes to howl beyond his patio and struck out into the starry night.

His luck held as he browsed the shelves and found Dr. Kaplan's diet book, the one that Nina had raved about, that had helped her to shed thirty pounds and keep them off, and feel healthier and more energetic, too. It gave him the opening he needed.

He was about to dial the cell number of Elias Salazar, the head of security, to request Dr. Kaplan's room number, when he saw Dr. Kaplan emerge from the main building looking distraught.

As he approached her, his detective's eyes sized her up: wearing drawstring pants and a tank top, this woman clearly practiced what she preached. Healthy, in peak athletic form. Ophelia Kaplan could skin a mammoth with her bare teeth.

Mentally, however, she seemed troubled. Something on her mind. Abby Tyler and the adoption issue? He was tempted to inquire but didn't want to expose his hand. He thought of the data Nina had uncovered on this woman. Was Ophelia Kaplan aware of her unusual origins?

"Pardon me," he said, catching her attention. "I'm sorry to bother you and I know you must get this all the time, but would you autograph your book for me? I mean, my book?" he added with a self-effacing smile.

She turned, startled, as if so preoccupied that she had forgotten that other people existed on the planet. "Sure," she said, "no problem," and took the book from him.

"I saw you on Jay Leno. You handled him brilliantly."

"That makes you and my mother who thought so." Ophelia would never forget that night, in front of millions of TV viewers, explaining the rationale behind her thesis: "Bread only came on the scene ten thousand years ago, Jay. Our bodies can't possibly be adapted to consuming it. Let's say something brand new to our physiologies is invented today, something that doesn't occur in nature, that our bodies are not used to metabolizing, that in fact wreaks havoc with our digestive systems and causes all sorts of physical and metabolic ailments, yet we start eating it by the ton and it becomes a daily staple in our diet. Do you think that in a mere ten thousand years this will become a health food?"

Jay Leno had leaned forward and said, "Dr. Kaplan, are you talking about Twinkies?"

She opened the cover of the book and poised her pen on the title page. "Who should I make it out to?"

He faltered. Did one sign books to dead people?

But if she were alive, Nina would be thrilled to have it. "To Nina," he said softly, "the greatest adopted sister a brother ever had."

A question stood briefly in Ophelia's eyes, then she wrote and signed her name and handed him the book.

"I only just learned my sister was adopted," he added in as casual and friendly a manner as he could.

Ophelia stared at him. He saw no reaction in her eyes to the word "adopted." Then she blinked and said, "If you will excuse me," and turned on her heel like the assertive woman she was, and walked away.

Jack watched her for a moment as Ophelia raked fingers through her short dark hair, and realizing she was another dead end, turned down a path and walked aimlessly among ferns, fronds and splashing fountains. It was all so strange. Three women brought here on a fake contest prize and weren't aware of it. They didn't know Abby Tyler, and yet there was a connection because it was written in Nina's notes. But what was the connection?

It occurred to him that perhaps Tyler had lost a child to the illegal adoption ring and was searching for her, but why not run a simple DNA test? It was what Nina would have done. Why bring the three women here on false pretenses? So it must be something else.

Had Abby somehow gotten wind of Nina's investigation? That Nina had been collecting names of babies stolen long ago? But then there was Nina's folder in Tyler's bungalow. But even more perplexing was Tyler herself. She was clearly hiding out here. None of his research on her background had turned up the smallest press item, nothing in the gossip magazines or society columns, which for someone with her wealth and social connections was odd. So what was she hiding from?

But most significant was Abby asking him when the murder had taken place. It was so unexpected. As if she were saying, *which* murder was he investigating? So what murder was she thinking of?

He stopped and looked up at the stars, so low and dense and brilliant in the desert sky that he almost thought he could reach up and scoop a handful.

Nina can you ever forgive me? I should not have let you go off to that late-night meeting on your own. I know better!

Realizing he was close once again to being overwhelmed with grief, he pulled himself together and pushed back the tears, because an emotional detective was one who had lost his edge. He would not cry for his sister until he had found her killer.

CHAPTER TWENTY-FOUR

THE SLIDING GLASS DOOR TO HER PATIO STOOD OPEN, admitting the fragrances of wisteria and honeysuckle, and the song of restless coyotes in the distance. A knock at the front door. The masseuse, finally, with his folding table.

Vanessa took in the brooding dark good looks and slender body beneath tennis whites. He was new to the resort. "You look French," Vanessa said, letting him in. "Are you?"

His eyebrows arched. "Oui, madam. I am impressed. You have an eye."

"What's your name?"

"Pierre."

"Well, Pierre, I've had a hard day and need to get some knots worked out of my muscles." She gave him a long, measured look. "Your hands are nice. I'm sure they will work magic."

Vanessa turned and untied the sash of her satin dressing gown, letting it drop to the floor. She was naked underneath. It took Pierre a moment to unfold and set up the massage table, covering it with a clean sheet and fresh pillow. While he busied himself with his supplies—lifting oils, creams and lotions out of his bag—Vanessa stretched unselfconsciously on the table, on her stomach, face resting on her hands.

He began with her shoulders, using heated oil the scent of peonies. Vanessa closed her eyes as she felt his strong hands work into her muscles. Down her back, massaging, kneading, melting away all the tension of the day. His fingers worked her buttocks and then moved down her thighs, her calves. She sighed as he worked her feet, limbering up every tight little joint.

She felt her mind and spirit, like her body, also loosen up. She was floating on a cloud without a care in the world except the feel of Pierre's hands on her.

He began to work back up her calves and thighs, more slowly now and with less pressure, fingertips gliding over her oiled skin. He was no longer massaging but caressing. First her outer thighs, and then the inner—slowly, teasingly. She parted her legs. Pierre's hands followed her lead, sliding in and up, fingers touching her moist place.

His hands swept down the inside of her thighs, up over her buttocks, kneading tenderly, and then up her back, down her waist and then, gently, under her arms, up and back, as if he were stroking a purring cat, each time his hands going a little lower, moving teasingly closer and closer to her breasts.

She arched herself a little so that Pierre's hands could slide beneath and cup her breasts. He massaged them, toyed with the nipples, making delicious strokes on her oiled skin.

As he drew his hands down to her thighs again, pressing here, rubbing there, Vanessa entertained a fantasy: she and Zeb making love beneath the stars of Africa. She opened her legs wider and Pierre slipped a finger inside, with such maddening slowness that her impatience grew. He brought her to a quivering brink, and then withdrew. She moaned. He entered again, going deeply, his thumb finding another spot. When he touched her she nearly cried out. He played her like a musical instrument now, composing the most delicious melodies on her flesh. Her breathing grew rapid. Her skin was on fire.

She imagined Zeb, naked and hard, lowering himself onto her, his hands on her knees pressing them apart, forcing her legs as wide open as they would go. Then she felt him plunge into her, vigorously, possessively. While Pierre increased his rhythm, using finger and thumb to send exquisite ripples of pleasure through her body, it was Zeb whom felt, rock-hard and thrusting.

When the orgasm began, she clutched the sides of the table. Flowing from her toes, through her legs and into her abdomen, the wave crashed over her in myriad hot, ecstatic sensations. To her delight, that wasn't the end of it. She felt another wave follow, rolling up from her toes and through her body like a delicious, tingling heat. A third wave, and then another until she at last she lay spent while Pierre covered her with a sheet and put away his oils.

Finally she sat up, reached for her robe and turned to Pierre who was waiting expectantly. Vanessa smiled. "You're very good," she said.

"Thanks," he replied, all trace of French accent gone.

"How soon can you start?"

"Right away."

Pierre had already had his medical check-up and blood work done, receiving a clean bill of health from The Grove's private physician. Vanessa never conducted an audition without one.

She was pleased with him. Picked up on the cues right away. She had said he looked French and he knew immediately what was expected of him. His accent was flawless and when she told him she thought his hands would work magic, he knew right away she was-n't interested in all-the-way sex. Many guests at The Grove were too shy or modest to come right out and say what they wanted, so they used hints. For the most part, The Grove's escorts were sharp and picked up the cues quickly. Rarely did one misread a signal and end up offending a guest.

Vanessa always personally put prospective romantic escorts through auditions, and to straighten them out on the rules of sexual conduct at The Grove. The female staff who were hired for their sexual talents were recruited from an exclusive escort service in Los Angeles and did not need the sort of auditioning Vanessa conducted, those ladies already knowing their craft. For the men, however, it was necessary. Back when The Grove had started offering intimate services to the lady guests, there were problems. "He came in two seconds," was the usual complaint. "Fell asleep and snored afterward. Acted like he was doing me a big favor." So Vanessa had taken the program in hand and shaped it into the class act it was today.

As Pierre snapped his supply case closed, Vanessa eyed his butt which was high and tight and round. She wasn't finished. There was still the final exam. Giving his crotch a significant look, she smiled and said, "Now I'm thinking you look more like a Sir Galahad."

With a grin, he picked up the cue.

An hour later, Pierre was strolling away from Vanessa's bungalow, where he had left her satisfied and sleeping. *Pierre*, he thought. It was as good a name as any. He had been known by so many aliases that sometimes he had to stop and think what his real name was.

Making sure there was no one around on the deserted path, he pulled out his satellite phone and hit automatic dial. As he listened to the ringing at the other end, he decided he was going to like this new assignment. He had worked undercover before, but never "under the covers."

Pierre didn't know who he was at the resort to hit, but he hoped the order didn't come too soon. This playground was full of gorgeous movie stars, celebrities, and rich bitches. He could have some fun before carrying out his real assignment.

When the other end picked up, Pierre quietly said two words: "I'm in." Then he rang off. He laughed. He couldn't wait—for either job.

CHAPTER TWENTY-FIVE

*S*ISSY HADN'T MEANT TO READ ABOUT THREESOMES. THE BOOK, *Thirty Steps to Better Sex*, had simply fallen open to that chapter. And when her eye had caught the illustrations, shockingly graphic, she had been unable to look away.

So *this* was how three people did it she thought as her eyes took in the multiple limbs and lips, breasts and buttocks, and his/her genitals. She felt guilty looking at the book, but excited, too, so that despite herself she was drawn into the fantasy…

Her doorbell rings. It's the neighbor from the next bungalow, dressed in a black leather corset that pushes her breasts up so there is no missing the nipple rings. Black garter belt and fishnet stockings, stiletto heels. Her pubic area is shaved. She has come to invite Sissy to a private party. Sissy is shocked and wants to close the door, but the woman takes her by the wrist and, with a wicked smile, draws her out onto the path and into the next cottage.

The man is wearing a black leather jock strap and a studded dog collar. His smile is welcoming so that Sissy finds herself unafraid. She was wearing only her bathrobe when the neighbor came, and they tell her now to remove it. She is bashful. Although they have locked the front door, and the garden is walled for privacy, Sissy is worried someone will see.

So they help her out of the robe, their fingers brushing her bare skin as they draw the garment from her breasts, shoulders and arms. She reflexively covers her breasts and the woman laughs. "Don't by shy," she whispers and, pulling Sissy's arms away, teases her nipples.

Sissy is instantly on fire.

They lead her to a chaise upholstered in hot pink satin. The woman presses Sissy back onto the pillows and says, "Open your legs, dear. Wider."

The man leans over for a look. "Nice," he says with a smile.

They cover Sissy's eyes with a silk blindfold and slip her wrists into soft handcuffs and anchor them to the head of the chaise. And then they begin.

She never knows which part of her body they are going to touch, if it is going to be gentle or sharp. She doesn't know who is doing the touching, the man or the woman. Lips on one nipple, sucking, and then another mouth on the other nipple. Fingers exploring her moistness. Something touches her mouth, pressing, wanting to get in. She parts her lips and tastes chocolate. She opens her mouth wider and realizes it is a chocolate-dipped strawberry. She bites down and chews slowly while a soft fluttering teases the insides of her naked thighs.

And then something hard slips into her, filling her. And suddenly it starts vibrating. Sissy cries out. She has never experienced anything so exquisite. "Oh God oh God oh God," she screams as she explodes in orgasm.

The book fell from Sissy's lap as she sat back in the chair, hot and bothered and shocked at herself.

She had never been so confused in her life. Emotionally, she was angry and hurt over Ed having an affair. But physically, she felt as if skyrockets inhabited her body. And now she was fantasizing things she had not even known existed.

She had committed adultery, too, something Sissy had never in all her life thought she would ever do. Or, if she ever should commit such a sin, she had always imagined it would make her feel wretched beyond salvation. She felt no such thing. She wasn't in love with the two men she had had sex with. Was that what made the difference? Don't give your heart away and it isn't betrayal.

Was Ed in love with his Linda?

Sissy realized that that was the crux of her pain. If it was just sex…

Her thoughts amazed her. If she had learned of Ed's cheating before coming to The Grove, she never would have said, "If it was just sex." There were no fine lines. Sleeping with another person was wrong. Period. But now that she had done it herself, she saw the fine distinctions. Sex with a stranger was one thing, falling in love, another.

Ed had called the night before, while she was out—being carried by a United States Marine because she had twisted her ankle. She hadn't seen the message light until she woke this morning. "Sorry I missed you," Ed said. "You must be having a good time. Everything's fine here, don't worry about us."

Everything's fine here.

How stupid did he think she was? Hadn't he checked in at home? Didn't his mother tell him Sissy had called?

Pain and anger were starting to give way to indignation and annoyance. He could at least give her credit for catching him. Well, it was a beautiful morning and she still had four more days at this fabulous resort before she had to return to Rockford and figure out what to do with the rest of her life.

As she stepped from her cottage into the sunshine, she ran into the couple next door. Sissy was instantly embarrassed, recalling her fantasy with them. Could they read her thoughts? The blonde was tall in spiked, strappy heels, a mini skirt that barely concealed the tops of her stockings and garter belt, her mammoth bra-less breasts visible through her gauze blouse. Sissy thought that if she dressed like that on the streets of Rockford, Illinois she'd be arrested.

And then Sissy realized the man with her wasn't the man who had grinned at Sissy from the garden Monday morning and yesterday in jodhpurs. But the way they held onto each other told her they weren't strangers either. The woman sent Sissy a wink and a flirty wave—as if she could read Sissy's thoughts—and they disappeared, giggling, into the bungalow next door.

Sissy stared after them. She had thought they were honeymooners, but now, remembering the "escorts and companions" that the resort offered, she wondered if her next door neighbor was in fact a secretary from Detroit or a nurse from St. Louis, spending her year's savings on a fantasy fling with several bed partners at The Grove. In another age, Sissy would have been shocked. But a lot had happened in the past two days.

She thought of Alistair on the Japanese bridge. So polished and perfect, his sexual technique impeccable. In fact, looking back, he was *too* perfect. He had been incredibly deft and discreet with the condom. Did he work at The Grove? Was the Japanese garden his beat, where he waited for lonely frustrated females to find him? And the Marine lieutenant, so perfectly masculine and masterful, yet getting permission every step of the way. Also slipping into a condom before she was aware of it. Fantasy partners?

Strangely, it didn't bother Sissy that they might be. After all, she *had* enjoyed it both times. And she wasn't looking for a relationship, just a pleasant physical interlude. Men had been doing it for thousands of years.

But the love—that was the vital part. If Ed loved Linda then he was rejecting Sissy, and Sissy had already been rejected twice. That would devastate her.

Calling the Guest Services office, she asked to be connected to Ms. Coco McCarthy. Sissy remembered what Ms. McCarthy had said in the boarding lounge back at LAX, that she was a psychic, and she had offered to give Sissy a reading.

The woman at Guest Services said she would forward the message, so Sissy waited by the phone, hoping Coco would call right back. And when the phone did ring, she picked it up with a thumping heart, realizing she was pinning high hopes on what Coco could tell her.

But it wasn't her fellow contest winner who was calling but Vanessa Nichols, asking Sissy if she would care to have lunch with Abby Tyler at Ms. Tyler's private residence.

But Sissy needed to straighten things out first. "Can we make it dinner?" she asked.

"Certainly, Mrs. Whitboro. I shall come for you at seven, to escort you."

Sissy was about to leave when her phone rang again and it was Coco, saying she would be happy to do a reading. "I can be there in half an hour."

"I cannot command my gift," Coco explained when they settled on the sofa in Sissy's blue and orange living room. "I've tried. It just doesn't work that way. And for some reason I can't explain, I am more open psychically to women than to men."

"Maybe women are more spiritually open and aware," Sissy offered, suddenly nervous, wondering if she should go through with this. Didn't the Catholic Church frown upon psychics and mediums and involvement in paranormal activities?

"When I picked up your purse in the boarding lounge Sunday night," Coco said, "I received a very strong flash that you were going to experience a shock here."

"I did. But I need to know more." Sissy started to tell Coco what the problem was, but Coco stopped her. "It's best if I do a 'free' reading. This way I have no preconceptions to cloud the message. All right, give me something to hold. Something related to the problem." Coco had left the crystal back in her room. The crystal was for *her*, nobody else.

Sissy handed Coco the jeweler's receipt for the watch.

Silence settled over them, filled with morning breezes and distant laughter. Coco closed her eyes and relaxed.

Sissy twisted her fingers and chewed her lip.

Coco breathed softly. Let the breeze play through her hair and over her face. Images and sensations filled her head. Finally she said: "Delgado."

Sissy waited for more. "Is that all?"

"I'm afraid so." Coco set the claim check aside.

"Is it a person's name?"

"I don't know."

"Could it be *Linda* Delgado?"

"I have no idea. It just came to my mind. It might mean nothing. I'm sorry I can't be of more help," she said rising.

"Thank you for coming," Sissy said.

After Coco had gone, Sissy looked at the phone by the bed and knew what she had to do. Dialing Directory Assistance, as calmly as she could she asked for the number of Linda Delgado in Chicago, Illinois.

CHAPTER TWENTY-SIX

*H*E STOOD NAKED AMONG THE FOLIAGE, LIKE ADAM IN EDEN. But as Vanessa drew near, she saw that Zeb wasn't really naked, just shirtless, his wiry torso glistening with sweat. It made her think of the day she first met him.

"I've found someone to take care of the wildlife," Abby had said a year before, when the veterinarian who took care of the exotic birdlife, the resident desert tortoises, the domestic cats that kept down the rodent population, and the occasional wildlife—foxes and coyotes—that strayed into the resort, left to get married. Abby used a hotel employment service in San Diego to recruit her staff; they had found Zeb and forwarded his impressive résumé to Abby. "He's perfect. He was a game warden in Kenya."

"He's *African*?" Vanessa had said excitedly. Her love affair with Africa went back to her childhood.

Abby had been interrupted by a phone call and gave no further details except to say he would be arriving on the evening flight. Picturing Sidney Poitier, Denzel Washington and all the fine black men she could think of,

Vanessa had spent two hours getting ready, discarding outfit after outfit before deciding on the Moroccan caftan with the gold embroidery. To let him know she was a "sister."

And when Vanessa saw the handsome black man emerge from the plane into the desert evening, her heart did a somersault. He was even more impressive than she had expected, with his thick black moustache and dignified bearing. He had barely reached the bottom of the steps when she was offering her hand, effusively welcoming him to The Grove, so glad to have him become part of the family, not letting him get a word in edgewise until the baffled man managed to withdraw his hand from her grasp and comment on how he had heard of The Grove's hospitality, but this was off the charts. And that was when the man behind him, a *white* man, said, "I believe, Miss Nichols, that you are looking for me," and Vanessa learned of another kind of racial prejudice. Back in the sixties, growing up in Texas, she and her friends had been refused service in whites-only diners. She even remembered the separate drinking fountains. But she didn't hold it against white people because, after all, they also marched and carried signs and helped to get the laws changed. She had no idea that she was not as color blind as she had thought. African meant black. How could a white man be African?

She soon learned that Zeb was born in Kenya to English settlers. He hadn't even gone away to school in England, as other colonists' children did, but had sat side by side with native children in the mission school at Nyeri. He spoke Swahili and wore shirts made of kanga cloth, and told tales of the Kenya highlands as if he were just as native as the natives. Which of course he was.

It made Vanessa's head spin. White men had never been her cup of tea. She had never even fancied light-skinned African American men, preferring her men dark and dangerous and powerful. In appearances, anyway. And now here was this stranger with a ruddy complexion, fifty-seven years old with thinning hair, but virile all the same, and out of his mouth came the romance of the continent she so loved and yearned someday to see.

Zeb was not the strong and silent type. Strong, yes, but far from silent. He loved to talk, and the tales he spun enthralled many a guest at The Grove.

Yet Vanessa sensed at the heart of his loquaciousness a carefully guarded secret. How could a man who talked and laughed so freely still give the impression of being mysterious?

It was what he was *not* saying that intrigued her.

She remembered the night she fell in love with him.

He had been drinking, heavily. An item in the morning's Los Angeles Times had upset him. Nine thousand pounds of illegal ivory had been found on sale in Nigeria. "Twenty years ago," Zeb had complained over a bottle of Foster's Lager, "there were over a million elephants in the world. Today, less than half that number exist. In some countries, Senegal, the Ivory Coast, they have been wiped out. Soon there won't be any."

Full of outrage, Zeb had shouted and pounded his fist. And then he had wept—for better days, old memories, and an Africa that was gone forever. "They called us white hunters murderers. But *we* were the ones policing the parks. *We* set the rules—no females were to be killed, and only one male per customer. We respected our prey. We did not allow senseless, random killing. We were tough regulators and we shot poachers on sight. But once we were outlawed, the poachers rushed in and no one is policing them!"

Vanessa had been deeply moved. But not without wondering why, if he felt so strongly about the issue, he didn't go back and fight to save the animals. It was all part of his mystery.

She espied him now among the foliage in the main aviary, his damp torso glistening in the morning sunshine. He lifted his hat to wipe perspiration from his forehead. It was a Dodgers cap, American baseball being his passion. From April to October, Zeb didn't miss a game. It was another facet to him that she found fascinating, and she decided she had never been so in love in her life. And never so miserable because of it.

She could never tell him the truth about herself.

As she rounded the curve in the trail that meandered through the gigantic aviary, she paused beside a blooming hibiscus, her heart and body aching with desire, and a question jumped into her mind: Why *not* tell him?

It suddenly occurred to her that, with Abby packed and poised to leave, and a homicide detective nosing around, a chapter in her own life was coming to a close. She and Abby had enjoyed thirty-three years of relative freedom, but now it was coming to an end and neither of them knew what tomorrow would bring.

This was probably going to be her last chance with Zeb. Why not tell him the truth about herself and her past?

Her heart began to race as the prospect of confessing to Zebulon Armstrong made her believe there could be a chance for the two of them—he harbored a secret, might he not therefore be sympathetic to *hers*? He didn't seem a man to judge others, and besides, the crime she committed was so long ago *and* in self defense.

Yes, she thought in sudden excitement, feeling the courage build within herself. I will tell him! Right now, blurt it out, in this private place among exotic birds and flowers, with the diffuse sunlight streaming through the overhead mesh that protected the aviary and the birdlife—in this garden that was as untouched and unspoiled as Eden—as pure as Africa itself! Tell him now because tomorrow everything was going to be different and all chances would be lost.

But as she took a step toward him, Zeb with his back to her, not knowing she was there, someone appeared on the trail up head, coming from the north entrance of the aviary, a female guest, leggy and blonde, running up to Zeb and squealing, "There you are! I woke up this morning and you were gone!" She flung her arms around his neck and planted a firm kiss on his mouth. Vanessa watched in shock as Zeb, not protesting, kissed her right back.

Stunned, Vanessa slowly backed down the trail until she was hidden behind large ferns and out of earshot. She did not want to hear what was said between the two.

What had she been thinking? How could she possibly imagine there could be anything between her and Zeb? They were from different worlds, different races. And she reminded herself that Zeb was a man of strong morals and ethics, that he lived by a strict personal code. How could she explain that the man she had killed was a pimp, that she had done it in self-defense? How to explain the burning of White Hills prison, where the inmates were subjected to cruel treatment? She was glad the blonde had shown up. It stopped her from making a fool of herself.

CHAPTER TWENTY-SEVEN

*A*BBY HAD A RECURRING DREAM.

It started with a knock at the door. *"Ms. Tyler?"*

"Yes."

"I'm from the District Attorney's office." He always had a Texas accent, but his clothes varied. *"We've been reviewing your case and we've come to the conclusion that you are not guilty of killing Avis Yocum after all. The conviction has been overturned. You are exonerated."*

But last night, for the first time, the dream had been different: *She opened the door to find Jack Burns standing there, informing her that her conviction had been overturned. He then took her by the hand, and she said, "Where are you taking me?"*

"To freedom," he said, and when she stepped through the door saw that they were at the beach.

They walked barefoot along damp sand, moonlight illuminating their way while silver-crested waves crashed on the shore. Abby realized she was in her nightgown, made of transparent gauze that fluttered against her skin.

The feeling awakened all her senses. She felt sharply sexual.

When had Jack shed his leather jacket? Where was his shirt? His skin was wet as if he had just emerged from the water, starlight sparkling on sculpted muscles. She wanted to lick the salt from his skin.

He turned suddenly, pulled her to him and captured her mouth in a deep kiss. Breathless, she kissed him back as the surf lapped around their ankles, tugging at them to join the creatures of the sea.

Jack stepped back to remove his jeans, slowly peeling them down his legs until he stood magnificently naked in the moonlight. Then he reached down for the hem of her nightgown, sodden with water, and drew it up her body and over her head. His eyes swept over every inch of her nakedness, and then his hands followed, as they explored Abby's every curve and hollow. She touched him, too, the sinewy archer's arms, the hard chest, the jaw that begged to be kissed.

Taking her again by the hand, he led her into the chill surf and dived into a massive, crashing wave to surface with Abby in his embrace, their mouths coming together in an electrifying kiss as the undulating ocean lifted them and lowered them, Jack's strong arms supporting Abby, her legs locked around his thighs. He thrust into her, out on the waves, moonlight shining on their hair and shoulders, and the tide floated them in and back, as they rode the Pacific locked together.

Pressing his lips to her ear, he murmured, "Swim away to the ends of the earth with me."

And she said, "Yes…"

She had awakened to find her sheets in a tangle and her nightgown up around her waist. She had burned with sexual desire that even now, hours later, continued to glow inside her as she stood at the door to Jack's bungalow.

He had surprised her by telephoning that morning and inviting her to breakfast. Abby had both wanted to accept and decline. She didn't like the affect he was having on her. No man had made her feel so weak and so alive. But she also needed to know why he was there. She had discovered that Jack Burns had had conversations with Coco, Sissy and, last night, Ophelia. This alarmed her. If he was investigating his sister's murder, then why

was he talking to *them*?

She knocked.

The blue work shirt was open at the collar, the sleeves rolled up, and his short hair went this way and that, as if he hadn't combed it yet. She looked at his mouth and wondered if he kissed in real life the way he had in her dream.

"Hello!" he said, standing aside to let her in. Jack had not seen Abby since the day before at noon, when she had introduced him to Elias Salazar, her head of security. Jack had thought he would run into her after that, but she was a difficult lady to pin down. Besides the demands of running so exclusive a resort, she also had a full social calendar. He had tried to finagle dinner with her but she already had evening plans. He needed to know why she had been investigating his sister, and what Abby had on her. So he had called first thing that morning and invited her to breakfast. To his surprise, Abby had accepted.

And now here she was, and Jack was thinking she looked as fabulous in the morning as she did at other times of the day when he should be thinking of a way to find out what information she had on his sister.

He saw her eyeing his gloves. "I've been working on my equipment," he said, and she saw the tall archery bow propped against the wall, the arrows laid out on newspaper on the floor. Abby was surprised to hear classical music coming from the stereo. Brahms or Schumann. She had pegged Jack Burns for a jazz man.

Jack was staying in the Sierra Nevada cottage. The exterior was like all the other cottages—stucco painted in muted desert tones, purposely designed to be inconspicuous— but the interior resembled a rustic mountain cabin with a large stone fireplace, cowhide furniture, Indian rugs, and paintings of elk and grizzlies. Abby thought that Jack, a rugged man, fit right in.

She glanced toward the bedroom, where she saw the four poster bed made of rough-hewn wood, the old fashioned quilt thrown back, sheets rumpled. The maid had not yet done the room. Jack's pillow was indented where his head had lain and Abby pictured him in bed and recalled riding the warm ocean current, his hardness inside her—

"Room service hasn't arrived yet," he said as he knelt on the floor to screw the cap back onto a bottle of pungent smelling liquid.

Abby was intrigued by the archery equipment. It looked at home in this replica of a fur trapper's cabin.

"I make my own arrows," Jack said as he gathered up pliers, knife, sand-paper, wax, and paint. "It relaxes me. I love the smell of the cedar, the feel of the wood between my fingers. Cresting them with my own colors. Doing my own fletching."

"Cresting? Fletching?"

He closed the toolbox. "Painting rings around the shafts and sticking the feathers on."

When he saw how she looked at the bow, as she had the day before when he had come back from shooting in the desert, he had a sudden idea. Jack had been at the resort for two days and three nights and had yet to obtain her fingerprints. The opportunity was perfect.

Still wearing the soft work gloves, he retrieved a polishing cloth and picked up the bow. "Have you ever held one of these?" he asked, carefully wiping the wooden grip.

"I've never even *seen* one," she said.

"Let me show you." He pulled something out of his pocket and handed it to her. "If you're right handed, put this on your right hand."

She slipped the glove on. "It's missing some fingers."

"You only use three fingers to draw a bow string. On the end joints, here," he said, touching her lightly.

Abby felt a jolt and wondered why she was doing this.

But Jack was handing her the bow and she took it. Abby found it to be surprisingly light, about two pounds, even though it was nearly as tall as herself. "It's so big!" she gasped.

Jesus, he thought. She made it sound sexual.

Maybe this was a mistake, Jack thought, recalling his dream about making love to her on a desert mesa. The dream had been so real he had to remind himself he had *not* touched her in intimate places, had not kissed her to breathlessness. Even now, he could still hear her ecstatic cry echoing in the deep, red canyons. "Okay," he said, "it's sixty pounds of draw weight. You'll need help."

Standing behind her, Jack placed his hand over hers and hefted the bow so that their left arms were aligned and parallel to the floor. Then he reached around for her right hand and hooked her fingers over the string. Abby felt his chest against her back. Jack inhaled the fragrance of her hair, inches from his face. He was instantly aroused.

"Don't pull with your arm, pull with your back." His voice was low, his lips close to her ear. Abby was stunned by the intimacy of the moment— romantic classical music on the CD player, the living room suffused with golden desert sunlight, and Jack Burns's hard body against hers. It felt just like it had in her beach dream. Would the rest feel the same?

"You have to maintain a high level of tension or the arrows will fly inconsistently," he said, drawing her arm back, his fingers around hers on the bow string. His chest was now firmly against her back, their arms lined up and touching, his arms encircling her in an embrace.

As he drew the string toward her face, he said, "People prefer different anchors, you have to find what is comfortable for you." His fingertips lightly touched her cheek. "Here," he murmured, "or here," and he touched her chin. Her skin was warm, reminding him of the secret fire he suspected deep within her.

They aimed at the garden wall. Abby could barely speak, his closeness was so intoxication. "Isn't this dangerous?"

"It's safe. We're just going to hit that wall." Her scent was sweet and delicate, not like a perfume but as if Abby were a flower grown in one of her own gardens. Why the hell was he doing this? Jack wanted to know more about Abby Tyler, but not *this* much more, the feel of her against him, the scent of her hair, the warmth of her skin. This was dangerous knowledge.

He should stop now. He *could* stop now—her prints were on the polished bow grip. Instead, he said, "Just push against the handle with your palm, fingers relaxed," warm breath on her cheek.

The bow wobbled and Abby suddenly laughed. Jack laughed with her as he found himself enjoying the moment, forgetting for an instant why he was there. "When you want to let go, you simply relax the fingers. Don't 'pluck' the string."

They released the string together. The arrow shot into the garden and Abby's right arm flew back in recoil. She fell against Jack and for an instant he held her in an embrace, holding her tight against him, her face upturned to his. And then they heard the arrow strike the stone wall and

Abby snapped her head around, saying, "Did we hit something?" and Jack dropped his arms, stepped away to be free of her.

He was angry with himself. Why had he let this happen? Once her prints were on the grip, he should have just taken the bow back, saying how it was too much draw-power for her, that she should start out on a lighter bow. Instead he had gone ahead with the demonstration. Why? He knew why. It was an excuse to be close to her. To touch her.

Taking the bow by the upper and lower recurves, careful not to contaminate the grip, he laid it on the bed. He had Abby's fingerprints at last. A full, clean set.

"Well," she said, stepping away from him, suddenly flustered, wondering what had just happened. She looked at her watch. "Room service is late. I hope we aren't having trouble in the kitchen again."

Jack was anxious for her to leave now. The minute she was gone, he was going to call Guest Services and get himself a seat on the first available flight out. Get the bow to headquarters, have the grip dusted for prints, run the prints through the FBI database—

"That waterfall should be running."

"What?"

"The waterfall in your garden. It should be going."

"I turned it off," he said. "It was distracting me."

She became thoughtful, then said, "That had never occurred to me. I always thought the sound of trickling water was relaxing. I wonder if other guests have found the waterfall or fountain in their garden distracting."

She reached into the pocket of her beige linen slacks and brought out a slender, micro-cassette recorder. She spoke briefly into it—"Note: meet with Gordon re private fountains and waterfalls, on/off switches"—then she restored the small machine to her pocket and said with a smile, "I like to make improvements when I can."

He shifted his weight. He wanted her to leave. He wanted her to stay. "You designed this place?"

"I'm a landscape architect. At least, I was until I became a hotelier." Working two and three jobs, going to night school, obtaining her degree had all been for one end: to find her child. And good private detectives did not come cheap.

"You're staring at me, detective."

He fumbled for words, and she said, "I know, you don't find many women in that profession. Once I had my license, it was impossible to find a job. Most established landscape architects did not want to hire a woman back then, and those who agreed to take me on, would not give me creative freedom, and didn't listen to me when I suggested they were doing something wrong." Abby's growing-up years in her grandfather's nursery had taught her more than any college classes could. But who cared?

"So I decided to go independent, find clients on my own." She remembered the day she had pulled up to the curb on a street in Bel Air and surveyed the scene.

She smiled at the memory. "A new house was being landscaped," she said to Jack, "and the men were putting the tall trees on the wrong side of the property. They should be on *this* side, to mask the noise of the traffic on Sunset Blvd. The walkway to the pool was straight, it should meander and be planted with a sequence of visual experiences—shrubs, flowers, bird bath, benches. And the flowers! The prevailing wind in the area was westerly for half the year, offshore for the other. But the flowers they were putting in bloomed during the westerlies, which meant the fragrance would be wafted into the neighbor's garden with no benefit to the owner of *this* house!"

Jack was noticing how animated she became, talking about flowers and prevailing winds, and he was thinking of Crystal Creek Winery, the brochure he had kept even though he had put aside his dream of buying the place, when his doorbell chimed. Abby paused in her story while he admitted the room service waiter, who mumbled apologies for the breakfast being delivered late, immediately reddening when he saw his boss. After the man left, Jack said, "Did you land the job?" He had her fingerprints. He could leave. Why was he doing this?

For Nina. Yes, it was for Nina.

"I found the owner in the back and told him my observations. He said, 'What would you say if I told you these were my own ideas?' I was blunt with him. 'You won't be happy once it's done,' I said. He challenged me. So I pointed out that he was placing water-loving plants under a drought-loving tree. For the plants he would have to over-water it and the tree would die. And it was a very expensive tree."

She poured coffee from the silver service and handed a cup to Jack, as if this were her room and she were the hostess. "We walked over the property for an hour and when we were done, he fired the landscaper and hired me. He was my first client and that led to many more."

She didn't tell Jack Burns the rest: that that first client's name was Sam Striker, a wealthy realtor, and that sixteen years ago, Sam had brought Abby out to the desert to show her his land. "Bought it dirt cheap," Sam had said. "My friends called me crazy, but I hired a geologist and he said there was artesian water here, it just needed a way to come up. That's what I did. Brought up the water and then I planted these trees."

Abby had been astonished. Barren wasteland as far as the eye could see, yet here was this grove of greenery, as if transplanted from the banks of the Nile.

"There's plenty more water underneath," Sam had said. "The geologist tells me it could last a hundred years or more. I figure to make this my retreat. Marry me, Abby. I'll protect you." By then, she and Sam had become lovers and he knew her story. "Bounty hunters will never find you. We'll build something special here."

"Sam," she had said that day sixteen years ago. "I'm fond of you but my child—"

He put a finger to her lips. "I know. Your child comes first. I won't get in the way. I'll help you in your search. But I want to take care of you. You brought so much beauty and tranquility into my life. Let me do the same for you."

"So," Jack Burns was saying now as he surveyed the breakfast offering on the room service cart—eggs, fruit, muffins—"As a landscape architect you were able to afford this property?"

"Oh no. My husband owned this land."

He turned and looked at her. "I didn't know you were married."

"I'm a widow. After he died and left this property to me, I decided to develop it into a retreat from the outside world."

Jack noticed a careful avoidance of her husband's name. But now he had a new lead to go on: a search at the County Hall of Records would give him the name of the owner of this land, prior to Abby Tyler.

Her pager went off. "Pardon me" she said, and spoke into her cell phone. "I'm sorry," she said to Jack, pocketing the cell. "Crisis at the health club that needs my immediate attention." She was reluctant to leave. The reason she had accepted his invitation to breakfast was that she hoped to learn more about him and the murder he was supposedly investigation.

She started for the door, then stopped and said, "Is that your sister?"

Jack turned to see where she was looking. Standing on an end table was a color portrait in a pewter frame. A pretty young woman with long blond hair. Jack's favorite picture of Nina, taken when she was twenty.

"She's lovely," Abby said.

Fury rose in him, suddenly and swiftly. He had been lulled into complacency by this beguiling woman. How could he fall for her, while she stood there blatantly lying, pretending not to know Nina?

The feel of her in his arms as they had drawn the bowstring back.

Jack mentally kicked himself. He was weakening, forgetting why he was here!

When she saw his features twist with emotion, she thought of the news articles she had requested from the Palm Springs *Sentinel*, special-messengered to The Grove, and which she had read before coming to his bungalow. When Vanessa suggested that Jack Burns was here on false pretenses, saying, "How do you know he's investigating his sister's murder? He could be here for *you*," Abby had requested the back news articles. And what she read had shocked her.

It explained some of Jack's mystery. He was burying his emotions. His sister's death was too recent, the wounds too raw—he was living a surface life. But it was an unhealthy way to live, perhaps even a dangerous one.

"Would you like to talk about it?" she asked gently.

"You have to go," he said in a tight voice. "Crisis at the health club."

She followed him to the door, distressed with this sudden turn. What was it about his sister? He had talked to Ophelia, Sissy and Coco. Was Nina adopted? Had she been searching for her birth mother? It stood on Abby's lips to tell him about herself, that she too was involved in an adoption search, but that would mean telling him everything—the murder, the escape from prison, the bounty on her head—and she suspected that Jack Burns followed a strict code of ethics when it came to police work. Once he knew that she was wanted by the FBI, he would have no choice but to arrest her.

"Detective, when you told me you were investigating your sister's murder, I had some news articles brought in from Palm Springs. I read about it. I am so sorry. If there is anything I can do to help."

"There's nothing," he said in such a painful tone that Abby's heart went out to him. "Very well," she said, "but if you should change—"

"It's just that my sister was very special to me. I was fourteen years older and I always looked after her. I took care of her. She depended on me. I let her down."

Abby heard in his voice a tone she herself had once spoken in. Jack was blaming himself for Nina's death.

"We can't always save those we love," she said, laying a hand on his arm.

He turned a furious expression to her. "Nina walked into a dangerous situation and I didn't do a damn thing about it. She left a message on my phone—a damn phone message, saying she was meeting someone later that night, someone who wanted to remain anonymous—" His words came out harsh, splintered. "She said she had stumbled upon something big, she said—I came home late and fell asleep on the sofa. I was on a case, I was exhausted. I didn't check my messages until the next morning when it was too late— " His voice broke.

"She left a message? Then how could you have helped her? Jack, it's not your fault. She had no way of knowing when you would hear the message."

He snapped the door open, and sunshine and desert breezes spilled inside. He had the fingerprints. There was nothing more here for him. He would leave on the next plane out.

"Jack, in her message, did she *ask* for help?"

He stood silently by the door, a tortured look in his eye.

"I know what it's like to blame yourself for something like this. The guilty feelings. But it was nothing you had any control over. I know, I've been there."

His stance was rigid and she knew he was fighting for control. She wanted to tell him that it was the malleable trees, like palms bending beneath a storm, that survived. Not the sturdy oak that became uprooted and was toppled.

She stepped outside and turned. "If you want to talk about it, I'm here," she said, wondering how she could help, but knowing that there wasn't much time. She knew that Jack was due to check out of The Grove on Saturday.

The same day she herself was leaving.

CHAPTER TWENTY-EIGHT

*T*HERE WAS SOMETHING ABOUT FLYING AT THE SPEED OF SIX hundred miles per hour that always made Michael Fallon horny. It was the image of himself shooting through open space in a phallus-shaped vessel. He could not concentrate on what his secretary was saying.

She was a looker. Tawny curls bent over a steno pad, smooth legs crossed at the knee so that one silken calf swung as she wrote. Her blouse was unbuttoned down to plump cleavage. She had a narrow waist and wide hips, the way Michael liked them. His concentration drifted. "Where were we, Miss Jones?" he said.

"The Governor and his wife, Senator Watson and wife, Arnold Schwarzenegger and Maria..." They were reviewing the RSVP's to the guest list for his daughter's wedding reception.

"I'll give you a million bucks if you unbutton your blouse," Fallon said with a sexy smile. Outside, fleecy clouds engulfed the private jet while inside soft music filled the luxuriously appointed cabin. Uri Edelstein was snoozing a few seats away—flying always knocked him out. But not Michael. He was suddenly rock hard.

Laughing softly, Miss Jones set her pad aside and slowly undid the buttons of her blue silk blouse, giving her boss a good view of mammoth breasts barely contained in lacy cups. Her real name was Ingrid and she had been a Vegas stripper before she learned shorthand.

Michael got up and went to the back of the plane. She followed. He pulled a curtain across the small galley and leaned against the wall. Ingrid knew what was expected of her. Secretarial skills were only part of her job. Kneeling, she unzipped his fly and took hold of his erection. Some gentle caressing and then she took him into her mouth. Michael didn't move, letting her do all the work. He didn't even touch her. He closed his eyes and thought of jet planes and speed, and soon came in her mouth.

She left him right away, to return to her seat while Michael stepped into the small john to clean himself. Sex always brought out his fastidious nature. As he restored himself and washed his hands, and made a mental note to give the secretary a bauble from Florida, a diamond bracelet maybe, the captain's voice came over the intercom: "We will be landing in a few minutes, sir."

Fallon was paying a visit to his mother.

If Michael didn't know who had sired him, he knew at least where and when the deed had taken place: at the Flamingo Hotel during its inaugural opening in 1946. "Born with Vegas," Fallon liked to brag. Born in the glory days of crime and men like Lucky Luciano, Meyer Lansky, Bugsy Siegel. Now *there* was juice. Anybody not liking them moving into town and building casinos with Mexican drug money and millions of dollars made on heroin was either bribed, frightened, or killed into silence. The moxie! Bugsy Siegel had killed thirty men by his own hand, and countless others through his goons. Bugsy had gotten away with so many gangland executions that he believed murder wasn't a crime if it was done by him.

Though Michael had never met the man, and Siegel wasn't Italian, Fallon admired him: Bugsy had single-handedly created and built the Flamingo Hotel. Without it, Fallon wouldn't walk the earth today.

Michael was ten years old and snooping through his mother's jewelry, hoping to find something to sell—but it was all junk, they were so poor—when he came across The Chip. He was only a fifth-grader, but he knew what a teal colored gambling chip signified. Someone had gifted his mother a thousand dollars. It came from the Flamingo. There was even a date on it: December 1946, so it had been made specially for the opening of the new casino. She had never cashed it in. Kept it as a souvenir. A reminder, Michael decided, of the night she had slept with one of the big juices.

When he was fifteen he read a book about Lucky Luciano. Even though the gangster hadn't been in Vegas in '46 but was hiding out in Cuba, young Michael fantasized that Luciano had snuck into the United States to be present at the Flamingo's grand opening and had stayed long enough to entertain a certain little waitress named Lucy Fallon before being caught by the Feds and deported back to Italy.

Over the years, Fallon devoured every news report he could find on that auspicious casino opening. One reporter had even described it has having "the gaudy opulence of a top hoodlum's funeral," which was ironic considering Bugsy Siegel was assassinated seven months later when a gunman at the window of his Beverly Hills home shot him through the head with such accuracy the police found Bugsy's right eyeball fifteen feet away.

And Bugsy's girlfriend, Virginia Hill, nicknamed by the FBI "a fabulous woman of mystery," had slept with every top Mafioso in the country before landing in Bugsy's bed. It was after Hill that the Flamingo was named—for her long legs that Siegel was so crazy about. She had chutzpah. In 1951, the Kefauver Committee was investigating rackets and fraud in Vegas and subpoenaed Hill to testify. When the distinguished politician asked her the secret of her success, she replied, "Senator, I'm the best goddamned cocksucker in the world."

Michael had kept a secret scrapbook filled with the news articles he had collected on gangsters, trying to figure out which one was his father. The latest, added only weeks ago, was the obituary of an old Vegas mobster, Carlo Bellagamba, who had been forced out of Nevada by the Feds back in 1970. He died of a heart attack in Chicago (in a whorehouse, it was rumored, trying to screw two women at once). Fallon had stared at the youthful photo of the deceased, taken from old police files, studying the Italian features, looking for his own in them, silently asking: *Were you my father?*

The charge nurse greeted him warmly and escorted him down a corridor crowded with beds, wheelchairs, and old folks in varying stages of alertness.

Michael had been trying for over fifty years to learn his mother's secret. Maybe this time she could be persuaded. After all, Lucy was seventy-eight and had recently moved into a nursing home because of a fall that had broken her hip. She needed daily medication and could only walk with the aid of a walker. Maybe the idea of being so close to facing her Maker would loosen her tongue. And the scrapbook would help. He would turn the pages and say, "Is this him? Is this the one?" Making it easier for her.

She was in a private room, propped up against crisp pillows, a pink bed jacket around her thin shoulders. "Mikey!" she said in pleasant surprise. She looked at him with shining eyes. Her handsome son. Nearly sixty but so fit, so dark-haired.

"Ma," he said quietly. "Who was my father? Tell me his name." If it was really bad—like Lucky Luciano—Michael would say she had been raped. But he needed the name to start his spin on it.

Lucy pressed her lips together. She had never told him as a matter of her own personal pride. Couldn't he see that? She had thought he would drop the subject long ago. What did it matter who his father was? Lucy wanted to keep her dignity. As long as she never uttered the man's name, she kept her honor.

"Mikey, listen to me. It won't change your life one iota. You've done well. You're rich. You have power. Leave me my one little bit of dignity, *please.*"

Fallon recognized intransigence when he saw it and knew he would not be getting any information from her.

The wedding was in three days. Too much was riding on it—Mike Fallon had wagered his entire life and fortune on those vows being spoken. He could not risk a slip of the tongue by his sentimental old mother. It didn't matter how much Francesca and Stephen might be in love, if the Vandenbergs should catch wind of scandal—the bride's grandfather a notorious gangster!—they would cancel the wedding and Stephen (Fallon knew *his* stripe well) would comply.

Without even saying good-by, he left the room and ducked into a protected doorway to flip open his cell phone. He still had connections in Florida. It had to be done right away. He didn't care about the details—the hit man could disguise himself as a visitor or a doctor, and he could use a pillow or lethal drugs—all Michael cared about was that it happened soon and that it looked like a natural death.

CHAPTER TWENTY-NINE

*S*O YOU'RE SAYING, DR. KAPLAN, THAT PROSTITUTION *ISN'T* THE oldest profession?"

Hearing the radio DJ's voice on the cassette tape made her hackles rise again, just as they had during the original on-air interview. Ophelia had recorded their informal chat and was now incorporating the transcripts into her newest book: *In Defense of Our Ancestors.*

Focusing on her work kept her from obsessing on the possibility that she was pregnant—a fact that she would not know until the pregnancy test kit arrived.

"I'm sorry, Dr. Kaplan," the nurse had said the night before. "The drug-store in Palm Springs got the order wrong. I had to requisition it again. But I assure you, on the very first flight in the morning…"

Ophelia looked at her watch. Nearly eight. The jet should be arriving any minute. She lifted her face to the blue sky and thought how deep and endless it was. The same sky that people had lived beneath millions of years ago.

Ophelia's people.

"So what *is* the oldest profession, if not prostitution?" The DJ's voice drifted away on the perfumed breeze. Ophelia was sitting in one of The Grove's flower gardens, riotous with spring blooms. And as she listened to her response, she simultaneously typed on her laptop keyboard: "Archaeological evidence points to cave dwellers as living in groups separated by gender. The women and children on one side of the shelter, males on the other. Women did not need men, or mates, for protection and food. They had the group. Therefore there was no need to 'sell' sexual favors. Humans engaged in sexual intercourse the same way animals in the wild do. It wasn't until humans began pair bonding, and a woman found herself dependent upon a male for protection and food, that sex was used as barter. Prior to that, there were more important professions already in place. The healer or shaman. The medicinal herb gatherer. The keeper of fire. Without these the clan would perish, and so such members of the group would have been held in high esteem and been lavished with favors by the clan."

"Dr. Kaplan?"

Ophelia stopped typing and squinted up at the person standing against the morning sun. The nurse. "The plane has just arrived and I am on my way to meet it. I should have the supplies in a few minutes. If you would care to come to my office—"

"No," Ophelia said quickly. "I prefer to conduct the test in private." After all, that was why she was here, away from David and her mother and her sisters. This was something she had to face alone.

The young woman smiled. "Very well. I can meet you at your suite in, say, fifteen minutes?" And she was off, long black braid swinging energetically across her back.

Fifteen minutes. And Ophelia would know her fate. And the fate of her marriage.

"I'm glad we see eye to eye on the issue of children," David had said when they started to discuss the possibility of marriage. David did not want children. "Too dangerous," he said, referring to the damaged gene, for which he had tested positive. "We have each other, and our work." Ophelia had agreed. After what her sister went through with Sophie's incurable illness and death before the age of five, Ophelia had vowed she never wanted to have babies and was thrilled to have found a man who agreed.

I'll meet you at your suite in fifteen minutes...

Ophelia turned off the recorder and closed her laptop. Gathering the rest of her things, she rose from the marble bench and in that instant the breeze shifted, and a floral scent she had not detected earlier suddenly washed over her.

Ophelia staggered, reached out for the lamp post to steady herself. The scent was overpowering. Cloying—too sickly sweet to be pleasant. But familiar. She didn't know the name, what flower it came from—but she *knew* it! Where from? What did the fragrance mean?

Her vision was suddenly filled with other sights: a hospital room crowded with flowers, a waiting room filled with people, and Ophelia as a child, suffocated and scared.

A memory? But of what?

She followed the sickly perfume until she homed in on the specific flower in the garden, standing tall and white, the label identifying it as narcissus. It nauseated her. And terrified her. She broke out in a cold sweat and she felt suddenly dizzy. Stumbling to the marble bench, she quickly sat down and pressed her forehead on her knees.

After a few minutes, the attack passed—or whatever it was. But it had left her drenched in perspiration and shaky in the legs. And as she got unsteadily to her feet, a memory flashed in her mind: Ophelia sitting on her grandfather's lap at a family gathering. He was not elderly then—she recalled thick black hair and a deep laugh. She had been very little. But something had happened, *Zayde* Abraham had said or done something that had hurt her. She had blanked it out. David had tried to help her recall it, even suggesting hypnotism, to no avail. He believed Ophelia's competitiveness and drive to over-achieve was rooted in that moment.

What had her grandfather done?

Ophelia hurried from the garden, from the past, from radio DJs who accused her of being promiscuous, from the sickly scent of a flower that terrified her.

The package was already in her room. The nurse had wisely ordered two.

Her heart thumping wildly, Ophelia opened the first box.

"Tay-Sachs Disease is caused by the absence of a vital enzyme called Hexosamindase A." The physician's voice cool and objective, as if lecturing on the life cycle of a frog while Ophelia and her sister sat in stunned silence. "Carriers of the disease can be identified by a simple blood test that measures hexosaminidase A activity. Both parents must be carriers in order to have an affected child. When both parents are found to carry a genetic mutation in hexosaminidase A, there is a twenty-five percent chance with each pregnancy that the child will be affected with Tay-Sachs disease."

"What are the odds?" Ophelia had asked. She and her sister sitting close together facing the doctor behind the desk, Ophelia there to give her sister support because the brother-in-law wouldn't come. They already knew most of this information because of Sophie, who had died at age five of TSD. What were the odds of it happening again?

"A person's chances of being a TSD carrier," the doctor had replied, "are significantly higher if he or she is of Eastern European Jewish, that is, Ashkenazi, descent. Which I understand you are. Approximately one in every twenty-seven Jews in the United States is a carrier of the TSD gene."

They had left the doctor's office unsatisfied, and six months later her sister's husband walked out on her.

And then Ophelia met David who was of Ashkenazi extraction and already knew he was a carrier. He had been tested when he came close to marrying several years prior. "I don't want children," he had said when their relationship was growing serious. Ophelia said she didn't want children either, that she was dedicated to her career. Whether or not she meant it at the time she couldn't say. She wanted David, she wanted a career. Children were vague little shadows in the sidelines. And at Sophie's grave she had vowed: *This will never happen to me.*

And so she had not submitted to the genetic test. She was on birth control. Her chances of getting pregnant were remote. Still, everyone said, she should have the test. When asked why she didn't, Ophelia couldn't explain it other than to say "It isn't necessary." But David thought it was because Ophelia didn't want to be told she had a defect. Ophelia had to be successful and perfect in everything. Mutant genes were for other people.

As she collected a urine sample and unwrapped the test stick with shaking hands, she wished now she had undergone the genetic test. Was there a child, at that moment, growing within her that was destined to die before its fifth birthday?

She dipped the test stick into her urine and watched the stick turn color. Unlike the previous test kit that provided two pink lines as proof of pregnancy, this one spelled it out in words.

After sixty seconds, tiny black letters appeared ghost-like on the stick. *You Are Pregnant.*

CHAPTER THIRTY

*C*OCO SITS IN HER FORTUNE TELLING TENT AT THE CHARITY FAIR, *waiting for the next customer. Finally, the curtain parts and sunlight delivers a dark stranger. He closes the curtain behind him so that the little tent is cozy and intimate, lit only by candlelight. He sits opposite Coco and waits expectantly. She is surprised. Men don't usually go to fortune tellers. She wonders why he is here.*

He is Mediterranean-handsome. His name will be Carlo or Dimitrios, she decides. "Give me your hands," she says, already feeling herself turn on, just by his looks, his nearness, but now by his hands transmitting his heat to her and she senses a sudden, mutual attraction.

She tries to concentrate but the olive-skinned stranger is delving her with his Rudolf Valentino eyes.

"It is warm in here, is it not?" he asks in an accent.

"Yes," she whispers.

He removes his jacket to sit in an open-necked shirt, dark chest hair curled near the collar. So Coco sheds the gypsy shawl she wears for effect and feels his eyes slide over her bare shoulders, down to her bosom. The elastic neckline of her peasant blouse is pulled down, and she realizes she has let too much cleavage show.

"You are a passionate man," she murmurs, receiving his masculine vibes loud and clear.

His eyes delve deep into her own, then they travel over her body, undressing her, seeing her naked, lingering here and there with such intensity that she can feel them on her.

"I must have you," he says abruptly.

He stands, filling the tent with his height and dominance. Coco trembles. She knows it will be a stunning conquest. But dare they? With all those people out there on the fairground, anyone walking in at any minute.

She doesn't care. She rises to meet his embrace, melts into his strong arms, presses her mouth to his. She tastes garlic and wine. He sweeps tarot cards and crystal from the table and settles Coco's butt on it, pushing up the gypsy skirt and forcing himself between her thighs.

"Wait," she says, embarrassed to realize she forgot to put panties on that morning.

He does not wait. Pulling down the elastic of her blouse, he exposes her breasts and helps himself to exploring, fondling, caressing them.

His kisses deepen. He is rock-hard against her. She is glad now she forgot the panties. Her fingers manage the zipper with a passion of their own. He springs out with impressive force.

With one hand he spreads her open and makes for the target. Coco clings to him with her arms around his neck. As they kiss, she opens her eyes.

His dark hair has turned to blond. His swarthy skin is now white.

Kenny!

And he says, "Someone's at the door."

Coco opened her eyes.

It was bad enough she had the hots for him, but did he have to intrude upon her private fantasies?

Damn it, she had a man to find.

That morning, after returning to her cottage from giving Sissy Whitboro a psychic reading, Coco had spent an hour with the crystal until it had finally come through with new information on her soulmate. More fine tuning from the spirit world informed her that he wasn't specifically well-traveled or worldly. What he was, was *wise*.

It hadn't come to her as a word but as a *feeling*, as if Daisy had invited a wise old soul to visit Coco's brain and parade through it as if to say, "This is who you are looking for. Someone like me." She pictured Sean Connery, Mahatma Gandhi, Albert Einstein.

But not Kenny.

And yet, as she had prepared to put the crystal back in its case, she had slipped into her ongoing fantasy with him. Why couldn't her libido fall into step with the spirit world?

The second time, she heard the knock that had startled her out of her trance.

Probably the maid. Coco's room was a mess.

It was Kenny, standing there in the noon sunshine in Bermuda shorts and a shirt covered in palm trees, and she was both thrilled and dismayed to see him. Could he tell she had just been entertaining naughty thoughts about him?

"I want you to know something about me," he said solemnly. "Is there somewhere we can talk?"

Coco was about to say no when she noticed the tiniest dribble of hardened egg yolk on his shirt, like a Christmas ornament on one of the palm trees. She wanted to weep with compassion. Kenny remembered every single fact known to humankind except where to put his napkin when he ate soft boiled eggs.

The Village offered a delightful outdoor café where diners enjoyed omelets and croissants next to a trickling fountain.

"Do you know who it is yet?" Kenny asked between bitefuls of avocado and bean sprouts sandwich.

Coco wished she hadn't told Kenny about her search for her soulmate. In the bright sunlight, in the company of all these normal looking people, it seemed so ridiculous. "The crystal is never specific. I receive generalizations. More like feelings. But once in a while a detail sneaks through. My last case was a missing child. They gave me her teddy bear and I sensed right away that she was in a dark place, and tied up. I almost missed the important clue because I tensed up. That's the important thing. To stay relaxed."

"What was the clue?"

"A sound. Sometimes, if I'm lucky, I'm clairaudient. I heard a factory whistle and the cops were able to locate it. They found the little girl, barely alive, but alive."

Coco sipped her wine. "You said you wanted to tell me something." The sunlight did nice things to Kenny's hair, giving it little gold tips here and there. She wondered what it would feel like to rake her fingers through all that luscious blondness. She remembered the very realistic kiss in her fantasy, when he turned from Dimitrios to Kenny. Would it be as good in real life?

Reaching into his pocket, he brought out a photograph and said, "I'm going to show you something I never show to anybody. I carry it as a reminder."

Coco stared at the picture. It was a young man standing beside a San Francisco cable car. But the car seemed dwarfed next to him.

"Who's this?" she asked.

"Me, at three hundred and fifty pounds. That's what I looked like when Vanessa Nichols found me.

Her eyebrows shot up. "This is *you*?"

"I was a sugar junkie. The guys at the water cooler making me perform, making bets on how much I could remember of something. I'd go home at night and console myself with candy bars."

He picked up a bean sprout and popped it between his lips.

"And then one day Mr. Memory was born. I quit my software engineering job and became a lounge act. My size wasn't a detriment to my show since I was a freak anyway. So I earned good money and channeled it all into food. One night Vanessa Nichols caught my act in San Francisco. We talked, and she offered me a job here. She said The Grove would help me get off the sugar." He squinted into the sunlight. "I didn't think anything could help. But this place gets to you." He brought his gaze back to her, two brown eyes filled with sunshine. "It's like there's some kind of magic in the air, or in the water. The first few weeks I was here I recognized my self-destructive behavior and did something about it. That was three years ago."

Coco watched the nicely formed fingers pick up the rest of the bean sprouts and deliver them to Kenny's nicely formed lips. "My God, you look great."

"It's still a struggle. I get cravings." He gave Coco a long look, turned his fork over and over, moved his iced tea glass, cleared his throat. "The fact is, I'm a coward. I'm just hiding here, I'm not really living. I'm afraid to go back out into the world, afraid I'll return to the sugar addiction."

He reached across the table and rested his hand on Coco's. She caught her breath. Emotions washed over her—Kenny's emotions and her own, colliding, swirling. But she didn't draw her hand away.

"I told you I spent time at the Carl Jung Institute in Switzerland. They keep writing to me. They want me to help them. They think my unique brain might hold a clue to the causes and cures for diseases involving memory, such as Alzheimer's. I want to help them, Coco, but I'm afraid that if I leave this place I'll be three hundred pounds again."

Coco was so rocked with emotion that she couldn't speak. Her chest tightened, her throat closed up. As she opened her heart to him and engulfed him with compassion, something dawned on her that gave her such a shock she nearly jumped out of her chair. She wasn't just attracted to Kenny, she was falling in love with him.

"Mr. Memory!"

They both jumped, and a shadow blotted out the sun. Coco looked up to see two young women standing over them, giggling, eyes bright. "We caught your act last night!" they both exclaimed, crowding around Kenny as if Coco weren't there. They were twentyish and deeply tanned in bikini tops and shorts. "You were fan*tas*tic! How do you *do* it? Let us buy you a drink!"

They actually pulled up chairs and enthused all over Kenny with such heat that Coco thought they were going to assault him right there. "Ladies—" he said, flustered and embarrassed. The taller one pressed her large breasts against him and breathed, "You are *so* smart!" Coco recognized the signs. She saw it in the groupies who hung around cop bars, looking to get laid. She decided to made a quick exit, shoving her chair back and muttering, "Thanks for the lunch," before Kenny could stop her, and as she fled, she looked back and saw him autographing a napkin while one of the girls whispered in his ear.

CHAPTER THIRTY-ONE

*J*ACK HAD NEVER KNOWN SUCH PAIN.

Not even at Nina's funeral. Since the morning of her death, he had worked hard to suppress his emotions, and although they surfaced at night in bad dreams, during the day he was able to keep himself in control.

Until Abby Tyler came along. *His arms around her as he helps her to draw back the bowstring.* She affected him in a way no woman had. There was a strength to her, and a vulnerability. But he also sensed a deep well of compassion, as though you could tell her anything and she would not judge. You knew you could rest your head in her lap and pour out your pain and she would take it into herself and give you peace.

He wished he could do that. His sister brutally murder, raped and made to look like a junkie. He could not take it in—not now, maybe never. The only way to survive was to bury the emotions as deeply as possible and live a surface life. But there was something about Abby that exhumed his whole bundle of emotions. He had to get out of his room, out of the resort. Find control in the bow and arrow.

Zeb was just returning from a desert run with a carload of guests. When Jack asked if any of the vehicles was available, Zeb consulted his watch and said, "We do not like guests to go driving out by themselves. It is too dangerous. However, I will be happy to take you, sir. Where would you like me to drive you?"

"As far out as we can go," Jack said, stowing his archery gear in the back of the Jeep.

Resting his arm on the rolled down window, he closed his eyes and felt the warm, dry breeze on his face. Once he had her fingerprints, Jack had wanted to leave the resort. But all flights out that day were full, no one was leaving by car, and there were no private planes to be hired. He could call for a limousine from Palm Springs, Guest Services had said. And then it occurred to him that Abby's prints might not even be on file anywhere, so he had called the County Hall of Records for the name of the Grove's property owner prior to Tyler. Abby said she had inherited the property from her deceased husband, so the former title deed would give Jack the name of the man she married. After that it would be a simple call to the marriage license bureau and he should have everything he needed to gain access to Abby Tyler's carefully hidden past.

In the meantime, the pain was insupportable and the only thing that would help him fight it down was to shoot targets until he was exhausted.

As they raced across the trackless desert, Jack saw nothing for miles around but dunes, cacti, Joshua trees and the occasional desert tortoise. "Not like Africa, I'll bet," he said to his companion.

"Not the part of Africa I'm from," Zeb replied. As his eyes swept the desert ahead, with its painted rocks and azure sky, into his mind walked the only person in the whole world who seemed to understand him when he talked about the ivory poaching and the doomed elephant. Vanessa Nichols. Who visited him in restless dreams and sleepless nights.

That morning in the aviary, he had glimpsed her hurrying away. Had she seen the blonde kissing him? He hoped not. But if she had, he prayed she had heard him say to the blonde, "Last night was a pleasant interlude, love. Why don't we keep it that way?" Zeb wasn't looking for a relationship.

It was only ever an in-the-moment thing for him, the sort that happened at resorts and on cruise ships.

The truth was, his heart was already taken. Not that he had given it willingly. When Zeb left Kenya it was with a promise to himself that he would never love another woman again as he had loved Miriam. And so he would never again fall in love. In the years since, he had come close several times but had quickly moved on, to avoid catastrophic involvement, and thus his heart was the measure of how long he stayed in any one place. But while in the past he had never actually fallen in love, this time he had.

With her African princess features, the large slanting eyes, high cheek bones, and full, lush lips over big beautiful white teeth that made him want so badly to kiss her that he ached, Vanessa reminded Zeb of Africa.

A *painful* reminder.

Zebulon Armstrong, former white hunter now taking care of birds and guests at a resort in the California desert, yearned to go home, to set foot on the red soil of East Africa, to drink in the rarefied air of Mount Kenya, to be among his own people again— yet unable to return, ever.

He had liked it at first, when he started working at The Grove a year ago and Vanessa reminded him of Africa, triggering fond memories. But now the memories, and her nearness, were becoming too painful. It was time to be moving on.

"I understand you're investigating a murder, Mr. Burns."

When Jack gave him a startled look, Zeb explained, "The head of security, Elias Salazar, told me. He and I are both baseball fans. We follow the games and have a friendly rivalry going, although what he sees in the Giants is beyond me. You a fan of the game, Mr. Burns?"

"I like sports to move a little faster."

Zeb laughed. "I hear you. A lot of people don't catch the secret charm of baseball."

"And what is that?"

"The waiting! Watching for that next big hit. The pleasure, Mr. Burns, is not in the act, but in the anticipation."

Jack gave him a look. Zeb could be talking about sex.

"So how goes the investigation, Mr. Burns?"

Casually asked, but Jack had the feeling that this was not a casual conversation. Recalling the man Abby had introduced him to the day before, the resort's head of security had the look of a tight-tipped secret-keeper. And Abby had assured Jack of Salazar's complete discretion, so he doubted the man had gossiped to Zeb about Jack's business at the resort.

Was Abby behind Zeb's offhanded inquiries? It wouldn't surprise him. She wanted to know what murder he was investigating, or maybe she was even more interested in what he had *found*.

"It's too early to tell yet," he said as he squinted at vultures circling in the distant sky. Something dead, out there on the desert.

The engine suddenly made a strange sound, started coughing and slowing down until the Jeep came to a stop. In the middle of nowhere. "What happened?" Jack said.

Zeb scratched his head. "I'll take a look." He got out and was soon under the hood, making distressed sounds over the hot motor.

"What is it?" Jack asked, joining Zeb under the hood.

"Happens all the time in the desert. Sand gets into the works. It'll take me a few minutes. Not to worry."

Jack surveyed the landscape. Nothing but sand and cacti as far as the eye could see. "What's that sound?" he said, feeling a chill go up his spine.

Zeb paused to listen—there was yelping among nearby rocks. "Coyotes," he said. "Pups, from the sound of it."

"Are they dangerous?"

"They can be if they think their pups are threatened. Just don't go over to those rocks."

While Jack retreated into thought, Zeb retreated back under the hood. He pulled a small portable radio from his shirt pocket and tuned it to a sports station to catch the Dodgers playing at Chavez Ravine. However, for the first time since he had discovered a passion for American baseball, he could not focus on the game. He could think only of Vanessa. He desired her so much that it kept him awake at night. Not that she returned the sentiment. Always professional toward him. Friendly, yes, but never flirtatious. Polite and businesslike. Besides, Zeb wasn't hoping for a relationship with her. Not with any woman.

But most especially not with Vanessa Nichols. Realizing he had come to the point, once again, of having to make a life-changing decision, he picked up a wrench and went savagely after the fuel pump.

While Zeb worked in concentrated silence, Jack felt the desert wind on his face, heard the cry of a hawk, and fought down the anguish that refused to stay buried.

When his captain and fellow detectives had offered condolences, when neighbors had said how sorry they were to hear of Nina's passing—when anyone under the sun mentioned his sister, Jack had always been able to maintain control.

But not with Abby Tyler. She had looked at Nina's photo, said, "She's lovely," and Jack had felt his emotional wounds rip wide open.

"It haunts me, Jack," Nina had said during one of their last dinners together. At Mario's in Santa Monica, over linguini in clam sauce—Nina's favorite. She had been searching for her birth mother for three years and had collected a mountain of data. All pertaining to other people.

Jack's parents had left him and his sister some money, but Nina also made good money as an advertising executive, and so she had been able to afford to hire more than one private investigator. She and Jack would get together and she would update him on what she had found. "So many names, Jack, so many people who had been torn from one another. I found websites where adoptees and birth mothers can post information. Children searching for their mothers, women searching for their children."

While a storm had battered the Pacific Ocean beyond the restaurant windows, Nina had let her food go untouched as she had said, "It's tearing me up, to think of the heartache and anguish and fear. What about my own mother, Jack? Was she just a girl and they forced her to give up her baby? Was her back turned for a moment and when she looked into the carriage, the baby was gone? I have to know. I have to find her."

"You'll find her, little sister," he had said, because even though they now knew Nina wasn't really his sister, she still was, nothing was going to change that. Jack had helped when he could, making use of law enforcement data bases, tracking down leads on his own time. But it wasn't enough. *I should have done more.*

The desert wind kicked up and tears sprang to his eyes. Pulling out a handkerchief, he wiped them away. "You all right?" Zeb asked.

"Sand," Jack said.

"That'll happen. When the wind acts up around here, you have to protect your eyes."

Jack wondered if he should set up his target right there and get to work wrestling his emotions back into their locked room. And then he thought: No, stay focused. Stay on the job. "How do you like working at The Grove?"

Zeb straightened and wiped his forehead. "Abby Tyler is the best boss I've ever had. She treats her employees as well as she treats her guests. She's like a mother to everybody. Not that she's old enough mind, it's just the way she is. A nurturer, if you know what I mean. If an employee is sick, Abby sends flowers."

Jack heard a special tone in Zeb's voice, making him wonder if Zeb had ever been intimate with Abby. And then he wondered: did she have a lover? Did she avail herself of the resort's bedroom services?

Damn it, he told himself, don't go there. Jack had always been able to compartmentalize his life—romance in one place, police work in another. But Abby Tyler was blurring the boundaries, making it difficult for him to concentrate. He was here to find a killer, not love.

"The first time I met her," Zeb was saying, "I was taken with her accent. People tell me my accent is exotic, but to my Kenya ear, the way Abby talks is downright out of this world."

Jack stared at Zeb. Then he thought back. He hadn't noticed an accent. Or had he? Now that he thought about it, a slight accent had slipped out while they had coffee in her bungalow Monday night. And then just that morning, when they released the bowstring together and she fell against him, laughing. Did she work at hiding it, and that when she was tired, or off guard, it slipped out?

Could this be the break he was hoping for?

"Where is she from?" he asked without sounding overly interested.

"Don't know. I'm no expert, but somewhere in the American South, I would guess." Zeb slammed the hood down. "Fixed! We can be on our way now."

"You know what? I've changed my mind. If it's all the same to you, I'd like to head back to the resort." Get back and engage Abby in a conversation, this time paying attention to the accent. He hadn't wanted to encounter her again, expose his vulnerability to her, but for Nina's sake he would.

Zeb was only too glad to go back. He had arrived at a decision, and he wanted to set it in motion. It was time to move on. He had made up his mind: he would give Abby Tyler his notice in the morning.

CHAPTER THIRTY-TWO

*T*HE DAY IT HAPPENED—OPHELIA KNEW THE EXACT MOMENT. As a prominent psychiatrist, with a prestigious practice and holding professorships at a major university and teaching hospital, David was often called as an expert witness in high profile murder cases. Six weeks ago, he took the stand in what was to be the pivotal moment of a sensational trial because the defense's position was an insanity plea and everything hinged upon what Dr. David Messer had to say.

Ophelia was sitting in the back of the packed courtroom, watching her handsome fiancé as he calmly fielded questions first from the prosecution and then from the defense. Listening to his rich voice ring out over the mesmerized spectators, Ophelia observed how the female jurors watched him, and the women spectators. They were entranced by him. Possibly even fantasizing. Ophelia became aroused. David, so attractive, in control, the man with the power at that moment, in his three-piece pinstriped suit, his black hair styled perfectly. Watching him was a turn-on, and knowing that every other woman in the court room desired him.

As the opposing counsels fought over David, passions rose, the atmosphere became charged. "Dr. Messer, you do admit that the defendant hears voices?"

"Yes."

"Voices that sound very real to him?"

"Yes."

"And you admit that they *order* him to murder people?"

"Yes. But he doesn't have to *act* upon those orders."

"Move to strike!"

"Your honor, may we approach?"

A hurried and heated discussion at the bench, all eyes on David who had caused the furor, everyone tuned to him—the judge, the attorneys, the jurors, the court reporter, the bailiffs, and spectators—every single person focused on David the alpha male of the clan, and Ophelia was positively on fire.

When recess was called, she sought David in the crowded hall, where reporters had immediately surrounded him and women devoured him with hungry eyes. She caught his attention and when he saw her high color, her secret smile, he broke away, grabbed Ophelia's hand and hurried her down the hall and around the corner. The first unlocked door they came to, David pulled it open, drew Ophelia inside and closed the door without bothering to lock it as he swiftly lifted her skirt and pulled down her panties. It was a small conference room, the polished wooden table oval-shaped and large enough for Ophelia to lie back while David thrust into her, both thinking of the unlocked door and the crowd in the outer corridor.

And that was when it happened. When, for some reason, Ophelia's birth control pills failed and conception took place within her.

Now, in her impossible French gaudy suite at The Grove, Ophelia opened the second pregnancy test kit and tested herself again. Hoping, *praying* that the first had been a false positive.

But the second test strip left no mistake. She was pregnant.

Her world tilted, spun her around and fell away from beneath her feet. This strong woman who led protest marches and spoke before enormous crowds, reached out to steady herself, so great was her sudden fear.

Her mouth ran dry. Her heart raced. *What am I going to do?*

She went straight to the phone and called her doctor. "I'm pregnant. How can I be pregnant? I'm on the Pill."

Dr. Cummins did not sound as upset as Ophelia thought she should be. Didn't she know the world had just come to an end? "Ophelia, the Pill is not one hundred percent effective. Still, it *is* rare for it to fail. Are you taking any new medication since your last visit?"

"No, of course not." Then: "My ophthalmologist put me on tetracycline for conjunctivitis."

A pause at the other end. "Ophelia, tetracycline can render some birth control pills ineffective. Your eye doctor should have asked if you were using oral contraception."

"All he told me was that tetracycline made me more susceptible to sunburn. I was using sunscreen when I should have used a condom."

"Ophelia, you're upset. I understand. Now, listen to me. Come in for testing on the amniotic fluid. If it's positive, we can terminate at once."

Terminate! "No."

"Right now it's just an embryo. It isn't even a fetus yet…"

Fetus.

It's a baby! My son or daughter! Not something you dissect in a high school biology lab.

She hung up.

She felt numb. She felt crazed.

Her eye fell upon the work spread out on the ornate, glass-topped coffee table, her current book-in-progress: *In Defense of Our Ancestors*. And suddenly she despised her ancestors, those distant Jews who had handed down their bad blood. Because of *them* Ophelia faced giving birth to a doomed child.

Abortion was wrong. It went against Nature's law and God's law. The prehistoric woman attempting to cause a miscarriage would have been ostracized by the clan, because the death of a child meant the death of the clan. Survival was the only law. How many abortion clinics had Ophelia picketed? Handing out leaflets. Carrying signs. Shouting at the women who walked through those doors. Calling them murderers because she refused to believe there was "another side" to the issue.

But now she was suddenly on the other side.

She paced furiously, back and forth between the Louis Quinze chairs, wringing her hands.

How could she possibly go through with the pregnancy?

Ophelia was thankful now she had won the mysterious contest and come to The Grove. This was something she had to sort out on her own, away from the influence of her very opinionated family. Away from the suffocating compassion of David.

As she pulled her swimsuit out of the shower, where she had hung it to dry, deciding she would swim laps to clear her head, Ophelia caught the scent of white narcissus again. But it was impossible! There were no flowers in her room.

And yet the fragrance was there, thick and cloying, making her sick to her stomach. Frantically she went through the oils and lotions provided by the resort, dumping shower gels and body washes down the drain, rinsing the bottles. She went through the drawers and shelves—had a prior guest left behind a rotting bouquet of white flowers, now turning brown, decaying, filling the air with their sweet death-scent?

She found nothing. And finally she realized the perfume was in her mind. But why? What did the white narcissus mean?

Zayde Abraham, that day many years ago. Ophelia sitting on his lap. What had happened?

"Ophelia has been a fighter since she was very little," Mrs. Kaplan proudly told David when the two had started dating. "Always competitive. Even at age six. Had to be the best at everything."

As Ophelia now fought the fragrance that was making her ill, she realized that her aggressiveness somehow stemmed from that moment on her grandfather's lap.

She suddenly couldn't breathe. She needed to get out, into the fresh desert air, and think. She didn't want to lose David. The one man with whom she could be weak and vulnerable. The one man who saw through her Amazonian bravado and recognized the lost little girl underneath. David, who might head for the hills if he knew she was pregnant.

Seizing bathing suit and towels, and seating her sunglasses in place, swallowing for courage and praying that the answers would come, Ophelia opened the door and there, in the hall, with suitcase in hand, stood David.

CHAPTER THIRTY-THREE

*S*ISSY DIDN'T WANT TO HAVE DINNER WITH ABBY TYLER. SHE wanted to get on a plane and fly to Chicago, march into Ed's room at the Palmer House and say to Linda Delgado how *dare* she steal another woman's husband.

She had obtained Delgado's phone number. It appeared numerous times on Ed's secret phone bills, coinciding with his stays at the Palmer House. Which meant Ed called her the night before he went to stay there.

Sissy had done nothing with the new information. Instead she had gone to the Village with Ed's secret credit card and enjoyed a shopping spree, treating herself to new and exotic treats she never would have looked at before, returning to her room with shopping bags full of Godiva chocolates, Hermès scarves, perfume and jewelry, and had sat down for one last, cleansing cry before she dried her eyes and vowed she was going to get through this and on with her life, come what may when she returned home.

One thing was certain: Ed was not going to get the kids. Two mothers might have rejected her, but Sissy was not going to be like them. Adrian and the twins were going to know a mother's love. But first she was to have dinner with Abby Tyler. After that, Sissy was going to start planning her new life.

Well, *after* she had tried one of the resort's fantasy companions. Or two.

The private investigator's report said: *Baby girl, born Odessa, Texas, May 17, 1972, sold to Johnson family in Rockford, Illinois. Given the name Sissy. In 1990 married Ed Whitboro of Rockford.*

The table in Abby's private dining room had been set with cold dishes— prawns on minty papaya salad with Thai peanut sauce on the side; chilled potato soup; eggs in tomato aspic—so that they would not be disturbed by people serving them. Finally, Vanessa brought Sissy to the bungalow, made introductions and then left.

With a racing heart, Abby looked at Sissy's eyes and saw the eyes of a hippie drifter thirty-three years ago. And did Sissy also have Jericho's smile, the laugh and dimples of the grandfather Abby had so loved but had driven to an early death because of scandal?

Abby decanted frosty white wine and invited Sissy to sit. The china and crystal sparkled; a delicate fragrance came from the floral centerpiece. "Ms. Nichols mentioned something about family problems," Abby said as she took the other chair and unfolded her napkin. "Nothing serious I hope."

"I don't know yet. I think my husband is cheating on me." Sissy wasn't in the habit of divulging personal problems to strangers, but Abby Tyler had a way about her, like a good therapist, listening as if she cared, inviting one to unburden oneself. "I know it's devastating news for any woman, but for me, it's like a triple curse."

"In what way?"

"I was adopted when I was a baby."

Abby's fork stopped halfway to her mouth. "Adopted?"

Sissy chose a plump prawn, dipped it in the peanut sauce. "I knew from early age, but I didn't know the details until I was older. When I turned eighteen my mother believed I should know the truth. It explained a lot. My mother was a cold woman—my adoptive mother, that is. It wasn't her fault. She couldn't have children and hoped that adopting one would bring out the maternal love. It didn't. I had felt rejected by her all my life. And of course I was rejected by my birth mother."

"You don't know that," Abby said cautiously, keeping her trembling hands in her lap.

"Yes, I do. My mother said I wasn't adopted through legal channels."

Abby sat in frozen silence.

"My mother told me that the day I was brought to their house, by a man and a woman, the man asked for extra money, which made my father suspicious. My parents had thought the adoption was legal. But the man wouldn't hand them the baby until my father paid an extra five thousand dollars. So he went to the bank and got the cash. He tried to get more information from the couple—where I was born, how my birth mother decided to give me up—but without success. And then a week later the woman showed up on our doorstep and said that for five hundred dollars she would give them the information they wanted."

Sissy took a sip of wine and Abby struggled to remain calm. Tell me, she thought, tell me you are my daughter.

Sissy resumed: "The woman gave my father an address in Odessa and he flew there to find my birth mother. It was a home for unwed mothers and the girl had already gone home. More money changed hands and he got the girl's address. She was only sixteen and her parents had forced her to give up her baby."

Abby felt her hopes start to fade—but she stopped herself. They were dealing with baby brokers, how could they believe anything they were told?

"My father didn't give them his name or where he lived. He told them he didn't want the girl changing her mind and wanting her baby back. She assured him she wouldn't."

"And that was it?" Abby said, unable to help herself. "I mean, how can you be sure…?"

"When I turned eighteen my mother told me the whole story, including my birth mother's name. She said she wouldn't blame me if I wanted to meet with her. And so I did."

Abby stared at her.

"I found her in Dallas. When she opened the door and took one look at me, I thought she was going to faint. She let me come inside but it wasn't a happy reunion. She had since married and had more children. She showed me their pictures. Her daughters looked like my twins. She showed me a picture of herself when she was eighteen and it could have been me. But other than the strong resemblance, there was nothing between us. She had never loved me and never would. So I went away, leaving her in the past."

"I'm so sorry," Abby said, for Sissy as well as for herself. This woman was not her daughter.

"It's all right. Since I've been here at The Grove, I've been finding out things about myself. I'm stronger than I thought I was. Ms. Tyler, I don't know how I managed to win that contest, but I am awfully glad I decided to collect the prize."

Abby offered dessert—chocolate-brownie cake smothered in hot fudge sauce—but Sissy declined, saying she would have dessert later, in her cottage.

After Sissy left, Abby enjoyed a slice of the rich cake in the solitude of her bungalow, feeling strangely disappointed yet upbeat at the same time. Sissy was not her daughter. That left Ophelia. And now that she thought about it, the resemblance was there.

But Ophelia had declined all invitations to meet, even for coffee. Abby looked at her watch and considered going to Ophelia's suite, and then remembered that the fiancé was there. He had telephoned that morning and asked for a seat on one of the flights. He wanted to surprise his fiancée, he said. So Abby wouldn't intrude, not tonight. But in the morning she would call over there, invite them both to breakfast.

Taking the dessert plate into her small kitchen, she returned to the living room to find an envelope on the floor. It had been slipped under her door.

An ordinary white envelope, no name, no writing on it. Sealed. She was about to open it when she was startled by a knock at the door.

It was Jack. And she felt the familiar jolt at his sudden appearance.

"Is this from you?" she asked, holding up the unopened envelope.

"No."

She looked up and down the path. "Did you pass anyone?"

He shook his head. "What is it?"

"I don't know. I just found it under my door. Please, come in."

But he remained on the threshold. "I just came to apologize for my be-havior this morning. It was unfair of me to treat you that way. I was angry and shouldn't have taken it out on you."

Jack had hurried back from his drive into the desert with Zeb, eager to talk to Abby, to listen to her accent. But she had been unavailable, involved with resort matters that demanded her attention, and then an evening din-ner date.

Was she purposely avoiding him?

There was only one thing to do. He had walked straight up the path to her bungalow and knocked on the door.

She looked up at him now and moonlight sparkled in her eyes—a *warm* sparkle, Jack thought, marveling that only Abby Tyler could make moon-light seem warm. "You don't have to apologize," she said. "It was a terrible thing that happened to your sister. I can understand it must be difficult to talk about."

And there it was, just as Zeb had speculated: the barest Southern accent. As if she worked at overcoming it.

After returning from the drive, there was a fax from county records informing Jack that the previous owner of The Grove was Sam Striker. A quick phone call to marriage records and Jack had what he needed. Samuel E. Striker and Abilene Tyler. Married at Los Angeles County Courthouse in 1988.

Her place of birth was listed as Bakersfield, California, but a call to their courthouse disclosed no birth record for a baby by that name. She must have been born somewhere else, a town she was keeping a secret.

As she spoke now, suggesting he talk to someone about Nina, saying she knew an excellent grief counselor, Jack listened to the cultivated speech of someone who has overcome an accent. No, not Southern, he decided. Not exactly. Jack would bet the farm on Texas. Because the facts suddenly fell into place.

Abilene. Tyler. Two Texas towns.

"Well, that was all," he said, "I just wanted to say I was sorry," and when she invited him inside again, he saw behind her, in the living room, the roll top desk with the folders on it. He still didn't understand why she continued to lie about knowing Nina. Not just knowing her, but collecting data on her. Jack wanted to just come out and ask, yet he could not as it might jeopardize his investigation. What if Tyler were connected to the murderer? She could tip him off and the man might never be found.

So Jack just said good night, eager to get away from her spell, but wanting also to stay and be spellbound, and Abby watched him go, her emotions colliding as she thought of her growing desire for Jack, her wish to help him heal, thinking also of Ophelia who was her daughter, and of the flight she must take from The Grove in two days, and the frightening, unknown future that lay before her.

After she closed the door, she remembered the mysterious envelope. Opening it, she found it contained an item clipped from a current newspaper. Abby frowned as she began to read: *"Darryl Jackson, who escaped from prison thirty-two years ago, was captured last week in Maryland, the California Department of Corrections said Monday."*

Her horror grew as the significance of the article dawned on her: *"Jackson, 62, was one of the longest-running fugitives from California, had served little more than five months of a fifteen year sentence..."* Abby's eyes skipped to the end of the article. *"There are only two California fugitives who have been on the run longer than Jackson. One escaped in 1965 and the other in 1966. State officials are still looking for 296 escapees."*

Abby's blood ran to ice when she saw at the bottom, scrawled across the newsprint in red ink: *"You're next."*

CHAPTER THIRTY-FOUR

*Y*OU CAN TELL A LOT ABOUT A MAN BY THE WAY HE TREATS A woman in bed. And I'm telling you, Coco, this one is a sicko!"

She awoke suddenly, eyes snapping open in the darkness as she struggled to orient herself. Fumbling for the light beside her bed, Coco turned it on and looked at the time. Eight o'clock in the evening. Then she remembered: she had taken a nap to get rid of her headache. But the nap had only dredged up a bad memory, an incident long forgotten, her sister telling her about a man she was dating who had done terrible things to her in the bedroom. It made Coco feel queasy now, just remembering it.

And then she thought: *Kenny doesn't have that luxury.*

As she went into the bathroom to run the shower, wondering where she should go for dinner, she couldn't get the photograph out of her mind, Kenny standing next to the cable car, three hundred and fifty pounds and unrecognizable as the Kenny she knew at The Grove.

A tormented man, frightened of the world, and of his weakness. A man unable to run from hideous memories, unable to bury them as everyone else could. It made Coco go cold with dread, the thought that she would remember every bad thing, every negative experience, every horrible event that happened in her life. It would make her insane. She wanted to take Kenny into her arms and tell him everything was going to be all right. She wanted to make slow and gentle love with him all through the night and the coming days, to kiss him and kiss him and never stop.

But Kenny was never going to leave this place. What possible future was there for them?

Beneath the invigorating spray, Coco made a decision. Tonight she was going to ignore the uncooperative crystal and go in search of Kenny. Buy him coffee and explain why she kept running away from him. Offer advice, urge him to go back out into the world, go to Switzerland and help discover a cure for Alzheimer's.

Feeling better than she had in a long time—it was good to feel in control again—Coco toweled off, blow-dried her hair, dabbed a little make-up on, then selected stretch denim leggings and knit tank top under a beaded tunic.

She was ready.

Kenny was searching the crowded lobby for Coco, hoping she would come, when his eyes fell upon a couple on the other side of the indoor waterfall, in a tight embrace, kissing.

We wouldn't be on the other side of the water, we would be under *it.*

The thought surprised him. Kenny usually tried not to fantasize because the fantasies sometimes became memories. But he couldn't help himself. He knew exactly how it would come about.

He's hiking through the redwoods outside San Francisco. Silence and purity all around him. He hears noises up ahead, rude laughter and gunned engines. Emerging through the trees, he sees in a clearing three tough bikers riding circles around a female hiker. She is swinging her walking staff at them, but it is only making them enjoy their taunting all the more.

Her sunhat has flown off, exposing a riot of burgundy curls. She is putting up a good fight but is no match for the bullies. Instantly unshouldering his backpack, Kenny charges at them. His black belt in karate comes in handy as he fights them off one by one, chopping, kicking, twirling to send them packing.

Then he turns to the woman, who is on her knees, nursing a scraped elbow.

"Let me help you," he says, and melts at the sight of her lush lips.

"How can I ever thank you?" she whispers as she holds onto him. She says her name is Coco and that she would have been dead if it hadn't been for his bravery.

They are both covered in dirt and leaves, and the day has grown hot. It is humid among the redwoods and ferns. Kenny knows of a place where they can wash off the grime.

The lagoon isn't far, but by the time they reach it, Coco is eager to get her clothes off and plunge into the water. She strips with no modesty and runs into the lagoon, her large breasts bouncing in a way that make him spring to attention. She turns and beckons, rosy nipples calling to him. Her waist is narrow, her hips wide and inviting. Earth mother. He likes how her eyes widen at the sight of his erection, how she keeps her eyes there as he walks toward her, slowly entering the water until he is in it waist-deep.

She holds out her arms, saying, "I have never before met such a strong, courageous man."

"It was nothing," he says as he pulls her to him, feels those luscious firm breasts against his bare chest. Under the water, his cock slides between her thighs and she responds with a wide-eyed grin.

"I've never seen such incredible martial arts moves," she says as she runs her hands over his muscular chest. She is breathing heavily. There is high color in her cheeks.

He slips his hands behind her, takes hold of her generous derriere, and yanks her to him. "I know a few other moves as well," he says.

She laughs and her kiss takes him by surprise, it is so hard and demanding, her tongue taking possession of his mouth. Her long red nails dig into his back, sharp and exciting. He feels like an animal, and she is fabulously wild in his arms.

She startles him by suddenly pulling free and plunging under the water, to take his erection into her mouth. It is a shock, to go from cold water to warm mouth, and maddeningly erotic. She comes up for air and he does some sucking himself. Her breasts are a feast and he could stay there all day.

But they swim to the waterfall where the icy droplets are stimulating on *their hot skin. Kenny gives her pleasure with his finger, and then slides himself in so that she pulls herself up and curls her legs around his thighs, buoyant in the water. She rides him in this wet world, screaming beneath the roaring falls, her breasts pillowing his face.*

"Hi there!"

Kenny snapped himself back to the entrance of the Java Club, where he had just finished his act, and saw Coco coming toward him. "I was hoping you would come," he said, flustered and red-faced, hoping she wasn't psychic enough to pick up the fantasy he had just been enjoying. "I'm a little embarrassed at how we parted earlier, when those two young women interrupted us."

"It's all right," she said, picking up interesting vibes from him, suddenly feeling inexplicably warm and tingly.

"It's the stage," he said, clearing his throat and stepping back from her as if he needed air. "There's something about performing that makes a person special. Do an act on a stage and women throw themselves at you. But work as a plumber and they say, 'Did you see the beak on that guy?'"

Coco laughed. But Kenny was wearing the tuxedo from his act and it made her think of her fantasy with the sequined costume so that her laughter was more to cover up her nervousness than from amusement. Could he tell by looking at her what she was thinking?

He took her elbow. "Let me buy you a drink."

They went to the bar in the lobby, opposite a pair of double doors with a sign that said WEDDING CHAPEL. When he saw how Coco stared, Kenny said, "If you arrange it in advance, they bring in a Justice of the Peace. There's a wedding going on right now, in fact."

Coco ordered a large Mai Tai and thought of how to begin. She didn't want him to think that this was a date, that their relationship was going any farther than this. She had come to explain.

"Kenny, do you *never* leave The Grove?" she asked, easing into the subject.

"Do you want to hear something pathetic?" he said, looking at her hair, eyes roaming the wild curls as if he wished he could go for a walk among them. "Three years ago, when I first came here, I arrived in my own car. I didn't leave for six months. By then I was losing weight and sticking to a program. I decided to take my day off in Palm Springs, take in a movie, do some shopping. Instead I went on a binge. Just like an alcoholic. I sat in my car and stuffed candy bars and donuts into my face. I was out of control. I came back and haven't been away since. My car sits there—I let other employees use it. Because I'm afraid of myself."

"But you can save yourself. You can leave, go to Switzerland, do something noble with your gift."

He laughed softly.

"Kenny, are you wise?" she said abruptly.

"What?"

"Do you consider yourself to be a wise man?"

"Why?"

"Because that's what my soulmate is, a wise man. That's what the crystal told me."

"Is this a joke?"

"I wish it were! I care for you, Kenny, more than I have cared for a man in a long time. But we don't have a future. I would know if we did! Listen," she said, speaking quickly now that she had begun. "I lived with a man once. We were engaged. We had plans, the house picked out, even babies' names, we were that serious. He was getting ready for a business trip. London. I was consulting my crystal when I saw the plane go down in the ocean. I begged him not to go. It was an important meeting. It meant a big promotion. But I was so scared, so hysterical, that he believed me and cancelled the trip."

Kenny waited. The chapel doors opened and music poured out.

"The plane didn't go down," Coco said urgently, raising her voice above Mendelssohn's *Wedding March*, "it made it to London. My fiancé lost the promotion and we broke up. Not because of the missed promotion but because he said he couldn't live with someone who was going to predict the future everyday and run their lives according to a chunk of crystal. I couldn't blame him. It took me a long time to get over him and after that I swore no more close relationships."

"So you're going to live alone for the rest of your life?" People started to come out of the chapel, carrying bags of confetti.

Coco shook her head. "I'm going to let the crystal decide for me."

"That crystal is a crutch, Coco, like sugar was for me."

"No," she said, getting to her feet, stepping away from the bar. The sound of applause filled the lobby as the bridal couple came out. "Kenny, I really connect with you, you set my skin on fire when you touch me, but you aren't the one!"

He jumped up. "Forget what the crystal says!"

"I can't! The man I am looking for is destined to stay with me forever. With you and me it will end someday. I can't bear any more endings."

"For God's sake, Coco, everything ends—relationships, life, even time itself. You can't stop living because of that!"

She started to turn away, Kenny reached for her, and in the next instant they were engulfed by the crowd pouring from the wedding chapel, people cheering and shouting congratulations and throwing confetti.

"Coco, please, let's talk about it."

She reached for him but was swept away by the happy mob. Kenny pushed after her, stretching his arm toward her, while Coco was carried backwards, startled and laughing at the same time.

When the crowd began to scatter, Coco freed herself, laughing breathlessly. Kenny reached her as the last of the revelers ran past. "I guess the happy couple," he started to say, and then a man brushed past Coco, knocking shoulders with her, hurrying on, and Coco snapped her head around, a shocked look on her face.

"What is it?" Kenny said.

"One of those people—That man—" She turned huge eyes to him. "That man is going to kill someone!"

"What!" He searched the crowd that had now mostly vanished into the evening air. "Which man?"

"I don't know. It happened so fast. But I *felt* it. I'm sure of it. He's planning a murder. Kenny, we have to tell someone!"

Five minutes later they were in the security office, Coco cradling a tumbler of whiskey as her teeth chattered in fear. "I have never felt anything so... horrible."

Abby was there, as well as the senior security staff, listening to the report in puzzlement. "Are you sure?" Elias Salazar said. "Maybe it was something you overheard or—"

"I *sensed* it. There were no words."

"Miss McCarthy is psychic," Abby said. "She works with the police." Her own face had blanched, the usual sunrise tones in her cheeks washed away from fear. She couldn't tell anyone about the news article and the words, "You're next." Had Coco bumped into the man who had slipped the envelope under her door?

"It was so *cold*," Coco said, while Kenny stood behind her, hands on her shoulders. "It was as if I had woken up in someone else's nightmare."

Salazar sat down and faced her, his voice solemn as he said, "You're sure it was murder on his mind? Maybe he was just angry and *wishing* he could kill someone?"

She shook her head and lifted the tumbler to her lips with both hands. The brandy was warm as it went down. "There was no anger, no emotion. Calculated. Like the brain of a pure killer."

"Do you have any idea who the target is?"

She shook her head again and was overtaken by a fit of shaking.

"Any little thing might help us. Did you get a sense of how he was going to commit the murder?"

"A gun, I think...yes, a gun."

Salazar looked at Kenny. "Did you see the man?"

"No, but I can give you descriptions of everyone who came out of the wedding chapel."

Salazar was familiar with Kenny's act. "I'll need to get hold of the wedding guest list."

"I'm not sure he came from the chapel," Coco said. She was exhausted. Psychic flashes sometimes drained her. "May I go back to my bungalow now?"

"Yes, of course," Abby said. "I'll have one of the guards escort you."

"That's all right," Kenny said. "I'll take Miss McCarthy back."

They made their way through the breezy evening, saying nothing, and when they reached her front door, Coco said, "I feel sick. When I sensed his thoughts, it was as though *I* wanted to commit murder."

She and Kenny stood beneath the lamp of her porch light, unaware of a shadow that moved in the bushes nearby, a man who had followed them and who now watched and listened—a man with a gun.

Coco's face was ghost-like, her eyes two dark hollows. And the way she trembled, Kenny thought she was not the same brash woman who had stood up during his performance and boldly said, "I'm next!"

"Hey," he murmured, drawing her to him, his arms tight around her. He felt her hands grip the fabric of his shirt, holding onto him for life. She shook in his arms like a frightened kitten. He was overcome. He hadn't meant to kiss her, not at such a vulnerable moment, but his body acted on its own. And Coco kissed him back, her lips moist and desperate against his, her arms curling around his neck to draw him down.

"I'm scared," she whispered.

Gently taking her face in his hands, he said, "Coco, I have a solution to our dilemma."

"A solution."

"Marry me," he said, unaware of the smile it brought to the lips of the man who watched in the shadows.

CHAPTER THIRTY-FIVE

BBY TYLER HAD OFFERED A TRIPLE FUDGE BROWNIE CAKE, warm from the oven, drenched in hot creamy fudge sauce and sweetened whipped cream. So by the time Sissy returned to her bungalow, she had decided to call Room Service and request one. Adding a bottle of Cristal to the order, she went into the bathroom and started hot water running into the tub.

Room service arrived and Sissy, salivating at the enormous rich cake drenched in hot sauce, decided to indulge later, to savor the feast to come.

Returning to the bathroom, where the tub was now full and steaming, she uncorked the champagne and set it on the marble. As she about to slip out of her peignoir and into the foamy bath, she heard a sound. Turning, she saw a stranger in the doorway. How had he managed to sneak in without making a sound?

She held her breath as she stared at him across the candle-lit chamber: he was tall and lean and wore a black pinstriped suit. He looked dark and dangerous.

"Who are you?"

"Special security," he said, his eyes moving lazily up and down her body, lingering at her breasts. "Management sent me to make sure you're okay." He undid the button of his suit jacket and Sissy glimpsed a gun in the waistband of his trousers. She gasped.

When he drew near she saw the dark irises surrounding black pupil; mink lashes to match thick black hair on his head. His neck was well muscled, shadowed by a sculpted jaw. She looked down at the gun and felt her heart race.

"A lady as beautiful as yourself," he said in a hard, authoritative voice, "should not be bathing alone. Anything could happen."

He reached out and drew aside the peignoir, exposing her breasts, a sensation so erotic that the breath caught in her throat. Picking up one of the fluted glasses of chilled champagne, he sipped first, then offered her a sip, and after she drank, he slowly tipped the glass to allow the rest of the cool wine to trickle onto her bare breasts, the sudden cold startling her, stimulating her.

He stepped back as, with dark eyes fixed on hers, he slowly undressed, first the jacket and shirt, leaving the gun dangerously exposed in his belt. Sissy couldn't take her eyes from it. She had never seen a gun in real life. When the shirt fluttered to the carpet and pooled there, he unbuckled his belt, and unzipped himself, catching the firearm before it fell. He held it for a moment, as if he were considering using it, then set it down. Finally he drew down his pants, stepped out of them as strong thighs rippled in the candlelight. He was already aroused, the sight of his erection causing her heart to skip a beat.

In one sweeping motion he slid an arm around her waist and pulled her to him; he pressed his mouth to hers as he pushed the peignoir from her shoulders, sending it to the carpet. His mouth tasted of expensive champagne. She wondered what the rest of him tasted like.

He scooped her up and carried her down into the steaming bath, kissing her, his tongue engaging hers. Lowering her into the hot water, so that it lapped over the sides of the tub and spilled onto the thick pink carpet, he eased her back against the sloping marble, bringing her legs up so that her knees were bent, and he knelt between them. He took one of her nipples into his mouth. She groaned. He released it and took the other. Her fingers dug deeply into the hard muscles of his back. She closed her eyes and imagined dangerous assignments—cops chasing killers down rain-slicked streets, long nights in dark smoky interrogation rooms.

She helped him with the condom, using her lips and tongue to unfurl it the length of his shaft. It was pink and tasted strawberry.

His hands on her waist, he thrust into her until the water churned and foamed, and steam rose in perfumed clouds. She flung her arms around him, curling her legs over his thighs to lock him deep inside her as she closed her eyes and delivered herself up to pure sensation and pleasure. The gun was so close. It terrified her and excited her. When she started to arch her back and release a yell, he allowed himself release, so that they shuddered together, feeling pleasure against pleasure, clutching each other, until she collapsed into the water, panting and amazed.

She said not a word as he quietly disengaged himself and, picking up his clothes and the pistol, left. Sissy closed her eyes as the steam swirled over her and grinned with satisfaction.

So *that* was what The Grove's fantasy lovers were all about.

As Pierre made his way back to the employees' dormitories, wishing he could stay in one of the guest suites but that was the price of being undercover, he whistled a tune and hoped the man who had hired him took his time ordering the hit. Pierre had done a lot of jobs for his boss, but never one that had been this pleasant.

At least now he knew who his mark was. Abby Tyler. When he saw the security guard outside her door, he laughed. That wasn't going to protect her. Pierre wondered what was in the envelope he had slipped under her door before his rendezvous with the lady in the bath. It must have been something important, because he saw her now, as he passed by her bungalow, silhouetted in a golden window, her face upturned to the stars. No doubt worrying about the message in the envelope, Pierre thought as he moved on.

CHAPTER THIRTY-SIX

A RE YOU SURE YOU'RE GOING TO BE OKAY?" ABBY SAID, worrying about Vanessa's decision to stay at The Grove.

It was because of the news article that had been slipped under Abby's door: *"You're next."* She had been found out. It was only a matter of time before the anonymous sender approached her with a demand for money, or an arrest warrant. Abby had had her old suitcase packed and ready to go for some time, and always it had been with the idea that when she left The Grove, Vanessa would remain in charge.

But now it was too dangerous for Vanessa. "The police know I escaped with a black girl," Abby said as she applied the last of the cover-up to the shadows beneath her eyes. She had not slept all night. "Everyone knows you and I have been friends for many years. It doesn't take rocket science. All they need is your fingerprints. And you can't prove you didn't drive that car in the liquor store hold-up where two people were killed. How can you prove you abandoned the car?" Abby put her hand on her friend's arm. "Please, Vanessa, for my sake. Get yourself to safety."

But Vanessa crossed her arms and tipped her chin. "I am not going anywhere. You created this resort and I'm not going to let strangers run it. Run it into the ground, most likely." Her tone gentled as she said, "But you shouldn't still be here. It's too dangerous, Abby. Go now while you can. I'll take care of things."

Abby shook her head. She still had to meet with Ophelia Kaplan. If Kaplan did not know she was adopted, Abby would say nothing. It would be enough to know that her daughter was living a good life, happy and surrounded by love. Then Abby would leave The Grove and not look back.

"All right, I'm going to see Ophelia now. Wish me luck." The two embraced.

Ophelia and David had alternately argued and made love through the night until, when dawn came, David fell into an exhausted sleep.

Ophelia had laid all her fears before him, argued for aborting the pregnancy, against aborting it, blamed herself, blamed him, blamed her ancestors. In the end, Ophelia was no closer to the answer of what to do about the pregnancy.

David's solution was to go straight to Ophelia's doctor and undergo an amniocentesis. If the baby was normal, then they would go ahead and have their child. "And if the test proves positive for Tay-Sachs?" she had cried.

David had resorted to a cliché. "We will cross that bridge when we come to it."

Now she stood over him, with dawn light spilling through the open window (she had discovered, thank God, that the Eiffel Tower view could be removed, like a shade), watching him sleep in the gaudy Marie Antoinette bed.

Last night, when she had found him on her threshold, Ophelia had been by turns relieved and outraged. "I knew something was bothering you," he had said. "Monday night, when you drove off like that. And you haven't returned my calls."

Ophelia had been unaware of the message light blinking on her phone. She blamed it on oversight, but knew that David read deeper meanings into it. She had wanted to tell him she was all right and send him away, but he stood there looking so handsome and in charge, a man with whom she could let down her defenses, and Abby Tyler *had* gone out of her way to make room for him on the evening flight out of LA—"She was surprisingly accommodating," he had said—that Ophelia had finally stepped aside and let him in.

He had taken the news of the pregnancy like a good Freudian analyst—calm, detached, asking her what she thought of it before offering an opinion of his own. If he was scared, he didn't show it. And if he held opinions as to how the pregnancy happened—surely she had to know that tetracycline interfered with oral contraception, Ophelia always read the inserts in medications—that it was a subconscious wish to get pregnant, he kept them to himself. And he didn't bring up the issue of why she had never gotten herself genetically tested, as everyone else in both their families had—which was how David knew he was a carrier—although he had once hinted that perhaps Ophelia didn't want to discover she was defective. None of this ever came out in so many words, but now as she stood over him, watching him sleep, with the memory of his touch still imprinted on her skin, she wondered if he was right about the fear of having a defect, and if he was right to think she had committed some sort of unconscious self-sabotage. But if so, why?

She had almost asked David about the white narcissus last night, how she had first picked up the scent in the garden, and then imagined it everywhere. But that would have been a whole new issue to lay at his feet. Right now, there was the pregnancy.

And what to do about it.

Ophelia calmly brushed her teeth, washed her face, and dressed in bleached jeans and a long-sleeved shirt. The desert was cold in the morning. Walking shoes, sunglasses and sun hat. She left him a note. "I have gone to think. Will be back soon."

Six hours later, she still had not returned.

"Abilene Tyler," Jack said into the phone to his friend at the police forensics lab. "I think she was born in Texas. Run a search on birth records. 1950's in Abilene and Tyler, Texas."

Jack hung up and, squinting at the morning sunshine in his walled garden, came to a decision.

He had invented various reasons for not being on his way back to LA once he had Abby's fingerprints. It all had to do with Nina, he kept telling himself. But it was time to face the truth. Tyler herself was the reason he was still here. She had a hold on him that he found increasingly difficult to break.

It was time to make that break. Whatever his friend in forensics uncovered, Jack would address it back at the police station in LA. Where he could be in control of his emotions again.

Holstering his gun and slipping into his leather jacket, he set off in search of Abby Tyler.

Her mind was on Ophelia as she hurried along the path and nearly collided with Jack as she rounded the corner at the aviary.

"Detective!" she said. Jack had also been on her mind. The pain he was in, and wishing she could help him.

"I'm glad I found you," he said. "I just learned that I'm needed back at the station, so I will be checking out."

"But you're booked here until Saturday," she said, thinking that after Saturday she might never see him again.

He avoided her eyes. "Can't be helped. I'd appreciate it if you could arrange for me to have the first available seat on a flight out."

David was frantic with worry. Where was Ophelia?

Scribbling a quick note in case she came back while he was gone, he struck off in search of someone in charge. A staff member escorted him to Abby Tyler, who was by the aviary, talking to a man in a leather jacket.

"Dr. Messer," she said in surprise.

"I'm worried, Ms. Tyler. I think something has happened to my fiancée. Ophelia left early this morning to go for a walk and she hasn't come back. It's just not like her to do that."

Abby masked her sudden alarm. Zeb had reported unusual coyote activity in the past few days. Several females had given birth recently and the males were aggressively searching for food. "I'm sure she'll be all right. The trails around the resort are very safe and clearly marked."

"You don't understand. She's pregnant."

Abby retrieved a small walkie-talkie from her pocket and paged Vanessa. "Get Zeb and the security staff. Have them go out in all the vehicles they can round up." She turned to Jack, her face white, her voice trembling. "I will see about that plane reservation as soon as I can, Detective."

"Put it on hold," he said. "I'm joining the search party."

CHAPTER THIRTY-SEVEN

*S*ISSY WOKE UP SMILING AND STRETCHING. SHE HAD NEVER felt so good.

Last night, after her dinner with Abby Tyler, Sissy had returned to her bungalow to order two special desserts: one involved cake, the other "Special Security" and a gun. And now she woke on this sun-filled Thursday morning thinking of the coming evening, and something special that she would like to try. One of the fantasy rooms perhaps.

But first she had to take care of something.

She was calm as she dialed the number. The person at the other end picked up after the first ring. "Linda Delgado."

"Ms. Delgado, this is Sissy Whitboro. Ed's wife." She paused to let it sink in. "I know Ed has been seeing you."

A slight hesitation. "Yes."

"Well, I just wanted you to know that you can have him. I'm getting a divorce." Sissy hung up and felt a mixture of sadness and relief. She still loved Ed—you don't just cast off fifteen years of love and marriage and children and shared memories. But this was a new morning, and she was a new Sissy.

The phone rang almost immediately. It was Ed. "Linda just called me. Oh God, Sissy, how did you find out?"

"The secret bank statements, the credit card charges, the hotel receipts. Did you think I would never find out?" She was disgusted.

"Oh God…"

"Just answer me this, Ed. Did you have an affair?"

"Sissy—"

"Be honest with me. Yes or no."

"Yes…I did…"

She swallowed painfully. "Then there is nothing more to talk about. Not now. Not on the phone. After I get home."

"Sissy, wait—"

The phone rang throughout the day but Sissy wasn't there. She was at the Village, shopping with Ed's secret credit card.

CHAPTER THIRTY-EIGHT

WHERE ON EARTH *WAS* SHE?

A fast walker, embroiled in her thoughts, Ophelia discovered she had strayed far from The Grove. In fact, she could no longer see it. And with the sun directly overhead, she had no idea which way was north, south, east or west.

Deciding to take a rest, she sat among an unusual grouping of boulders and opened her water bottle. Once the sun headed toward the horizon, she could get a fix on her location and head back to the resort.

She was surprised to find herself sexually aroused. Maybe it was the pregnancy hormones, or the desert. The wind was old, as if she had walked back in time. She imagined the Native Americans, a thousand years ago, making their dramatic trek westward in search of water and farm lands— the Anasazi who seemed to have vanished mysteriously. But did they really? She closed her eyes and lifted her face to the sky. Her body cried out for its blessing. Setting down her pack and water bottle, she unbuttoned her shirt and slipped it off her shoulders.

The wind's breath was erotic. It made her think of David, his finger-tips lightly dancing over her skin. Her breasts ached. Removing her bra, she closed her eyes and let the sun and desert breeze envelope her in an ancient embrace. She suddenly wanted to be naked. To run free among the dunes and feel the shadow of the red-tailed hawk glide over her skin. She wished her hair were long, to brush her bare back in teasing caresses. Imagining it were so, she stood up, bent her head back, closed her eyes, and held her arms out cruciform, to open herself to the spirits and the earth's sexual energy.

David materializes before her—a different David, resurrected from the primal past, copper-skinned, long-haired, clad in buckskin loincloth. This warrior knows nothing of pinstriped suits and analysts' couches. He is tied to the land, in tune with the rhythms of nature. His needs are basic and raw: to hunt and to mate.

The spear he carries is bloody at the tip. He is panting as if he has run a great distance. He immobilizes Ophelia with his intense, hungry gaze.

Yes…

The smell of his sweat, pungent and strong, fills her nostrils. And another scent—animal. She has never felt so wild.

The loincloth comes away with a tug and she sees what a magnificent male he is. She will show him how much woman she is. She brings him down to the hot earth and presses him onto his back. Removing her own buckskin skirt, she straddles him, watching his face as she lowers herself onto his erection. He moans with pleasure. Her thighs are strong, she can ride him forever.

But before he releases, he lifts her off and takes command.

He puts a hand on her abdomen as he worships the magic within. They have created life. They are close to the gods. The warrior gives her pleasure in a gentle way that surprises her. This was not the vigorous coupling that had conceived the child; now he is tender and mindful of her condition.

While he is moving in a forceful rhythm, he reaches down and touches her magical place and brings her to orgasm, then finishes himself and they both laugh and embrace and thank the gods for the sun and the sky.

Ophelia opened her eyes and squinted at the ochre wilderness dotted with boulders, cacti and Joshua trees. Filled with her deep love for David, for the man who was her partner and equal, but who was also her warrior and champion, she understood how basic and simple all of life was. She had allowed herself to become caught up in a race that she did not want to run. Now she knew why she had come to The Grove. Because the answers, all along, were here.

Reaching for her shirt, she scanned the horizon. How far was she from the resort? There were no telephone poles or roads, no signs pointing the way. To get a better lay of the land, she started to climb up the boulder, but her foot slipped. She lost her grip and tumbled headlong between the big rocks that were older than time.

CHAPTER THIRTY-NINE

*T*HREE HOURS LATER THE SEARCH PARTY HAD COME UP WITH nothing. Ophelia was nowhere to be found.

Kenny knew about the missing guest and wanted to join the search, but he was worried about Coco. The night before…her brief foray into the mind of a cold-blooded murderer. She had looked so wretched when he left her that he had spent a sleepless night in worry.

The man who had followed them from the security office—an armed security guard who had waited politely until Kenny had said good night—was no longer stationed outside her door. And now she wasn't answering her doorbell.

Where was she?

Last night, on this same step, he had asked her to marry him. First she had looked shocked and said, "You're crazy." Then she had frowned and said, "You're serious." The she had just said good night, assured him she would be all right, that she wanted to be alone, and had left it at that.

But Kenny couldn't leave it.

Pushing through dense shrubs that embraced the small dwelling, he found a window with the drapes parted, and peered in to see Coco emerging from the bathroom wearing a terry cloth robe, her hair wet from the shower.

Continuing around the side of the house, he found the garden gate unlocked. As he quietly went through, he broke out in a sweat. Part of him wanted to turn back, but the greater part made him press on. He was about to make one of the biggest decisions of his life.

The last time he had left The Grove, he had gone on a sugar binge and nearly gone over the edge himself. He had not left in the two and a half years since and was terrified to do so now. But Coco needed his help.

He tapped at the glass door, startling her. There were shadows under her eyes but she smiled as she drew the door open and said, "Kenny! How unconventional of you."

He put his hands on her arms and searched her face. "How do you feel?"

"I didn't sleep. And then I went for a walk. That man is still here, I can feel it." She looked up into his eyes so full of concern. Last night he had asked her to marry him. He had called it a solution, but Coco knew that marriage would only make matters worse, locking them into a relationship they would both eventually want to get out of.

"I came to talk to you about my proposal."

"I can't think straight."

"Then let's get out of here. I still have my car."

She stared at him. "You'd do that for me? Leave The Grove?" But she looked uncertain. And when she glanced at the crystal orb, sitting on its wooden stand, Kenny said, "Make this your own decision, Coco. Look, just Palm Springs. How's that? There and back." And already he was thinking of the donut shop on Palm Canyon Drive, and the Baskin Robbins ice cream parlor on Mecca Avenue, and the drug store with its huge candy counter. And they terrified him.

Twenty minutes later they were on the road, passing two of the resort's vehicles that were out searching for Ophelia Kaplan. The sun soon set and night fell over the desert. Coco and Kenny said little, she thinking of her scare the night before and wishing she could find a cure for her psychic curse, he feeling his heart race as he left his haven. Kenny turned on the car heater and tuned the radio to an FM station that played soft melodies. Coco's head fell back and soon she was asleep.

"Wake up, Coco." A soft voice, a gentle hand on her shoulder.

She opened her eyes and was confused for the moment. Where was she? Then she realized she was sitting in a car. But it wasn't moving. And Kenny didn't have his hands on the wheel but was turned sideways in his seat, gently shaking her awake.

"What happened?" she said, stretching. "Are we in Palm Springs?" But then she heard a strange roar and smelled something odd. She sat up. "Where are we?" She peered through the window. She blinked at the moonlit beach, the breakers crashing on the shore, and, beyond, the Pacific Ocean stretching away to the starry horizon.

"Unless California finally had the Big One and Palm springs is now beach front property, we are not where you said we were going."

"We're in Malibu."

"You brought me here on purpose?"

"I kidnapped you."

"Why?"

"Because you need to break from your dependence on that crystal, Coco. This was the only way I could think of doing it."

"Take me back."

"I only have enough gas to go another ten miles. And that gas station is closed for the night."

Now she saw the scenery to her left, through Kenny's window. Palisade cliffs, a gas station and convenience store, and a small highway motel.

"We're in luck," Kenny said. "We got the last vacancy."

The cabin was small and rustic, but clean, and the bathroom was surprisingly polished and shiny with little soaps in new wrappers. There was only one bed, and it wasn't king-sized.

Coco stood in the center of the tiny room with her hands on her hips. Outside, there was only the silence of the night and the whisper of the ocean. And Kenny sitting on the edge of the bed, looking sheepish. "I'll give you a Hershey bar if you take me back," Coco said.

He smiled. "I see you haven't lost your sense of humor."

"Who's joking?"

Their eyes met. The moment stretched. The salty perfume of the sea invaded the room, filled their heads. And the rhythmic throb of the surf...

They reached each other in two strides, lips meeting, fitting, tasting perfect. Arms encircling, drawing tight. Coco's finger's feasted on gold-tipped surfer-blond hair while Kenny's discovered firm breasts with hard nipples. The lovemaking was urgent because they were starved and because they knew they had a lifetime to engage in more leisurely intimacy. Hot tears streamed down Coco's cheeks and into their joined mouths as she thought in joy that this was the man she was going to spend the rest of her life with, and Kenny cried, too, because this was the first of many wonderful memories that were going to fill his mind from now on down through the years.

Later, as they lay contented in each other's arms, Coco said, "Maybe soulmates aren't all what they're cracked up to be. Maybe we don't *find* them, maybe we create them."

"Want to hear something funny?" He got out of bed and Coco watched his naked back as he went to where his pants were draped over a chair. He was slender and not muscle-bound. He told her that as a kid he had dreamed of becoming a karate champion but had never even made it to "pink belt," he was that uncoordinated. But never had she seen more perfectly sculpted buttocks. They still bore the red imprints of her fingers where she had dug in and held onto him as he had thrust into her. Just thinking about it made her arousal spark anew.

Then Kenny came back to the bed and Coco's eyes were riveted to his heavenly cock that, unlike the rest of him, had not lost weight while at The Grove. Kenny was well endowed and that had come as a delightful surprise.

She saw that he had brought back his wallet. "Remember last night when you told me you were looking for a wise man? You asked me if I thought *I* was a wise man? And I asked you if that was a joke?" He handed her the wallet, opened to his driver's license.

Her eyes widened and her jaw fell. "Oh my God," she whispered. "Kenny *Wiseman*? But why didn't you tell me?"

"Because I wanted your decision to be with me to come from your heart, to come from within yourself, not because the crystal told you to."

She put her arms around his neck to draw him down and kiss him passionately. "Kenny Wiseman," she said, filling her mouth with his name. "You thought you were a coward, hiding out at The Grove, afraid to go back into the world, afraid you would return to the sugar addiction. But you aren't a coward. You did a brave thing, taking me away from my insanity, bringing me back into the real world. Leading me to where I belong, right here with you. Kenny, I want to take you home to meet my family. I just know they will adore you." And he would never be an orphan again.

"Let's go to Switzerland," she said. "Let them study you and find a cure for Alzheimer's."

"It's a big decision," he said and she knew what he meant.

Looking back at her sexual encounters at The Grove, she saw that they weren't bad, she had chemistry with them, and in fact any one could have blossomed into a relationship. Yet she had found fault with each. Was it on purpose, because deep down inside she really wanted Kenny? "I don't have to consult Daisy or any crystal," she said. "I know what I want to do. I want to go to Switzerland with you."

"Would you be happy there? Without your police work, what would you do?"

She grinned as she reached for him. "Maybe the Swiss police can use a good psychic."

CHAPTER FORTY

*T*HEY CALLED IT JUICE. JUICE WAS POWER, MONEY, SOCIAL standing and clout. Juice was how things worked in Vegas, how one succeeded, survived. Gregory Simonian once had juice.

Years ago—before the newspaper editor's wife kissed his cock, before being called a "gangster" in the man's paper, before marrying Gayane Simonian—Fallon was unmarried and in the Wagon Wheel casino playing blackjack. He was winning big and the pit bosses figured he was counting cards so they reported it to Simonian who had him thrown out. Fallon had laughed it off but had secretly plotted revenge.

Marry Simonian's daughter and take over the casino.

Tonight, as Michael Fallon went to the gold and marble bar that filled an entire wall of his penthouse living room and poured himself a scotch, he smiled as he remembered the day, long ago, when he had been thrown out of the Wagon Wheel by Gregory Simonian. "Fuckin' Albanian," Michael had said on the sidewalk. He was twenty-two years old and his pride had been hurt.

"I think he's Armenian," said his best friend Uri, who was with him.

Albanian, Armenian. Simonian was a dead man.

But then Michael caught a gander at Simonian's daughter and had a better idea.

Simonian had thought his daughter was safely hidden at the Barrington Academy for Young Ladies. Maybe from ordinary men, but not from Michael Fallon. His dossier on the girl included photos, hobbies, friends, and a list of all her likes and dislikes. Not too bad looking either. Seducing her had been a piece of cake. Spotting her at her favorite hangout in town, flirting with his eyes, then with his body. Michael had always had a way with the ladies, charming them, treating them well and being generous afterward. He had thought of getting Gayane pregnant and forcing Simonian to insist on a shotgun wedding but decided instead to try the respectable approach, it might come in handy someday.

Michael had not only expected Simonian to fight the relationship, he had *counted* on it. Fallon knew one thing about females: deny a woman what she wants and she will want it all the more. Gayane had threatened to get married without her father's blessing—this was, after all, Nevada—and Simonian, caught between the proverbial rock and a hard place, decided that it was better to keep his daughter's favor and at the same time keep an eye on the bastard Fallon by giving him a job in the casino.

On his wedding night Michael made gentle love to Gayane, not out of tenderness or affection but so that she wouldn't have an excuse to go crying to her father that her marriage was a failure. The loveless union didn't bother him because it was just a stepping stone to his true ambition: owning the Wagon Wheel.

And then love blindsided him, hitting him square between the eyes when he wasn't expecting it. He completely forgot Gayane, lying dead on the bloody sheets, as his attention was suddenly focused on the baby in his arms.

Francesca, for whom he would kill.

Had killed.

And Fallon intended, after Francesca's wedding on Saturday, to keep a close eye on Stephen, making sure he was keeping Francesca happy. Making dead sure…

They had made love on satin sheets the color of peaches and sunsets, and now Francesca lay awake, wondering about her future.

Stephen was a fabulous lover, considerate, taking his time, making sure she was satisfied. Afterwards, she always loved watching him as he slept. But tonight was different. With the wedding only a day away, Francesca continued to be conflicted. *Am I really doing this to please Daddy?*

Francesca and her father were so close, and had been for so many years, that she often didn't know where her own identity ended and his began. In retrospect, many things that she had thought were her wishes turned out to be her father's. Francesca had never had a burning desire to go to business school. But she had gone as her father wished and convinced herself it was a dream come true.

And now the wedding.

She loved Stephen. She wanted to be with him. But her feelings for him were so inextricably tangled with her feelings for her father that she wasn't sure of her own motives anymore. Francesca had hoped that the closer she got to the day of the wedding, the more certain she would be that she was doing the right thing. But here it was Thursday and the wedding was day after tomorrow and the only certainty that had grown in her was that she was not doing this for herself but for her father.

"I owe it to him," she had told her shrink. "Daddy so badly wants to be accepted into the Vandenbergs' circle."

"So you will sacrifice your life for him?" Dr. Friedman had asked.

Her father didn't know she was seeing a therapist. He would hit the roof if he found out. But going to Father Sebastian for counseling hadn't helped. "Marriage is more than just physical love," the priest had said—a man who had never been married.

"I took my mother from him," Francesca told Dr. Friedman. "She died giving birth to me. I owe him something in return."

Slipping out of bed so not to wake Stephen, Francesca walked softly across the thick carpet to the dresser where her mother's photo stood. Gayane Simonian at twenty-one. Hauntingly beautiful. Dead at a young age because of the child within her. "I had to choose," Francesca's father had told her, "the doctor said there was internal bleeding that he couldn't stop unless he took the child out. He could save Gayane, but the baby would be sacrificed. Or he could save the child and Gayane would be sacrificed."

When Francesca was fifteen she ran away. She had seen the pile of new toys in the corner of his office, for her upcoming birthday—dolls and tea sets, even a rocking horse. He was so involved in his casino and getting rich that he hadn't noticed that Francesca was growing up. And so she had told herself she ran away because her father didn't care and wouldn't notice. But that wasn't it. It had taken Francesca a long time to come to terms with the guilt she had carried within her since she was old enough to know her mother had died giving birth to her. When his men brought her back to Vegas, Fallon had not punished her, had only asked *why*. He gave her everything. Francesca had never needed for anything in her life. She was his princess. That was when she had broken down and sobbed that she didn't want to live with her mother's death on her head.

She would never forget the shocked look on his face when she shouted at him: "You ignore me! It's because I remind you of Mama."

He had stammered, "I don't ignore you, Francesca. I love you. Don't I give you everything you want?"

"Things!" she had cried. "You surround me with strangers and give me things! I never see you. And I know why. You think I killed Mama!"

He had pulled her into his arms and they had cried together, and then everything changed. No more bodyguards and chaperones. No more tutors and strict hours and rules. No more sitting in the penthouse with strangers while her father was downstairs running the casino. They became close after that, father and daughter doing things together, going places. He took her on a cruise around the world and then a three-month tour of Italy where she learned about her roots. He assured her over and over that she was not responsible for her mother's death. That it was in God's hands, that sometimes nature worked that way and it wasn't up to us to question.

Francesca had accepted it, but sometimes, late at night, such as this night, she would stand on her balcony and look over the sea of colored lights, look beyond them to the black and silent desert and wonder...

"Honey?"

She turned. Stephen was sitting up in bed, his hair tousled in a boyish way, his eyes dreamy.

"Go back to sleep," she said softly, and pushed away a memory that had a habit of surfacing at moments like this. Erik. The skydiver she had loved so desperately and deeply six years ago. She had thought she would never get over his death. And for a long time she had been consumed with the idea of seeking revenge. Erik had been careful about packing his own parachute, someone had deliberately cut the strings. But who? Speculation was that it was a competitor, or an old rival from his past. After a while, Francesca saw the futility in avenging Erik's death and in the end, she accepted that there was no evidence that he had not simply been sloppy with his chute and it was just one of those unfortunate accidents in a risky sport.

Stephen did not go out for sports. He was a cerebral man. And she loved him. But did she love him enough? she wondered again as the lights of Las Vegas flashed behind her. How did you know when you wanted to spend the rest of your life with someone? Her father had said he fell in love with Gayane at first sight. He hadn't even known who she was, hadn't known that she was Gregory Simonian's daughter. And when he found out he had been afraid Gayane's father would not approve. But Simonian had welcomed Michael Fallon with open arms. Francesca wished she could have been there to see it, to know her mother and grandfather. She always loved it when her father told her stories of those days, and what a shock it had been when Gregory was killed in the freak helicopter accident, how it had devastated her father and it had taken him months to recover.

That was when he had built the Atlantis. "I was grieving so hard over your grandfather's death that I plunged into my work. It was what saved me. That, and you."

In all her life, Francesca and her father had clashed on only one issue: flying.

The first time she rode in his private jet, in the cockpit because she was the boss's daughter, Francesca had fallen in love with the freedom of the sky. She was too young at the time to know that her new passion for flying stemmed from the constricted life she lived, a life of constant vigilance from an over-protective father who worried every minute of his life that his daughter might get kidnapped. While other little girls collected dolls, Francesca collected model airplanes. She glued them together and hung them from her bedroom ceiling. Mike Fallon periodically took them down, saying little girls shouldn't be doing such things. But no matter how many frilly toys, dollhouses, plastic babies and teddy bears he gave her, Francesca secretly smuggled airplane kits into her room and glued together tiny Beechcraft Bonanzas and little Grumman Wildcats.

But her true desire had been to fly an airplane of her own.

She got her way when she was fifteen and had terrified her father when she ran away. He promised her flying lessons as soon as she turned sixteen, and for her eighteenth birthday he gave her her own Piper Cub. After that, during college and law school years, Francesca filled her spare time with logging hours in the air. It was the only time she felt truly free and at peace.

"I can't sleep," she said to Stephen.

He got out of bed, handsomely naked, and came to her, slipping his arms around her waist. "It's just pre-wedding jitters."

She closed her eyes and pressed her face to his chest so he wouldn't see her tears.

"You're trembling."

"I'm cold." *I'm frightened.*

Had she agreed to marry Stephen because he had said that children were not a priority for him? That he didn't mind if they never had children, since their two careers came first? Had he spoken words that her terrified mind needed to hear? Because Francesca's secret fear was that what happened to her mother might happen to her. The thought of having children made her heart stop, even though a doctor had told her she was perfectly healthy. Hadn't Gayane been perfectly healthy, too?

"Stephen" she said impulsively. "Let's elope."

"What?"

"Let's go away, right now, to Mexico, or Canada. Let's find a parson in a small town no one has heard of and let it just be you and me." As she spoke, the words tumbling from her mouth, surprising even her, Francesca saw a whole new life for the two of them, living in a mountain community with a small business practice that left time for flying and traveling…

He drew her to him and held her tight. "And what would your father say?" he asked with a soft laugh.

And just like that, her dream vanished.

CHAPTER FORTY-ONE

I DON'T LIKE THIS WIND," ZEB SAID AS HE GRIPPED THE steering wheel. The wind, moaning and buffeting the SUV, had an ominous feel to it. If it should develop into a sandstorm, they would never find Ophelia Kaplan.

Vanessa was frantic with worry. Ophelia had been missing for hours. It was late. Night had fallen, casting the desert in darkness, and now the Santa Anas were sweeping down from the northeast, threatening to engulf the region in clouds of sand.

On top of that, they had heard coyotes barking. Not the yelping that sounded like little girls laughing, or the howling that was almost musical. But the sharp, threatening bark of coyotes protecting their dens. Abby had ordered everyone to carry guns, just in case.

Why had Ophelia left the resort? Her fiancé had said she was facing an important decision and had gone for a walk to clear her mind. Vanessa had noticed Dr. Kaplan's distracted manner since her arrival at the resort. Did it have something to do with the pregnancy?

Vanessa's worry was mixed with excitement and hope. Not only had Abby found her child at last, but now there was the prospect of a grand-child! She wished there could be a real reunion, with Abby publicly claim-ing her daughter as her own. Unfortunately, if Ophelia didn't know she was adopted, and if she was happy, Abby had no intention of revealing the truth. Besides, Abby's future was laid out for her, in the packed suitcase and one-way airline ticket, plans that did not include a daughter. Or anyone else.

Vanessa had seen how Abby looked at Jack Burns, how her cheeks flushed pink when she saw him. After years of denying herself the love of a man, here it was, practically dropping into her lap. Too late.

Vanessa looked at Zeb, his profile tight as he scanned the dark desert for signs of Ophelia. He had been uncharacteristically quiet all day. Worry-ing about the lost guest? Or was it something else? Last night, when he had brought the last of the desert safari groups back to the resort, instead of un-winding over a drink as he always did, Zeb had offered Vanessa a cool "good night" and retired to his quarters. Did something happen while he was out with the guests? She wanted to ask, but she had never invaded his privacy before and she wasn't about to start now.

"What's that?" Zeb said suddenly, pointing ahead.

Vanessa squinted through the blowing sand. A flicker of light!

Zeb turned the steering wheel and headed toward the frail beacon. As they neared, the headlights illuminated a cluster of boulders. "There!" Van-essa said. "Isn't that a person?"

Zeb brought the vehicle to a jolting stop and was out and running be-fore Vanessa even opened her door.

"Thank God," Ophelia said weakly. "I saw your headlights…" She was shining a pen light on a key chain. Her clothes were dirty, her hair and face a mess. "I slipped and couldn't get free. I thought I was going to die out here."

Zeb was immediately on his knees, inspecting Ophelia's foot pinned be-tween the rocks. The wind whipped around them, churning up the sand, fill-ing their eyes with grit. While Zeb levered the boulders apart with a crowbar from the SUV, Vanessa was on the walkie-talkie, informing security at the resort, and the search parties, that they had found Ophelia and were bringing her in. "She's injured," she said against the howling wind. "Inform the nurse."

Zeb drove at top speed back to the resort where Abby and David met them. Ophelia was transferred into a guest cart and spirited away, with Zeb and Vanessa following.

Abby sat anxiously at Ophelia's side, not wanting to leave. In her lap was a letter, written long ago. It was addressed to her daughter, and it spoke of love and devotion and promises. Abby had expected to read it to Coco, and then to Sissy. Now she knew it was meant for Ophelia.

But the nurse was saying, "I need to tend to her, Ms. Tyler. I'll send for you when you can see her."

Abby hesitated. After all these years, all her searching and sleepless nights—to be sent away now? She looked at the letter, the envelope yellowed with age, and another person came into her mind, someone in pain like herself, who needed healing.

Leaving David to sit with Ophelia, Abby struck off in the direction of Jack Burns' quarters while Vanessa and Zeb, leaving the main building and stepping into the windy night, paused to look up at the treetops being whipped about.

"I don't like the look of that," Zeb said. "We might be in for a blow. I'd better button down the aviary."

"I'll help," Vanessa said.

The aviary was a beehive-shaped structure built of wire and mesh to give the feel of being outdoors. It had been equipped with a tarpaulin that could be lowered in case of sandstorms or other inclement weather, to protect the birds. But when Zeb threw the switch, nothing happened. The mechanism was stuck.

"I'll call maintenance," Vanessa said.

But Zeb stopped her. "There isn't time," he shouted, squinting at the top of the cage where exotic birds flew frantically in the wind, batting their wings against the mesh. "They're frightened. They'll hurt themselves."

He surveyed the structure and knew it was dangerous to climb in this wind, but the cover could only be released manually. "I'm going up!" he said, and Vanessa watched with her heart in her throat as Zeb scaled the enormous cage. He clung like a fly, scaling inch by inch as the birds shrieked and flapped their wings. Each time his foot slipped or he lost his grip, Vanessa pressed to her hands to her mouth in terror.

It seemed to take forever, as the wind increased and Vanessa had to crane her neck to see, Zeb lost in the overhead darkness, the birds creating an unearthly cacophony that blended with the howling wind. And then suddenly: a loud crack and a rushing sound.

Vanessa jumped back as the tarpaulin come rolling down. Inside the aviary, the birds grew quiet.

Finally, Zeb was back, jumping to the ground.

Vanessa rushed to him. "Are you all right?"

He laughed. "I'll live."

She was so flooded with relief that she impulsively threw her arms around him. "You are a hero!" And her mouth was on his before she even knew what she was doing.

Zeb held her to him. It had been a long time since he felt like a hero. It was a good feeling.

And then he drew back, suddenly serious. "Vanessa, there is something I have to tell you."

The thing that she knew had been on his mind all day. And he was so solemn now that she didn't want to hear it. But she remained silent and let him speak.

"I'm leaving The Grove. I'll be giving my notice tomorrow."

Her emotions plummeted. She stepped back. "Where are you going? Back to Africa?"

He shook his head. "I can never go back there."

She waited. The night wind whipped around them, tugging at clothing and Vanessa's long hair. Massive ferns and fronds thrashed together until it seemed as if even the stars might be blown from the sky. Zeb took Vanessa's hand and drew her into the protection of a stone wall, standing close to her, his voice filled with passion as he said, "I want you to know something about me, something I have never told anyone." His face was close to hers as he spoke. "After hunting was outlawed in Kenya, I became a tour guide, leading photographic safaris. But when I saw the atrocities that were being committed by poachers, the utter disregard for the endangerment of animals, I became outspoken against the government and their hunting policies. I was reckless. Friends warned me to shut up but I couldn't, I was so angry. When

I received anonymous threats on my life, I didn't stop to think. Vanessa, I was married. When my wife was killed suddenly and unexpectedly in a car accident, I became bitter and left. I can't go back."

She wanted to weep for him, and to comfort him and take away his pain. "Are you so sure? You left twenty years ago."

Zeb looked up at the tree tops thrashing against the black sky. Windy up there, but not down here in the protected windbreak of the oasis.

He looked at Vanessa. Raised a hand to her hair, and then to her cheek. "My wife kept warning me to keep my mouth shut, that the walls had ears. I wouldn't listen. I didn't think the secret police would go after *her*."

"I am so sorry," she said.

"Now you know why I can't go back. You understand, don't you?"

"I know about murder and I know about police." And then it all came out in a rush, as if the words had been building up for twelve months, crowding behind her lips, waiting for the moment to make their bid for freedom: the pimp who knocked her teeth out, Vanessa cracking his skull with a baseball bat, the conviction and life-sentence, the year at White Hills Prison, the fire and the escape. She left out the girl named Emmy Lou who became Abby Tyler because that was Abby's story and none of Zeb's business, but she wanted him to know the truth about her, and if he turned away because of it, then that was that. But he didn't, he listened in amazement and she barely had the last words out, "I've been on the FBI's wanted list ever since," when he was kissing her hard on the mouth.

She kissed him back, pulling him to her in a desperate embrace. For thirty-three years she had been alone. Except for Abby, Vanessa had no one. Once, she had gone back to her home town in Texas to learn that her mother had passed away, her sisters had all married and moved to other cities. There was nothing there for her anymore, nothing left of Mercy. So she had closed that chapter in her life and never looked back.

But now, in this man's arms, tasting his kiss, feeling herself catch on fire, Vanessa knew that a new chapter was opening up.

"My God," he murmured, looking at her, filling his eyes with the sight of her. "My God…"

"Zeb, your wife's death. Are you so sure the secret police did it?"

"What do you mean?"

"You said it was a car accident."

"But they arranged it."

"How do you know?"

He blinked. He opened his mouth and closed it. And then something occurred to him for the first time in his life: that he *didn't* know for sure what had caused the car to crash.

"It could have just been a coincidence," Vanessa said in her gentle, wise way. "Sometimes we think the universe revolves around *us*, that the whole world is talking about *us* and is concerned solely with what *we* are thinking and doing. In reality, the world doesn't give a damn because it is too busy worrying about itself. Sometimes," she said solemnly, "a car accident is simply a car accident."

Relief overwhelmed him—the thought that maybe Miriam's death wasn't his fault, the washing away of the guilt he had carried for so long. Not all at once, but it was a beginning.

The wind picked up, catching them in a small whirlwind. He took Vanessa by the hand, and they ran through the thrashing greenery until they reached his quarters, a small suite behind the business offices.

It was Vanessa's first time in Zeb's room and it came as a surprise. She had expected an East African theme with drums and animal trophies. Instead she found one wall fitted with shelves stocked with paperback mysteries and science fiction novels, and another covered in framed baseball cards, autographed posters, a catcher's glove in a case, and, on a special stand under a spotlight, a baseball with a single signature on it. "That," Zeb said with pride, "is an Official National League baseball autographed by Hall of Famer Sandy Koufax, 1959 and 1963 World Champion, three-time no-hitter, perfect-game pitcher. The crown of my collection," he said as he looked deep into her eyes. "And I would give it up in a minute to spend this night with you."

They kissed again, more tenderly, with no fierce wind whipping about them just gentle light and the faint sound of music coming from his stereo. They kissed as they explored each other's bodies, relishing the contrasts of white on dark, hard on soft, their opposites being such an erotic turn-on that they didn't make it to the bedroom.

Zeb pressed his face between her large brown breasts and felt the pain in his heart begin to dissolve. This woman was not Miriam, she was not Africa, she was herself, Vanessa—solid, warm, and compassionate. And when Vanessa opened herself to him she opened herself to Africa, because he made love to her with more than his body, but with his voice, in an accent that made her think of endless blue skies and snow-capped mountains embracing a dark-raced people who had lived on the red soil of Kenya since before the beginning of time. His mouth, imprinting kisses on her body, was stamping her with a new identity. He murmured endearments in Swahili. She closed her eyes and they were making love on Mt. Kilimanjaro.

"I've been wanting to do this since the night we met," he said afterward, as they lay in each other's arms.

"You are one slow white man."

"And you are one beautiful black woman." He looked into her eyes, almond shaped, slanted, exotic, and marveled at this gorgeous creature who had brought him back from a fatal brink, made him feel like a man again.

And made him think of lion-colored savannahs beneath the equatorial sun, thorn trees and vast grazing herds, snow-capped Kilimanjaro in the distance, and at his side, this incredible woman, leading him home.

CHAPTER FORTY-TWO

$\mathcal{W}$ HILE VANESSA AND ZEB WENT OFF TO TAKE CARE OF THE caviary, and guests sought shelter from the wind, and staff covered the swimming pools, anchored furniture, closed up the outdoor bars, Abby hurried toward Sierra Nevada Cottage.

She hadn't wanted to leave Ophelia, but Ophelia was suffering from exhaustion and dehydration, and had injured her foot. The nurse had promised to call Abby when Ophelia was well enough for a visit.

So Abby had decided to see Jack one last time. Tonight was her only chance. Because of the threatening note, "You're next," she had moved her departure from The Grove up a day. Someone knew her true identity. Abby wanted to be reunited with her daughter before that happened. Any minute now, federal authorities could arrive with a warrant and handcuffs. This time tomorrow she was going to be a thousand miles away.

Jack carefully dismantled the bow and sealed the grip in a plastic evidence bag. He was leaving The Grove first thing in the morning.

He thought of Abby. What a surprise she had turned out to be. Abby Tyler respected her guests' privacy, she didn't seem to pass judgment on them or their strange requests, she wasn't a gossip, didn't say mean or malicious things about anyone. A woman who did not kowtow to the rich and famous. A classy woman who grew things only from the natural water underground, as if the desert were giving her permission to plant an oasis there, as if she had struck a bargain with the land.

And warm. He might not know much else about her, but Jack sensed Abby's deep warmth, as if a hot desert afternoon had settled within her and continued to shimmer and glow. He was drawn to that warmth. It would drive out all the coldness in his life, the chill of corpses and unsolved murders.

But she was hiding something. And lying.

Bow, arrows, quiver and target in their cases, he gathered up personal things from around the cottage. He set the photograph of Nina on the fireplace mantel along with the brochure for the winery. They were linked by fate. The brochure had been in his pocket the night Nina died. He had had an appointment with the owner of the vineyard the next day—an appointment he never kept.

Jack turned his eyes to the wind-blown garden beyond the "cabin" doors. He had hoped that, by now, he would have found Nina's killer and started to envision his future once again. He could not. The winery was still a faded dream that seemed destined never to be brought back to life. Jack wondered if even he himself could be brought back to life.

A sound at the door made him think of the wind, something rolling by on the path. But when he heard it again he realized someone was knocking.

"Ms. Tyler!"

"I hope it's not too late?"

He stared at her, thinking the windswept look suited her. And with her blouse the color of sunlight, tucked into sunset-orange slacks, it was as if she had brought daybreak with her. "How is Dr. Kaplan?" he asked.

"She's resting. The nurse said she'll be all right. Detective, I came to show you something."

He looked at the envelope in her hand and his guard went up. Reluctantly, he stepped aside and she entered. The wind came in with her, like a pushy intruder, rushing past Abby and Jack to sweep through the living room that had been made to look like a cabin, over the rawhide furniture, the Indian rugs and along the mantel of the stone fireplace.

As Jack shouldered the door closed, the draft sent papers sailing from the mantel to flutter down to the floor and land at Abby's feet. Jack bent to retrieve them but Abby was quicker.

She raised her eyebrows at the brochure for Crystal Creek Winery in Rancho California. Curious—the vineyard pictured on the glossy paper was lushly green and fruitful—she read the description. Thirty acres of grape vineyard and wine-making facility that produced ten different wines, indoor and outdoor wine tasting areas, located on the slope of a hill that afforded visitors a spectacular view of the valley below. Midway between Los Angeles and San Diego, with fifteen other wineries in the Valley, Crystal Creek was popular on wine-tasting tours. It sounded delightful.

Numbers and dollar signs were scribbled on it in ink, and the words *down payment*.

"Detective Burns," she said, returning the brochure and photo to the mantel, "I brought something for you to read. It's something private, that I wrote long ago. I've never let anyone read it. But I think it can help you."

She held him with those eyes again, steady and unblinking, looking as if they had seen everything in the world and knew what it was all about. "I don't need to read anything."

"It troubles me that you are in pain."

"That's my own business," he said. Then he noticed a windswept lock of dark hair on Abby's cheek and, in a move that shocked them both, reached up and gently brushed it back.

Abby's pink lips parted in a small gasp. Jack felt his cheeks redden. It had been an impulse. And now he still felt the warmth of her skin on his fingertips.

Flustered, amazed at the shock his touch had sent through her, Abby cleared her throat and held the envelope out. "Please, read this. It will help."

He turned a furious expression on her. "You want to help? Then tell me about Nina. Admit you know her."

"Why do you keep saying that—"

"Goddam it, I saw the file, Abby. I know about the file. So stop lying and tell me the truth."

"Jack, I don't know what—"

"Just go," he said, turning away. "If you're not going to be honest with me, then just get out of here."

She stared at him, feeling hurt and angry, and then she turned and headed to the door. It surprised Jack. He hadn't thought she was a quitter. But when he saw that instead of reaching for the doorknob she began punching numbers into the keypad on the wall by the door, he ran to her, shouting, "What are you doing?" Grabbing her wrist.

"It's the master code for the security system." She wrenched her arm free of his grip, hit a final button, and a high pitch sound beeped. "We are now locked in."

"What!" He tried punching in his own code.

"You can't override it," Abby said as she strode to the sofa and sat down as if prepared to stay there forever. "I want you to read something, a poem," she said, holding out the envelope. "And after you have read it, you can decide for yourself if I am lying to you."

He eyed the envelope warily, drawn to it, yet frightened of it. "No," he said.

"All right, I'll read it to you."

He tried not to listen, determined not to let this woman manipulate him, but her voice was firm and compelling, and it drew him like a moth to a flame.

"To my precious child," Abby read, "wherever you are: I waited…to count ten tiny toes and fingers/To hold you in my arms and to kiss your sleepy eyes/To say, 'I love you. I'm your Mama.'/But you never came. You were not there./'Where's my baby?' I cried./They told me you were dead, but they lied./You lived. You were strong."

Despite himself, Jack was drawn to her. He sat next to her on the sofa as wind swept through the garden and gentle words filled the night.

"On my lonely path/You are my companion/Kept in every beat of my heart./Sacred. Close. Alive./Others tore us apart/Yet I blamed myself for so long/Searching for you is where I find healing/Hope gives me strength/I will *never* give up."

She raised her head and looked directly at Jack as she recited the final lines: "I loved you then/I love you now/I love you always. I wait…"

Silence rushed in behind her words as their eyes held, and the desert wind moaned beyond the walls. Jack swallowed with difficulty as he watched Abby fold the paper and slip it back into the envelope.

"There was a time, Jack, when I was in so much pain, I thought I could not live. And then one night, when I reached the bottom of my despair, I took a pen to paper and laid my feelings down in words. It helped a little. I kept this poem with me and read it over and over, and as time went by, it became a balm to my pain. The person I wrote this poem to has never read it, has never heard these words, and I don't even know if she ever will, but it has helped me to cope with a trauma that nearly destroyed my life."

He could barely speak. "What does this have to do with me?"

She laid her hand on his shoulder. "Write to Nina. Tell her how much you love her and how sorry you are that you weren't able to protect her. There is healing in words, Jack."

"I'm no poet—"

"It doesn't have to be a poem. Write her a letter. Tell her what's in your heart."

Pain engulfed him as he suddenly remembered all the good things about Nina that he had buried beneath his grief, surfacing now like brilliant little suns: Nina's amusing laughter that ended up on a squeak, the way she could never properly tell a joke which made it all the funnier, her soft heart for animals and the stray cats she was always taking in, and her generosity when she opened her wallet to a friend in need.

He broke down and cried. Abby sat at his side, waiting. Finally, he said in a strained voice, "My parents were in a car accident when Nina was eight. My father was killed and Mother was seriously injured. She never fully recovered and had a hard time taking care of a child. I had just graduated from college, so I came home to help my mother and Nina. That was when we grew close. I think I became more of a father figure to Nina than an older brother. I lived at home and worked various jobs, supporting them, until I joined the Police Academy. Nina eventually got a college degree and went into advertising, but we always stayed close, and took care of our mother."

He looked at Abby, then at the paper in her hands, seeing it through eyes blurred with tears. "Who is your poem written to?"

"I had a child taken from me. The hour it was born."

Sudden understanding dawned on his face. "That's why you're involved in the black market adoption ring."

"How do you know about *that*?"

"Through Nina. Abby, you have a file on her. I saw it on your desk. I didn't open it, but I saw several papers and what looked like the edge of a photograph. Monday night, when you left the room to get the security pass, I saw the folders on your desk. Nina was trying to locate her birth mother. In her investigation she compiled the names of other adopted children. The three women, Ophelia, Sissy and Coco—Nina had those names. That's why I came here, to see if I could find out something from them. I saw their folders on your desk, and I saw Nina's."

"I have a file on Nina?"

"I thought you knew! I thought you'd been lying to me about it."

"Jack, my private investigator followed many leads and then he narrowed it down to one of three. But I told him to send me all the files he had collected, even though they did not pertain to me, because I am going to turn the information over to a non-profit organization that is attempting to unite abducted children with their real parents. Jack, I've never even looked at those other folders. I didn't know one of them was your sister."

He ran his hands over his face, and when he looked at Abby she saw the depth of his grief in his eyes. "I'm sorry," he said. "I shouldn't have accused you of lying."

Abby wanted to do more, take him into a comforting embrace and hold him to her breast, but he was vulnerable, so she laid her hands on his and said, "Jack, write a letter to Nina, like the one I wrote to my daughter."

His fingers curled around hers and Abby felt the calluses from years of shooting arrows into targets. Desire flared deep within her.

And then he pulled her to him and kissed her hard on the mouth. Abby was suddenly on fire. *Yes!* But as his embrace tightened, she thought: *No!* And pulled back. "Jack, I have to tell you something. Something I have never told another soul."

She told it quickly, before courage failed her, while Jack listened somberly to the story of her past. She ended it with, "My baby was born in prison and she was taken from me. They told me she was stillborn but I later learned that the warden was selling babies to a blackmarket adoption ring. I have been searching for her ever since." The rest—the prison escape, the bounty on her head—she couldn't talk about right now. Jack was a policeman and would be duty-bound to arrest her. Perhaps after all this was over…

"With the help of a private investigator, I traced her to three possibilities. And now I have narrowed it down to one. Ophelia Kaplan."

His eyes widened. "The woman who got lost in the desert today?"

"I believe she is my daughter. She doesn't know it yet. We haven't had a chance to talk."

Jack groaned. He wanted to kiss her again, make love to her, let Abby dissolve his pain and he, hers. But his emotions were turbulent and they frightened him.

The night air became charged as he said with passion, "Don't let her slip through your fingers, Abby. I would give anything to have Nina back. Don't lose your daughter. Go to her. Right now. Tell her the truth."

"I can't, Jack. It isn't fair to Ophelia. She is an individual and she has her own life. I can't let my needs and wants be more important than her happiness."

And suddenly he saw something for the first time: that Nina had been her own person, an individual, making her own choices, and that at some point a parent, or an older brother acting as a parent, has to let the child go his or her own way. "Nina knew her investigation was leading her into dangerous territory. I warned her to be careful. She wouldn't listen."

"Jack, you need to not only forgive yourself, you need to forgive Nina as well."

And it struck him what he and Abby had in common: he losing a sister, she losing a daughter. And both finding them again. Two people hurting, two people blaming themselves for something that happened to love ones.

"Abby, I came here not only to find out who murdered Nina, but to find out who her birth parents were. I owe it to her."

"I'll help you in any way I can. I have collected tons of data that you are welcome to go through."

"You are one amazing lady," he said, lifting his hand to her hair.

"It's about hope," she said, wanting to kiss him. Wanting to deliver herself into Jack's strong arms and surrender to desire. "A flower always turns toward the sun. No matter how you reposition it, the flower will always find the sun. Humans are like that about hope. No matter the circumstances, we always turn towards it."

And he realized she was right. He had lost hope. But now, maybe, he could find it again.

He drew her to him and kissed her again, gently this time, touching her neck, her shoulders, marveling at this woman who had come into his life, feeling the warmth within permeate his skin and muscle and bones to go straight to his soul. And Abby, nearly weeping with joy, leaned into him as her heart opened up for the first time in thirty years.

The phone rang, startling them. It was the nurse reporting that Ophelia was well enough for a visit. "Go to her," Jack said, not wanting Abby to leave but knowing she would be back. "Good luck."

She paused at the door and said, "Write a letter to Nina. Even though she's dead, write to her as though she were going to read it. Tell her everything that is in your heart, Jack, and you will begin to heal."

After she was gone, he rose and went to the desk, pulled out blank stationery and a pen, drew up the chair, and sat down to write…

CHAPTER FORTY-THREE

ABBY PRESSED THE BACK OF HER HAND TO HER MOUTH WHERE Jack's kiss still burned.

She had never felt so alive. Years ago, when she had vowed never to fall in love, she had thought it would be an easy oath to keep. Not even with Sam Striker, for whom she had developed a deep fondness, had Abby felt so electric and in tune with the world.

Dear Sam. Fifteen years her senior, bald, in poor health. The new garden had been for his remaining time on earth and the landscaper he had hired was doing it all wrong. But Abby stepped in and created a healing wonderland of trees and shrubs, gazebos, ponds and waterfalls. It hadn't spared Sam from the cancer, but it had prolonged his life long enough for him to provide her a haven in return, in the form of his name. He was right, no cops looked at the wife of wealthy realtor Sam Striker and connected her to the fugitive on a wanted poster.

"Someday you will fall in love, Abby," he had said in his final weeks, when the desert resort they had built together was nearly finished. "And I hope that lucky man realizes what a prize he has won."

Did Jack feel about her the way she felt about him—this sudden, un-expected rush of passion and desire? Abby would have to think about it later, explore her new and frightening feelings. Right now, something more urgent demanded her attention.

After thirty-three years of preparing for this moment—three decades of running, hiding, frightened of being caught, searching for her daughter, terrified of learning that her baby was dead, bringing the poem to show Ophelia she had never forgotten her—Abby realized she wasn't prepared at all. Her heart galloped as she stood at the door of the Marie Antoinette suite.

Back in her bungalow, her suitcase was packed and waiting, a coat draped over it, purse sitting on top. The plane reservation had been made. These next few minutes with Ophelia were going to bring to an end a life she had known was only temporary. Tomorrow she would set off for a new one, far from this place.

She knocked.

David answered the door. A handsome man, distinguished looking with jet-black hair. They shook hands.

Ophelia was reclining on a rococo settee of pink silk upholstery and gilded legs. If she wore an Empire-style gown, Abby thought, Ophelia could be a lady in the Court of Versailles. But she was wrapped in a no-nonsense chenille bathrobe and looking very displeased with herself.

"I am so sorry, Ms. Tyler," she said, sitting up. "To put everyone to such trouble. To cause such worry. I can't imagine what I was thinking. Please, sit down."

The response caught in Abby's throat. Thirty-three years ago, waking up from the anesthesia to be told her baby had died, and then just weeks later, Mercy saying the baby was alive. That was the moment Abby's journey had begun. She had wanted to go back to the prison, fight for her freedom through legal channels. But the need to find her daughter was greater, and so she had begun her life as a fugitive from justice. Now that her road had brought her to this final dream-come-true, however, she was at a loss for words.

"These things happens," she said as she took a seat. "We're just glad you're okay."

As she looked at Ophelia, the child taken from her before she could even hold her in her arms, Abby thought of all the birthdays she had missed, all the "firsts" in a girl's life. It was on her lips to blurt the truth. But if she did, then the rest would have to come out, too, and how could she tell this woman that the man she thought was her father, Norman Kaplan, certified public accountant who, according to the private investigator's report, was known for his charitable works and philanthropy, was not really her father, that the man who had sired her was in fact a cold-blooded killer who had murdered an old woman for fifty cents?

Ophelia picked at a thread on her robe. "I had a difficult decision to make. I needed to be alone, to think."

Difficult decision? Abby now sensed a troubling undercurrent in the room. Something was not right here. She turned to David and said, "Dr. Messer, would you mind if I had a few minutes alone with your fiancée?"

He looked at Ophelia, who said, "I would love some ice cream. The desert sucked all the moisture from my throat."

After he had gone, Abby tried to think of how to begin. She had thought that Ophelia, in love, pregnant and about to be married, would be deliriously happy, setting Abby's mind at rest that her daughter was living a wonderful life. She said, "I hope you were able to make your difficult decision," and waited for Ophelia to volunteer an explanation.

"I apologize, Ms. Tyler," Ophelia said, struggling to rise from the settee. Her ankle was wrapped in an elastic bandage, her foot red and swollen. "I don't mean to drag you into our personal problems." She hobbled to an ornate armoire inlaid with pastoral scenes. Pouring two glasses of Evian, she said, "Tell me, how did I win the contest? I never enter contests."

Abby thought of telling Ophelia what she had told Coco and Sissy, about Sam Striker's philanthropy, but the falsehood had no place here. Abby needed to know the source of Ophelia's problems, needed to know if and how they were going to be resolved.

Ophelia handed Abby a glass—no asking, Abby noticed, Ophelia was a woman who took charge—and returned to the settee. Her eyes moved to the closed door again and Abby knew by her troubled look that she wasn't really interested in the contest.

Abby had to take the plunge. This woman was her daughter. For thirty-three years, Abby had not been there for her. Now she would be. "Do you want to talk about it?"

Ophelia looked at her hostess. Ophelia had heard somewhere that Abby Tyler was a recluse. She had created this resort fourteen years ago and hadn't set foot outside since. A trim, attractive woman in her late forties, tastefully dressed, her most striking feature was her eyes—direct, open, like windows to an understanding soul. "It's because of my pregnancy," she said quietly.

In the desert, trapped among the rocks, all alone with the wind and the sand and the sky, Ophelia had gone to find answers but instead had experienced a stunning epiphany.

As she had walked beneath the sun and listened to the silence, she had thought it was like a prehistoric world, innocent and untouched, like the landscape that had given birth to humanity's ancestors, themselves innocent and untouched. The wind had encircled her, whispering, fanning her face with hot-cold breath and she had felt her soul slip backwards in time. The world of books and TV shows and picket lines faded as the colors of the desert brightened, and her senses grew sharp until she could almost understand what the red-tailed hawk, circling overhead, was saying to her in its echoing cry.

When Ophelia had paused to rest, she squatted on rocks and imagined herself wearing animal skins, eating roots and berries, and caring for her young. She reached within and found her primal self, Cro-Magnon Woman, a female for whom there were no questions, no dilemmas, no painful decisions to make. Life was life. That was the sum total to the equation of her existence. The question of keeping or destroying the life in her belly would never come up. Life was sacred and vital to the survival of the species.

A talk show host had once asked Ophelia if she practiced what she preached, making a joke about what her cave in Beverly Hills must look like, asking where she found mastodon meat on Rodeo Drive. Making it sound like she couldn't possibly practice what she preached, her world being so different from that of humankind's hominid ancestors.

But Ophelia knew now that she *could* practice what she preached. It didn't matter the clothes, or type of dwelling, or the fact that Neanderthals never drove cars. This was something *within*.

Now, back in the modern world, Ophelia said to Abby, "I went out into the desert because I had an important decision to make regarding my baby. I wasn't supposed to get pregnant. My oral contraceptive failed. Ms. Tyler, I am of Ashkenazi Jewish descent and so is David. He tested positive for a mutant gene that causes a disease called Tay-Sachs."

"I've heard of it."

"Then you know what it would mean if I brought this child into the world. Which is why I considered abortion."

Abby's hand flew to her throat.

"But it never went beyond a brief consideration. I'm keeping the baby, Ms. Tyler. He or she might not live long, but then none of us is guaranteed a long life. But while my child is alive, he will know love and joy and happiness. David and I are going to see to that."

Abby looked at her in confusion. Was Ophelia not her daughter after all? "You tested positive for Tay-Sachs?"

"I haven't had the genetic test yet. I intend to do that as soon as I go home."

"But if the test comes back negative," *and it will!* "then you have nothing to worry about."

But Ophelia said, "I would worry every single day of my life. How can I trust a lab test when I couldn't trust a birth control pill? I would go from doctor to doctor to make sure, and when would I be satisfied? The cloud would always be over me, did the lab make a mistake, am I going to give birth to a child that will die before its fourth birthday?"

There was more: the excitement of her and David's intimacy lay in its spontaneity, keeping them both keenly interested in each other, always watching for the signals, the romance staying fresh and thrilling. Would they lose all that? Would the worry of pregnancy turn them into cautious partners who watched the calendar and carried condoms?

Abby rose from her chair and went to the fireplace where rococo figurines and gilded clocks stood on the mantel. Outside, the desert wind whipped the trees and shrubs of The Grove in a wild late night dance. Abby turned to Ophelia. "Dr. Kaplan, what if you weren't of Ashkenazi descent?"

"But I *am* of Ashkenazi descent."

"Hypothetically," Abby said. "For the sake of discussion." The moment was here. She drew in a steadying breath. "Dr. Kaplan, I need to tell you something about myself. When I was sixteen years old," she said, returning to her chair, "I had a summer romance with a boy who did not stay in my life for long."

Ophelia listened, wondering about the change of subject.

"A murder was committed in our small town, I was accused and arrested. I didn't do it, but I had poor defense—my public defender even dozed off during the trial." She cleared her throat. "I was pregnant at the time and didn't know it. When it was revealed by the jail doctor, it caused a sensation. This was in Christian Bible Belt country. The men in the jury box were outraged. I was found guilty and sent to prison."

Abby paused to take a sip of water while Ophelia waited and wondered what this story had to do with her.

"My baby was born in prison and," Abby met Ophelia's eyes. She struggled for control. "They took my baby from me and sold it on the black market."

She left it at that, to let Ophelia take it in. Ophelia no longer looked patiently polite or puzzled, but deeply concerned. "That's awful," she said, thinking of her own baby, just weeks into life, but already a person, a soul.

"When I got out of prison, I began searching for her. It took years, a lot of money, and many private investigators. I hit dead ends, followed false leads. I collected facts and dates and names and compiled them into a database. I subscribed to clipping services and had them send me news articles that mentioned illegal adoptions, blackmarket baby selling, adoptees searching for birth mothers, mothers searching for babies taken from them. But in all that growing information, nowhere did I find any threads that might take me to my own child."

She took another sip of water. "And then, finally, the last detective I hired got a lucky break."

Ophelia watched Abby set her glass aside, rise from the Louis XIV chair and go to the window. It was closed, but the howling of the Santa Anas could be heard on the other side. Abby saw a world in turmoil. Her precious, delicate resort at the mercy of desert winds.

"He tracked down the warden of the prison where I gave birth to my child. Previous private detectives had tried to interview the woman, but she wouldn't talk about the past. This time, however," Abby turned to face Ophelia, "my investigator found the retired warden to be in the advance stages of liver failure and she *wanted* to talk about the past. During her years with the Texas penal system, she had been involved in various illegal activities and, I guess, being close to death, she wished to unburden her conscience. She gave my investigator a lead."

While Ophelia wondered where this was going, Abby went on to explain how her private detective narrowed the trail to one man: Spencer Boudreaux whom he found in a seedy hotel and who was willing to talk for a bottle of red wine. "He had 'run babies,' he said, back in the sixties and early seventies. Although Boudreaux himself was hazy on details, he said the nursemaid had had a sharp mind and would be able to fill in the blanks. My investigator found her and she provided other names that led my investigator to more information until he finally narrowed it down to three infants that could have come from White Hills Prison on the night of May 17, 1972."

Abby paused then, her heart pounding. Now was the moment she could stop, walk through the door and leave Ophelia ignorant of the true facts of her birth. Were it not for the pregnancy and Ophelia's fears for her child, Abby would do just that. But Ophelia needed to know the truth. That she was not of Jewish descent and therefore could not possibly carry the mutant gene.

Ophelia frowned. "May 17, 1972 is the day *I* was born."

"I know," Abby said. She had brought the papers with her, just in case. As she reached into her shoulder bag and brought out a folder, she said, "My daughter was born in the early hours of the seventeenth and was delivered on the evening of the seventeenth to this address. This is why I have reason to believe that you are my daughter."

"What!" Ophelia took the folder and opened it, scanning the words on the papers within.

"We know that Boudreaux already had two babies in the car with him when he stopped at White Hills prison," Abby said. "We just couldn't determine which of the three was the one he picked up that night. I have since ruled out the other two candidates, so that leaves just you."

Ophelia gave her a blank look. "You think I'm your daughter?" She handed the folder back. "It's a mistake. I know who my family are."

"Dr. Kaplan, you didn't win a contest. It was a way to bring you here—"

"Ms. Tyler, I was *not* adopted. Your private investigator made a mistake."

"The facts are there," Abby said, pointing to the folder. "I'm sorry. I had not intended to tell you. It is not my place. You have your own life. What right do I have to disrupt it, and the lives of all who are connected to you? But circumstances have changed. You are not of Ashkenazi descent. My ancestors were Scottish. Your baby is not in any danger."

"This isn't possible," Ophelia said, getting to her feet. "My mother would have told me—" And then suddenly the room was filled with the thick scent of white narcissus. It overwhelmed her.

Abby shot to her feet. "Are you all right?"

Ophelia reached for a chair to steady herself. "Oh my God…"

Abby watched, holding her breath.

"I have a memory," Ophelia said suddenly, "it was buried for years, but when I was in one of your gardens yesterday, I smelled white narcissus and it brought the memory to the surface. I have been trying to remember. It had something to do with my grandfather. I was sitting on his lap…"

She stopped and stared. "I remember!"

The Santa Anas howled beyond the window, sending palm fronds thrashing against the glass panes.

"I was seven years old. It was at a family gathering. I remember trying to put my arms around my grandfather's neck. He pulled them away. He lifted me from his lap and set me on the ground. And he said to my mother." Ophelia turned wide eyes to Abby. "He said, 'She is not one of us and never will be.'"

Ophelia looked down at the paper lying on the coffee table. *Baby girl delivered May 17, 1972 to Rose and Norman Kaplan, 633 Dos Padres Drive, Albuquerque, New Mexico. They named her Ophelia. Graduated 1995 from UCSB with a degree in Anthropology…*

The ormolu clock on the mantel ticked and then chimed. Ophelia looked up. She saw Abby Tyler's pale face, the anguish in her eyes.

Ophelia went to the phone and dialed. Time seemed to stop as she waited for the other end to pick up. Abby heard a crash outside and the frantic shrieking of birds in the aviary.

"Hi Dad," Ophelia said with a dry mouth. "Is Mom there? Yes, everything's all right. I sound strange? It must be the connection. I know it's late but…I need to talk to Mom for a minute."

Ophelia placed her hand on her abdomen as she waited, the scent of narcissus suffocating her. *She is not one of us.* The names and address on the private investigator's report, the irrefutable facts. It couldn't be!

"Mom? I need to ask—Yes, I'm fine. Listen. I need to know—Mom, I said I'm fine. Just listen. I need to ask you something." Ophelia drew in a deep breath. "Mom…was I adopted?" She listened. "It's not a silly question, Mom. There is a woman here who claims *she* is my mother. She even has papers."

Ophelia listened. She frowned.

"What is it?" Abby whispered.

"My mother says we need to talk. But not over the phone."

"Invite them to come here. I will send the private jet."

"Mom, is it true?" she said into the phone. Abby saw Ophelia's knuckles go white, she gripped the receiver so tightly. "*Am I adopted?*"

She listened, and nodded wordlessly. Abby saw her swallow with difficulty, and remembered the dry throat. Fetching her a glass of water, she handed it to her as Ophelia said, "Mom, they're going to send a private jet to pick you and Dad up." Her voice was raw. "Can you—Can you come right away? First thing in the morning?" She looked at Abby, who nodded. Then she said, "Okay, yes, I know you love me. I love you, too, Mom."

Ophelia held the phone out. "My mother wants to talk to you."

Abby took the phone, paused for courage, then put it to her ear. "Mr. Kaplan, this is Abby Tyler," she said calmly. "Your daughter Ophelia is here with me. I think…I have reason to believe she is *my* daughter. The papers that were given to me—I beg your pardon?" Abby glanced at Ophelia, who had gone shockingly pale. "Yes," Abby said. "May, 1972. Through a man named—" Abby closed her eyes. "Yes, Bakersfelt. The same man. I beg your pardon? I understand, Mr. Kaplan. We'll talk about it when you get here. My assistant will call in a few minutes to make your flight arrangements. Good night."

After she hung up, Abby said to Ophelia, "They'll be here in the morning."

Ophelia's voice came out a whisper. "What did my mother say?"

Abby could hardly find the words. "She said it's true. They adopted you thirty-three years ago."

CHAPTER FORTY-FOUR

*S*ISSY HAD AWAKENED THAT MORNING WITH A DIVIDED HEART. Last night had been so wonderful, spectacular in fact—the fantasy room decorated like a castle tower, with suits of armor, stone walls, tapestries. Sissy had been costumed in a gown with a tight bodice and full skirts, a lace cap on her head, her hair done up in ringlets over her ears. She had been given needlepoint to occupy her time, and just when she thought she had been forgotten, a man had come through the window, literally flying in, so that Sissy had jumped and screamed, and then she had seen the doublet and breeches, the magnificent plumed hat, and he was impossibly handsome with black hair and a rakish smile, and when he begged her not to let the night guard know he was in there—he, "A captain of the King's Musketeers,"—Sissy had fallen right into the role.

Sissy had wanted to try something in one of the sex manuals. She had thought she might have to point it out to him, explain what she wanted, but it hadn't been necessary. A little wine, some flirting, a few signals from Sissy, and things were underway.

On Tuesday night, with the Marine lieutenant, Sissy had tried something she had never done before, and she had enjoyed it. Last night, the tables were turned. She had laid back in a dreamy haze as her companion had made love to her with his tongue. She had never imagined it could be so delicious. And when she came, her orgasm was explosive.

The delightful part was that, after the oral lovemaking, her companion was still able to perform in the more conventional manner, using his lovely penis to bring her to more peaks of pleasure.

Such a wonderful week—Alistair on the bridge, the Marine Lieutenant on leave from combat, her bath partner with the gun, and finally last night—Sissy felt as if she walked in a new body. Every molecule danced with energy. Today was her last day and she was not looking forward to leaving.

But at the same time she missed her children and couldn't wait to take them into her arms, to hear about soccer practice and spelling exams and what movies they had seen. She missed Ed, too, and dreaded the inevitable confrontation that must take place between them. She was definitely leaving him. Sissy might have had sex with four strangers, but she had not given her heart to a single one.

Toweling off from her invigorating shower, she tried to focus on today. Like Scarlett O'Hara she would deal with the future when it arrived. For now, she still had twenty-four hours at The Grove and she intended to make full use of it.

When she heard the knock at the door, she thought it was room service. She had ordered filet mignon with scrambled eggs, papaya juice, kiwi fruit and a devilish crispy cheese bread found only at The Grove. Cinching the sash of her silk robe tightly about her waist (she wore nothing underneath), and thinking of the room service waiter last Monday and the come-on look he had given her, and thinking she might just invite him in to share a little breakfast with her, she opened the door.

And received a shock.

"Ed!"

"Hi Sissy." His eyes widened. "My God, you look wonderful!"

"What are you doing here?"

"We have to talk. May I come in?"

She stood her ground. "How did you get here?"

"When you wouldn't answer your phone I called the manager, Miss Nichols. I told her my problem and she got me a seat on this morning's flight in. Sissy, listen to me."

Seeing Ed after nearly a week's absence upset her balance. He was still cute, with his dimples and sparse hair on top and horn-rimmed glasses that made him look like a little boy. Fifteen years of memories washed over her— high school prom night, their wedding, the honeymoon, the birth of their first child, all the Christmases and birthdays and Ed falling in the snow and Sissy burning their first dinner, and four-year-old Adrian learning to say, "Hail Mary full of grapes." It was hard to believe this man had cheated on her, had hurt her the way he had.

She stepped aside and he came in. As soon as she closed the door, the words poured from his mouth. "Sissy, I love you. I didn't fall in love with someone else. It was just curiosity. I just wanted to know what it was like. I thought I was missing out on something."

She listened calmly while her emotions churned. She refused to cry, but tears threatened.

"It started at Gary's bachelor party, remember that? Someone brought a couple of strippers and, well, one thing led to another and I discovered I liked it. It was exciting. I tried to stay away, Sissy. But I got kind of addicted."

"The sports club," she said in a tight voice. "Two nights a week with Hank Curly?"

He reddened. "I've been going to that place out on the highway beyond the city limits."

Her jaw dropped. "The one that's called a *gentleman's* club?"

"A buyer from Oregon, Hank Curly, introduced me to the place. I just couldn't stay away. Call it a midlife crisis. I don't know. I'm not proud of myself. But I wasn't having affairs, Sissy. I didn't fall in love."

She pressed her lips together and tipped her chin. Ed's jaw was covered with stubble. Shadows lurked beneath his eyes. He looked wretched. Still, he was the one who had done the hurting. "Did Linda like her watch?"

He groaned. "Sissy, I am so sorry you found out about that." He reached into his pocket. "The jeweler could have told you I ordered this at the same time." It was a beautiful gold bracelet with both their names inscribed on it.

Sissy felt a small crack in her resolve. "You didn't answer my question."

"Linda didn't accept the watch. She said it was inappropriate." He pulled a card out of his wallet and handed it to her. "Linda Delgado is a marriage counselor. She said it wasn't ethical to accept a gift from a client."

Sissy stared at the card.

Ed said, "I was a mess, Sissy. I didn't know who I was or what I wanted anymore. I only knew that I wanted to find my way back to you, back to *us*. Father Ignatius recommended this woman. She counsels Catholic couples. I went out of town because I didn't want any of our friends to find out."

"Why did you go to a therapist? Why not come to me?"

His blush deepened. "Because, well, it was embarrassing, Sissy. Linda Delgado's specialty is sex therapy. I couldn't talk to you about it. I mean, our Saturday nights, I'm sorry Sissy, they just aren't enough." He ran a tongue over his lips. "Sissy, I love you, I will always love you. I'm not trying to excuse what I did, but I want you to know that it was never love. It was just sex."

He fell silent and as he waited for a response, noticed differences in her appearance. Had she lost weight? Gained weight? Had her freckles faded or did she have a tan? Her make-up was different. No, it was the silk robe that he had never seen before, the way it was tied around her waist emphasizing the fullness of her breasts, the erect nipples pressing against the fabric. He swallowed with difficulty. He was confused. He had never seen Sissy quite so...*sexy* before.

"I'm sorry," he said. "I know you don't see it as 'just sex.' That sleeping with another woman is wrong even if there is no love—"

She put her finger to his lips. "It's possible that I do understand what you mean by 'just sex.'" But she didn't elaborate, and she wouldn't tell him about Alistair and the others. Some things were best left secret.

He took her hand between his. "Sissy, I'm here to beg your forgiveness and ask you to give me a second chance."

She smiled and said, "It isn't entirely your fault, Ed. There must be something wrong with me if you felt you couldn't be open and honest with me. So I forgive you, Ed, and I will give you a second chance, because I want a second chance, too."

"Then you'll go with me to see Dr. Delgado? I'm still not cured. I still crave the excitement—"

"Ed, we don't need therapists. We can work things out ourselves, and The Grove is the best place for it," and with that she led him to the bedroom, knowing now what had been missing in her life, excitement and romance, just as it had been missing from Ed's, and she thought of the surprise that lay in store for Ed when she guided him into a new world of passion and intimacy, realizing that if it hadn't been for The Grove she might not have forgiven Ed and given him this second chance. But she had had a taste of it herself, with Alistair, the Marine and the others. She understood the fascination of sex with an exciting stranger. But from now on, she and Ed would be those exciting strangers for each other as together they explored the unknown territory of erotic love and Sissy introduced him to role-playing, costumes, and sex toys.

First thing in the morning, she was going to request an extension of her stay at The Grove. Using Ed's credit card, of course.

CHAPTER FORTY-FIVE

ABBY WAS TO HAVE LEFT THE RESORT BY NOW, BUT BECAUSE of Ophelia she had postponed her departure.

Last night, after Abby made arrangements for the Kaplans to come to The Grove, Ophelia had said she wanted to be alone with David. Abby understood. They all had a lot to think about. She was glad Ophelia had David for comfort and support. She herself had wanted to go to Jack for the same thing, but she knew he was making peace with his sister and Abby did not want to intrude. She had then called Vanessa's bungalow only to get her friend's voice mail. Occasionally Vanessa did not spend the night in her own bed. And so Abby had passed the night alone with her memories and fears, thinking of the past but determined to face the future, unable to sleep, and wondering also about the person who had slipped the "You're next" note under her door. She had expected to hear from them again. But they had not made a move. What were they waiting for?

Finally morning had come and now Abby stood at the landing strip, awaiting Mrs. Kaplan's arrival. Mrs. Kaplan, who was about to have her daughter taken from her.

The winds had died, the air was calm. The resort was covered in dust and sand, and the staff was already at work sweeping the walkways, scooping debris out of the pools, rolling up the tarpaulin on the aviary.

The plane's engines could be heard before the craft itself was in view. Abby braced herself. Standing between Abby and David, Ophelia waited for the woman she had thought for thirty-three years was her mother. Her emotions were in turmoil. Not to belong to the family she had thought she belonged to—after all these years! Her sisters and brother. The myriad aunts, uncles, cousins. *Zaydeh* Abraham saying, "She isn't one of us."

But that also meant her baby wasn't one of them, probably not even Jewish. And no longer in danger of dying of Tay-Sachs disease.

The jet taxied to a halt, the stairs unfolded to the ground. The Kaplans were the first to disembark.

Norman and Rose Kaplan were in their late sixties, plump and gray-haired, Rose shorter than her husband, and when they approached, Abby offered her hand for a handshake. But instead Rose Kaplan placed her hands on Abby's cheeks and said, "My daughter's mother," with such tenderness that Abby wanted to cry. "We took good care of your baby. We loved her as our own. I am sorry she was taken from you. We did not know this. We were told she had come from a Jewish orphanage, that her mother was dead."

They rode in a guest cart to Abby's bungalow, where Vanessa was waiting with refreshments.

While Vanessa poured tea that no one touched, Abby offered a brief summary of her past and the subsequent search for her child, showing the Kaplans the private investigator's report. Mr. Kaplan wordlessly went through the papers, then set them down with a sigh. "Because we were told the baby's mother had died, we were never afraid she would show up some day."

Ophelia stared at her parents. David sat at her side on the sofa, holding her hand. "Then it's *true*?" she said.

Rose turned sorrowful eyes to her. "Your father and I were married five years and still no sign of a baby. I went to specialists. They said I couldn't

have children. We decided to adopt. But we wanted a Jewish child. Our lawyer said he knew of a man who handled special cases like ours. We were
in the waiting room and I overheard him on the phone with a man he addressed as Mr. Bakersfelt. A week later he called to say a Jewish woman had
died in childbirth. The baby was a healthy girl who had our coloring, our
ancestry, he said." Mrs. Kaplan twisted her handkerchief. "But he said there
were other couples ahead of us. And he hinted that there was a way to push
us to the top of the list."

"Money," Ophelia said.

"He said it would be a donation to an orphanage. A worthy cause. Our
ten thousand dollars would make everyone happy all around. So we paid it."

"And then," Norman Kaplan interjected, "six months after you came to
us, your mother discovered she was pregnant. That was your sister Janet.
And after that came Susan and Benjamin. Like you hear about, adopted
babies making women pregnant." He smiled sadly.

Ophelia's face looked as if sculpted from white marble. "Why did you
never tell me?"

"We intended to. But each year, we said next year. We were afraid it
would make you less of our own. As it was, my parents couldn't accept you."

That day on her grandfather's lap. Ophelia realized now that her grandfather's words were at the root of her lifetime of competitiveness, to prove
herself. "What does white narcissus signify?"

"You remember that? You were so young. Your grandmother was sick in
the hospital. People brought white narcissus, her favorite flower. When we
brought you to visit, my father, *Zaydeh* Abraham, would not let you in the
room. He had been opposed to the adoption and said he would never accept
you. I didn't know you were aware of it."

A heavy moment descended upon them, as each struggled with new
thoughts, new emotions. "Mother," Ophelia said, going to sit at Rose Kaplan's side. "Mom, I have news. I'm pregnant."

The older woman gasped, then pulled Ophelia into a embrace. "Praise
God," she sobbed.

Abby watched as they held onto each other, as Ophelia told Mrs. Kaplan
about her fears, the possibility of Tay-Sachs, that it was why she had come

alone to The Grove, and Abby's heart went out to Rose Kaplan, weeping on Ophelia's shoulder, Ophelia also weeping, not wanting to let go of the woman she had known as mother.

Finally Mrs. Kaplan drew back and dried her eyes with a handkerchief. She offered Abby a sad smile and said, "Such irony. We wanted a Jewish daughter, but now, thanks be to God, it is a good thing she isn't. The baby is safe."

"You two have much to catch up on," she added as she composed herself.

But Abby looked at Rose in horror. She had not intended for this to happen. "I have to go away," she said.

"For how long?" Ophelia said in alarm.

"Perhaps for a very long time. I had never planned to reveal myself to you. But with your pregnancy, you needed to know that your child was not in danger—" The words caught in her throat. "But I have to go. Today. You will probably never hear from me again." She couldn't drag her daughter, newly found, into what she planned next.

When no one said anything and the moment grew tense, David rose and said, "I think we need to step back and absorb all of this."

With relief, everyone agreed.

"We tried so hard to make Ophelia ours," Mrs. Kaplan said to Abby as they went to the door. "We even changed her birthday. Isn't that silly?"

"I beg your pardon?"

Mrs. Kaplan reached into her purse and produced the original birth certificate, the document that had accompanied the baby. "We decided to make the day she came to us as the day she was born. But you see?" She handed the faded paper to Abby. "Ophelia is really three days older."

Abby stared in shock. The document was similar to the ones she had for Sissy and Coco, both born on May 17 in nearby Amarillo. But this one said May 14—*Boston, Massachusetts.*

Ophelia was not her child.

An hour later she was seeing the four of them off on The Grove's private jet back to Los Angeles. Although Abby had offered them all the services the resort had to offer, Ophelia was anxious to be back among her family. The idea of being adopted was going to need some getting used to. But in the end, the Kaplans were her people. And if they had been lied to about the baby's origins, that perhaps she had not come from a Jewish mother, it didn't matter. "I might not have been born Jewish, but I am Jewish all the same."

Such an emotional shock: the accidental pregnancy and then discovering she was adopted. It was too much. She needed to stand back and sort it all out in a clinical fashion. But, for the first time, David stepped in and instead of making a subtle suggestion that usually ended with, "Do what you think is right," he said, "No. Don't step back from your emotions. Go with them. For once, stop being a scientist and just be a feeling human being."

Dear David. How she loved him. "I was so opinionated and arrogant. How could you stand that?"

He smiled. "Because you are also smart and brave and act on your principles. You don't just pay lip service like so many people do."

She had also learned a lesson. Someone had once said to her, outside an abortion clinic that Ophelia was picketing, about walking in someone else's shoes. Now Ophelia *had* walked in another's shoes and she understood something for the first time. Not all women entering a clinic had the same stories, one could never know what they were going through, what had driven them to walk through those fateful doors. We on the outside cannot judge, Ophelia understood now, it was between those women and God.

The memory of what her grandfather said also explained much. Ophelia had never gotten around to the genetic testing. Everyone asked her why, and even she couldn't explain it. David had said it was because she didn't want to be told she had a defect. Ophelia had to be successful and perfect in everything. But now she realized that buried deep inside her was the memory of her grandfather saying "She isn't one of us." Subconsciously, she knew the genetic test would have confirmed it.

She also wondered now if her passionate study of prehistoric humans also had its roots in her grandfather's rejection of her. What he said at the time wouldn't have made much of a conscious impact on a five-year-old, but the seed was planted, it settled in and grew in her subconscious, the fact that she had no history. And so she had gravitated to the study of people without history—because she related to them, and was searching for herself among them.

With a promise to come back, and the prayer that Abby found her daughter, Ophelia said good-bye. They watched the plane lift into the air, Abby silently wishing Ophelia and David all happiness, then Vanessa said to her friend, "What are you going to do now? Are you leaving The Grove?"

Abby wordlessly shook her head. She couldn't leave. The disappointment that none of the three women turned out to be her daughter was crushing. But she would not be deterred. Her child was still out there, and Abby was determined more than ever to find her.

"I don't understand," she said as the drone of the jet engines faded in the sapphire sky. "Did the private investigator miss something?" She recalled what he had said about Spencer Boudreaux, a wino living from bottle to bottle. How accurate could his memory be after all these years? And the nursemaid, in her seventies, who admitted to having been on many baby runs across many states. And then something occurred to Abby. "Vanessa, are you sure my baby was a girl? Did you actually *see*?"

Vanessa turned to her friend, wishing she could ease her pain, herself crushed with disappointment, and said, "I had never attended a birth before. There was a lot of blood. I got faint. I had to sit down, so I never actually saw the baby being born. The warden washed it and wrapped it in a blanket and handed it to me. No, I didn't see for myself, but I could have sworn I heard the warden refer to the baby as 'she.'" Vanessa massaged the back of her neck. She had spent the night with Zeb and had gotten little sleep. "But now…I couldn't swear to it. Abby, the baby *might* have been a boy."

Abby knew one thing: she was not going to spend the next thirty-three years searching for a *son*. Boudreaux and the others were no longer alive, but there was one man, she knew, who had the answer.

A dangerous man, the private investigator had warned, who made people disappear. But Abby had no choice. All the leads the investigator had followed—Boudreaux, the nursemaid, the warden, and others—were deceased. That left only one man who had connections to the ring that kidnapped her child.

Gangster or no, Abby was going to confront Michael Fallon.

CHAPTER FORTY-SIX

M R. FALLON," THE CLIMATOLOGIST SAID. "WHAT YOU ARE proposing simply cannot be done. This is the desert and we—"

"Fuck the desert," Michael said. They were riding in the back of his stretch limo, blueprints spread out between them. "If you can't deliver, I'll find someone who will."

"Very well, Mr. Fallon," the man said, backing down. "I will get to work on it right away."

The car stopped and the architect got out.

Fallon's plan for a vast outdoor rainforest had failed once before. The water costs were sky-high and the plants did not thrive. The climate and soil of the desert simply could not support such a scheme. It made him hate the desert even more. But he was determined to have his way. The rain forest would be the Atlantis's "traffic stopper," something every super casino required. The Luxor had its sphinx and Treasure Island its pirate ships. The Atlantis had to do better. It had been on the cover of *Time* and featured in

National Geographic. Michael Fallon made the cover of *People,* and *Forbes* placed him on its annual list of the four hundred richest Americans, his worth estimated at $200 million. He was unofficially recognized as the most powerful casino owner on the Strip.

Which was why he was in a dark mood this Friday morning. The Vandenbergs. They should be *honored* that his daughter was marrying their son. Instead, they were showing their disapproval in a hundred little ways—not inviting Fallon to a cocktail reception for the engaged couple, a party which all of Nevada society attended. Mrs. Vandenberg dropping hints that the pair should take more time to think about their commitment. "Take separate vacations," the bitch had said. And Stephen Senior, chairman of a charity golf tournament to which pros and celebrities had been invited, slighting Michael Fallon by pointedly leaving him off the guest list.

You would think their precious son was the Second Coming, the way they treated him. But thirty-three-year-old Stephen was nothing remarkable in Fallon's book. He had selected the boy for his pedigree and because he looked like he could take orders. Michael Fallon intended to have a hand in the running of Francesca's marriage, whether the Vandenbergs liked it or not. And he was going to see that the wedding went ahead, despite Mrs. Vandenberg's subtle campaign to sabotage the plan.

Michael Fallon had insurance. He had discovered the Vandenbergs' nasty little well-kept secret about their only child.

The limousine pulled to the curb and stopped. Fallon was on his way to Confession but he had a quick appointment first.

Dr. Rachel Friedman's office was on the fourth floor. There was no receptionist. The therapist herself opened the door.

"Mr. Fallon," she said, extending her hand.

"Thanks for taking the time to see me, doctor, I know you're a busy woman." He gripped her hand and looked into her eyes. Nice looking woman, classy and mature. As they shook hands, he felt the quick, reflexive grasp of her fingers that he always felt when a woman connected with him, and when he saw the pulse throb at her throat, he thought he would love to get this lady into bed.

"Have a seat, please. What can I do for you?" Dr. Friedman felt as if she had already met this man. Her patient, Francesca, spent most of her sessions talking about her father. And she had heard about him around town. Michael Fallon was as handsome in real life as in his news photos, and the charm was everything others said it was. But there was more—just sitting in the chair opposite her, he exuded power, it seeped from his pores as sweat did on other men. She wondered what he was like in bed.

"I have to tell you," he said, laughing nervously, tugging at his French cuffs. "I wasn't picturing a beautiful woman when I found out my little girl was going to a shrink. I had someone older in mind, you know, plainer. If you don't mind me saying, you are quite a looker, doc."

Rachel wondered if it were an act, the self-consciousness, but she was flattered all the same.

"And smart, too," he said, whistling at all the diplomas. "Me, I never finished high school." He blushed. "It's about my daughter, doc. I'm worried about her."

Dr. Friedman said nothing.

"I know she's been coming here—"

"She told you that?"

He reddened and laughed self-consciously. "I had her followed. I'm her father. I protect her. She was going somewhere once a week, regular as clockwork, and I got worried, you know. When I was told she was seeing a shrink—pardon me, psychologist, it scared me. Is she all right?"

"I'm sorry, Mr. Fallon, but that is confidential. I cannot divulge what is said between me and a patient."

"Are you sure? I am her father. And I'm just worried. I mean, you don't have to give me details, just, you know, the general topic she came to you about."

She gave him a reassuring smile. "Speak to Francesca yourself. I have a feeling she would welcome it."

He looked around the office, fingers tapping on the arm of the chair. "I don't know. I have a feeling she isn't telling me something. She's getting married tomorrow."

"It's in all the papers."

"Big wedding," he said with a grin. "For my little girl. Maybe you could just let me look at her files? You wouldn't exactly be *telling* me anything, would you?" He winked. "You know, our little secret?"

"My files are confidential as well, Mr. Fallon."

He nodded. "I understand. A father can't help trying." He fell silent, fingers tapping the arm of the chair, emerald pinkie ring catching the overhead light. His eyes grew shadowed and unreadable and Rachel felt a small excitement spark within her. She had been trained to be impervious to the manipulative tactics of patients, had years of experience dealing with people from the very timid to the extremely aggressive. But Michael Fallon eluded categorization. She felt the woman inside herself step around the clinical therapist and cross her legs in a way that made her skirt rise above her knee and catch his eye. She looked at him expectantly. She suspected he was unpredictable. It excited her.

"Thanks for your time," he finally said, rising. "I just thought I'd try, but I respect that you have to protect the privacy of your patients. Say, that's a beautiful painting. Is it real?"

"Yes."

"Must have cost a fortune. I take it business is good?" He held up a hand. "Not that you're in business. You're a doctor, you help people. Now me," he spread a hand on his chest, "I'm a businessman. And business is good, if I may brag a little here. As a matter of fact, I'm expanding. Diversifying, they call it."

She walked him to the door, liking his tallness, his expensive scent, the self-mocking laugh. "What are you diversifying in, Mr. Fallon?" Surprised to find herself disappointed that the meeting was so short.

"The carpet cleaning business. No, seriously. I'll show you." He opened the door to the outer office and beckoned to a thick-bodied man, who slipped in and closed the door behind himself. "Tony," Fallon said, "give me some of that carpet cleaner. Maybe the doc here would like a piece of the action, you know, invest in my new company."

The man reached into his overcoat and produced a small bottle of brown liquid. "Now this," Michael said, unscrewing the cap, "is the strongest, most efficient carpet cleaning solution in the world. Gets any stain out. You see that spot there?"

She looked down, frowning. She saw no spot. The carpet was new.

"Watch this," and he dribbled a few drops to the floor.

Smoke and an acrid smell rose up. Dr. Friedman jumped back, looking in shock at a black hole sizzling in the wool.

"What the heck?" Mike Fallon shouted at the other man. "You brought the concentrated formula. We've ruined the doctor's carpet."

"It's all right," she said, waving a hand in front of her face, the smell was so strong.

"I am so sorry, doc. This stuff has to be diluted before you put it on the carpet." He waved the bottle around and Dr. Friedman took another step back. "The base of this solution is acid, it'll eat through anything, even human flesh. You have to be sure you don't get it on your skin because you'd be disfigured for life. Let me buy you a new carpet," he said with a disarming smile.

Rachel Friedman hung in a frozen moment, looking into Mike Fallon's charming and handsome face, at the bottle of acid, at the large man blocking the outer door.

"What an impression I've made," Fallon said as he screwed the cap back on and handed the bottle to his companion, shaking his head. "I come here to ask about my daughter and end up ruining your carpet. Let me replace it, please."

His eyes remained on her, the smile was still there, but now it sent a cold chill through her.

Taking another step back from Michael Fallon, sudden fear squeezing the breath from her lungs, she said, "The carpet is fine, please don't worry."

"Worry, that's all I do these days. Francesca getting married and all."

"Mr. Fallon, now that I think about it, I don't think it would do any harm for you to look at your daughter's file…" she said, cursing herself for her cowardice and for taking on as a patient the daughter of a mobster. She would call Francesca first thing in the morning and recommend she see someone else.

"Thanks, doc," he said as he accepted the files. "Let's you and me have dinner together sometime. What do you say?"

The limousine came to a halt in front of the church and Mike Fallon made a dramatic ascent up the stone steps, making sure everyone saw. Inside, he eyed the confessional booth warily.

When he was a child his mother had forced him to go to Confession every Saturday night so he could take Communion the next morning. She never knew it, but little Mikey Fallon always lied to the priest. He couldn't tell him the truth, could he, and risk the man ratting on him to his mother or, worse, to the cops? When he was eighteen he stopped attending church altogether, and only started going back after Francesca was born. Even then, he never again went to Confession.

But now it was necessary. Tomorrow Francesca was going to have the biggest goddam Catholic Mass wedding there ever was, and how would it look, all the Catholics heading down the aisle to take the wafer while the father of the bride sat like a sinner in the pew? Of course, confession had changed since he was a kid—now it was called celebrating the sacrament of Reconciliation—but he still had to go through with it. Others were waiting to go in, mostly the older generation who didn't trust a confession that didn't go through a priest. If his mother were still alive, she would be among them, kneeling, a scarf covering her head. But Lucy was dead. Fallon had received the call from Miami the night before—Lucy had suffered what appeared to be a heart attack.

The secret of his father's identity had died with her. But at least it also meant Francesca would never learn the truth, and protecting Francesca from his past was what Michael lived for.

When it was his turn, he parted the curtain and entered the stuffy little box, waited tensely, and when the panel slid open and he saw the vague outline of Father Sebastian, Mike Fallon crossed himself and whispered, "Bless me Father for I have sinned. It has been forty years since my last confession. These are my sins."

The night before, Fallon had done what he considered a fair and frank examination of his life. And everything he had done, was for Francesca. Would the priest understand that? If you did it for your child, was it still a sin? "I missed a coupla of Sundays at church. I cursed a few times. I might have taken the name of the Lord in vain now and then, but only because I was pushed to it." Of the rest of his sins—stealing, fornication, lying, murder he made no mention. Those were all business anyway.

His cell phone rang. "Pardon me, Father," he muttered, and took the call.

"Jesus," he said out loud in the confessional. Abby Tyler had contacted him. She wanted to meet.

The conversation was brief. He said he would take his private jet. After ringing off, he placed a call to a contact who in turn was to get in touch with Fallon's man inside The Grove, canceling their contract. Fallon had decided to take care of things himself. The same way he was going to take care of the Vandenbergs.

Then he called McCarran Airport and told them to get his jet ready and to page the pilot. Michael wasn't even going back to the Atlantis. He wanted to get this last loose end taken care of.

CHAPTER FORTY-SEVEN

*J*ACK WANTED TO BE WITH ABBY MORE THAN ANYTHING AT THAT moment. To hold her, kiss her, tell her how grateful he was. A partially written letter to Nina lay on his desk. Not perfect, but it was a start. But more than that, to tell Abby he wanted *her* in his life. But she was enjoying a reunion with her daughter and he didn't want to impose.

As he dismantled his archery equipment and packed it away, he thought about the future and how everything had changed. He was flooded with new emotions that he needed to think about and sort through. Jack knew he was not the same man he was when he had arrived at The Grove five days ago, but he had lived for so long with pain and rage that he didn't know how to let go of them. Even after starting the letter to Nina, there was still something inside him he couldn't exorcise. Somewhere along the way, anger had become his blood and vengeance his breath. So he would go home, come to terms with Nina's death, and think about what to do next. Probably turn in his badge and his gun, then take over ownership of Crystal Creek Winery. He would invite Abby to come and stay…

There was so much he wanted to share with her, his past and his passions, and to learn about her, the rest of her story after the birth of her child in prison, how she had managed to get acquitted, what it had felt like to be exonerated after such an ordeal.

Amazing woman! She had re-awakened his dream to own a vineyard. The first thing he was going to do when he got back to LA was call Crystal Creek Winery and see if it was still for sale. If not, he would find another one, or start his own. It felt strange and good to have a future again, and something to live for.

As he polished the bow grip—he didn't need the fingerprints any more— he listened to the wind beyond his door. It was already blowing strong and the day was young. And then he heard another sound: his fax machine. It had hummed to life and now a printed sheet was coming out.

It was a note from his friend at Forensics: "Your intuition about the towns of Abilene and Tyler was an inspiration, Jack. My search brought up Tyler Abilene, born in Abilene, Texas in 1938, who in turn gave birth to a daughter in Little Pecos in 1955—Emily Louise Pagan. The dates and other details match. You aren't going to believe it, Jack. Your pigeon's got a price on her head."

A second sheet came through—an FBI Wanted poster for a girl named Emily Louise Pagan.

Jack stared in shock. The picture was of a sixteen-year-old girl, but the resemblance was there. And the description of her hobbies—horticulture and gardening. And then he read the rest...

He felt the world tilt around him as the words *lies* and *betrayal* thundered in his mind.

Abby hadn't told him the whole story! About setting the prison on fire, escaping in a stolen car, killing two people in the commission of a liquor store hold-up. She had conveniently left all that out while pretending to be honest with him.

He cried out. It felt like a sledgehammer against his chest. Jack wanted to put his fist through a wall. He had fallen for the oldest trick in the book: being seduced by a pretty face. The old rage and bitterness, not far below the surface, flared up, hotter than ever.

He came to a grim decision. He had no choice. She was a fugitive at large. And he was a police officer. *Graduation day at the police academy, his badge newly pinned to his uniform, hand raised as he recited the words of the policeman's oath to protect, serve, and uphold the laws of the people and city of Los Angeles.*

Strapping on his gun and badge, he folded the wanted poster into his pocket and went out into the wind in search of Abby.

CHAPTER FORTY-EIGHT

Mrs. Vandenberg was acting strange.

Not that Francesca had hit it off with her in the first place, Stephen's mother being an unreachable woman. Even so, as she stood before the tall mirror while the seamstresses made a last minute adjustment on her train, Francesca could swear her future mother-inlaw, who was overseeing the whole delicate operation, was unusually agitated.

"Turn around, dear," Mrs. Vandenberg said, as she cast a critical eye over the twenty-thousand-dollar wedding dress. "White really isn't your best color, is it?"

Such a thing to say to a bride! Francesca curbed her irritation. Stephen was familiar with his mother's personality and had promised that he would not allow her to interfere once they were married.

But mothers-in-law had a way of swaying their sons…

They were interrupted by a knock at the door. A maid entered with a special delivery package, addressed to her father, marked Urgent. Francesca looked at the return address. Miami, Florida—from a doctor. She set the package aside and carefully slipped out of her wedding dress. After Mrs. Vandenberg and the seamstress had gone, Francesca went back to the package and frowned at it.

Her father had been called away on business. Uncle Uri had gone with him and they wouldn't return until evening. Just how urgently did this require attention? Thinking it was something she could take care of—Francesca frequently handled legal matters for her father—she opened it.

The package contained two items: a death certificate for a woman named Lucy Fallon, and a sealed envelope with instructions written in a careful hand: *To Be Given To My Son Michael Fallon of Las Vegas, Nevada— upon my death.*

Francesca stared at it. Daddy's *mother*?

Thinking it had to be a mistake, she picked up the phone and dialed the number on the letterhead. A nurse answered. Francesca asked to speak to the doctor who had signed the death certificate and was told he was away for the weekend.

"I'm calling in regard to Mrs. Fallon and the circumstances of her death."

"Are you a relative?"

"Michael Fallon is my father," Francesca said, hoping the nurse would say, "That name is unfamiliar to us. This is a different Mrs. Fallon."

But the woman said, "We tried getting word to Mr. Fallon. Doctor was hoping he would come in time, as his mother was asking for him."

Francesca hung up. Her father had a mother in a nursing home in Florida? All these years, a grandmother she didn't know about? *Why?*

And then other, darker questions crept into Francesca's mind. Rumors she had heard over the years, whispers of her father's supposed connection to Murder Inc many years ago. She had dismissed it as the usual Las Vegas mythology—like Elvis still being alive— but now she wondered...

He hadn't said where he was going, hadn't given her a number in case of an emergency. She didn't even have Uncle Uri to turn to for answers, because Uri had accompanied her father.

There was only one way to find out. Francesca called downstairs to have her car brought around, grabbed her purse, keys, and the sealed envelope, and drove out to McCarran Airport.

Her sporty Cessna 172 was kept in the same hangar as her father's Lear jet. The mechanics knew her. They told her that her father and Mr. Edelstein had flown to a destination in the Mojave Desert called The Grove. She had heard of it. After a careful preflight check of her plane, Francesca took off into a due south heading, wondering why she was doing this, why she couldn't let it wait until her father returned in the evening.

But she knew why. The wedding tomorrow. She didn't want to marry Stephen under a cloud of secrets.

Stephen Vandenberg pulled up to the hangar, the tires of his Maserati squealing. He had been told Francesca was here and he had to see her right away. An emergency had come up. But she had taken off for a place called The Grove, the mechanics informed him, and Stephen had to make a split-second decision.

This could not wait.

Consulting a map, he determined that, at top speed, he could make it to The Grove in three hours. Not that he would beat Francesca there, but with luck, before she learned the bad news from her father. Stephen wanted to be the one to break it to her.

Francesca was nearing her destination. A wind came up, suddenly and unexpectedly, buffeting the aircraft. She called the tower at Twentynine Palms Marine Base for a weather update and was told a storm was building to the east. They advised her to turn around.

A little wind didn't daunt Francesca. She had flown through storms before. And The Grove was just up ahead. Thanking the tower, she signed off.

But the air began to haze with dust and landmarks below were starting to become obscured. Then she looked to her left and saw something that made her blood run cold.

A massive brown wall, growing and rolling from out of the desert. A sandstorm! And she was heading straight into it.

CHAPTER FORTY-NINE

FALLON LIKED BEING ABOVE THE WORLD, SAILING THROUGH THE sky like a god. From up here, in his private jet, he felt like a lord over the desert he so despised.

He was in high spirits. Everything was falling into place, his lifelong dream of being a member of the most upper crust was going to come true in twenty-four hours. The childhood poverty, the stigma of being a bastard, the years of crime, doing the dirty work other men didn't want to soil their hands on, and even later as a respected businessman, having to put up with socialite women looking down their aristocratic noses at him—tomorrow, Michael Fallon was going to own the world.

All it had taken was one simple letter to the Vandenbergs, informing them that he knew the secret about their precious son that they had guarded fiercely for many years, and he had hinted that any plans to block the wedding would result in nationwide publication of that secret.

Which left Abby Tyler as the last stumbling block. He had tracked down and taken care of everyone who knew anything about his past. With Tyler erased, his past would be erased. Starting brand-new, with a clean slate that Fallon was going to fill with wealth, position and power.

He laughed out loud, he felt so good. Because whatever Abby Tyler thought she had on him, she wasn't going to have a chance to use it. Fallon was sure of that. He had a surprise for her.

Stephen Vandenberg raced down the highway with an eye out for Highway Patrol. He had taken off for The Grove because he had received shocking news and he wanted Francesca to hear it from him first. But now he pressed the accelerator to greater speed for another reason—he had just heard a radio report about a massive sandstorm engulfing the Mojave Desert. And Francesca was flying a fragile aircraft.

Praying she had time to turn around and outrun the storm, Stephen pressed the pedal to the floor and the Maserati shot down the highway.

Jack arrived at Abby's bungalow with grim resolve. He didn't want to do this, but she was an escaped fugitive. And Jack had his duty.

When Abby opened the door, looking worried and distracted, he saw her quickly slip something into the pocket of her slacks, but not before he saw what it was: an airline ticket. He had arrived just in time. Wanting to get this unpleasant task over with, he reached behind his back for the handcuffs that were tucked into his belt, but Abby said, "I'm glad you're here, Jack. Ophelia Kaplan isn't my daughter after all. A man is on his way, I believe he has information about my child."

His hand paused. "A man?"

"From Las Vegas. Michael Fallon, he owns the Atlantis hotel."

Jack stared at her. Was she aware who Fallon was? A tough guy with legendary mobster connections. "Listen, Abby," he began, but was interrupted by her pager. The security escort at the landing strip reporting that her visitors had arrived.

Fallon and Uri Edelstein disembarked the private jet, bending their heads into the Santa Anas that were blowing from the east, and were taken to a private bungalow where Tyler was waiting for them. Not bad looking, Fallon thought when he saw her, fit body tastefully dressed, rich but understated. In other circumstance, he would have gotten her into his bed. To his surprise, she had only two people with her, a black woman in an Arab caftan and a stranger in a leather jacket. If the meeting had taken place at the Atlantis, Michael would have been surrounded by a staff of security men.

Still, he wasn't going to underestimate her. Abby Tyler had managed to elude federal authorities for over thirty years. She wasn't stupid. And while this meeting might be taking place on her turf, Fallon was going to have the upper hand. Find out what she knew about him, and then make certain the information was secure. He expected to have this wrapped up within the hour and be on his way back to Vegas.

Abby braced herself. She was glad Jack was there. She had been warned her that Fallon was dangerous, and when he came into the living room, he *exuded* danger. Handsome, of confident bearing, dressed in a stylish suit with diamonds and platinum adorning his fingers and wrists, Michael Fallon was the personification of a man in power. And a charmer, Abby decided. She knew men like him, and knew he was not to be trusted.

There were no introductions. Before Abby could speak, Fallon took the lead and said, "What is this nonsense about me having information on the whereabouts of your child?"

Abby handed him a sheaf of papers, photocopies of her private investigator's report. It was thick and stapled at the corner. Fallon glanced through them, thirty-thousand dollar watch glinting with each flip of his wrist.

The atmosphere grew charged with tension as the moment stretched and Fallon read dates, names of birth mothers, descriptions of stolen infants, routes traveled, names and addresses of adoptive parents and amounts of cash handed over. Peppered throughout the prodigious report was the name Michael Fallon.

Jack Burns watched Fallon with loathing. If only half of what he had heard about Fallon's criminal activities were true, the man should be executed. Jack particularly did not like the way Fallon had walked in here, acting as if he owned the place, smug and disrespectful to Abby.

Vanessa looked on with trepidation. She, too, sensed Fallon's power. And he had come to this meeting slick and confident. Even now, as he read the mountain of evidence against him—that would put him away for life—he appeared to be unperturbed. How much did he know, she wondered, and who was the man with him?

Fallon tossed the papers onto the coffee table. "The word of winos, crackpots and people who are conveniently dead," he said dismissively. "There isn't an iota of truth in there."

"Mr. Fallon, where is my child?" Abby asked.

He sized her up. Tyler had a stronger spine than he had expected. If he told her the baby from White Hills prison had been the fourth in the shipment, that it had died and was buried in the desert, would she drop this challenge, or would she escalate her fight? He decided to keep the information secret for now. "Suppose I know something," he said. "I'm not saying that I do, but if I have information, what will you give me in return?"

"What do you mean?"

"I'm a businessman. I'm not in the habit of giving away things for free."

"You stole my child. You had no right. Tell me where he or she went."

He didn't say anything. The wind roared outside, dry and electric, making the back of everyone's neck prickle.

Jack spoke up. "Tell the lady what she wants to know."

"It's all right, Detective," Abby said. "I can handle this."

Fallon laughed. Detective! Was that supposed to intimidate him? He inspected his manicure. "I have no idea what you are talking about."

Abby pointed to the sheaf of papers. "There is a record in there of a child taken on the night of May 17, from White Hills, Texas. *My* child. Where was he taken?"

Fallon shrugged and said, "I have no idea where your child is," enjoying the moment as he wondered how far he could take this. To what extreme would this woman go for the information? It was like playing a fish on a line. Toy with her until he reeled her in. Then gut her and throw her into a frying pan.

"A man who worked with you, Spencer Boudreaux, told my investigator that you had once bragged you were keeping a record of the adoptions. Insurance, you called it."

He tugged at the starched French cuff of his four-hundred-dollar shirt.

"I want those records," she said.

Fallon picked a speck of lint from the sleeve of his dark suit. "This so-called information that *supposedly* connects me to baby trafficking, Miss

Tyler—you realize that when you expose that information, you only expose your own involvement—a convicted murderer giving birth in prison. An escaped felon wanted by the FBI. You'll be arrested."

Now Abby knew who had sent the threatening "You're next" article. It alarmed her to think Fallon had an agent working for him inside The Grove and she had not known about it.

When he saw the look on her face, he said, "Yes, I know who you are."

"I want those records, Mr. Fallon," she said, undaunted.

Vanessa shifted nervously. She would die before she went back to prison. And Jack stiffened, suspicious of the man with Fallon. He looked like a lawyer or an accountant, but he could also be Law.

Fallon savored his next words. Watching a woman beg for mercy could be a real turn-on. "You said I bragged that those records are insurance. I have insurance, all right. But not the kind you are thinking of." Reaching into his breast pocket, he brought out a white envelope. "I have here a federal warrant for your arrest. I am here, Miss Tyler—or should I say Miss Emily Louise Pagan?—to take you back to prison."

"Grove ground control!" Francesca shouted into the radio. "This is Cessna 1277 X-ray. Can you read me?" She mentally kicked herself. She knew better! She had grown up in the desert, had taken her first flying lessons in the desert. It was the discovery of an unknown grandmother—Why had her father kept Lucy Fallon a secret?—that had clouded her judgment. Now she was flying into a sandstorm with no way out. She tried another frequency. "This is Cessna 1277 X-ray calling The Grove resort. I am five miles south. Request landing instructions!"

The winds whipped up to 40 miles an hour. Visibility dropped to a brown-out. Francesca turned on her landing light but could not see the ground. "Grove, this is Cessna 1277 X-ray. I need help!"

She turned on her taxiing lights and looked for the landing strip. But it was as if she flew through a brown sea. The plane bucked and shuddered. A heavy object struck the front of the plane. Francesca saw flames. She lost control. "May day! May day! I'm on fire! I'm going down! Grove control, can you hear me? Grove—"

The wind shrieked past Abby's private bungalow, the lights flickered, trees thrashed in the garden. Abby said to Fallon, "Arrest me then." And she held out her arms, wrists together.

All eyes turned to Fallon. He was unfazed. "I mean, it," he said, not taking her bluff seriously.

"And *I* meant it," she said. "All those names, dates, places, data on birth mothers and adoptive families. Hundreds of them. All leading back to you, Mr. Fallon," she said, pointing to the photocopies. "I will expose them."

He laughed. "Who would believe you, a woman on the FBI's wanted list?"

"It doesn't matter who believes me. I will deliver the data to newspapers around the country. To *60 Minutes.* To organizations that are dedicated to reuniting children who were wrongfully taken from their birth mothers. They don't need to believe me. They have only to look at the data."

Fallon pursed his lips. "You realize that Texas has the death penalty. It means the electric chair for you."

But she spoke with passion. "You stole my baby from me and sold him to strangers. You victimized women all over the country. You treated children as merchandise. If I cannot be reunited with my own child, then I will see to it that others are. If I am executed, at least I will know that some good came out of my own victimization."

He blinked. Cleared his throat. "You must think I'm stupid. Either way, I lose."

"Give me your records," she said, "I will combine them with my own, and I will delete all mention of your name, as well as Karl Bakersfelt, Spencer Boudreaux and any others that could ultimately implicate you."

Fallon studied the ruby ring on his right hand, adjusted his Montblanc cuff links. He thought of the Vandenbergs, Fallon's doorway into the world of politics. No longer satisfied with just being a businessman, Michael Fallon had his eye on the governor's chair. "Your baby was the fourth one in the May 17th shipment," he said matter-of-factly. "But it died,"

"Bastard," Vanessa whispered.

"I want proof," Abby said, standing firm, although a tremor run through her body. "Show me the record from that night."

"I have a better idea," Fallon said, thinking of the agent he had planted here at the Grove, who had been ready all week for the signal to take this woman down. Fallon would give the hit order the minute he and Uri left. "Give me the originals of these photocopies and I won't have you arrested."

She tipped her chin. "Give me *your* records and I won't tell the world about you."

His eyebrows arched. "You would risk going back to prison, to face the Texas death penalty, for a bunch of strangers you don't even know?"

"I might not know those children, the adoptive families, the birth mothers, but I know what they have gone through. I know their anguish. If I can never hold my own child in my arms, then at least I can help other mothers to hold their children in their arms."

Fallon glared at her. This was not something he had anticipated. As they stood deadlocked, each waiting for the other to back down, with Vanessa and Jack and Uri watching, the wind rose and howled and rattled window panes and sent debris flying against the outer walls creating a hellish cacophony, and when the door flew open, everyone jumped. Zeb stood there, a handkerchief to his face. "Abby! A private plane just went down near Indian Rocks. The pilot identified herself as Francesca Fallon."

"What!" Pushing Abby aside, Fallon bolted out into the wind

"Wait!" Zeb called after him, but the wind had swallowed him up. "Abby, he'll get lost in that sandstorm."

"Where in relation to Indian Rocks did the plane go down?"

"We don't know."

"Okay. Zeb, send search teams north and east of the rocks. You and Vanessa take the west. I'll go south."

"You can't go out there," Jack said, putting his hand on Abby's arm.

"I am the *best* person to go out there. I know the terrain like the back of my hand. And I've been in sandstorms before. Besides, if anyone is hurt on my property, it is my responsibility."

"I'm going with you," Uri said. When Abby started to protest, he said, "Francesca Fallon is my god-daughter."

Zeb gestured to him. "All right, you can come with me."

Jack and Abby made their way through the storm-battered resort to where the vehicles were parked, jumping into an SUV and plunging into the sandstorm. As Jack drove through the brown-out, Abby unpacked the emergency supplies that all Grove vehicles came equipped with.

"Can't see a damn thing!" Jack shouted as rocks, grit, sand and fragments of cactus flew into the windshield.

Abby broke open a box of paper surgical masks—the desert survival kit included food rations, packets of water, and medicine—and prayed Francesca Fallon was still alive.

"Listen, Abby, that man is dangerous. He's known for making people disappear. He's especially known for keeping his past a secret. Rumors a while back of a pit boss who had made a reference to Fallon's connections with Murder Inc—" The SUV hit a boulder, flew into the air and landed with a crash. "A month later they fished his headless body out of Lake Mead."

The vehicle slammed into another rock and spun out of control. When it came to a rest, the front wheels were buried in a sand drift while the storm howled around them.

"I'll go on foot!" Abby shouted as she reached for the first aid kit. "Jack, you'd better stay here. I know this terrain."

But he grabbed a face mask and a flashlight and jumped out after her.

They held onto each other as they headed into the storm, but within minutes they were separated. "Jack?" Abby turned in a circle, trying to see him in blowing sand. She could barely breathe. Grit found its way under her sun glasses and stabbed her eyes. "*Jack!*"

She pressed on, going against the wind that nearly knocked her off her feet. The storm blew hot and cold and pelted her with sharp grit and debris. When she tripped over a rock, the first aid kit flew out of her hand. She could not see beyond a few inches, and a moment later the metal box was buried.

Abby struggled to her feet, calling, "Hello?" only to have the wind snatch the word from her mouth.

Finally she saw a dense shape ahead, and when she reached the downed Cessna, she saw a young woman lying half out of the charred, smoldering aircraft, her forehead bleeding. Abby helped her up, tried to assess her condition, but the sandstorm was so thick it was like nighttime and Abby's flashlight provided little illumination. But she heard the young woman moan and say, "Where am I?"

"You're all right, Ms. Fallon," Abby shouted above the wind. "I'll get you to shelter."

Helping Francesca from the plane, Abby stopped to feel the wind. She saw which direction it was coming from, where the grains were flying, listened to the gusts whistle past her, and knew where Indian Rocks lay.

They staggered together through the storm, Abby supporting the younger woman. The wind howled and shrieked, pulled at their hair and clothing, and sucked the breath from their lungs. When they reached a stone wall, Abby frantically felt along with her hands until she found an opening and dragged Francesca inside just as the young woman collapsed.

The cave provided little shelter. It was too shallow and cramped, and then Abby's flashlight beam caught on something that made her blood freeze. Small animal bones, scraps of fruit and berries.

They were in a coyote den.

Fallon plunged blindly through the sandstorm until he stumbled upon the wreckage of the plane, finding the door flung open, blood on the windshield. Where was Francesca? Then he saw the FedEx envelope on the seat. As the wind howled around him, buffeting the small aircraft, threatening to bury it and Fallon with it in a sand drift, he could just make out the inscription on the envelope. And he knew why Francesca had flown here.

Handkerchief covering his mouth, he squinted through the blowing sand. In the near distance, the flicker of a flashlight. Pulling out his gun, he threw himself into the storm.

Thinking of coyotes, hungry and threatened, Abby said, "We can't stay here. There is a small tunnel leading into the rocks. Can you walk?"

Francesca pressed a hand to her bleeding forehead. "I'm dizzy...but yes...I can walk."

Abby put her arm around the young woman's waist and helped her over the cluttered floor. "Am I at The Grove?" Francesca asked. "Is my father here?"

Abby didn't respond as she kept her flashlight aimed at the floor, thinking of snakes and scorpions, forced out of their dens by the storm. The passageway was narrow and low, they had to push through with their heads down, rocky walls scraping their arms, sand sifting down onto their hair.

"Wait," Francesca said when they came to an open space, coughing and fighting for breath. "I must sit down. My head…"

Abby helped her down, then pulled off her face mask and sunglasses, and surveyed their shelter with the flashlight.

They were in a small cave with tunnels branching off. She tried to think. Years ago, she and Sam had explored these caves with an Indian guide. There was a way out of this subterranean warren, but which way? The wrong direction would lead them to abandoned mines that had been declared hazardous decades ago.

Suddenly she saw a circle of light sweep over a far wall. "In here!" she shouted, her voice echoing off the cavern walls. "Jack? Zeb?"

But it was Fallon, holding a small flashlight from the Cessna. He ran to Francesca and gathered her into his arms. "Baby, thank God! Are you okay?

"Daddy, I am so sorry!"

He dabbed at the blood on her face with his silk handkerchief, then he looked at Abby. "Do you know a way out of here?"

She had been listening to the drafts, feeling the ebbs and flows of the cool breezes shifting through the caves, sniffing the air, feeling the walls for dampness. Indian Rocks stood over an earthquake fault line, which was the reason for the artesian wells that fed The Grove. But the water could be both beneficial and deadly. One of these tunnels led to an underground lake.

Finally she said, "That way."

They had to stoop at times when the ceiling grew low, tripping over the uneven floor as they followed Abby's frail flashlight beam. The air grew heavy. Their ears popped.

Hearing a sound, Abby brought her companions to a halt.

"What is it?" Fallon snapped, Francesca leaning heavily against him. He was worried about her head wound.

"Listen!" Abby said. "Is that—?"

Then it came more clearly, someone calling out, "Hello?"

"Jack! Here! We're in here!"

Footsteps approached and suddenly the chamber was flooded with light brighter than sunlight. Francesca cried out and covered her eyes. Jack turned down the power on the fluorescent lamp he had taken from the SUV.

"Thank God!" Abby said, running to him. "I was terrified when I lost you in the storm." She looked past him. "Where are the others?"

"I have no idea." He cast a suspicious glance at Fallon.

"I think if we follow that tunnel there," Abby said, "we will come out on the north side of the rocks. Let me have your lantern. The light is much better." She turned her back. "I'll just take a look—"

The shot was deafening. Francesca screamed. Jack flew backward and slammed against the wall.

Abby spun around. She stared at Fallon and his gun. Then she ran to Jack's side. "Are you all right?" she said as she peeled his shirt away and inspected the bullet wound.

"I'll live," he said with a grimace, thinking of the gun beneath his jacket. "What the hell—?"

The shoulder wound was deep and bleeding profusely. Abby quickly removed her blouse, folded it into a thick pad and slipped it under the bloody shirt. Eyeing her lacy cream camisole, Jack said with a tortured smile, "You'll catch cold."

"What happened?" Francesca was saying as she brought her hands from her eyes. The light from the lantern was still too bright. It made her head throb. But she saw her father's gun, and the other man lying on the floor. "You *shot* him?"

"I had to, baby, he was going for his sidearm."

"I wasn't..." Jack groaned.

"I don't understand. Daddy, what's going on here? Why did you come to this place?"

"I wasn't going to tell you, I didn't want to frighten you. These people have been blackmailing me. They're threatening to reveal information about my past, long ago, fabricated lies, but it could be damaging to *you*. I came here to negotiate with them. They're demanding five million dollars."

"That's not true!" Abby said.

"But...to shoot him? Daddy, you could have killed him."

"It was to protect you, baby. If the blackmail didn't work, they planned to kidnap you." He took Francesca's arm. "Let's get out of here. You need to be seen by a doctor."

"We can't leave him!"

Fallon looked at Jack. "You're right. We'll take them to the authorities." But Fallon intended to finish the job before they found their way out.

They limped into the northern tunnel, Abby in the lead, supporting Jack, Fallon helping Francesca, gun still in hand.

Finally she could go no further. "I'm dizzy," she said. "And I'm thirsty."

"There's water near here," Abby said, holding tightly to Jack.

They came upon an underground stream that trickled cool and clear. The cavern was spacious and the air smelled fresh. While Abby tended to Jack's wound, Francesca said, "Daddy, who is Lucy Fallon?"

He smiled and smoothed back her hair. "She's an old lady in a nursing home and the staff were trying to find her relatives. I got a call from them weeks ago, but I told them I was no relation. My name isn't even really Fallon, it's Falconelli! It's an administrative mix-up. That's all."

"But it said on the envelope 'For my son Michael Fallon of Las Vegas.'"

"It's just a mistake, sweetheart. They're looking for another Michael Fallon. I feel sorry for the poor old woman. I wish I *could* be her son."

Abby scrutinized Jack's face. He was shockingly pale. Reaching into her slacks for a handkerchief, she tenderly wiped the dust from his cheeks and forehead. "Jack, why did he shoot you?"

"I have no idea. I wasn't reaching for my gun. He doesn't even know I've got one."

She glanced over her shoulder, thinking of ways to get out of the tunnels and away from Fallon. "Let me get you some water," she said, and left him.

Jack watched Abby, his heart aching at the sight of her pale back and slender shoulders, the thin silk camisole held up by barely-there straps. Abby Tyler, strong and vulnerable at the same time.

He shifted his gaze from Abby and saw Francesca turn toward the lantern light. He stared. "My God," he whispered. And in that instant he understood the real reason Fallon had come to The Grove, and why Fallon had shot him.

Jack did some quick thinking as he watched Abby. She obviously was not yet aware of the truth. But Jack knew that the minute she realized who

Francesca was, she would not be able to mask her reaction, Fallon would see, and their lives would be worthless.

Jack groaned loudly. Abby ran back to his side, water cupped in her hands. "What is it?"

"The bullet moved." He pulled her down to him and pressed his lips to her ear. "Pretend you're inspecting the wound," he whispered. "Don't let Fallon know I'm talking to you."

Abby glanced at Fallon, who was pacing anxiously.

"Abby," Jack whispered hoarsely. "Francesca…"

"What?"

"Don't react. Don't let Fallon know—"

"Know what?"

"Francesca…she is your daughter."

She frowned. "What are you talking about?"

"In my pocket…folded up. The wanted poster—Abby, the picture of you, it looks just like Francesca. And the description of your hair, red-gold. Francesca's…"

Abby chanced a quick glance over her shoulder and saw Francesca in the lantern's glow, her hair catching the light in red-gold highlights. And suddenly the memory of something her grandfather had once said: *"I remember the day your Mama brought you home, Emmy Lou. A week old and all smiles and shiny copper hair. That hair of yours made folks comment. It looked like someone had been polishing pennies and you got mixed into the bunch and got your head polished as well."*

Francesca Fallon, her daughter? Was it possible?

"I don't see the bullet, Detective," she said in a tremulous voice.

"Abby!" Jack whispered sharply. "Hold it together. Fallon shot me because he intends to kill us. He knows that as soon as we saw Francesca, we would know the truth. As long as Fallon thinks we don't yet know the truth, we have a chance. But if he thinks we've figured it out, we're dead."

"But Jack, if you're right…I have to tell her we aren't going to hurt her. Jack, she needs to know!"

Her voice had gotten too loud. Fallon looked over. Jack brought Abby's face down and caught her mouth in a hard, deep kiss.

Fallon turned back to Francesca. "Can you walk, baby? We have to get going."

She nodded.

Fallon waved his pistol. "You, on your feet."

Abby started to rise and Jack whispered, "Wait." Scooping up a small handful of dirt, he smeared some on Abby's cheeks. She understood. Francesca had not yet seen her face. But once she did, and saw the striking resemblance, would she ask questions? What would Fallon do then?

Would he go so far as to kill Francesca to keep his secret safe?

Abby struggled with her emotions. Now that she saw Francesca in the light, she knew she was indeed her daughter. Francesca's eyes came from Abby's grandfather, her mouth belonged to Abby's mother, and the red-gold hair a perfect match to her own. And, in profile, Francesca's fine, straight nose was that of the hippie drifter who had stolen and broken Abby's heart.

It was all Abby could do to keep from running to her, taking her into her arms and holding her…after all these years. My daughter! Abby's heart cried out.

As she reached for Jack, Fallon said, "Not him. He stays. You come with us."

When she started to protest, Fallon showed her the gun and said, "Leave him or I'll finish him off."

"Daddy!"

"Just go ahead, baby. Everything's going to be all right. His friends will find him. But we're taking this woman as insurance. As long as we have her with us, they won't hurt you."

"I won't leave Jack," Abby said.

"If I kill him, you will."

"Go," Jack said.

"Listen," Abby said to Fallon. "You two just go. Follow this stream. It leads to the aquifer. There is a water-processing station there. I promise, you will never—" Her voice broke. "You will never hear from us again."

"I don't take risks. Now get over here and pick up that lantern."

"Go," Jack whispered again. "I'll be all right."

She knelt quickly and kissed him on the mouth.

But when she joined Fallon, and he said, "Not that way, we go this way," Abby protested. "We must follow the stream."

"And find your friends waiting for us at the end? That was your plan all along, wasn't it?"

"I had no plan! I didn't create the sandstorm or make the plane go down. Mr. Fallon, listen to me—"

He aimed the gun at her. "I could just as easily do this here." Francesca slumped against him. Her color was bad.

"All right," Abby said. "We'll go your way. But we have to get…your daughter medical attention."

With a final glance at Jack, Abby went into the tunnel, taking the lantern and plunging Jack into utter darkness. He heard their footsteps fade away, and then he was alone.

"Mr. Fallon, you have to believe me, this is not the right way," Abby said after they had gone several yards.

He wasn't listening, and when his face caught the lamplight, she saw a deadly look in his eyes that alarmed her.

With a groan, Francesca collapsed. Abby ran to her side.

Fallon stood over the two women, watching Abby, hearing the worry and fear in her voice, saw how gently she touched Francesca. "What's going on?" he said softly.

And Abby realized what she had done. She looked up at him. "The fourth baby didn't die, did it?"

When Fallon remained silent, Abby said, "Why?" pain in her voice. "Why did you take my child?"

Fallon glanced at Francesca, her eyes closed, her breathing slow and deep. And he came to a decision. "I needed a baby," he said, because Abby Tyler might as well know why she was going to die. He would carry Francesca out to safety and tell her the two criminals had met deserved ends.

His voice seemed to come from deep inside the cave's shadows. "I married Gayane Simonian to get her father's casino hotel. When she was pregnant, I had to protect her. I had enemies. Gayane would have been vulnerable in a hospital. So I arranged for the baby to be born at home."

Fallon's eyes focused on the cave wall, as if he were seeing the past unfold on the rocky surface like an old movie. "When Gayane died in child-birth, and then the baby a few minutes later, I knew I was going to lose everything. So I called a man I had once worked for, asked him if he had any deliveries in the works. He had four, he said, from Texas. He told me the name of the motel on the highway. I bundled up my dead baby and drove out there. I selected an infant and switched them."

He closed his eyes and saw the babies on the motel bed, all girls, one with an extra finger on each hand, the second too small and quiet, the third Jewish, the driver said. Fallon had wondered if she could she pass for Italian when he saw the fourth—the nursemaid, inexperienced with babies, had mistakenly thought it had died but it had merely fallen asleep. This one was crying lustily now, fighting to live, small hands waving in the air, ready to seize life. With reddish gold wisps of hair and eyes that looked straight at him. "Came from White Hills Prison," the driver said. "Mother is serving life for murder." That was the one Fallon chose and named Francesca. When he returned to the Wagon Wheel, he paid off the nurse and doctor, sent them away, not telling them about the switch. And then he presented the baby to his father-in-law, Gregory Simonian, who accepted her as his grandchild.

The rest—holding the baby in his arms, feeling the soft bones and curves through the little blanket, Fallon having never known love before, feeling a strange new emotion flood his heart, forgetting that she wasn't his, his mind over the years editing out the night of her birth and the little corpse buried in the desert—he did not say any of this to Abby. Francesca was *his*. Nothing was going to make him give her up.

"Boudreaux said you were serving life for murder. The warden had as-sured me you had no family, that during the time you spent at White Hills no one visited you. So I knew no one would come looking for the baby. Especially not you, once you escaped and you were on the FBI wanted list. But I underestimated you."

Abby rose shakily to her feet. "What are you going to do now?"

"I can't let you live," he said.

"I'll give you everything on the adoptions," she said quickly, "all the files, the data. I won't tell anyone. I have an airline ticket. My bag is packed. I'll disappear."

Fallon's voice came from far away, from a place that filled Abby with dread. "It's not enough. You're too much of a threat. Francesca is getting married tomorrow. She is my passport into a world that I've been fighting to get into since I was a boy. I handpicked the man she is going to marry. I've worked for years toward that goal." He frowned at the wall as another scene from the past played out there. "She almost married a worthless skydiver, you know, but I took care of that."

He raised the gun and Abby braced herself.

Jack felt his way along the rough walls, as blind as a mole since Fallon had taken the lantern, his shoulder throbbing. He was following the water upstream. He knew that if he went downstream, he would reach safety. But he couldn't abandon Abby.

His legs grew weak. The floor seemed to fall away from under him. *So this is what it's like to die.*

Suddenly, light flooded the chamber and Jack heard Zeb Armstrong say, "Are you all right, Detective?" Gentle hands taking him, Vanessa saying, "He's hurt!"

A few minutes later, Jack felt better. They had revived him with water and a tonic from the first aid kit. Vanessa cleaned and bandaged his wound, stopping the bleeding, and gave him a pain killer.

"Fallon took Abby at gunpoint."

"Which way did they go?"

He pointed upstream. "There's more. Francesca Fallon is Abby's daughter."

"What!"

"We have to go after them. There is no telling what Fallon will do now that his secret is out."

"Can you walk?"

"I'll make it."

Jack led them in the direction Fallon had taken the two women. They stopped short when they arrived at three tunnels branching away before them.

"Mr. Armstrong, do you know your way around down here?"

Zeb shook his head. "There's a reason the local Indians call these caves haunted. People go in and don't come out."

"Welcome to the Hotel California," Jack muttered as he surveyed the three branching tunnels.

"We could split up," Zeb offered, "but we only have the lantern and one flashlight. Which means we can only search two tunnels."

Vanessa inspected the mouth of each, scanning the rocky walls with her flashlight. "What's this?" She bent and examined the fresh scratch marks in the rock.

Zeb ran his fingers over the scratches. "Fresh. About waist level."

"Abby used her wristwatch to mark the way!"

They moved cautiously into the tunnel, encountering more scratch marks, hearing the wind now, realizing they were not far from an entrance. But they had arrived at another fork in the tunnels. Jack peered ahead into the maw of darkness and recalled what he knew of the layout of Indian Rocks.

As if he were competing in a field archery competition, unmarked-distance, Jack listened for the wind above them, noted the movement and direction of the cave drafts, mentally calculated the exterior distances...

"There's an opening not far from here," he said, remembering when he had gone after a stray arrow and found a crevasse. "We can use it to back-track and head Fallon off. Come on!"

"Daddy?"

Fallon spun around. Francesca was sitting up.

"Is it true?"

He looked down at her, the gun still in his hand.

"You married my mother to get the casino? Is that true?" She rose unsteadily to her feet. "And Erik? You had him killed?" *The worthless skydiver.*

She looked at Abby and now saw what she had been blinded to back in the main cave: her resemblance to this woman.

"Please don't kill her." Francesca held her hands out, pleading. "You're still my Daddy. It doesn't matter how I came to be your daughter. You adopted me. Let's go home. Let's forget about these people. I'll marry Stephen. Everything will be just like it was."

"No," he said. "We can't trust her not to show up and ruin everything. Trust me, baby, we have to be free of her. I want your life to be perfect. It's what I've lived for." He reached out to touch Francesca's cheek and Abby seized upon Fallon's brief distraction. Swinging the lantern hard against his head, she grabbed Francesca's wrist, and ran.

"Are we lost?" Francesca asked minutes later. She was numb with shock. Her father confessing to abducting her as a baby, saying he killed Erik. It was like a horrible dream.

Abby turned this way and that, sensed a change in the air, and said, "Up ahead, that's the way out."

But they went just a few yards when Francesca said, "What's that sound?"

They held their breath as they listened. "Huffing," Abby said. "A female coyote calling to her pups."

And then there she was, directly in their path, her bushy tail raised horizontally—a sign of aggression.

"Don't move," Abby said. "If there are pups, the male could be nearby." Abby ran a dry tongue over her lips. "Back up slowly," she said, putting herself between Francesca and the growling coyote. "Watch your step. Don't hurry. Don't make any sudden moves."

The animal stayed put, alert and ready to spring, as the two woman moved cautiously away. "She won't follow us," Abby said. "She's just protecting her den."

They backtracked through the passageways, pushing through massive cobwebs, stepping over old bones until they came upon a corridor hewn from the rock by manmade tools. Abby recalled that back in the thirties, miners had dug here. Rotten timber beams still supported the ceiling.

When they heard a sound, they thought the coyote had followed them. But another variety of desert predator had found them.

Fallon.

"I can hear the wind!" Vanessa said. "We must be near an entrance."

"It sounds like the storm is dying down," Jack said.

"What's that up ahead? It looks like—Oh my God!"

Fallon aimed his gun. "Francesca, come here."

But Francesca had lived all her life with the guilt of having killed her mother. She was being given a second chance. "No. I won't let you do this."

"Francesca, do as I say," Fallon said more sternly as he cocked the pistol.

And then: "Drop it!" Jack Burns stood there gripping his service revolver with both hands, aiming it at Fallon.

Fallon spun around, fired. The bullet struck a rotten beam, splitting it. The ceiling began to give way. Abby grabbed Francesca and ran toward Jack. They covered their heads as the ceiling crashed down in a thunderous roar. When the dust cleared, they saw the tunnel blocked completely with rocks, sealing Fallon on the other side.

Abby fell into Jack's arms. "Thank God you're okay," he said, holding her.

"Jack, we have to get Fallon out of there. There was no other exit."

But Zeb was grabbing Vanessa's arm. "The rest of the ceiling's about to come down. Quick! This way!"

Fallon dug frantically at the rock slide that had cut him off from the others, trapping him in a small chamber. Sand sifted down as he clawed until his fingers bled. He was hot and suffocating. He stripped off his jacket and threw it down. As the air grew thick with dust, Fallon thought he heard his mother's voice. But that wasn't possible. A phone call yesterday: "The job in Miami has been taken care of." How was it done? Poison? A pillow over the face? *Did Lucy know it was her son who had ordered her murder?*

As sand rained down from the ceiling, he remembered Rocco Guzman years ago, buried up to his neck in sand and turning purple. He thought of all the other graves out there in the desert around Las Vegas.

And a little one—Gayane's dead baby—buried behind a cheap motel on Highway 91.

He grabbed the lantern and swept it over the rock pile, searching for places to dig. The light fell upon a white object on the cave floor: the envelope he had found on the passenger seat of the Cessna. He had forgotten all about it.

Tearing it open, he examined the contents in the fading light of the lantern. It contained a death certificate, the thousand-dollar teal poker chip, and a letter.

Lucy Fallon's last words, dictated to a nurse three months prior: *"Dearest son, I am old and have not long to live. The priest has heard my confession. I am ready to meet God. This chip was given to me the night you were conceived. It was given to me by your father. I kept his name from you because*

I didn't want you to follow in his footsteps. But you did anyway. You are so like him, that charming evil man. I make no excuses for what happened that December night during the grand opening of the Flamingo Hotel. I was young, naïve and dazzled. He seduced me.

"You want me to tell you that your father was Bobby Bavacua or Tony Cuzamano, men with glamour in their names. But the man who sired you was Benjamin Siegel, the monster whom everyone called Bugsy. When I told him I was pregnant with his child, he laughed at me and had me thrown out."

Fallon stared in amazement as the sand sifted down, more heavily now.

Bugsy Siegel, lynchpin of the Jewish mob! He laughed. Michael Fallon in his Giorgio Armani suit and Bruno Magli loafers and Italian tie and watch, his hair styled by a barber named Scorcese, Michael Fallon who had lived all his life as the proudest Italian on earth, now thought: *What a kicker. All these years I've been going to the wrong goddam church.*

A chunk of the ceiling suddenly gave way, and sand and rock rained down on Fallon's head. "No!" he shouted. He began to dig again, clawing at the stone and debris, frantically tearing at the rubble until his fingers grew raw and bloody. He began to sob. *Francesca!* His lungs hacked up dust until pain shot through his chest. *We'll go away together. We'll forget what happened here...*

A fragment dropped from the ceiling and caught the back of his head. Fallon saw stars and planets. He slumped onto the growing pile of dirt and lay there until his arms stopped moving. Blood trickled onto the rising mound of sand around him, he tasted blood and grit as darkness closed in around him and the lantern was extinguished.

As he was plunged into the darkness of a grave, and sand filled his lungs, he realized he wasn't a bit surprised this was happening. Michael Fallon had always hated the desert. And after fifty-seven years of fighting it, he conceded that the desert had finally won. .

The sandstorm had moved on and Riverside County Sheriff's search and rescue teams were scouring the caves for Michael Fallon. Among the volunteer searchers was a Grove employee who had been working under the name of Pierre. When he had received the call that his assignment had been cancelled, he had accepted the dismissal with equanimity, having decided to stay on at the resort, maybe drop out of the contract killing business altogether, the ladies here being so grateful.

The resort's nurse was seeing to Francesca's head wound, with Vanessa at her side, thinking of the night she was born. And now here she was, reunited with her mother at last.

Vanessa looked over at Abby who was giving a report to the sheriff, and she thought how ironic to see her friend conversing freely with a law official. *How far we have come since those days at White Hills.* It would never cease to amaze Vanessa the special magic that life can hold.

She and Zeb had plans to go to Africa. The night before, after making love for the first time, before Fallon and the sandstorm, they had talked until dawn about Africa and Zeb's passion to preserve the endangered wildlife. Vanessa had re-awakened his old dream. In a few days they were leaving for Kenya, both of them "going home."

The sheriff finished his interview, thanked Jack and Abby, and left. "How are you doing?" Jack asked when they were alone. His arm was in a sling, a proper bandage in place of Abby's ruined blouse. A paramedic had draped a blanket around her shoulders, but one of the silk straps of her camisole peeped through.

Abby filled her eyes with the sight of him. Jack's face was smudged, there was a wisp of spider web in his hair. It amazed her to think that she did not even know this man five days ago. "I'm fine," she said. "And you, Jack?"

He was thinking what a gracious hostess she would be at Crystal Creek Winery, what a special place she could turn it into. But he needed to know: "In your bungalow, Abby, I saw a suitcase. It had a coat thrown over it, and your purse. And I saw the airline ticket."

"Yes," she said. "I'm going away."

He waited.

"Jack, last night I didn't get a chance to finish my story. I was never released from prison. I escaped. I have been wanted by the FBI ever since. I have a bounty on my head. That's why I have been hiding here."

"And now you are going to run again?"

"No. Ever since I was wrongly convicted I have wanted to fight to have the ruling overturned. But I couldn't do it until I found my daughter. She was all that mattered. Once I found her, and was satisfied that she was happy, then I was going to turn myself in and begin the fight for acquittal. When the private investigator told me he had finally traced my child through an illegal adoption ring, I contacted a criminal lawyer in Houston. He agreed to take my case. His team has been studying the trial transcripts and searching for witnesses."

Abby's lawyers were already tracking down the people who had been in the roadside nursery at the time of Avis Yocum's murder—tourists her own court-appointed attorney hadn't bothered to look for and who would certainly remember being in the nursery that day because it was Labor Day and a girl with red-gold hair had taken their pictures in front of a giant saguaro cactus named Horny Sam.

Abby's team had also located the driver of the Greyhound bus, long since retired but who remembered picking up a girl that particular morning, at a deserted crossroads in New Mexico, because it was the first time he had ever picked up a passenger there. So Abby was in the process of being cleared of involvement in the liquor store hold-up and killings. When asked what happened to the black girl Mercy, she said she had no idea.

"Jack, Abby Tyler is leaving The Grove and never coming back. It will be Emily Louise Pagan who returns."

He marveled at her courage. She could disappear again under another name. Instead, she was going to fight for her innocence.

Jack brought out the Wanted Poster and tore it into tiny pieces, placing them in Abby's hand. "I don't think I could have arrested you anyway. Not after everything I've learned in the past few days. The most important of which is that it's impossible to think clearly with clenched fists."

Her eyes filled with tears. "And I have learned that the heart expands. I thought for years that I only had room in my heart for my daughter. But the heart always makes room for more."

He brushed a strand of hair from her cheek. "You and I haven't been living in the present, Abby, but in a twisted sort of combined past and future.

When a question arose, we would say we would cross that bridge when we came to it. Always with an eye on those bridges. But you know what? Not a single person in the history of mankind has yet managed to cross a bridge before he or she came to it. We are both going to have to learn to live for today and let tomorrow take care of itself."

He drew her into his arms and kissed her, in the desert sunshine, in front of Zeb and Vanessa and Uri Edelstein and Francesca and the sheriffs.

Abby looked over at the caves, where weary men were coming out with dusty faces. "Do you think they'll ever find him?"

Jack shook his head. "The desert has claimed him." Jack suspected something else about Michael Fallon—that he was the man behind Nina's murder. Now that Jack had a solid suspect, he would be able to follow evidence and clues, and certain of Nina's notes that had been undecipherable— a notation: "MF"—and Jack had no doubt that they would all lead to Mike Fallon. Her case, and Nina, would be laid to rest at last.

Jack's gaze went to Francesca, who had a white bandage on her forehead. He foresaw a long and joyful road ahead for her and Abby.

Thanking the nurse, Francesca turned to her father's lifelong friend and said, "Uncle Uri, did you know?" But her eyes were on Abby, who was looking back at her. Mother and daughter, spellbound in the moment, each wondering how to cover the distance between them.

Uri Edelstein had not lasted long out in the storm, forced to take shelter until it was over. He was dust-covered and fatigued. And he had lost his best friend. "That you weren't Michael's real daughter? No. He didn't tell anyone. But I had my suspicions a few months ago, when an informant told us that a woman named Abby Tyler was asking questions about Michael's past. We got hold of an old photograph of her. I saw the resemblance, but I didn't say anything. But when we arrived here, the minute I saw Abby in person, I realized the truth. And I understood why Michael had come here. Tyler's existence threatened his plans."

Jack and Abby walked up then. "Miss Tyler," Uri said, "there is a special safe in Michael Fallon's office at the Atlantis. I don't know what's in it, he never showed me the contents. But he called it insurance, and told me that in the event of his death, I was to burn the contents of that safe and make sure the information did not fall into other people's hands. I have a feeling, Miss Tyler, that the adoption records you are seeking are in there. I will turn everything over to you."

"Thank you, Mr. Edelstein."

Abby turned to Francesca, tremulous with love and anticipation. How beautiful her daughter was! "How do you feel?"

"Better, thank you. The nurse gave me something." She held her green eyes on Abby. "I still can't believe it. You being my mother…"

"Would you believe me," Abby said, "if I told you I have a picture of you, taken when you were sixteen years old?"

Francesca gave her a surprised look.

Reaching under her hair, Abby lifted the gold chain from around her neck and brought it into the sunlight. At the end of the chain was a gold locket. She snapped it open to reveal the face of a smiling girl. Francesca's eyes widened. "Where did you get this?"

"It is you, is it not?"

"Yes! It was taken at Lake Mead, one summer…"

Abby shook her head. "That isn't you, Francesca. It's my mother. Your grandmother, who died when I was very young."

Francesca stared at the picture.

"I'm sorry," Abby whispered. "You were taken from me but I never gave up looking for you." Abby reached out and touched Francesca's red-gold hair. "Underneath the brunette dye, my hair is the same color as yours. With a touch of gray," she added with a smile.

With tear-filled eyes, Francesca handed back the locket, but Abby said, "Keep it."

"Tell me," Francesca said, suddenly needing to know, "tell me about my real father."

Abby stared at her. This was a moment she had known must someday come. For thirty-three years she had played it in her mind, over and over, scripted and rehearsed, each time with changes, trying different beginnings and endings—"Your father was a cold-blooded murderer,"—trying to strike a balance between truth and hurt feelings, "Your father was handsome and exciting." *"I knew your father for only a few weeks. I slept with him and never even knew his name.*" Finally, Abby said, "I loved him very much," and, at the time, it was true.

Francesca turned her face into the wind. The day was clear, the sky blue, the storm long gone. "I can't believe my father stole babies. But then, he wasn't really my father." Things started to fall into place. The rumors she had heard over the years, things other kids had said to her, cruel and taunting… her father a gangster…

Suddenly, her whole life was a lie. Everything had been taken from her. And yet, strangely, a new life had been given to her in its place. As if, the instant one door was closed, another opened up.

This woman…this strong, courageous woman…her mother. And suddenly they were in each other's arms, Abby holding her child at last, Francesca feeling the love and warmth of a mother she never knew. They cried together, and laughed, and then drew back to touch each other's hair, study each other's face, to let the tears run freely, until finally Francesca broke down and sobbed into her hands. "Daddy is gone." And Abby held her and comforted her in the soft desert wind and sunshine.

"Francesca!"

They turned to see a Maserati come speeding toward the rocks, the driver waving an arm and shouting.

"Stephen!"

They ran to each other and met in a crushing embrace. "Francesca, thank God you're okay, I was so worried about you in that storm! I got here as fast as I could but I had to pull over until the sandstorm passed, my God I've been worried sick!" He kissed her hard, held her tight, then drew back to inspect the bandage on her forehead.

"I'm all right. Stephen, why are you here?"

He spoke in hurried, disjointed sentences, about a letter his parents had received from her father, threatening to reveal something from their past if they did not go through with the wedding. "Francesca, I don't care what my parents think. I'm going to marry you, whether they approve or not." He took her face in his hands. "When I was in college I was arrested for drug dealing. It was no big thing, a little pot, but it's on my record and my parents are very straight-laced and think if word got out it would be the end of the world. Your father was afraid my mother was going to force me to back out of the wedding—"

Francesca silenced him with a kiss. "I have a lot to tell you, too," she said. "About my mother. And about my father." As they held tightly to each other beneath the warm desert sun, she realized that, when they were all trapped in the tunnels, her main fear was that she would not live to see Stephen again. Not that her doubts about loving Stephen had vanished in an instant. But at least from now on she would know that whatever she felt for Stephen, it would be for himself, not to please her father. And she also realized something else: the fear that she could die in childbirth, because her mother had, was gone.

Jack took Abby by the hand and led her away from the others. He said, "I am going to continue to search for Nina's birth parents. And when I find them, and if Nina was kidnapped, I am going to tell them all about her, what a wonderful person she was, and bring closure for them."

Then he took out the brochure for Crystal Creek Winery. "Charles Darwin said that it's not the strongest of the species that survive, nor the most intelligent, but the one most responsive to change. I have made no progress, Abby. When Nina died, I died too. I haven't been living. I *want* to survive. I want to live. Starting now, with you."

She looked over at Francesca, red-gold hair shimmering in the afternoon sun, and the handsome young man embracing her; and she thought of Jack Burns, the most exciting man she had ever met, and Abby knew that the life of Emily Louise Pagan, put on hold for thirty-three years, was about to begin again.

Printed in the USA
CPSIA information can be obtained
at www.ICGtesting.com
JSHW022208140824
68134JS00018B/933